THE ORCHID KEEPER

The Orchid Keeper

The tenth novel in the Sean O'Brien series

By

Tom Lowe

Kingsbridge Entertainment

Also By Tom Lowe

A False Dawn

The 24th Letter

The Black Bullet

The Butterfly Forest

Blood of Cain

Black River

Cemetery Road

A Murder of Crows

Dragonfly

Destiny

The Jefferson Prophecy

Wrath

The Confession

This book is a work of fiction. All characters, incidents, organizations and events portrayed in this novel are either products of the author's imagination or are used fictitiously. Any resemblances to any person, living or dead, is merely coincidental.

The Orchid Keeper – Copyright © 2019 by Tom Lowe. All rights reserved. No part of this book may be reproduced, scanned, stored in a retrieval system, or transmitted in any form or by any means – electronic, photocopying, Internet, recording or otherwise without the written permission from the author. Please do not participate or encourage piracy of copyrighted materials in violation of the author's rights. *The Orchid Keeper* is published in the United States of America by Kingsbridge Entertainment, Windermere, FL.

Library of Congress Cataloging in—Publication Data - Lowe, Tom.

ISBN – 9781691682935

The Orchid Keeper by Tom Lowe – First edition, September 2019

The Orchid Keeper (a Sean O'Brien Novel) is distributed in ebook, paperback print, and audiobook editions. Audible Studios is the publisher of the audiobook.

Cover design by Damonza.

Formatting by Ebook Launch.

The Orchid Keeper by Tom Lowe © First edition – September 2019. Published in the U.S.A by Kingsbridge Entertainment. All rights reserved

Acknowledgments

My thanks and deep appreciation for the people that helped put this novel together. To my wife, Keri, who works tirelessly as my first reader and superb editor. A big thank you Helen Ristuccia-Christensen, Darcy Yarosh, and John Buonpane for their extraordinary beta reading skills. To Howard King, Ph.D. for his expertise with botany. Thanks to the talented team at Ebook Launch. To the graphic designers with Damonza. And finally, to you, the reader. Thank you for reading and being part of the journey. I hope you enjoy *The Orchid Keeper*.

"As we got further away, the earth diminished in size. Finally, it shrank to a marble. That beautiful, warm living object looked so fragile, so delicate, that if you touched it with your finger … it would crumble. That changes a man."

- James Irwin, Apollo astronaut

For Helen Ristuccia-Christensen
and Darcy Yarosh

ONE

As a young boy, Joe Thaxton was never afraid of monsters. During his childhood and teen years he spent a lot of time outdoors, learning to fish and hunt. Monsters were never under his bed or in his head as a child. But, today, that was going to change. Thaxton watched a real monster appear through the camera lens of his aerial drone. It would prove to be the most foreboding sight in his life.

Thaxton, late-forties, skin bronze from running charter boat fishing trips, stood on his wooden dock in Florida's Indian River Lagoon, flying his drone almost a mile upriver. Unnatural images appeared on the screen in his hands. Images he'd never seen. He looked closer, the corners of his pale blue eyes creasing, staring in disbelief. He used the remote-control toggle switches to fly his drone high over the river, looking for signs of schooling sea trout and redfish in the flats. He saw a giant. And it was coming toward him.

Thaxton set the controls down on a wooden bench for a moment, reaching into his shirt pocket, removing his glasses for a closer look. The breeze carried the briny smell of salt water and baitfish. Two white pelicans sailed over the river, flapping their black tipped wings, heading east toward the Atlantic Ocean less than three miles away. Thaxton pulled the bill of his baseball cap lower, just above his thick eyebrows, the beige cap sweat-stained, a logo of a sailfish in the center, his curly brown hair jutting out from the sides. "What the hell …"

he mumbled, using the toggle switches to fly the drone higher above the long and wide river. The greater the perspective, the worse the nightmare. As far as he could see, the river was covered in a chemical-green color as if the massive body of water, more than a mile wide, turned into solid-green Jell-O.

He licked his dry lips, lowered the drone to about one-hundred feet above the surface, and flew it slowly down the center of water that often reflected the blue sky—water so clear in the tidal flats you could watch crabs scurry across the sandy bottom. Today, it appeared to be teeming in a green slime that moved silently, as if it had a sinister mind and will of its own, threatening to smother the very soul of the river beneath a pea-green soup that stretched as far as the eye could see.

Under his loose-fitting shirt, Thaxton felt a drop of sweat roll down the center of his back. He'd lived around the Indian River all his life. He and his brother had fished with their father for years in the northern section of the river near Titusville and Mosquito Lagoon. And he knew most of its 121-mile coastline on both sides of the waterway, from its start near Ponce Inlet in the north to Stuart in the south, where the water empties into the Atlantic Ocean. The Banana River and St. Lucie River all make up the massive waterway.

He stood on his dock near Port Salerno and watched his world about to change. His dock, one of the longest in the area, grand-fathered in at a length of one-hundred feet, had a small, thatched-roof sitting area at the end. He kept a 16-foot Boston Whaler tethered to the dock. His commercial flats charter boat was moored at the Ocean Drift Marina, less than two miles from his home.

Thaxton made his living as a guide, and the waters of the Indian River Lagoon were his primary source of income. His wife, Jessica, worked as an elementary school principal. They'd bought their waterfront home twenty years ago, back before the real estate prices became unaffordable. They'd struggled, saved, and managed their money, forgoing expensive vacations to stay home and enjoy what they considered a slice of paradise in Florida.

As Thaxton watched the video monitor receiving the live images from his drone, he had a feeling that everything, from the way he made a living to the lifestyle he shared with his family, was about to change.

His fingers trembled while flying the drone and recording video, the sinister images giving the river the appearance of aquatic death. The river looked like the water suffered from some bizarre kind of nuclear fallout, changing the entire biology and morphing it into a river of green slime.

His phone buzzed in his pocket. He looked at the caller ID and answered. His wife calling. Jessica said, "It's Sunday. Maybe time for a break from playing with your new toy. I think you have some kind of drone fever. Big boys and their new toys. I'm making lunch for Kristy and me. Would you like a sandwich? I can bring it out and the three of us can have a picnic on the dock."

"My appetite is suddenly gone."

Jessica Thaxton stood in her kitchen, peering through the window overlooking the bay and the dock. She could easily see her husband holding the drone controls in one hand the phone in the other. She smiled. Attractive face and a fine nose, light brown eyes, dark hair that was just beginning to show signs of gray. She said, "You didn't have breakfast this morning. Why aren't you hungry?"

"Because I just saw something that sickened my stomach."

"What?"

"Something in the river?"

"What? Another dead manatee?"

"No."

"Please, God, don't tell me you spotted a body floating."

"No. Nothing like that. Maybe even worse."

"What could be worse than a dead body?" She half smiled and sipped a cup of coffee.

"The death of a river and a way of life for a helluva lot of folks."

"Joe, what are you talking about?"

"You need to see this thing. I'm getting pictures of it from the drone, and the drone is less than a half-mile upriver. Whatever it is … it's coming our way, and it looks like it'll be here soon. And there's no way in hell to stop what's coming."

"You're scaring me. Is it safe for me to come on the dock?"

"I don't know. I do know that, in the time I've been watching it, the stuff is moving with the flow of the river, it's a slack tide, so that means the current is running about six knots. By the time I retrieve my drone, it will probably be coming right in front of our dock."

"Joe, what is it?"

"I don't know for sure. Something in the water. Something I've never seen in more than forty years on this river."

Two

Ten minutes later, Joe Thaxton piloted his Mavic drone to within one hundred feet of his dock, the drone buzzing like a swarm of angry bees. Two sea gulls circled once above the drone, squawking and fussing, as if they were giving it a verbal warning to stay out of their air space. Thaxton guided the black drone to the center of his dock, near the thatched roof lean-to. He worked the controls, gently setting the drone down and shutting off the four rotor motors. In the abrupt silence, he could hear the lap of the river water, the flow of the current against the pilings, the sound of the family dog, Rodeo, barking in their backyard.

Thaxton leaned down, picking up his drone, removing the data video card, and folding the rotor arms so he could fit it in the carrying box. He stood and looked up, the green carpet on the water now visible and coming his way. He scanned the river, no sign of any boats, rare for a warm and sunny Sunday afternoon.

"Daddy! We brought you a sandwich."

Thaxton turned around. His six-year-old daughter, Kristy, running down the dock toward him. Rodeo, their yellow Lab, trotted next to Kristy, a crooked dog smile on his bright face. Jessica followed, carrying a wicker basket in one arm. Kristy stopped running, walking the last twenty feet. A spattering of freckles dusted her nose and cheeks. Her auburn hair was combed neatly and pulled back in a pink headband, her blue-gray eyes going wide. "Did you fly your drone today?"

"Yes. I was flying it over the river."

"Can I fly it too?"

"I'll teach you, but we'll need to start lessons in a wide, open field with no trees or water."

She grinned, one of her teeth missing. "Okay. Mommy made you a sandwich. I helped a little bit."

Thaxton looked over to his wife as she set the basket on a round, wooden table under the thatched-roof lean-to. He said, "Thank you both."

"You're welcome." Jessica looked at the river, her eyes scanning to the east, toward the ocean. "I don't see anything."

Thaxton gestured with his hand. "That way. You can see the green from here."

His wife looked to the northwest, her eyes narrowing some, breeze blowing her hair, "What is it?"

"My guess is that it's some sort of algae bloom."

"We've had those in the past."

"But nothing like this. Let me show you what I saw from the air." He inserted the video card in his tablet and hit the play button. Within seconds the screen filled with the chemical green, the point-of-view changing to a wider perspective, the green appeared endless.

"Oh my God," whispered Jessica. "I've never seen anything like it. Where's it coming from?"

"What is it, Mommy?" asked Kristy.

"I don't know. Daddy just found something in the water."

Thaxton pointed. "The current is bringing it our way. It's just a matter of time before it's out in the open ocean."

They stood, watching the green monster grow closer. Thaxton said, "I'm betting, because of the recent rains, the gate keepers at Lake Okeechobee have released a lot of water and, for some reason, the stuff is on fire."

Jessica shook her head and folded her arms across her breasts. "It's like they did a massive toilet flush and all the crap is coming our way." She frowned. "It looks like some kind of toxic waste … like Jell-O that's gone through a weird kind of nuclear reactor spill, as if its glowing, and not in a good way."

"I've got the footage. I have to report this to the DNR and Florida Fish and Game."

Within thirty seconds, the green water was less than one-hundred feet from the end of their dock. Kristy said, "My nose is burning."

Jessica eyed her husband. "Joe, let's go inside. I don't like the way things are looking."

"You take Kristy back to the house. I want to use my phone to capture some of this on video as it comes ashore on our property and our neighbors' properties."

The wind abruptly shifted direction, blowing from the northwest, the breeze skimming across the continuous surface of green. Kristy said, "Something stinks. Like dead fish."

Jessica shielded her eyes from the sun with one hand, staring at the approaching green tide. "Look! I can see hundreds, maybe thousands of dead fish bobbing in that sea of green. It's killing everything it touches. The odor is putrid." Rodeo barked, snorting through his nose, panting.

Kristy's face tightened, reddening, her lungs gasping. "I can't breathe!" she managed to shout. "Daddy! I can't breathe?" She fell to her knees, holding her small hands to her chest, her breathing labored, lungs wheezing.

"Kristy!" shouted her mother, bending down and holding Kristy's face in her hands, looking into her daughter watering eyes. "Joe! Call 9-1-1! She's having some kind of respiratory attack."

Thaxton bolted three steps to his wife and daughter, scooping Kristy up in his arms, her body convulsing as she tried to suck in air. "We've got to get her inside! You can call 9-1-1 as we go back to the house."

He ran, looking down at his daughter, her face contorted, desperate for air. Her eyes seemed far way. She couldn't focus on her father's face—her mind elsewhere, as if it had left her contorting body. Thaxton sprinted down the dock toward his backyard and house. He had never felt so frightened, so helpless. "Kristy! Breathe! Try for short breaths. Breathe! Stay with me, Kristy." His wife and dog ran behind, the rancid stench of decay and toxins in the wind, chasing them. The smell of death coming from a river of poison.

Three

Florida Everglades

The last time I bought flowers for a woman, I placed them on my wife's grave. I thought about that driving east on State Road 41, from Naples to Miami, through the heart of Big Cypress National Preserve and the Florida Everglades. I knew the place. It was marked by a small sign. Hand-painted. Neat lettering. Maybe the man who'd erected the sign didn't want it to be easily read, at least not by most of the motorists speeding across the state through a land filled with towering cypress trees and dark water. I believe I knew why the sign looked more like a postscript. And that was the charm of the merchant of the Everglades. Perhaps hermit would be a better title. Maybe the entrance gate would be unlocked. Maybe it wouldn't. I'd soon find out.

It had been a few years. The old man was in his early seventies when I'd first met him. *Was he still alive today?* The sign was coming closer, about a mile away. I'd stopped there years ago and bought an exotic orchid for my wife Sherri. She'd kept it in a corner of our home in Coconut Grove, the soft sunlight from the eastern window exposure was just what the orchid needed. A few months after her death from ovarian cancer, it seemed like the orchid itself had lost its will to live. I'd watered and cared for it the best I could, trying to replicate what she'd done so well, so effortlessly. One day, the final bloom folded, petals withering, dropping to the floor. The orchid's once vibrant shades of lavender and pink, bowed over, never straightened, and died.

My name is Sean O'Brien. A few months after Sherri's death, I'd left Coconut Grove and moved north to the center of the state, selling our home and buying a ramshackle cabin overlooking a remote oxbow on the St. Johns River. Leaving Miami, I'd piloted an aged, 38-foot Bayliner up the Intercoastal Waterway, finding a slip for it in a rustic marina near Ponce Inlet. The used boat and old cabin—both in constant need of repair, became my therapy after Sherri's passing and my resignation as homicide detective from the Miami-Dade PD.

Max, my ten-pound dachshund, slept in the center of the seat beside me as I drove my black Jeep east on Highway 41, often called the Tamiami Trail. I glanced down at her. "Hey kiddo, I'm going to be stopping in a few minutes. You need a bathroom break?"

Max's head shot up. She stood, stretching, eyes bright and animated. She was a reddish doxie with permanent black eyeliner around animated, brown eyes. Small in size, but she had the heart of a lioness supported by four little legs. Max was my wife's final gift to me. The cancer not only destroyed our opportunity to have children, but also our life together as best friends and lovers, ending abruptly into a deep and cavernous void. Maxine, as Sherri originally named her, became the child we never had, drawing me out and bringing comic relief just when I needed it most. At my height, almost six-three and 200 pounds, together, Max and I make quite the odd couple.

The sign came into view. Same place as it was years ago. A small white board nailed to a rustic cypress post, not near the highway, but at least twenty feet to the right, off the shoulder of the road. You had to be searching to see it, and you had to slow down to read it. It looked like the lettering, black script, had faded to a grayish color. It read: Orchids for Sale. I slowed my Jeep, easing off the highway onto the grassy shoulder and then stopping at the entrance.

The galvanized gate was open.

In this place of minuscule signs, that was a good sign—assuming he was still alive and in business, as much as it could be called a retail business. I pulled a little further from the highway and turned off the motor. Max stood in the seat, trying to hang her head out, but at her size she could just rest her chin on the open window. She looked back at me, made a quick snort, and I said, "Okay, you know the rules. There's a canal on this side of the road. What can live in a dark-water canal in the Everglades?" Max tilted her head, her nostrils wet. I smiled. "Gators. And one would love to take you to lunch. So, this means we'll have to use a leash when you go pee. I can't chance you bolting near the water."

I took the leash out from the center console, snapped it to Max's collar, holding her in one hand, opening the door and getting out of the Jeep. I set her down and walked toward the sign. The old road leading into the swamps was covered in pea-sized gravel, broken oyster shells and knee-high weeds. A breeze delivered the scent of tannin water, the decay of ferns and leaves in a stew beneath tall cypress trees. The warm air was moist, humidity soaking into my pores like a sauna. Even Max looked like she might break a sweat as she sniffed the grasses and squatted to pee, glancing back at me over her left shoulder. A mosquito buzzed near my face.

To my right and left, the canal ran adjacent to the road as far as I could see. Black water. Gnats orbiting in a cluster near the canal. The long ditch was dug during construction of the road back in the late 1920s, the roadbed fill dirt coming from the canal. It was a massive engineering feat at the time. At least seven men died building the Tamiami Trail, which made ground transportation possible through some of the most hostile country on earth, the Florida Everglades. I thought about that engineering endeavor as I watched a wood stork sail over the giant cypress trees. Its wingspan was close to six feet, the wing feathers black and white, like piano keys in flight. The storks, known by old-timers as iron-heads because of their bald, leathery heads, are as close to a flying dinosaur as you can find today—the pterodactyls of the Everglades.

A long, black snake slithered across the driveway, less than fifteen feet from where Max sniffed a fallen palm frond. She spotted the snake and barked once. Within two seconds, I heard the sound of a single splash coming from the canal to my left. I watched the water and could see bubbles coming to the surface, the trail of bubbles moving closer to us.

I knew it was an alligator under the surface moving stealth-like toward a dinner bell—the bark of a dog.

"Come on, Max. Let's get in the Jeep. As I recall, the drive through the swamp to the orchid man's cabin is at least a hundred yards. Let's go see if Chester Miller is home." I swatted a mosquito, picked Max up and got back in the Jeep. I drove slowly, making sure the rough path hadn't become engulfed in water since I was last here. Within seconds I'd entered into a place time had overlooked—a place like nowhere else in the world. It quickly grew dark under the midday sun, mammoth cypress trees with thick canopies stood like stoic sentinels as the drive wound around their trunks, some with a diameter wider than a car.

Max stood on her hind legs, the humid air through the Jeep's window delivering a potpourri of ancient scents she never smelled. She looked back at me for a second. Max, my fearless dachshund, had a look I rarely saw in her eyes—a look of trepidation.

Four

Joe Thaxton never sought the limelight. Never looked for fame. Had a general disgust for professional politicians. But now he knew that the only real way to draw attention to the degradation of Florida's once pristine waterways was to hit the source, and to hit it hard. That's how he was raised. *If you commit to do something positive*, his dad would say, *do it with everything you have. Never half-ass. Give it your all or don't play the game.* Thaxton thought about that as he drove to Channel Twelve in West Palm Beach. It would be his first of three scheduled television news interviews for the day.

There would be more to come.

Joe Thaxton was now a candidate for the state senate. He had a small but passionate and dedicated group of volunteers at his election headquarters in Stuart, working the phones, social media, hitting the ground and scheduling media interviews and rallies. At noon, Jessica and little Kristy would join him at a political rally in Stuart. He'd won the primary election by working twelve-hour days for months. His driving message was to do everything he could in elective office to restore clean water to Florida before it reached the tipping point of no return for the state's greatest assets—its rivers, lakes, and beaches.

His message, energy and drive were resonating with a lot of people in his district and across the state. So much so that the opposing candidate's party worked harder to solicit and receive more money than ever in the history of Florida's state senate elections. That development, combined with Thaxton's "downhome" campaign style, drew the interest of national news media. "I'm really your average Joe," Thaxton would say to anyone who'd listen. And now thousands were listening. "I may be your average Joe … but I have an extraordinary need to save Florida."

He parked in the Channel Twelve lot and got out of his pickup truck. He wore neatly pressed jeans and a denim shirt tucked inside his pants. His sleeves were rolled up. He entered the building and was met by a balding news producer in a sports coat with an iPad in one hand. "Mr. Thaxton," he said, extending his hand. "Thank you for coming. We'll be going live in a few minutes. We can get you into hair and makeup."

Thaxton smiled. "Not too much you can do about my hair. It's been windblown for so long as a fishing guide I can barely get a comb through it. As far as makeup goes, what you see is what you get." He grinned.

• • •

If there was a magical mystery tour in the Big Cypress Preserve, this had to be it. Chester Miller, perhaps the world's foremost expert on the cultivating and growing of rare orchids, may not be much of a sign painter, but he knew how to design an entranceway that complemented the natural soul of the swamps. The last time I was here, the drive in was impressive. Today, it almost took my breath away.

Orchids, bursting in rainbows of deep colors, hung from the cypress trees like holiday ornaments. Deep verdant green ferns lined both sides of the drive and the worn wooden fence posts. Bromeliads, many in shades of red, pink and canary yellow, draped from tree trunks and branches. Staghorn ferns, some the size of manatees, grew from colossal bald cypress trees that looked older than the nation. Dappled sunlight poured through the branches in natural spotlights, catching the helicopter movement of hummingbirds and butterflies. They darted in and out of the flowers as if they all shared the same frenetic mission, like teams of elves working overtime before Christmas eve.

Max turned a circle in her seat, stood on her hind legs, looking out the window, nostrils quivering as the scents of mysterious flowers and fauna, rich and yet sweet, came through the open windows like a personal summons in the breeze. I said, "If these flowers smell good to you, imagine the effect it must be having on the bees." She ignored me.

I drove another fifty yards down the gravel drive and could just see the cabin. It was as gnarled as the crooked cypress knees that stood up through the dark water like petrified wooden stalagmites. The exterior resembled the boards on an old barn, weather-beaten into the dark gray color of a solitary old elephant standing motionless in the shade of Serengeti trees. The cabin had a screened porch and three wooden steps leading up to it.

I parked and got out, then lifted Max and set her on the ground. Darting back and forth, her nostrils were not able to inhale the potpourri quick enough. To the right of the cabin was one of the largest banyan trees I'd ever seen in Florida. It appeared to have grown taller and wider since I was last here. If there was a tree of life in the 'glades, the ancient banyan might be a good representative. The dark green canopy of leaves was larger than two parachutes engulfed in the wind. Some of the limbs reached to the heavens, others grew horizontal from the tree. Their heavy weight, supported by prop roots, resembled snakelike tentacles, twisting down from the limbs, burying their heads in the dark earth.

I heard a door open and a man walk out onto the front porch, the boards groaning under his weight. I could barely see his silhouette behind the screen. Max stopped in her tracks, staring. Usually she would bark. But not now, and like the open gate and faded board near the road—I took that as a good sign.

And then I heard a sound behind me. Someone walking. Max and I both turned around at the same time.

Five

Johnny Nelson threw a cast net with the precision of a rodeo cowboy. But, Johnny wasn't roping steers or yearlings. He set his sights and skills on catching mullet. He parked his pickup truck near the water's edge at the southern tip of Pine Island north of Ft. Myers Beach. Newly married, Johnny painted houses for a living. He fished and threw a cast net to help put food on the table for his family—a four-month-old son and his wife. As a former Marine, he'd spent more than two years in parts of Syria and Iraq. When he wanted to throw the net as hard as he possibly could, he thought about his time in combat. Something about the desert, the lack of water, the smell of death and fear of the unknown that made him throw harder.

Johnny thought about his wife and baby boy as he walked from his truck to the shallow inlet where he often fished. He stood almost six feet in his Croc water shoes. Scruffy, rust-colored, half-inch beard. Military haircut. On his right upper arm, was a new tattoo—a U.S. Marines insignia of an eagle at the top of the world. Johnny walked waist-deep in the water. A boat ramp, closed since the last hurricane, was to his left. Some of the asphalt pavement on the ramp was gone from the storm, as if a backhoe had chewed it and spat out one-third.

He glanced over at the mangrove-covered keys across the bay, the aberrant smell of something rotting in the breeze. Sky hard blue, hot sun licking his bare shoulders. He readied the net, rope with a slip-knot in his left hand, lead weights at the bottom of the net. He tossed it high in the air, the ten-foot net spreading like a pancake hitting the surface of the water. A white ibis in the shallows made a clucking sound and flew away.

Johnny pulled in the net. Even without seeing it, he knew there were no fish. A few mullets made a difference in retrieving the net. He pulled it out of the water. Nothing. Not even a minnow. He tried three more times, changing the landing location each time. Still, he caught nothing. He walked to the far right. Closer to what was left of the boat ramp. Johnny stepped out of the water, walking down the ramp and back into the water. The odor of rotting flesh was stronger here.

As he pulled back and started to throw, something caught his eye. In the spider-like mangrove roots next to the shore was a dead baby manatee. The carcass just floating in the rippling of the water. Flies buzzed. A large crab ate part of the manatee's tail. Johnny slipped and fell on the slick, moss-covered surface, his shin hitting against something under the water. It was hard and sharp, like an oyster bar. Johnny could tell that he was cut. *Just a small cut*, he thought. He ignored it and cast his net in the opposite direction from the dead manatee. Nothing. After three more attempts, he looked at his watch and decided he had time to try one more place before heading home.

He walked carefully back up the derelict boat ramp, looking at his right shin. Blood oozing out of the wound and trickling down to his foot and between his toes. He'd get a band-aid from the glove box in his truck and continue fishing.

Johnny didn't know it, but this would be his last time fishing. Although he didn't catch mullet, he caught something else. Microscopic, but deadly. In a few hours, the first tracks of the unseen bacterium would show near the wound. From there, it wouldn't take long to attack a combat veteran, a man who fought bravely and dodged death in the Middle East, to fall victim to something in the water that would escape the tightest mesh of any cast net.

Six

Joe Thaxton sat in a chair on the television set of Midday Live and thought of his daughter, Kristy, the prime reason he was here. The reason he was out of his comfort zone and trying to make a difference for the health of Florida and the people who live and visit here. He took a deep breath through his nostrils and smiled. Opposite him was a reporter and host of the program. She wore a red dress, dark hair to her shoulders. Full red lips and curious hazel eyes.

"Stand by!" shouted the floor director standing next to one of the three cameras. "Coming up in ten." A few seconds later, he used the fingers of one hand to countdown and then he pointed at the host of the news program. A recorded voice-over narrative came from a speaker mounted to the studio wall, "From Channel Twelve, Eyewitness News, this is Midday Live with Rachel Moreno."

The host smiled, looked into one of the cameras. "Hello everyone. My guest today is certainly no stranger to the viewers in southeast Florida … or for that matter, the entire state of Florida. Joining us today is Joe Thaxton, a candidate for state senate. For those of you in the audience who may not have heard his story, Mr. Thaxton, who is a former fishing guide and holds a master's degree in marine biology, won a tough primary election by promising to go to the state capital in Tallahassee with one primary goal … and that is to restore the state's water quality within its lakes, rivers, and beaches. Welcome, Mr. Thaxton. Thank you for coming today."

"Thanks for having me. But, before we go any further, please call me Joe."

She smiled and said, "Okay. A large part of your message is that you are what you call yourself—the average Joe with an above average agenda. What do you mean by that?"

"I'm not a career politician. Although I've always voted, I never sought elective office until my daughter almost died from acute respiratory failure eighteen months ago when part of the Indian River Lagoon became a river of green slime. And, since that time, it's happened twice more. On the west coast of Florida, Fort Myers, Pine Island, Sanibel, Captiva, Naples and many other areas, they're dealing with the same thing. Tons of fish are dying. Manatees are washing ashore, dead. Florida residents and tourists are experiencing severe health effects from airborne toxic spores. This is causing throats to close, breathing difficulties, coughing, and burning eyes. And, for folks with asthma … it's extremely dangerous, especially for children, as my wife and I experienced with our daughter, Kristy."

"If you're referring to red tide, it seems that's been part of Florida for decades. Perhaps way before much of the development and industrial runoff began. Correct?"

"It's much more than a red tide blooming far out in the Gulf of Mexico. Yes, in Florida's history, there have been outbreaks of red tide, especially along the Gulf Coast beaches. But never have we had to experience and suffer puke green slime pouring into our waterways. It's happening when water management authorities give the okay to release millions of gallons of toxic water from Lake Okeechobee into two prime exits. One is the St. Lucie river, which empties into the Indian River and the Atlantic Ocean. The other is on the west side of the lake where the water is released into the Caloosahatchee River that flows to the beaches of Fort Myers and surrounding areas. When you have manmade toxins from one of the most polluted lakes in America hit the natural elements that contribute to a red tide, you have the perfect storm of contamination that's killing fish, mammals and causing dangerous respiratory-related health conditions to residents and tourists."

"In your opinion, what's causing these toxins in Lake Okeechobee?"

"It's not my opinion. It's from consistent data gathered from biology and science research. For decades, massive farming operations, including the sugar industry, have pumped water from the lake into irrigated fields, which are laden with pesticides and fertilizers, and then pumped the runoff water back into the lake. That's created a toxic soup. Today, a lot of that return dumping into the lake has ceased. However, the damage is done. Big Sugar owns or controls most of the farmland on the southern border of the lake. It's here where that water should flow through, not into the rivers like they flush a toilet of toxins into the two rivers whenever they want to."

"At this point, what can be done?"

"Almost twenty years ago, the state and federal government agreed to a Comprehensive Everglades Restoration Plan. The basic idea was to clean the water and restore its natural flow south of Lake Okeechobee into the Everglades and the Big Cypress Preserve. Some progress was made, but we still have a long way to go. Too much corporate greed and special interests lined the pockets of career politicians, and the original restoration agreement became full of roadblocks, amendments and holes. It's a sham and a shame. In 2014 the Florida taxpayers, in a special referendum, voted to fund the buying of farmland south of the big lake for water restoration. However, powerful lobbyists working for Big Sugar and big agriculture dammed the flow of that effort."

• • •

"Your dog is so cute," said the young woman who approached us. Max snorted a half-bark and sauntered over to her, tail wagging in a full-bore doxie greeting. "Can I pet her?" asked the girl who looked college-aged, blonde hair hanging below her shoulders. Pretty oval face in a natural sort of way. No make-up. No earrings. She wore a long-sleeve khaki shirt, jeans and lace-up black boots. She held a garden trowel, taking off a pair of dirty cotton gloves.

I said, "Max has never turned down a scratch behind her hound dog ears."

The girl smiled, blue eyes sparkling. She squatted down next to Max and petted her, using both hands. "How does a female dog get a name like Max?"

"Her real name, at least the name my wife gave her, is Maxine. A few weeks after my wife died, Maxine sort of assumed the personality of Max."

"I'm sorry for your loss." She pulled a strand of hair behind one ear. "What kind of personality does a Max dog have?"

I smiled. "You're seeing it. Rather bold. Friendly. Very unformal. Nothing pretentious, not that Maxine is a pretentious name … just a bit more formal. Actually, I wasn't the first to call her Max. A friend of mine, a guy who lives on his boat, called her Max first. Now, he often uses the name Hot Dog. Max comes to either name if you have food. Her affection can be conditional."

The girl laughed. She stood and smiled, the screened door opening with a rusty squeak. I turned and watched the old man, full beard, cane in one hand, walk down the three wooden steps, holding onto the railing with one hand. He stopped and inhaled, the breeze filled with the fragrance of flowers. The girl smiled, watching the old man approach. "That's my grandpa. I was a little girl the first time I remember seeing him, and it was out here. I must have been about five or six. And, the very first thing he asked me was if I believed in ghosts. I said I really didn't believe in ghosts. Then he smiled and said he'd take me into the Everglades and show me a real ghost. He did. Ever since, I've been a believer—at least in what he says. If you're lucky, maybe he'll show you, too."

Seven

Rachel Moreno waited for the TV commercial break to end. She looked at her notes and smiled at Joe Thaxton. As a local appliance commercial played in the background, she said, "One of the producers in the newsroom said a lot of people are calling in with positive comments. Some want to know if we'll take live questions on the air."

"I'm game," said Thaxton. "It's all about the people anyway, or it should be."

"Standby!" shouted the floor director. "In three." He pointed to her and the tiny lights mounted above the camera lens glowed red again.

"If you're just joining us, we're speaking with Joe Thaxton, a man who a year and a half ago was a fishing guide. His daughter became very ill from breathing toxic spores from an algae outbreak on the St. Lucie and Indian River waterways. He's running for state senate and is growing quite a base of supporters." She turned from the camera to Thaxton. "If you are elected to the state senate, what can you do?"

"Say hell no to lobby money. Say yes to Florida's clean water and health. I'll work hard to sponsor and pass a bill to change the status quo. I'll be tireless in my effort to protect our waterways, our beaches, the Everglades, and the health of our residents in Florida and that of the people visiting our state. When people no longer come and vacation because Florida's beaches are hazardous to their health, what's going to happen then?"

The reporter nodded. "You're talking about a potential disastrous economic effect, correct?"

"Absolutely. Think of the jobs that will be lost. Tourism is the number one employer in Florida. It generates close to a hundred billion a year for the state. Last year, more than 120-million people came here for vacations. What happens if that ends? Nobody will come to beaches where the lifeguards are wearing respiratory breathing masks. Who wants to step over thousands of dead and rotting fish in the surf and on the beaches?"

"Your critics, including the governor, dismiss you and say you're not a whistleblower but more of a rebel rouser doomsayer who paints an apocalyptic 'Henny Penny—the sky is falling' view of Florida's future, when that's not necessarily the path. How do you respond?"

"Before I was a fishing guide, I worked as a marine biologist. The scientific data paints a better picture than anything I can say. There's a direct cause and ill effect every time they flush Lake O, and we feel like someone just urinated on us. For far too long, the sugar industry has bought and sold politicians to get what it wants, and that's not in the best interests of Florida, its precious waterways, beaches, and its people." Thaxton smiled and said, "Rachel, earlier you'd mentioned the platform I'm running on ... it's really a platform of change and responsibility that I'm standing on as I try to offer positive change." He shifted his eyes from the reporter to one of the cameras. "And, for too long, the average Joe's in our state have suffered the consequences of corporate greed destroying the very thing that makes Florida unique among the forty-nine other states ... our 663 miles of sandy beaches. Our rivers and our lakes. Lake Okeechobee, the tenth largest in the nation, is one of the most polluted in America. That has to change, or Florida will turn into a cesspool that can never be drained. I have no problem standing toe-to-toe with the well-funded lobbyists and special interest groups because not to do so will only allow the environmental disease to fester and grow worse. And, one day, we'll wake up and learn our beautiful state—Florida, has terminal cancer. At that point, it's too damn late. When Spanish explorer Ponce De Leon first sailed here and walked our beaches, coves and woodlands, he called this new land *Florido* … or a place with flowers. That bloom is in danger of falling off the plant forever. But the good news is that it's not too late. It can be restored. It just comes down to choice: Do we want our Florida to be the land of flowers or the state of green slime?"

• • •

A dozen reporters, the news director and staff watched the interview on screens in the Channel Twelve news room. "He's charismatic and persuasive," said a middle-aged news director, his blue tie down a notch, a cup of black coffee in one hand. "You think he has a snowball's chance in hell?"

The executive producer, a woman with her dark hair pinned up, quick green eyes, watched the interview on one of the newsroom monitors for a second more. She turned to her boss. "Maybe. There's something about him that seems way beyond reproach. Sort of like the old movie, *Mr. Smith goes to Washington*. If he does get elected, he'll be the first politician to make a dent in the powerful sugar and agriculture lobby. Maybe he'll touch a nerve. And maybe something good will happen because of it."

The phone on her desk buzzed. She answered, and a receptionist said, "There's a man on line seven who says he has a hot news tip. Want me to put him through. I tried Leslie's extension, but just got her voice-mail."

"Put him through." The executive producer paused, glancing across the newsroom at the bank of TV monitors and said, "News desk. Can I help you?"

A man's voice, husky, slightly distorted, said, "We're thinking about blowing up your TV station for giving that freak time on the air."

"You're welcome to come in for an interview. Who is this?"

The news director could tell his executive producer was agitated.

The caller said, "Like that would happen. Tell your average Joe to check his car before he starts it." The caller disconnected.

The executive producer licked her lips, set the phone down and looked at the news director. "From what I just heard on that call, I'd say Joe Thaxton already is hitting a nerve."

"What'd the caller say?"

"It wasn't what he said … it was what he threatened to do."

Eight

Chester Miller stepped from his front porch holding a wooden cane in his right hand. His flowing silver-gray beard reminded me of the Spanish moss hanging from the large banyan tree on his property. His hair was bone white and hung to the collar. He wore bib overalls with a red-flannel shirt underneath. No shoes. He grinned, approaching us, a large-boned man who walked with a slight bend to his wide shoulders, his eyes smiling. "Welcome!" he bellowed. Max cocked her head. "Welcome to God's little acre tucked back here in the Big Cypress Preserve. Are you looking for an orchid? How may we assist you and your canine companion?"

I nodded. "As a matter of fact, I am looking to buy some orchids. And I'm a repeat customer. I bought an orchid from you about seven years ago."

The old man looked over the scratched glasses perched on the tip of his nose, as if he were seeing me for the first time, trying to place me, his right hand gripping the cane. "I don't get a whole lot of repeat customers. Not that I don't want them. But my little strand in the 'glades is not what the retail experts would say is the ideal location." He inhaled deeply and gestured all around him. "It's great for the flowers, not so much for people. I do remember you, though. And, if memory serves me correctly … I remember the type of orchid you bought. We'd spent some time chatting, walking. You were very interested. As I recall, you worked in law enforcement." He chuckled. "I only get a few customers a month, so it's not as if I have a mind like a steel trap. Although, I remember you and the orchid, your name slips my mind."

"It's Sean O'Brien."

He looked from me to the girl. "This is my granddaughter, Callie. Callie is here for a few months to help me with the orchids before returning to the University of Florida. We've been replanting some of the native species of orchids in the 'glades and Big Cypress Preserve. I'm not as spry as I once was when I traipsed all over the world studying plants. I'm Chester."

"Chester Miller," I said.

He grinned. "Impressive. You must have a thing for remembering names and faces."

"Some, not all."

"Well, I'm flattered to be included in that group you do manage to retain in your mind. Maybe it's my Santa Claus beard." He grinned.

"You're a hard man to forget. I remember spending almost an hour with you. I felt like I learned more about botany in that one hour than I have my entire life. You even offered me some of your homemade banana wine."

"I have a new batch fermenting. I'll cork a few dozen bottles soon. You'll have to stop in the next time you're traveling through the 'glades."

Callie smiled and said, "Grandpa will never admit it, but I'm convinced that he knows more about orchids than anyone on the planet. He's been studying them for more than a half-century. He has one of the best minds I've ever seen. He's the reason I'm majoring in biology and botany in college."

"Callie, my only grandchild, likes to flatter an old man." He glanced at me, his furrowed brow tightening. "You bought a dove orchid that day. Not any run of the mill dove, but one I had worked to propagate into a hybrid that's a cross between a pale white dove and the lady slipper." He smiled. "May I inquire as to the health of your orchid? Is it still producing blooms three times a year?"

"Unfortunately, no. After my wife passed away a few years ago, I attempted to do exactly as she had done so well with the orchid."

"I gather it had been a gift for your wife, correct? I hope she enjoyed it."

"Yes. It was a gift. Sherri loved it. I soon learned that I didn't have the green thumb that she did."

He chuckled. "And now, I assume, you're ready to try again? I have some orchids that are much more tolerant for folks who are, as you suggested, challenged when it comes to caring for plants."

"The orchid is not for me. I've learned my lesson. It's all I can do to keep Max fed and out of the mouths of gators here in Florida. I live on the St. Johns River in the center of the state. The orchid will be for a friend."

He nodded. "A lady friend, I presume?"

"Yes. And she doesn't live that far from here, so the orchid might do well in the same environment."

The breeze blew, limbs from a large weeping willow tree swaying like leafy ropes. A wind chime on one corner of the cabin tinkled for a few seconds. Chester motioned toward a greenhouse that looked like a Quonset hut or an old airplane hangar you'd see abandoned in airfields. It was made of corrugated steel and curved plexiglass panels. The plexiglass had yellowed. He said, "In that old greenhouse are some of the rarest orchids on earth. I've spent my entire life studying and working with nature to grow them. As a matter of fact, you're standing less than fifty feet from the rarest exotic orchid plant ever. I have waited more than fifteen years for it to bloom. I hope that I live long enough to see that happen. If you promise not to photograph it, and promise not to divulge the location ... I'll show it to you."

"You have my word. No pictures. No secrets revealed."

He chuckled, his gnarled, arthritic hand gripping his cane. "Follow me. We'll visit the greenhouse first. I want to hear more about your friend. That way I might suggest an orchid for her. I have cultivated some flowers in there that I believe have ancestral roots all the way back to the Garden of Eden. I like to think it was before evil arrived and caused the garden to go to seed." He laughed and came closer.

I could smell the odor of old clothes, dried sweat. He looked at his granddaughter. "Callie, if you will dear … lead us into the greenhouse." He glanced down at Max and then eyed me. "Please watch your pup. There are cottonmouth moccasins around here. Now we have pythons to contend with in the 'glades. I removed a large snake from the greenhouse last summer. Just like Eden, it's often difficult to keep a snake from slithering into the garden."

Nine

Callie led the way, followed by her grandfather. Max looked at me for a brief second before trotting behind them, her head high, stopping in her tracks when a lizard darted into a pile of green coconuts stacked at the base of a palm tree. "Come on, Max," I said, bending to pick her up. "Leave the lizard alone. You heard Chester's warning. There could be a snake hiding in that pile of coconuts."

We entered the subdued light of the greenhouse. The warm air humid. The sweet fragrance intoxicating—mysterious and yet gentle, soft as perfume veiled on a beautiful woman. More than two-hundred orchids and lilies filled almost every square inch. Dozens of orchids grew from pots lined up and down a long wooden table, stretching for at least fifty feet. Handwritten, three-by-five cards were positioned next to each clay pot and the plant it contained. Other orchids were placed on waist-high benches that wrapped around the inside perimeter of the greenhouse.

I'd never seen such a hodgepodge sea of colors in bloom. The blossoms seemed to be in striking natural still art poses. Motionless. Raw beauty. The hum of a bee somewhere in the mix. The orchids were of every shape and color in the known flower universe. Some had such a blend of colors—flamingo pinks, lavenders, deep purples and iridescent yellows and golds, they appeared surreal and delicate, like blown glass.

Callie stepped to the center of the table and pointed to a white orchid with pinkish-blue cascading colors, similar to rings, on the five largest petals. "This is my favorite so far." The center portion, the smallest petals, were like rubies, the tint of light through a glass of merlot. "Grandpa started experimenting, trying to create this flower when I was born. It took him a few years, but he did it. And he named it after me."

Chester laughed. "It took me longer than a few years. More like fifteen years. And then it took another two years for the orchid to bloom. I wasn't sure it ever would, but at the time Callie graduated from high school, the first bud appeared, and the rest is history. The scientific name is *Platanthera Calliope* … Calliope was the Greek muse who presided over song, poetry, and the arts. I simply shortened all that to one word … Callie."

She smiled wide, slight dimples in her cheeks. "Thanks, Grandpa."

I said, "I'd bet that one is not for sale."

"Correct, Sean," he said. "However, many of these are indeed for sale. When, and if I believe they're ready to move outside, I try to place them in the wild, sometimes building small wooden stands that I attach to trees. You may have noticed that driving on the property. I like to give my orchids a high elevation, so deer can't eat them, and they can look around and see what's coming."

I said, "The eye of the orchid."

"You'd be surprised what plants can see or at least feel with senses that humans don't possess." He pointed to the long bench behind me. "Every plant on that bench is for sale. The rest of these and some I have in the trailer behind the cabin are not for sale. The reason is that you're looking at some of the rarest orchids in the world. To wealthy collectors, they'd be worth six figures. However, I don't grow them for money. Never have. I grow them for the hope that I can use my experience to partner with nature to produce some of the most exotic flowers since Eden. That may sound pretentious, but I've spent a lifetime cultivating rare orchids from all over the world. There is a special quality about the orchid that holds a fascination with most folks. I've collaborated and worked with renowned botanists, biologists and research universities. And I've shared the flowers, photographs, and scientific data with thousands of interested people around the world. Regardless of all that, my ultimate goal is to replant the native orchids back into the Everglades. And I've made great headway, restocking a few thousand orchids."

Callie used her left hand to brush off some potting soil from the table. "I've been helping Grandpa upload the photos and information to a website I built for him. I think I've convinced him to do a few podcasts, too."

"We'll see," Chester said, propping his cane up against the bench. "Sean, tell me a little about your friend. Is she good with plants?"

"Yes, at least I think so. She has a lot of plants in her home, and she has a few on her back deck."

"You mentioned she lives not too far from here, correct?"

"Close to the Seminole Indian reservation in northern big cypress."

"Is she Seminole?"

"Her mother is full-blooded. Her dad was Irish-American."

"Over the years, I've made friends with the Seminoles. However, many of the elders I knew have died. What I know about botany pales in comparison to some of them … especially those who studied to be medicine men. I've learned a lot from people like Sam Otter. I haven't seen him in a couple of years. He's in his nineties. Maybe older. When he passes, a wealth of knowledge about plants and the interaction of plants as medicine will go to his grave. Not a lot of today's generation interested in that sort of thing."

"I am," Callie said, smiling.

"And you're one of the exceptions. The study, care, and cultivation of plants, especially exotic flowers, is work. Hard work and dedication. For a generation that seems preoccupied with short-term results, well … to each his own I suppose." He picked up his cane and shuffled around the table to a section of the bench and pointed to a tall orchid plant with purple and yellow petals. The center of the flower was scarlet red with flecks of pale yellow, like gold dust scattered at the entrance. He said, "That is an orchid I worked with Mother Nature to produce. About a decade ago. She's patient with me. I've grown more than fifty since then, shipping some to botanical gardens and others to patrons of the arts. It's living art. Perhaps your friend might enjoy that one."

I said, "It's very beautiful."

"What's her favorite color?"

I paused for a moment, my mind playing back the color of her clothes, the interior of her home, furniture, the color of her car. "I'm not sure. She seems to like wearing white and yellows. Blue as well, sometimes."

Callie smiled and said, "A woman's wardrobe is a good start. But that can be a lot of colors. Right next to the orchid Grandpa suggested is one I really love. I don't know the scientific name off-hand without reading the card under the pot. But it seems to bloom often, and just look at the colors." The flowers were snow white with teardrops of dark red and soft pinks in an alternating pattern."

"Tough decision ... so, I'll take both of them."

Callie and Chester grinned at the same time. "Excellent choice," he said. "We'll put them in a container, so they won't tip over in your Jeep."

• • •

The executive producer of *Midday Live* thanked Joe Thaxton for appearing on the program and walked him to the lobby of the television station. At the glass doors, she stopped and shook his hand, glancing outside to the parking lot. "Are you in the guest parking area?"

"Yes. I'm the only pickup truck parked there."

"We appreciate your time today. You didn't shy away from the issues or difficult questions. Live appearances like this help our viewers—the voters, to get a close-up look at the candidates. I wish you all the best."

"Thank you for having me."

"Where do you go from here?"

"We're having a rally in Stuart. I hope there's a good turnout. We've been getting larger and larger crowds. Seems people are very interested about the health of Florida's waterways and beaches, and they want to protect them."

"Absolutely. But with any hot issues, you'll have your naysayers. A lot of the people who deny climate change will say pollution for Lake Okeechobee, the rerouting of water, does not cause toxic outbreaks and has no effect on the increase of red tide."

"I believe these folks are in the minority. In any debate, the true facts trump opinion. In this case, the scientific data is there. If the naysayers will objectively look at the science, I think more and more of them will agree we have to start now to make the change."

"You're up against tremendous money from agriculture and the Big Sugar lobbyists. It'll be a tough fight."

"I'm used to that. Anything worthwhile takes time, drive and energy to change. I'm just hoping we raise the money to counter the attack ads we know are coming our way."

The producer paused. She opened the entrance doors and stepped outside with Thaxton. She glanced at his pickup truck in the lot, her eyes scanning the parked cars. A UPS truck pulled up to the TV station. A news crew, reporter and camera operator hustled out the door and walked quickly to an awaiting news van, Channel Twelve Eyewitness News painted in blue and yellow on the sides. The producer looked at Thaxton. "It may be nothing, but I wanted to mention something to you."

"What's that?"

"We receive a lot of nut job calls from time to time when we have political guests live on the program. You're not an exception to the general rule. You can't please all the viewers all the time. I received a call from a viewer—a man. It sounded like he was trying to disguise his voice."

"What'd he say?"

"He was angry that we had you on the program. He called you a freak and said he might come down and blow up the station. In the seven years I've worked here, we've had calls like these." She glanced back at the main entrance. "We have great surveillance cameras all around the outside of the building. A security guard is on duty twenty-four-seven. So, it was probably just another arm-chair anarchist calling to spew hate. I think the Internet and the anonymity of social media has spawned these people. Nonetheless, I wanted to tell you."

"Thank you. I hope it's an isolated incident. But I know I'm hitting a nerve. My campaign headquarters has received a few hate calls. Nobody's threatened to blow up our headquarters or a TV station for interviewing me, though. They just want me to shut up and go away. I'm called a tree hugger with an attitude. I can handle that."

"Be careful. This caller sounded angrier than most."

Ten

After I'd paid, and Callie helped me secure the orchids in the back of my Jeep, Chester said, "I promised to show you what, if it blooms, will be the rarest orchid in the world."

"It'll bloom, Grandpa. I have faith in you," Callie said.

"It's not me anymore. I've done my best to help nature spread her wings. It's up to the plant. It's alive and seems to be doing well. Just no buds yet. Come on, Sean."

With Max still in my arms, I followed the old man and his granddaughter to the left of the cabin, walking past an Airstream trailer, the silver exterior discolored and oxidized, tree sap blotted the roof, the door open, as if it had never been closed since it arrived and took root in the mire.

Chester pointed to the trailer. "I lived there for two years until I could rehab the old cabin. This high ground was put in as a work camp when they built the Tamiami Trail back in the late twenties. At one time, up through the fifties, there was a half-dozen shanties in here to house some of the workers. They used fill dirt from the canals to elevate these ten acres above the near constant water in the Big Cypress Swamp. I got lucky when I managed to buy it many years ago. Today, people can't buy government land and build homes in here. When I die, I'd like to leave the property to the Nature Conservancy."

Callie said, "Don't you talk about dying. You have a lot of good years ahead of you, Grandpa."

He smiled, the deep lines around his eyes crinkling. "We'll see. Come on, our guest has orchids to deliver to his friend." Max and I followed them to the right of the trailer. Chester pointed to a large cypress tree, it's base submerged in a few inches of dark swamp water. "Big Cypress, and the 'glades for that matter, are drying up. At any given time, you'd see at least sixteen inches of water around these cypress trees. Now it comes and goes like a bizarre tide. We don't get the summer rains like we used to out here. I think some of it is climate change mixed with the rerouting of the natural water flow through South Florida. It's hard to find wild orchids in the 'glades and Big Cypress Preserve because of the changes."

"Maybe things will eventually be restored," I said.

"Not in my lifetime." He motioned with the tip of his cane. "On that perch is the *paphiopedilum quetzal*. The scientific name for an orchid that I affectionately refer to as Persephone. She was the Greek goddess symbolic with the cycles of life and death … the change of seasons, from summer through winter and the renewal of life in the spring. I've gone through a lot of seasons with Persephone. Maybe this will be the year she awakens."

"Why does it take so long to bloom?" I asked.

"Because it's an extremely delicate breed—a hybrid of four of the world's most rare and exotic orchids, the Shenzhen, the Kinabalu of Malaysia, the Rothschild, and the Dragon's Mouth. It may never bloom. Inside the trailer is my mini-lab. Microscopes. Magnifying glasses. Tools as small as those a craftsman uses to build fine watches. In there are specimens of rare pollen I've collected from around the world, kept in sealed, air-tight containers."

I pointed to a bush that was really more of a small tree. It was filled with what looked like tiny apples. Green and smaller than golf balls. "I've seen bushes like that. What is it?"

"That's the manchineel. The Spanish called it manzanilla de la muerte, or little apples of death. The sap from that plant is deadly. The Calusa Indians, long ago annihilated from diseases the Europeans brought to Florida, shot Juan Ponce de Leon in the leg with an arrow dipped in the sap of a tree like that one. He died a slow death from the wound."

"Did you ever consider cutting down that tree?"

"No. It was here before me. It has a right to be here after me. Also, it more or less protects the orchid in the cypress tree. If someone should disturb the orchid, as in stealing it, they'd most likely brush against the leaves and the forbidden fruit of the manchineel would cause burns. To those with severe plant allergies, it might cause death if they're not treated in time." He paused, glancing at Max and then raising his slate gray eyes to me. "It's sort of like my watchdog. But this one makes no noise, the victim does." He looked down at his bare feet for a second. "I could talk all day. But you have more important things to attend to. Callie and I hope that your friend enjoys the orchids, and that they bloom often for her."

Callie stepped next to her grandfather and said, "If she doesn't like them, we offer a money back guarantee. Oh, I'd told you a little about the first time I met Grandpa when he asked me if I was afraid of ghosts. What he was referring to at the time is a very rare and exotic orchid that lives in the Big Cypress Preserve and parts of the Everglades. I don't know the scientific name, but Grandpa called it the ghost orchid."

"Do you have any here?" I asked.

"No," Chester said. "They're so rare that when I do find them, I take pictures and document the locations and the numbers of orchids. It's a sight to see, though, when I find one. I still get goose bumps in hundred-degree temperatures and humidity. The true canary in the mine for this land can be the ghost orchid. The more their habitat is changed or altered, the scarcer they become."

"For people really interested in the preservation of ghost orchids, Grandpa will sometimes take people out in the swamps to see them up close. That might be a fun trip for you and your friend who'll soon be gifted those beautiful orchids you just bought."

"I may take you up on that, thanks."

Chester reached in a front pocket of his overalls and pulled out a card. "If you'd like to go, call us. Callie will probably answer the phone. I might if I can hear it. I'd be delighted to host a tour for you and your lady friend. Do you have a card? Are you still employed with the Miami-Dade sheriff's department?"

"I do have a card. But no, I don't work there anymore. After my wife died, I decided on a new lease on life, a new way to make a living and a new place in Florida to call home. I sort of split my time between by cabin on the river in the center of the state and my old boat docked near Ponce Inlet."

"What do you do now?" Callie asked.

"I tried my hand at working as a charter boat captain. I wasn't good at finding fish. I wound up giving a few of the customers their money back. Now, I'm a free-lancer of sort. I can't find fish, but often I'm okay at finding stuff for people, or even finding people who've fallen off the radar." I handed Chester my card.

He looked through his smudged bifocals, grunted. "Sean O'Brien … and only a phone number. From what you said, I gather that you are a private investigator, correct? Seems like a tough way to earn a living."

"I don't do it for the money. I do it if someone's in dire straits to find something that might correct a life that's gone dramatically off course."

Callie smiled. "Rather than hunt the ghost orchids—you search for a different kind of ghost … people or I'd guess bodies, too."

"Sometimes. Law enforcement officers usually find the bodies. They don't always find the person who did it. Occasionally, a case grows cold and the files are put way on the back burner due to a lot of things. Sometimes I get lucky and can help. Not always."

Chester handed my card to his granddaughter and said, "Well, at least you try hard. That's noble, and about all anyone can ask of a person. I have a feeling that you might solve more than you don't." He grinned. "Maybe you ought to help the rangers in the Everglades National Park find the elusive pythons that are crawling amuck and swallowing deer and rabbits."

Callie said, "Those snakes are only out there because people who bought baby pythons as pets couldn't handle them as they grew too big for apartments and houses. They'd release the snakes into the 'glades. Some can get twenty feet in length."

Chester said, "Once they grow too big for the gators, the pythons have no natural enemies. Most people can be standing just a few feet away from one out here and never see it in the sawgrass because the snakes blend in so well. A python can come out of the brush and snatch your pup before you can blink. You're a big guy, Sean. But even you would have a very difficult time prying one of those snakes off once they coiled around something and started constricting. You'd have to shoot the serpent in the head."

I said, "I'll remember that." Then looking at Max, I said, "Come on, Max, we have flowers to deliver."

Eleven

Joe Thaxton drove to his next event a little faster than the posted speed limit. He would be speaking with supporters at a town hall meeting that his election committee coordinated. His campaign manager and two members of his volunteer staff were already there. Jessica planned to join him, too. Pulling onto I-95 north, he glanced into his rearview mirror, spotting a black Ford SUV and someone on a motorcycle. Within a mile on the interstate, the motorcycle roared past, the SUV staying behind him. Thaxton accelerated, moving close to eighty-miles-per-hour. The SUV accelerated, keeping within sight.

Ten miles later, the SUV kept the distance.

Thaxton thought about what the TV news producer had said, *Be careful. This caller sounded angrier than most.* He called his wife, the call going to her voice-mail. At the beep, he said, "Just checking in to see if you're going to be heading out to the rally soon. Did you catch the Midday Live program? Call me. Love you." He disconnected, looked in the rearview mirror, the SUV behind one car, but still in sight.

Thaxton turned on his radio, moving the FM dial to a talk radio station. The host, a man with a deep voice said, "In this hour of our discussion we're talking about the state-wide races and the race for a new governor. The current occupant of the governor's mansion has his sights set on a seat in the U. S. Senate. Two men are vying for the job in a race that's getting deeply personal and ugly. Before we get into that, let's see if any callers have opinions on the flurry of new appointments the governor has been making in the last couple of months of his administration. Ron, from Miami is on the line to join the conversation. What's on your mind, Ron?"

"Those eleventh-hour appointments are nothing but pure crony politics. Look at who he put on the South Florida Water Management Board. Not scientists or anyone seriously knowledgeable about the hydrology in the state. He appointed his pals—lawyers and corporate cronies to these positions. It's the worst case of the fox watching the henhouse. I hope that'll change with a new governor in Tallahassee. But right now, the best candidate we have to even suggest these changes isn't running for governor, although he should. He's running for a state senate seat. Joe Thaxton from Stuart, which is the epicenter for toxic algae blooms on the east coast. He's not afraid to call it like he sees it, and that's pointing to the fat-cat lobbyists working for corporate agriculture."

"We'll have Joe Thaxton as our guest this Friday during our first hour on the air. Maybe you'll call back with questions. He's not your average Joe, so please, don't come back with average questions, okay?"

The caller laughed. "That's for sure. I heard him say the other day, if a candidate refuses the influence peddling of the lobbyists, those lobbyists will just go see the opposing candidate and drop two-hundred thousand into their cookie jar. That kind of money is ridiculous and why we're in trouble to begin with."

The radio host said, "You're talking about how it's been in Florida for decades. Almost as long as the farm bills were first passed. Thanks for your call."

"No problem. Love your show. Bye."

"If you'd like to join the conversation, call eight-hundred, radio one-one, and the ones are digits, not the letters—that's number one for our talk-radio station ranking and number one for our host award rankings … eight-hundred, radio one-one. We'll take a short break and continue the conversation on today's political races in some of the most watched contests in the nation, happening right here in Florida. Stay with us."

Thaxton stopped at a traffic light and made the call. A woman answered the phone. "Radio-one-one with Don Berry. Would you like to join the conversation?"

"Yes. This is Joe Thaxton, candidate for state senate. I'm heading to a town meeting in my car, and I heard some of the show. Thought I might add a quick comment for a minute."

"Oh, Mr. Thaxton. Thanks for calling. I'll let Don know you're on the line."

"Thank you."

The commercial on the radio ended, and the host said, "Timing is a lot in politics. The last caller had mentioned the name of a man he admires who is running for office. Now, that doesn't necessarily qualify him as a politician, and that's his appeal. He calls himself the average Joe with an extraordinary message and plans for fixing the pollution too often experienced on Florida's beaches, rivers and lakes. Joe Thaxton is a fishing guide in the Indian River Lagoon, and now he's running for office after watching one too many toxic algae blooms in the habitat where he makes a living. My producer tells me Joe is heading to a town hall meeting. We have him on the line for a couple of minutes. Thanks for calling in, Joe."

"Happy to join the conversation. I know I'm booked with you for Friday, I just wanted to thank the last caller and say he's right on the money, no pun intended about the lobbyists. You're talking about people who have money to burn. Big Sugar's lobbyists work both sides of the aisle, republican and democrat, to get the votes they want to keep doing what they're doing. I believe folks should own property and be responsible land owners. However, when these massive sugar cane farms prohibit the natural flow of the water in Florida, hurting our national treasure, the Everglades, we need to look closely and ask …why? Why, twenty years after the Comprehensive Everglades Restoration Plan was passed, is so much of it the same as before it was passed. In 2014 the people of Florida voted to buy land south of Lake Okeechobee to begin real steps to restore the Everglades. That move has been delayed by the current administration and the cronies who don't care about what the people voted to make happen. In the meantime, the glades are drying up and water managers are flushing toxic water down two rivers, the

St. Lucie on the east coast the Caloosahatchee on the west coast. We got a huge problem. But it is fixable."

"Let's get into the solutions when you have a full hour on Friday's program. The question the last caller asked is why the heck aren't you running for governor. You'd have a lot better chance with your Everglade's restoration plan if you were in a higher office."

"One step at a time. If the people do choose to put me in office, I'm not gonna start by figuring out how I can keep that office. As a matter of fact, as soon as I can make a difference, I'm outta there. In terms of the governor's race, I can work with the candidate the people decide to elect as our next governor. This issue, clean water and good health in Florida, is way too big for party lines. It's going to boil down to the salvation of our way of life in the state."

"That's a scary but, most likely, path we're on as a whole. If you were governor, what's the first steps you take?"

"I'd ask for the resignations for most of the folks on the Water Management Board. I don't think we have to replace them with scientists. Science is certainly part of the perspective. I think we need people on the board who understand what's at stake, knowledgeable people who'll be there to take care of our fragile natural environment. We're at the tipping point. The water chemistry is already so altered it's often too dangerous to breathe the air or swim on some of our beaches, lakes and rivers. We can reverse that."

"We're looking forward to hearing your plan on Friday. Joe, are there still seats in your town hall rally today?"

"Absolutely, if we get too big a crowd for indoors, we'll move it outside. Come join us at 1212 Birdsong Street in Stuart. The folks at the national guard facility there have been kind enough to let us borrow the place for an hour." Thaxton looked in his rearview mirror, the black SUV now behind him. "And, if they're listening, I'd like to invite the driver in the Ford Explorer riding my tail to join us. I'll give you a front row seat."

The radio host laughed and said, "There you go. A special invitation from Joe Thaxton. Joe, thanks so much for calling in this hour. Looking forward to more on Friday. We hope you have a big crowd today. And maybe that tailgater will ease off the gas pedal and join you."

TWELVE

I was looking for the weather forecast on the radio when I found a storm. I normally don't listen to talk-radio, because it's often boring. Politics rehashed like tainted potato salad never has a good taste. However, while scanning the dial, I caught part of a talk show that piqued my interest. After spending time with Chester Miller and his granddaughter, Callie, the subject of the radio discussion was fitting—the degradation of the environment.

Max and I drove northeast on Highway 41 through the Everglades, and I thought about one of the things Chester had said: *The true canary in the mine for this land can be the ghost orchid. The more their habitat is changed or altered, the scarcer they become.*

I didn't see any ghost orchids out my open window, but there were miles of sawgrass. At one time the Everglades was often called the River of Grass. The sawgrass was there today, but not a river beneath it. Max slept on the Jeep's passenger seat, and I listened to a talk radio program, the subject resonating as I drove. The caller, a fishing guide running for state senate, had some salient points. I thought about one of the things he'd just said, *We're at the tipping point. The water chemistry is already so altered it's often too dangerous to breathe the air or swim on some of our beaches, lakes and rivers. We can reverse that.*

Living in Florida for years, I'd followed the history of the environment and man's influence. The Big Cypress Preserve and Everglades suffered massive crisscross scars, ditches dug across its face to divert the natural flow of water. The Army Corp of Engineers had good intentions, just bad results in terms of balancing the environment and the needs of wildlife with the desires of developers. The original canals, ditches and dikes were built to prevent flooding as Miami and the southeastern portion of the state were the promised land in the eyes of developers. Winter weary northerners, people with money, would flock like snow birds to sunshine and palm trees if the water levels could be controlled.

That meant literally draining the swamps. The result—a drastically changed hydrology, the River of Grass was dry part of the year, the blood-flow to the Everglades constricted to a trickle at best. For the wading birds, fish and animals, the land they knew for thousands of years was gone. What was left, especially in the headwaters of the 'glades, the land around and south of Lake Okeechobee was muckland. Dark black mud. To sugar cane growers and farmers, it was black gold. They bought up massive tracts of land as if oil was beneath it. Might as well have been.

I wished the candidate luck. He was going to need it taking on corporate agriculture and the sugar industry. I picked up my phone, slowed down and scrolled to find the number to a woman I hoped was home. This land, the 'glades, had been the home of her people—the Seminole Indians, since they fled here to escape from the U.S. Army and those who wanted to relocate the Indians from Florida to reservations in Oklahoma. The Seminole had refused to be escorted down the Trail of Tears. They'd been resilient, defiant, and were unconquered. I thought a lot of those traits were in the DNA of the woman I'd bought the flowers for, Wynona Osceola.

After earning her degree in criminology from Florida State University, she'd been accepted into the FBI. Preferring to work the job away from New York City or Washington DC, coveted locations for a lot of agents looking for visibility and a place to climb the ranks, Wynona preferred to hunt for criminals, not the limelight. She started in the FBI's Tampa field office. Two years later, she relocated to Miami. Nationwide, her arrest and conviction records were in the Bureau's top ten percent. After Miami it was an assignment in Detroit, and that would be her final chapter in the FBI. She'd worked an undercover sting to bust people thought to be aiding and abetting Islamic radical terrorists in the Middle East.

The home of a suspect had been bugged, Wynona and her partner on stake-out in a van parked in the dark a half-block away from the middle-class, ranch-style home. What they overheard through their earpieces was a fundamentalist father about to murder his teenage daughter in what he called an honor killing. The reason, he alleged she'd disrespected the family by flirting with a teenage boy.

By the time Wynona and her partner broke down the front door to the home, the father had already stabbed his daughter three times. Wynona shot the man once in the chest and then emptied her clip. One round at a time. Two seconds between trigger pulls, sending another seven bullets into his dead body.

The Bureau called her actions "excessive force." The FBI's brass demoted Wynona and took her off the streets. She was reassigned to a desk job. She quit, traveled the country for a spell, looking for nothing specific, except for trying to make sense of it, all the while searching for the elusive resolution to the unanswerable ... *why?* Why does a man butcher his daughter and call it an honor killing? Why is the face of evil often unrecognizable until the mask comes off? Why is good too often a victim? She eventually circled back and returned home to the Everglades and her family. Now she works as a detective with the tribe's police department.

She answered the phone. "Hi, Sean. How's Max."

I glanced over at Max. "She's asleep."

"Well, she's earned the right for a frequent nap, not that she needs beauty sleep like the rest of us. Are you calling from your cabin or your boat?"

"Neither. We're in my Jeep, and we're not that far from the rez. Have you had lunch yet?"

"No, and I'm starving." Wynona sat behind her desk in the Seminole Tribe's Police Department. She was the only woman in the large room. Two other detectives, both men, made phone calls and worked computer keyboards. Wynona glanced down at her left hand, looking at her nails, trying to remember the last time she had a manicure or a pedicure. She had long, raven black hair. High cheekbones. Misty, brown eyes that gave the impression of depth, like something enigmatic below the surface of still water.

"We can meet you at the "Glades Café," I said. "As I recall, they make a good burger. Frybread is outstanding. Would forty minutes work?"

"See you then."

• • •

Joe Thaxton drove down the interstate and called his wife, Jessica. "Did you see the *Midday Live* interview?"

"Yes. I thought it went very well. I'm proud of you and what you've been able to accomplish is less than two years."

"No pain no gain. I didn't want to ring any alarm bells, but in the last couple of weeks, we've received a few threats at the campaign headquarters—one in particular stood out."

Jessica set a cup of coffee down on her kitchen table. "Why didn't you tell me?"

"Because ninety-nine percent of telephone threats are just that … threats only."

"Joe, all it takes is the crazy one-percent to go off the deep end. What kind of threat?"

"The caller didn't ask to speak with me. He just said to my staff to tell me that, if I stayed in the race, it'll be the last race I ever run. The producer of the *Midday Live* broadcast told me some guy called in and threatened to blow up the TV station for having me on the program."

"Now you're frightening me. We need to go to the police. The best way to take on adversaries is not to be extorted or bullied by them, but to bring in the authorities to help stop them in their tracks. After this rally, promise me you'll call the police and report these threats, okay? I'll go with you."

"What can the police really do? We don't know who made the call. The caller ID indicated an unknown number, like the guy is using one of those non-traceable phones to make his threats. And, today at the TV station, the caller, of course, didn't identify himself. So, police have no place to look. We can't even file a restraining order unless we know who we're trying to restrain."

"We might not know a name, but we know the people behind it might be the ones you're challenging, the big ag and sugar cane operations in the state."

"Maybe. But I'd like to think they do their fighting using lobbyists and fistfuls of money, not in some cheap, mafia-style threats coming from guys who would break kneecaps. I won't be deterred or intimidated. Florida has suffered way too long."

"Be careful, Joe. I'll see you at the rally. I love you."

"Love you, too." He disconnected. Thaxton saw the sign to his exit, slowed and left the interstate. He stopped at the traffic light at the end of the long ramp before turning right. He looked in his sideview mirror and saw the black SUV come up very close to the rear of his truck. He looked up in the rearview mirror, trying to see a face or faces. Two men. Both wearing dark glasses, both with billed caps on their heads.

Thaxton turned right and drove two blocks before coming to a red traffic light. He stopped, the SUV pulling up to his left, the passenger lowering the window. Thaxton looked at the red light, wanting it to quickly turn green. He turned his head to the left. The passenger, a man in his early thirties, pulled a hoodie over his ball cap. The man stared at Thaxton for a second before using his index finger and thumb to resemble a handgun. He pointed his finger at Thaxton and pretended to pull his trigger thumb. Face deadpan. He lifted his index finger to his thin lips and acted as if he was blowing smoke from the tip of a barrel. He grinned, replacing his index finger with his middle finger, sticking his hand further out the window.

Thaxton turned his head, staring at the traffic light. *Green.* He accelerated, the driver in the SUV taking a left and driving in the opposite direction. Thaxton tried to get a good look at the license plate. He could tell it was a Florida plate. He couldn't make out the numbers and letters. But there was no mistake that the men had delivered a warning to him—a death threat.

Thirteen

I drove through the largest of the five Seminole reservations in Florida, thinking about the incongruities of time and circumstance. Big Cypress Reservation is about eighty-five square miles in size. It borders the Big Cypress Preserve southwest from Lake Okeechobee. Fifty years ago, most of the tribe lived in small concrete block homes that dotted the landscape of scrub oak, cabbage palms, canals and wetlands. Some of the elders lived in chickees, wooden structures with hard-packed dirt floors and thatched roofs made from dried palm fronds.

Today, there are plenty of ranch-style brick homes with late model cars and trucks in the driveways. The Seminole Tribe leveraged their status as a sovereign tribal nation, exempt from many federal or state laws, to secure gambling rights and turn the cards into a multi-billion-dollar industry, giving them ownership of the most lucrative casinos in the state. In addition, they own the Hard Rock Café brand, including its hotels, casinos and resorts worldwide. The Seminoles, who years ago, often made a living by wrestling alligators at roadside attractions for tourists and charging for airboat rides through the swamps, represent one of the largest businesses in Florida.

Where money flows, greediness often awaits downstream like hidden boulders beneath the fast water.

The massive cash flow removed abject poverty from the tribe, each member getting bi-monthly financial windfalls for life. But the Seminoles, like anyone, are not immune to the double-edge sword of the blessings and lacerations wealth can spawn. That's one of the reasons Wynona Osceola, as a detective on the reservation, isn't bored in her job. It might not offer her the challenges that her former position as an FBI agent once did, but she still investigates the dark side of mankind. And there is more than enough of that to go around because boundaries on a reservation can never contain or repel the ghosts of greed.

As I drove into the heart of the Big Cypress Reservation, I thought about how the infusion of cash provided many members of the tribe the opportunity to build businesses that prosper as tourists arrive by the busload to experience narrated tours through the swamps on airboats and swamp buggies. They can catch a snake show, gator wrestling, a rodeo, and visit Seminole culture, past and present, in a museum.

I slowed, lowering the Jeep's windows and turning off the road onto the parking lot adjacent to one of the largest restaurants. Max stood on her hind legs, nose out the window, catching the scent of fry bread and hibiscus flowers. The Gator Cafe resembled an immense, sprawling log cabin or an old Florida fish camp from the sixties, made from cut and treated cypress poles. Tin roof. A wide, wrap-around porch that circled most of the restaurant and offered views into a sprawling wetland. Philodendrons grew at the base of a dozen tall canary palms, the leafy green fronds swaying in the breeze.

I shut of the motor and turned to Max. "As I recall, they'll let you eat here if we get a table outside on that long porch." She snorted, eyes anxious. I lifted her up with one hand, locking the Jeep. I scanned the parking area, not spotting Wynona's car among the dozens of rental cars and three RVs. A family with a Kentucky license plate on their mini-van got out, the two kids running ahead. Mom shouting, "Stop running! That means you, Andy."

To my left, came a Toyota RAV-4, parking in the least crowded section. Wynona Osceola stepped out of the car. Even from a distance of about one hundred feet, she looked striking. Her black hair fell to the center of her back. She wore jeans, a white cotton blouse, and a dark blue business jacket, open. I could see her wide smile. Max began fidgeting. Although we hadn't seen Wynona in a few weeks, Max almost sang her excitement in a fast repartee, her barks rolling off her tongue like a rapper who could only yodel.

I made sure no cars were coming or going before setting Max down. She bolted in Wynona's direction, making a full circle around her shoes, barking twice, tail blurring. Wynona bent down and picked her up. "I've missed you, too, Miss Maxine." Wynona held Max close, receiving doxie kisses on her cheeks. "What a greeting," she said as I walked toward them. "My mom used to say dogs wag their tails with their hearts."

"I think your mom was spot on," I said, giving her a hug. "You're looking lovely."

She smiled. "Thanks. You're not so bad to look at yourself." She scratched Max behind the ears. "It's good to see you, Sean. Did you just happen to be in the area, near the rez, and decided to see if I was available for lunch?"

I smiled. "No. It was more preplanned than that. I know your birthday is this month. I wanted to give you an early present. It's here." I motioned for her to follow me to my Jeep. I opened the back and unbuckled the two orchids in their clay pots and held one in each hand. "These are for you."

She smiled, her eyes misting a moment. "They're so beautiful. You remembered me telling you that orchids are my favorite flowers. As a little girl, when my brother and I would go into the glades or Big Cypress with my grandfather, he'd use a bamboo pole to move his flat-bottom boat through the shallow water and point out various plants, animals, and flowers to us. My favorite was the orchids … especially the ghost orchids. They reminded me of something between a butterfly and a frog because they always had the beautiful white wings of a delicate butterfly and looked as if they were leaping from the trees, like frogs. Can I trade you Max for the orchids?"

"Absolutely." We made the exchange, and Wynona looked closely at the blossoms, her eyes filling with wonder and curiosity.

"Sean, these are the most beautiful orchids I've ever seen. Thank you so much. I have the perfect place in my house to put them. These don't seem like the kind of orchids you can buy in the grocery store. They're much too exotic and mysterious. Where on earth did you ever find them?"

"A place on earth that's hard to find. Actually, it's not too far from here as the proverbial crow flies. Off the Tamiami Trail is a nearly hidden spot that you have to be looking for to find. An old man lives back in the cypress swamps. He's traveled the world studying and buying orchids. He's a botanist who cultivates and grows some of the most beautiful and rarest orchids in the world. He's been replanting native orchids back in the glades. Over lunch, I'll tell you more about the pedigree and legacy of your new orchids."

"Sounds like these should come with registration papers or maybe a passport."

• • •

Johnny Nelson walked into the hospital emergency room with his frightened wife by his side. Amber Nelson stood a foot shorter than her husband, her vivid green eyes filled with worry, her mouth like a red knot. Her hair, the color of bailed hay left in a field, was pulled back in a tight ponytail. She held a baby on her hip, gently swaying back and forth as they met with the nurse receptionist. "My husband has a real bad infection," she said, licking her dry lips. "His leg looks like it's on fire."

The receptionist stayed seated, her computer screen reflecting off her glasses. She nodded. "We'll have the doctor look at it as soon as we can. First, I'll need to ask you folks a few questions and get you in the system."

After they gave her all the required information, they were told to have a seat in the waiting area with at least two dozen other people, many in for flu-like symptoms, deep coughing, hacking. One man with snow white hair, slumped shoulders, his left eye partially closed and filled with cataracts, sat in a wheelchair, his khaki pants stained from the loss of urine.

Johnny and Amber took seats in a corner area, a dwarf palm in a dark plastic pot near them, a TV screen on the wall, sound off, Wheel-of-Fortune on. "I hope we don't have to wait too long," she said, rocking her baby son in her arms.

Johnny stared at his leg. The cut on his shin looked to be alive, long red streaks splaying out like a sun flare, the wound oozing a milky green substance. He cleared his throat. "It's weird … I've had deeper cuts than this in combat. They all healed up fine. After a few days, they'd be scabbed and forgotten about, but not this time."

"That's 'cause there are things in that water that can kill you. Even in the two years that you did those tours of duty, the water in southwest Florida has changed. It's not like it was growing up around here. Late last summer, the red tide or something in the water got so bad, some people living in Sarasota couldn't sit out on their porches in the evening when the breeze blew the stuff around the canals and whatnot. A couple interviewed on the news said it smelled like dead fish for three weeks." She eyed her sleeping baby. "They had a child close to Michael's age at the time. The man said they were scared the baby would get a respiratory infection because they could smell it even through the air-conditioner."

"That's sad. Never should happen. Maybe I can just get a shot, a bunch of antibiotics and knock this thing out of me."

Amber looked at her husband's leg and put on the bravest face she could muster. "When we get you well, you gotta promise me you won't go back in there with your cast net. It's not worth the risks." The baby cried softly. Amber rocked her son with the reassurance in her arms that she wanted to feel in her heart. But the wound on her husband's leg shattered illusions with a painful reminder of the unknown that too often lurks beneath the water.

Fourteen

Joe Thaxton looked out into the sea of faces and paused, glancing at Jessica standing off to one side of the stage, which was a large outdoor gazebo in a park setting of palms and lofty oaks draped in Spanish moss. More than three hundred people, most in shorts and short-sleeve shirts, spilled out around the gazebo, the Stuart city water tower in the background, an American flag painted on the big silver-gray water tank. The air smelled of fresh-cut grass and roses in the wind. Thaxton said, "So, in conclusion, friends. I want to thank y'all for coming out here today to show your support ... not so much for me, but rather for what we all stand for. And that's clean water for every man, woman and child in Florida."

"Tell it like it is, Joe!" shouted a supporter.

"I plan to, and I plan to do a lot more than just telling. I'm a doer. This plague, which is what I'm gonna keep calling it until it's inoculated and gone—this disease called pollution is drastically interfering with the way we conduct our lives. The way we work and play ... and our health. When you can't take your child to the beach because of the fish kills, the stink, and the fear of catching something or worse—like dying, when our lifeguards are sitting in their guard stands and breathing through surgical gauze masks, this is beginning to look apocalyptic. It must change!"

"Take it to Tallahassee!" shouted a tall man.

"I will! That is with the help and support of people like everyone here today. No one can do it alone. We need a united front to face the polluters. We need an angry populace to demand accountability on the state water management boards. We need to tell Big Sugar and corporate agriculture their time with the current status quo is up. Because far too long they've lobbied and paid their way to greater profits by having laws written to their benefit. Guess what? These laws can be rewritten to turn back the toxic clouds of pollution that move insidiously like green slime along our waterways. If you send me to Tallahassee, you'll send me with more than a message. I have a plan that can work with agriculture and change antiquated septic systems, measures we need in place to save our lakes, rivers, beaches, and our health. Let's make this a win-win!"

The crowed exploded in applause. Thaxton signaled for his wife to join him on stage behind the podium. Jessica stood by her husband's side, smiling, his hand on her back. A mass of smiling faces and applauding supporters. And then she spotted two men in the back standing in the shadows of a live oak. They weren't clapping. Hands deep in their pockets. Dark glasses on hard faces of stone. One man whispering in another man's ear, both nodding. One using a pocket knife to scrape dirt from under his fingernails.

• • •

We sat in a remote section of the restaurant's expansive veranda, the orchids on the back part of our table, Max at our feet, the beauty of the marshlands across the vista, the sound of an airboat in the distance. We ate fried catfish, gator tail nuggets, kale salad and fry bread. I sipped black coffee. Wynona ordered water with a lemon slice.

I told Wynona about Chester Miller, his efforts to restore native orchids to the Everglades, and his extensive orchid research project tucked away in a raised spit of land surrounded by swamps. "So, the orchids you'll take home with you have quite a legacy by way of Colombia and the volcanic peaks and valleys of Malaysia. Chester has spent a lifetime studying and cross-pollinating some of the best of the best in the world of orchids. He's more than a botanist … he's a scientist who's cataloged orchid DNA back to the time the famed orchid hunters of Europe trekked to inhospitable jungles in South America and Africa to export the most fascinating plant Europe and Victorian England had ever seen, the mysterious orchid. Fast-forward a couple of centuries later and factor in mass production with greenhouses, orchids now are as available as sunflowers."

"But they're not the same," Wynona said, looking at the vivid, delicate petals. She lifted her eyes to mine. "There is still something mysterious about a beautiful and rare orchid. The shape of the flower—the variegated colors of the petals, the feminine lips into the inner sanctum, the womb, that seems to hypnotize bees into blind obedience—to carry the orchid seed on their wings and help flower a new generation." She paused, taking a deep breath, gazing at the wetlands beyond the veranda. Then she looked at me, something hidden in the complexity of her eyes. After a few seconds, she smiled and said, "Orchids hold a unique fascination. It's as if they've been around so long, they could tell us stories about the birth of the planet if we'd only listen."

"I think people like Chester Miller, and even his granddaughter, Callie, are listening. They're not focused as much on the birth of the planet as they are on its well-being. The ghost orchids you mentioned seeing as a little girl … Chester has studied and cataloged them in the Everglades, Fakahatchee Strand, and Big Cypress. He says the label ghost is applicable, not so much by the way they look, but rather because they're difficult to find. He calls them the canary in the coal mine in terms of the condition of the Everglades."

Wynona nodded and sipped her glass of water. "I think he's right about that. Although I haven't been in the glades or Big Cypress in a while, the last time I was there I can't recall seeing a ghost orchid. That was at least four years ago. This botanist you mentioned, Chester Miller …"

"What about him?"

"If I'm not mistaken, I believe he's friends with Sam Otter, the last of the renowned Seminole medicine men. You met Sam when you were helping to prove Joe Billie was innocent of murder charges. No one is sure of Sam's exact age. Some guess it's about a hundred and three years. Even when I was a little girl, he seemed to be old back then.

He's way up there in chronological age … but somehow time seems to have less of an aging effect on him and some of the other elders that I remember in the tribe. It probably has a lot to do with his lifestyle, diet, and his deep knowledge of plants and Seminole medicine."

I looked at my plate of food. "Let's hope catfish is among his favorites."

Wynona smiled. "I think Sam Otter has spent time with Chester Miller in the Everglades. I remember hearing about a non-Indian who was extremely knowledgeable about the flora and fauna in the glades. I heard that Sam shared a lot of information, handed down knowledge from generations of Seminoles about the ways of nature. Sean, that's like getting a dozen PhDs in plant science. What makes people like Sam Otter so fascinating is his ability to mix the sap and leaves of various plants and bark to obtain the specific medicine he seeks. Inside his chickee there are literally hundreds of canning jars. Many contain dried leaves. Some hold dirt, dried mud, mixed with plant materials. Others have hardened sap, pollens, and tree bark. None are labeled in the traditional sense. When he dies, all of that extensive knowledge and wisdom will go with him to the grave."

"Let's hope he can get an apprentice and log the materials and data."

"Where will he find someone to do that in today's Seminole Tribe? Those days are gone forever."

I smiled. "Maybe Chester Miller would be an apprentice. Even in his eighties, he's at least twenty years younger than Sam Otter."

Wynona laughed. "Now that would make a great reality TV show. Imagine, two elderly men, one in his hundreds, one in his eighties. Both in waders slowly walking through the glades, pointing out plants and flowers. Maybe the younger fella, Chester, would be scribbling notes like James Audubon when he first arrived in Florida and the massive flocks of wading birds would darken the sun at midday when they arose and took flight over the glades."

"Now, that's a visual. I'd watch that TV show. Sounds like something that might interest Discovery or National Geographic Channel."

"I know that Sam wouldn't be interested. Not that he's too old, and it's not that he's uncomfortable or intimidated by cameras. Among the Seminole, he's a revered and respected man. Maybe like the pope with Catholics. Sam mixes medicine with religion and helps members of the tribe to heal their bodies and their spirits."

"Did you ever see him when you were ill?"

"Twice as a little girl. I'd had a bad fever one time and a case of pneumonia the second time. Sam looked at me, my eyes, inside my mouth and ears. He placed one ear on my chest to listen to my heart and lungs. He looked at my hair and fingernails. He asked me a few questions in the native language. My mother had to interpret for me. Then he gave her these horrible tasting herb medicines for me and strict instructions on how to administer them. Within a day or two, each time, I was well again." Wynona inhaled deeply through her nostrils, slowly releasing a long breath. "There was another time I should have seen him, but I chose not to."

"When was that?"

"I think you might know. Let's order coffee, and I'll tell you."

Fifteen

Joe Thaxton and his wife, Jessica, stayed on the Gazebo platform, shaking hands and listening to stories people told. Most of the supporters were long-time Florida residents with tales to tell about the days before green-slime rivers and the red tides rolled up on beaches leaving dead fish. Some people had recently moved to the state and felt like they'd opened a Pandora's box when it came to green algae rivers and red tide. Each had an example for Joe to use as he built his platform and sharpened his toolset.

Joe's campaign manager, Larry Garner, a big man with a round, ruddy face, puffy eyes, graying hair, stood to one side of the candidate and his wife. Garner wore a dark sports coat, button down shirt and new blue jeans. He glanced at his watch and scrolled through his iPad, looking at schedules. They were running behind. The next appointment was to meet with the editorial board of the largest newspaper in the area. Garner hoped that the meeting would result in the paper endorsing the candidacy of Joe Thaxton for state senate.

When the handshaking line dwindled to a few people, Joe glanced at his remaining supporters, recognizing one man, nodding and then speaking to a woman who was next in line. "I appreciate you coming out here today," he said to the woman, mid-forties, wearing a blue sundress, matching high heels, a strand of pearls around her dark, tanned neck.

The woman looked at Jessica and then at Joe. "You two make such a nice couple. It was interesting and heartbreaking to hear y'all tell the story of your daughter the first time that green goop came floating down the river. By the grace of God, your little girl is okay, right?"

"Yes ma'am," Joe said. "We're blessed."

Jessica smiled and added, "Our daughter, Kristy, is just one of many children who can't tolerate that kind of toxicity in the air. It's like people who are allergic to peanuts. They can't go near peanuts or suffer grave consequences. Diet is a choice people can make, but that's not always the case when it comes to the environment. Often, you can be going about your daily life and come to realize you're being attacked by things in the environment. But like Joe says, we can change that before there's no change possible."

"I agree. You had quite a turn-out here today. Now, what y'all need are T-shirts and hats for people to wear and proudly show their support."

Joe turned to his campaign manager. "Did you hear that, Larry? We have requests for T-shirts and matching hats."

"They're coming soon," he said with a mail-slot grin. "We didn't want to make hundreds of T-shirts and have nobody to wear them. Now that we see the crowds are getting consistent and larger, we have the demand, and we'll pump out the shirts and hats."

The woman pulled a pair of dark, turtle shell glasses from her large straw purse. "I'd be happy to buy mine. On that note, how can I make a campaign contribution?"

Garner was quick to say, "You can write a check, payable to the Joe Thaxton for state senator candidacy or you can go online to our website and make a donation with your credit card."

She reached back in her purse and whipped out a checkbook. "No better time than the present."

"Thank you," Joe said, as the woman stepped aside and used the support of the wooden podium to write the check, Larry Garner making small talk as she chatted and wrote, a mockingbird chortling from a live oak.

Joe and Jessica turned to the last man in line and Joe said, "If it's not Captain Roland Hatter. How the heck are you, Roland?"

The man grinned, his brown face crinkling with sun lines on both sides of his pale blue eyes. He was tall and lanky, large hands and powerful forearms, the long-limbed build of a cowboy who'd spent half his life on a horse herding cattle. He wore a loose-fitting, short-sleeve shirt outside his blue jeans. "I'm doin' good," he said, shaking Joe's hand. "Hey, Jessica, it's been awhile. So glad to hear Kristy is well and doing fine."

Jessica gave Roland a hug. "I have to pick her up from school this afternoon. Thank you so much for coming out to the rally today."

"I was in the area, heard Joe on the radio, and decided to drop by. I'm glad I did. You got a helluva campaign goin' on. Years ago, you were asking me for pointers on how to find fish for your clients. And, now look at you … fishin' for votes. Well, you sure as heck got mine!"

Joe smiled. "Thank you, Roland. And you were nice enough to give me some sorely needed suggestions way back in the day. You still fishing the Mad Hatter outta Ponce Inlet, or did you get another boat?"

"Still got her. Wouldn't trade any time soon. I'm not out there on the water as much as I used to be. On account of the algae blooms and crap in the water, I've had more cancellations in the last couple of years than I have had in the nearly thirty years I've worked as a fishing guide. Dozens of guides like me are damn glad you're taking this thing on and tryin' to do something to turn the tide, so to speak. We're getting more and more green slime in the river and lagoon. People won't pay their hard-earned money to fish around that crap. I used to come in from a run and listen to a half-dozen booking inquiry messages just about every day. Now, if I'm lucky, I'll get a half-dozen inquiries in a week, and it's only if the news isn't showing green gunk on the water for miles."

Joe looked at the American flag painted on the water tank towering near the park. He said, "Together, we can change that. I think we have a good guy runnin' for governor. If he wins, and if I can get in there, I know I can work with him. He wants to restore the glades, fix the rivers and runoff so it won't kill the fishing industry and the people, too." Joe glanced at his watch. "We need to get going."

"I'll walk with you to your truck," said Roland.

Larry Garner thanked the woman who wrote the check as she turned and walked toward a parking lot. Garner said, "Joe, I'm parked next to your truck."

"So am I," said Jessica. "I need to run and pick up Kristy from school. I wish I could go to the newspaper editorial board with you. Maybe the next one. I know in my heart that there will be more opportunities for endorsements."

Joe, Jessica, Garner, and Roland followed a wide sidewalk meandering through the park toward the largest tree in the manicured setting of queen palm trees, azaleas, black wrought iron benches and old oaks with hanging moss. Jessica remembered seeing the two men standing near the largest oak. They were gone, but the smirks on their faces seemed to hide in the dark shadows falling over the verdant lawn. After walking another fifty feet, Joe abruptly stopped.

He stared at his truck.

"What the hell is that?" mumbled Roland.

"That's a crime!" said Garner, whipping out his phone.

The tires were flat.

All four punctured.

Jessica touched her hand to her mouth. "Oh my God! I can't believe this."

Sixteen

"Nine-one-one, what's your emergency?" the police dispatcher asked.

Larry Garner, pacing near Joe's damaged truck, phone in one ear, face flushed, said, "I'd like to report vandalism in Gazebo Park. State senate candidate, Joe Thaxton's pickup truck was vandalized. All four tires are slashed. A windshield wiper is twisted off. And someone keyed the paint on one side of the truck."

"Is anyone hurt?"

"Financially, yes. Physically, no."

"We'll have an officer there in a few minutes." The dispatcher disconnected.

Garner looked at Joe, Jessica, and Roland. "Police are on their way. This is beyond getting into the mud. This is an attack. It's an attack against Joe, his campaign, and his supporters who demand change."

Joe looked around the park, a worker in the distance using a leaf blower, two children playing on a swing set, their mother standing near them. He looked at the damage to his truck, the flat tires, the long scratch in the paint, the twisted wiper blade. "I never expected this kind of reaction. I'm hitting more than a nerve … I'm making them run scared. They're afraid their cushy way of life, making hundreds of millions of dollars, while polluting our rivers, lakes and beaches is going to come to a halt."

Roland shook his head, scratching the whiskers on his chin, his eyes searching the park. "Takes balls or plain stupidity to do this in a park that was filled with a couple hundred people just an hour ago."

Jessica moved her purse to her left shoulder and folded her arms. "Joe's received threats. He's obviously making some people nervous, making them take him seriously. I don't know if they did it, but I spotted two men standing near that big oak tree, and they looked out of place."

"What do you mean?" Roland asked.

"They never applauded at anything Joe said. Never smiled. Most of the time their arms were folded across their chests. One guy looked like he was using a pocket knife to clean under his fingernails. They wore dark glasses and baseball hats. It was hard for me to see their faces clearly, but there was no mistaking what their body language was saying. They looked like they despised everything Joe was saying, especially when you took questions from the audience."

Joe said, "I'm definitely rocking the boat. I never entered this race thinking it was going to be easy. I just didn't think I would be bullied by people who sure as hell don't want me to win."

Roland nodded. "You think the big ag money is behind this?"

"Who knows. I'd hope they wouldn't stoop so low."

"Could be the guy you're runnin' against, Scott Sherman. Maybe he's behind it."

"I don't think he'd get down this far in the mud. Somebody wants me to shut up, or to drop out of the race. I won't do either."

Larry Garner looked around the park. "Where are the police?"

"What are they going to do?" Jessica asked, her voice filled with frustration. "We've reported the telephone threats. Police, unfortunately, have no clue. They seem to say that threats are just that … threats. And, until someone commits some kind of physical crime, like assaulting my husband, they can't go after the culprits. We're told they can't enforce restraining orders if there is no one by name to restrain. In the meantime, I'm frightened that someone will try to hurt Joe."

Garner looked at the flat tires. "Well, there's the evidence of a physical crime. Maybe that'll give them something they can use."

Jessica said, "If anyone in the crowd saw something, it'd seem like they would have told us or called 9-1-1."

Joe said, "My truck was parked behind the audience. A guy with a sharp ice pick could have hit all four tires in less than thirty seconds. These threats are getting more violent, but they won't stop me. The mission is too great."

Roland cleared his throat, glancing around the park, up to the American flag on the water tank and then down, looking directly at Joe. "I've known you and Jessica for a long time. I know there is nobody better to run for that office with this agenda at this time than you. This is a huge issue, and that's why you're getting these threats 'cause you're stepping on toes and old money is taking you seriously, as they ought to. They stepped over the line with this kind of crap. Since the police don't seem to be able to help until some freak decides to stick the icepick in your back, sounds like you need to consider options."

"What options do we have?" Jessica asked.

"A body guard would be one."

Joe shook his head. "We don't have the funds for that. It's not like I'm running for president of the United States and need Secret Service protection."

Roland cut eyes to the flat tires and twisted wiper blade. "You need some kind of protection."

Jessica said, "You mentioned options, as in more than one. Is there something else?"

Roland shoved his hands in his pockets just as a City of Stuart police cruiser pulled into the parking lot. No lights flashing. Two officers in the car. Roland looked at them a second and then shifted his eyes to Jessica. "Yes. Maybe a private investigator would be the solution if you can find the right person."

"Again," Joe said, shaking his head, "we don't have the funds. Everything that goes into the campaign is needed to pay for expenses and to buy advertising time on television and radio."

Roland watched the officers slowly get out of their car. Moving with no real sense of urgency. He said, "There's a guy at Ponce Marina, well he isn't there a lot. But he has a boat there. I met him once. He's low-key. Tall fella with a lot of muscle. But more than that, he seems like somebody you'd want watchin' your back. I heard he was a former Delta Force leader who came back from tours of duty to become a homicide detective in Miami. He supposedly had the highest conviction rate in the history of the department. But something happened down there, and he left."

Garner looked up from his iPad and asked, "What happened?"

"Don't know for certain. I think he was asked to leave … sort of a Dirty Harry kinda thing. His boat showed up one foggy morning in the marina. They say he paid a year's rent for his slip, and then no one saw him for months. I heard he lives in a cabin somewhere out in the boonies on the St. Johns River. A good friend, Nick Cronus, who knows the guy well, said he'll take cases only if he feels you've gone the traditional route and didn't get help."

"Who is this man?" Jessica asked.

The officers arrived. Two men in their mid-twenties. Short haircuts. Police radios on their thick belts crackling with staccato noise. Roland leaned closer to Joe and Jessica, lowering his voice. "Guy's name is O'Brien … Sean O'Brien."

Seventeen

I listened as Wynona paused, looking out across the wetlands, her thoughts as distant as the flock of white herons at the edge of the horizon. She stared into the outlying vista of sawgrass, island hammocks thick with cabbage palms, where marshes and blue sky became one at the curvature of the earth. Most of the tourists were now gone, heading to alligator and snake shows, some people strapping into swamp buggies or airboats for a cursory trip into the edge of the unknown, the illusion of an exploration into an alien world.

Wynona looked at me. "Sam Otter is more than a medicine man or a healer. He's very spiritual and wise. He adapted parts of Christianity into the Seminole religion because he saw strong parallels in both, focusing on one god, the Breathmaker as he calls God. A lot of the annual Green Corn Dance is a spiritual event. As a people, the Seminole were never conquered. Never signed a peace treaty even after three bloody wars with U.S. Army troops through the 1800s. Although my dad was Irish, I feel a lot of Seminole in my blood or my heart. But I don't have that indomitable spirit." She paused and sipped her coffee, Max snoozing on the chair beside us, a soft breeze coming over the marshlands with the citrus scent of blooming water lilies.

"Why do you say that? You are definitely a survivor."

"But I'm not a warrior. There's a difference, Sean. Surviving can often be because of forced circumstances, situations beyond your control.

At that point, it can be a fight or flight scenario. The indomitable spirt that is the legacy of the Seminole probably goes back to the time Osceola sat at the peace treaty table, looked at the treaty, which had a condition incorporated in it that the Seminole be relocated from Florida to Oklahoma. Rather than sign it, he brought his knife down hard into the center of the proposed agreement, pinning it to the wooden table. A few years later, meeting under a white flag of truce, Osceola and some of his men were surprised, jumped, and taken as prisoners. He was thrown into an Army prison cell where he died of an infection. I may share his last name, but I'm not sure the valor is there. I'm sorry for venting. It's been a rough couple of weeks. There was a suicide on the rez. A teenage girl. Cyber bullied. She took an overdose of oxycodone."

I said nothing for a moment, the high-pitched faltering crow of a rooster beyond the tree line of palms. "I'm sorry to hear that. Wynona, that night a few years ago, when you and your partner kicked down the front door of a house in a Detroit suburb to stop an insane man from killing his teenage daughter … that was and is one of the best examples of valor and fearlessness I've ever known."

She leveled her eyes at me. "A lot of that had to do with the screams from a teen girl coming through our earpieces. We had no choice."

"You did have other choices. You could have called for backup. Brought in SWAT. You didn't have to charge in there, not knowing whether you'd be shot as soon as that locked door was kicked open."

"I've replayed it in my mind, even in a strange, slow-motion scenario, too many times. Could I do that again? I often ask myself that question. The single round from my gun killed the deranged father. The other seven rounds I pumped into his body had nothing do with defending his mortally wounded daughter. It had everything to do with my rage. That's not heroism. My partner was later murdered in a revenge killing because of that. I'm still suspicious and leery of almost everyone I meet. I've allowed that horrible night and its consequences to further define me and I regret that."

I said nothing, allowing Wynona to vent and have someone listen who deeply cared about what she was saying. After a half minute, she leaned back in her chair and said, "Could be that I'm dealing with some sort of post-traumatic stress. I don't know. Most days it's never a real issue. Other times, it rises up when I least expect it. A smell can trigger it. A certain sound. Even a color, like the color of that kitchen in the house that night." She smiled. "Maybe I should hang out with Sam Otter and learn more about the laid-back world of the elders. But I have a job to do, catching bad guys. And we have our share of them on the rez. Not only Big Cypress, but the other four in Florida. Your thoughts, Doctor O'Brien?" She smiled.

I met her eyes. "It doesn't take a psychologist to see you've gone through hell and back. Not only that night in Detroit, but the afternoon in the parking lot of a deserted banana warehouse when we were facing Dino Scarpa and some of the Miami mafia. You persevered, you won."

"And I took a bullet for it. If it weren't for you pulling me out of that dark rabbit hole, I wouldn't be here having lunch in the Gator Café today. It's the little things in life." She pursed her lips and then half smiled. She placed one hand on her stomach, as if she felt pain.

"Are you hurting?" I asked.

"No, I'm fine. Must be the fry bread." She sipped her coffee. "We put bad guys and their evil out of commission, and the world is a finer place for it. That's why I studied criminology. I just followed my heart. And the career, at least what's left of it, met me along the road to perdition. Unlike legendary Osceola, I don't consider myself as a warrior. I'm more of a strategist, trying to deliver a checkmate to those who make it their career to hurt others. But it's always a trade-out. A crossroads where your soul is trying to remain intact because it's all you have left."

"Everyone has an Achilles' heel. There are no perfect knights. There will always be a weak or a rusty spot in the armor we try to put around us. Everyone, to some degree, becomes the sum of our circumstances, the hairline cracks that are the scars of survival. Maybe these cracks are not always visible on the outside. But the inside, where it counts, where our moats and drawbridges exist to defend us. We just have to remember not to become a prisoner in our own castle."

She smiled, her eyes filled with depth and radiance. She said, "The compromise is to remain vulnerable. That's not always easy, Sean. If I'm in my castle, I'm going to be perched in the tallest spire, glass of wine, gazing out over the land. Not that I need rescuing, mind you. I don't. But if a wayward knight like you comes wandering along on your horse, well, I'd be the first to see you on the horizon. I've missed you." She reached out and touched my hand.

"I've missed you, too."

She looked at the orchids on the table. "You know, my birthday is still twelve days away."

"Just like the twelve days of Christmas, maybe you'll get a gift each day leading up to the big day."

She laughed. "As long as there are no turtle doves or a partridge in a pear tree, I'm good with that." She paused, stared at one of the orchids, then looked back at me. "I've never had a bucket list, per se by the definition of a 'to do' list before-you-die kind of thing. But that trip with you and little Max aboard the sailboat, *Dragonfly*, would have been at the top of the list, if I'd ever made one. I still think about that, our slow trek back from the Bahamas, stopping at the little islands that didn't even have names. They sure have staying power in my mind. I think about them often."

"Me, too. After what happened, it was a perfect antidote."

"After that, I fell in love with sailing." Her eyes searched my face. "I really appreciate the orchids. It's very thoughtful, but then you're a caring man. A man who guards his privacy and his friends with a passion."

There was the distinct sound of gunfire in the distance, somewhere beyond the sawgrass and cabbage palm spits of land. Wynona said, "It's already starting."

"What? A war?"

"No." She chuckled. "Hunting season. It's not for two more days, but too often the overzealous go out in the glades to shoot their guns up in the air. Sometimes it's too close to the rez, because what goes up must come down. Two years ago, a twelve-year-old boy was hit in the top of his head by a bullet that fell from the sky. He was treated in the ER, the round almost cracked the boy's skull."

"Isn't hunting prohibited in the glades?"

"Yes, unless you're hunting for pythons. The park service sanctions those guys—the reptile hunters. Big Cypress National Preserve, which borders the rez, is where hunters are allowed in some areas during the season. They hunt for deer, wild boar, turkeys, whatever is in season." She glanced at her watch. "I need to get back to work. How about you? Are you working any PI cases for clients?"

"No. It's pretty much by referral only. And since I haven't had any referrals in the last couple of months, I'd like to think the crime rate is down." I laughed.

"You, of all people, Sean O'Brien, know that's not the case. Well, since it appears that you have a little free time on your hands, I'd like to formally invite you and Maxine over to my home for dinner tonight. I won't be cooking gator bites, frog legs or catfish, but I can make a great lasagna and glades salad."

"Sounds good. What time?"

"Will seven work?"

"Yes. It'll give me time to buy wine and get Max some dog food. Not that she'll eat it after scarfing down four gator nuggets." Max, hearing her name, sat up, looked at the empty plates, raising her soft brown eyes up to mine.

There was a second sound of gunfire in the distance. Max turned her head and looked in the direction of the sound. For a brief second, Wynona's eyes became shielded, as if the visor on her armor shut. She pulled a strand of dark hair behind one ear, what she said earlier echoing like the rifle shot in the distance. *Other times, it rises up when I least expect it. A smell can trigger it, or a certain sound.*

Eighteen

It was dark, and Joe Thaxton sat behind his makeshift desk in his campaign headquarters, returning emails. Five of his volunteers had left for the night. Only one, Travis Sinclair, remained, finishing a phone call. Travis, tall and angular, was a political science major in college, now about to head to grad school. He ended his call, stood from a desk near the front of the office filled with placards and signs. He stretched, walked back to Joe and said, "If you don't need anything, I'm heading out."

Joe looked up from his computer screen. "I'm fine, Travis. Thanks for staying past five o'clock. I really appreciate your time and help with the campaign."

Travis smiled, lots of straight white teeth showing. "No problem. I so believe in what you're doing ... I wish I didn't have to go back to grad school. Working with you, I'm getting invaluable training in political science."

Joe rubbed his temples, his eyes slightly red. "I'm no expert, but as far as I can tell, there's not much science to it. I use the science and data measured from research to prove points about pollution. As far as this political thing goes, seems to me it's all about human nature. Giving the voter not what he or she thinks they want to hear, but rather sound reasoning and scientific data, allowing them to make up their minds if the candidate is the right person for the job. And I look at it as a job, not a career. I want to get in there, fix what's broken, make sure there are provisions in place to keep it fixed, and then leave. I'd rather be out on the water fishing. But I want to fish in water that's not covered in green grunge."

Travis nodded. "Your message is so right on the money … we have people calling to volunteer. Our contributions, even at the one-hundred-dollar maximum level you set, are growing. Giving the people a voice, finding candidates that adhere to the U.S. Constitution, making a positive change … all that is why I'm interested in this field. I appreciate you giving me a shot here, thanks. It's actually better than grad school."

"You're welcome. Now go home. Get some rest and come back to hit it hard in the morning."

"Sounds good. Oh, I almost forgot." He handed Joe a phone message slip. "The gentleman who called while you were on the phone said his name is Howard Allen. He didn't say who he's with, but he said it's important that he speak with you this evening if possible. He told me he's very impressed with the campaign, your message, and the professional way you're conducting the race. Seems like a good guy and a solid supporter."

Joe took the message. "Thanks."

"See you in the morning. Don't stay too late."

When Travis left the office, Joe pinched the bridge of his nose, looked at the phone number and made the call. A deep voice answered. "Hello, Howard Allen speaking."

"Hi, Mr. Allen, this is Joe Thaxton returning your call."

"Excellent. Thank you for the quick call back."

"No problem. How can I help you?"

"Well, that's what I wanted to ask you. You're running a tight ship, facing an incumbent state senator with solid name recognition, a long track record, and a deep war chest. Maybe I can help you."

"What'd you have in mind? We're always looking for volunteers."

"Perhaps my time would be better served simply providing you with the resources to conduct your campaign on a higher level. Your opponent will flood the television airways soon with slick campaign ads. The creation, production, and purchasing of TV advertising time requires a substantial war chest."

"You're right. I'm hoping that if we get enough donations at a hundred dollars each, we'll be in a position to produce and buy ads. But I don't want to throw mud in smear and attack campaigns. All my ads will stick to the facts, the science, and let people know why I believe I'm the person who can most effectively do the job."

"No doubt." There was a pause for five seconds. "Joe, you're not the average Joe as you contend. You can relate to the voters on a level that resonates with them. That's a natural gift that you have. It can't really be taught. The gift that we can help you with is finances, more than enough to be competitive in the race. I promise you this, you will need it. You can't win by posting pictures on social media and doing talk radio interviews."

"You said we … who are we?"

"A number of people in executive positions to fund your campaign. We can help take you to the winner's circle. From what we can tell, and I'm talking about politically savvy consultants who're closely following the race, you might parlay a win at the state senate level into the governor's office later. And because Florida is such a large state, doing a sound job in the governor's office could open the door for a run down the road to the White House."

Joe laughed. "I really appreciate the vote of confidence, it's flattering. But I have no desire to become president of the United States. Same goes for the governor's job. Don't want it. But I do want to work as a team member with whoever wins the governor's race so together, we can turn back the tide of water pollution in Florida."

Joe could hear the man release a long breath before saying, "I'm not sure if I'm making myself clear. You will never make it at the rate you're going. Granted, you'll build some initial interest and then the heat will fade. It'll fade because your opponent, Senator William Brasfield, will hit you with so many attack ads that even you won't know who you are after the defecation starts flying. We can change that with resources to go the distance."

Joe stood and walked toward the front of his office in a strip mall shopping area. He watched two teenage girls enter a Subway restaurant. He saw a homeless woman, dirty gray hair feathering over half of her wrinkled face, pushing a grocery cart filled with crinkled brown bags of her possessions, the woman's mouth turned down under the streetlights infused with a wash of blue neon from a dry cleaner's sign. Joe said, "Anytime someone's waved money at me, money I didn't earn yet, there's always a catch. What is it that you and your people want, Mr. Allen?"

"Nothing really. No big political announcements or declarations. What we'd like to see, however, is for you to tone down your rhetoric about pollution. As a marine biologist, you'd be one of the first to admit pollution comes from many sources, farming is not the sole reason. We believe you can still run an effective campaign without a lot of unsubstantiated finger pointing. Do you follow me?"

"Absolutely, I follow you all the way to the main source of the pollution and the money trail like yours that allows it to exist in the first place, harming our fish and wildlife, and ultimately the people."

"Joe, we're in a position to make incremental PAC funding in your campaign well into seven figures, okay?"

"No, it's not okay. I can't be bought, Mr. Allen."

"Stay average, Joe. See how far you get. You'll regret your decision. If our funding doesn't go to you, it goes to your opponent. We won't lose." The man disconnected. Joe looked out the window, the homeless woman pushing her cart across the parking lot, one hard rubber wheel out of alignment, and wobbling.

Nineteen

Later that evening, the home filling with the smell of baked lasagna, I watched Wynona do what I never did. And in retrospect, maybe I should have done it. She walked to a small end table near a large window overlooking her backyard and spoke to her new orchids as if they had ears. She said, "This is your home, your new spot in the universe. You can see out into the backyard, but you're far enough away from the window to keep the direct sunlight off your delicate floral faces." She turned to me and laughed, her hair down, wearing black jeans and a white button-down blouse.

I stood in the kitchen, poured two glasses of wine, Max stretched out on Wynona's couch. I said, "I'm thinking that's what I did wrong with some orchids I had. Forgot to chat with them."

She walked back across the room to me. "You have to make them feel welcome and at home. It's more than just water and light. It's giving the plants their own sense of feng shui. Plants may not have ears, but they are perceptive, and they have moods."

"Well, I think you not only put them in their happy place physically, but you've elevated their feelings." I handed her a glass of wine. "Cheers … long live your new orchid friends and happy birthday to you."

She touched her glass to mine, sipped the wine, the flicker of candlelight swaying in her eyes. She said, "I have a plant joke for you."

"Okay, but can you tell it in mixed company. We don't want to embarrass the new arrivals."

"It's rated G for all plant audiences. Ready for this … why do some plants go to therapy?"

"I have no idea."

"To get to the root of their problem." She giggled, turning to the orchids and saying, "Now, I hope you guys are not in need of therapy. If so, let's talk about it, and we can work through any orchid issues."

I laughed. "That's better than what the big flower asked the little flower when he looked down in the garden and said … what's up bud?"

"Very good, Sean. Did you hear that from your new friend in the glades, the orchid man … what's his name again?"

"Chester."

She set her wine on the table. "I love the name … Chester. You don't hear that name too often anymore. I never heard it on the rez, not that Chester wouldn't have been a good name for a member of the tribe. Oh, the lasagna." She moved quickly beyond the kitchen counter, grabbing thick mittens to lift a dish of bubbling lasagna from the oven. "Just in time. We can let it cool for a while before serving. In the meantime, I'll make a salad." She glanced across the room to a wide-screen TV monitor mounted on the wall. "Do you mind if we catch the news while the lasagna is cooling? I want to see if the local stations are carrying the story about a large-scale embezzlement that I'm investigating."

I picked up the TV remote control, glanced out the window, a three-quarter moon hanging low in the southern sky.

• • •

Amber Nelson stared at the moon from her bedroom window. She held her baby to her shoulder, standing next to the child's crib, rocking and humming nursery rhymes. Amber looked across the bedroom at her husband, Johnny, who slept with his injured leg propped up on a pillow. She heard him moan, mumbling something in his sleep. The baby cried.

Amber whispered, "It'll be okay, Michael. Daddy will get well. Don't you cry little one." She looked at her baby's face, moonlight coming through the window, and she sang, "Hush little baby don't say a word … Daddy's gonna buy you a mockingbird … and if that mockingbird don't sing … Daddy's gonna buy you a diamond ring." She rocked the infant and gently set him down in the crib. The baby was now drifting off.

Johnny moaned in his sleep. He was back in eastern Syria. He and a squad of ten men walking quietly through what appeared to be an abandoned town of adobe-style buildings, some reduced to rubble after a barrage of mortar and air strikes by U.S. forces. This was one of the last ISIS strongholds. It was the equivalent of their Alamo, a last stand for ISIS militants who still fought, refusing, like so many, to retreat and assimilate in the populations of Syria and Iraq.

Johnny and his men used hand signals to communicate, moving stealthily down deserted alleyways, the smell of charred human flesh still lingering in the desert air. The corpse of an ISIS fighter lay across the threshold of an open door to a two-story building. Flies buzzed and crawled around the bloated face and neck. Eight of the Army Rangers' men carried MK-16 assault rifles. Two held modified 12-gauge shotguns, both guns loaded with double-aught buckshot.

After forty minutes of searching through abandoned buildings, the men stopped in an alley to regroup. "We've counted thirty-nine bodies," said Jesse Farren, unshaven, lean face, the youngest in the group of Rangers, his southern Cajun accent from the swamps of Louisiana. "I wonder how many of these fellas are stittin' in paradise with seventy-two virgins?"

"You really think they believe that? Dying in battle gets them a ticket to paradise and women, c'mon."

"I got no clue."

There was a sound, almost human, as if a woman cried out.

"What the hell's that?" Johnny asked. "Sounds like somebody in pain."

Jesse turned his head. "No, it sounds like a goat." Seconds later, a small goat wandered into the alleyway, a rope around its neck, the rope tied to a broken piece of wood. "Looks like that goat's a survivor.

Must have come loose from his hitch. I'm gonna take the rope off its neck so it'll find water and food without draggin' that wood around the desert."

Johnny looked at the rooftop of a building across the street. The other men did the same, uneasy, the buzz of flies louder. "Why don't you just let that goat fend for himself? We got more work to do."

"This'll take a few seconds. Hate to see an animal suffer." He walked over to the goat, the animal bleating, its rib bones showing beneath its hide. Jesse held his rifle in one hand, using his right hand to work the rope off the goat's neck. When he removed the rope, dropping it to the ground, he said, "Go on now. You're free." Jesse turned around to face his squad. He grinned right before his head exploded with a single shot.

"Noooo!" Johnny said, sitting up in his bed, sweat beading on his forehead. He looked around the darkened bedroom, disoriented.

Amber, washing her face in the adjacent bathroom, came running to his bedside. "She turned on a table lamp. "It's okay, Johnny. You must have had another nightmare. Maybe you're getting them again because of all the antibiotics in your system."

Johnny looked up at his wife. She used a hand-towel to wipe the sweat off his brow. "I keep seeing Jesse Farren in my dreams ... right before he was shot. Right after he set a little goat free." He licked his dry, cracked lips, the taste in his mouth like gun metal. He looked from his wife's face to his propped-up leg, an expression of fear in his eyes. "It's not getting' better, Amber. Look, it's getting worse every hour."

Amber stared at the wound, her breath catching in her throat. "Something's not right. The doctor said the antibiotics would stop the infection. It's not working. We need to get you to a hospital."

Twenty

I tried to remember the last time I watched the local news on television. It'd been awhile. I picked up the remote control, turning on the screen. "Any particular channel?"

Wynona looked up from slicing a tomato. "It should be on channel seven out of Miami. They're usually the most thorough when it comes to reporting crime news, and sadly, that's about all they report."

The TV came on, the screen filling with images of Coast Guard boats on the sea in what appeared to be a search and rescue mission. A reporter off-camera said, "The small plane went down about a half-mile off the coast of Jacksonville Beach. Authorities say there were four people aboard. The pilot is the owner of the plane, believed to be a Cessna. He was flying from Savannah to Miami with his wife, daughter, and son-in-law. Officials don't believe any of the four people survived the crash. From Jacksonville Beach, Sarah Hernandez, Channel Seven News."

Wynona used large wooden spoons to toss the salad in a big glass bowl. "That's so horrible. Sounds like the entire family was lost in the accident."

The picture on the screen cut back to a dark-haired news anchorman behind the desk in the studio. He looked into the camera. "In other news, it's not politics as usual in some of the state's races. Joe Thaxton, the candidate who calls himself average Joe with an exceptional plan to restore the Florida Everglades, was a victim today. Thaxton's pickup truck was vandalized at his rally in Stuart. All four tires were slashed, one wiper blade broken, and a long gash carved into the truck's paint, front-to-back bumper."

The image cut from the anchorman to video of Thaxton's truck as it was loaded onto a flat-bed wrecker, all the tires flattened. There were images of Thaxton, his wife, and others watching the loading. The anchorman continued. "Joe Thaxton is the charismatic fishing guide who's making a hard-charging effort to win a state senate seat in an effort to sponsor legislation for water clean-up and Everglades restoration. He's gaining a lot of supporters, and they are not confined only to his district. He's acquiring a following across the state of Florida and even the nation. Thaxton's pushing an agenda, not only to restore the water flow to the Everglades, but to end the release of polluted water from Lake Okeechobee into two waterways—the St. Lucie River on the east coast and the Caloosahatchee River on the west coast. Apparently, not everyone agrees with his plan. Thaxton said that doesn't matter, and he will not be intimidated or bullied."

The image cut to Thaxton, his truck secured on the flat-bed, the bearded wrecker driver pulling away and waving at the camera. Thaxton said, "We expected to rock the boat with our message, but we never thought someone would be destroying property to scare us. We've received threating phone calls. All this means we're pushing somebody's button."

"Any idea who's behind this?" asked an off-camera reporter.

"I have an idea, but until law enforcement can find out just how far up the chain this goes, I'd rather not speculate."

The picture returned to the anchorman. "Police say the investigation will continue. However, they say there are no immediate suspects, and apparently no one saw anything because Thaxton's truck was parked to the rear of the large crowd. Estimates are that it was around three-hundred people who came out to hear him today."

I muted the sound. "I heard that guy on a radio talk show. He's articulate, focused, and now is apparently stepping on the toes of either his opponent, William Brasfield, or the people who bankroll the lobbyists. And, in this case, I'd say that's very deep pockets—irresponsible pockets."

Wynona nodded. "Just in my lifetime, I've seen water levels and the condition of the water drastically change for the worse in the glades. My mother said, when she was a child, the tribe would drink directly from the water that flowed through the glades, through the endless sawgrass. She said the water was crystal clear. Now, it looks like coffee."

The newscast segued into a weather segment, and Wynona said, "Let's eat. We can keep the sound off. I've had enough bad news for the moment."

We sat at an antique mahogany wood, octagon-shaped table in the dining room adjacent to her kitchen. Max jumped from the couch in the family room to claim her position on the kitchen floor near my feet. Wynona told me about the case she was investigating, and said she had reason to believe that the suspect had fled the state. "We'll get him," she added. "He was sloppy, an emotionally-fueled crime that left a trail. I'd wish he'd fled into the glades. I could probably find him easier in there. If I couldn't, Joe Billie could. He's not a cop, as you know, but he can track just about anyone or anything if he's asked."

"I haven't seen Joe in a couple of months. How is he?"

"He comes to the rez less than he used to. After the trial, it seems to have changed him somewhat. He's even more reserved and harder to find. Not that I go looking for him. But he has family here. I know they'd like to see him more. I guess he still lives in that old trailer near the center of the state. You, Sean, are probably his best friend. Not so much because you proved him innocent of murder, but because you two have always had each other's backs … way before the trial."

I sipped my wine, "To see him, I have to go find him. He's not fond of keeping his phone charged. He has stopped by my river cabin when he's been out in his canoe fishing."

She smiled. "He's one of the few people who don't check their phones every twenty minutes."

"The lasagna is excellent."

"I'm glad you like it. You said you had some orchids and they died. Did you buy them from Chester or somewhere else?"

"They were Sherri's orchids; and after her death, I inherited them. Max loved following her from plant to plant as she watered them. There were about a half-dozen or so. All very beautiful. She'd kept them alive for years. One-by-one, they seemed to bend their blooms over, like bowing their heads, and then wasted away. I didn't have Sherri's green thumb."

"No, but you had her heart … and she had yours. That never died. And it shouldn't. I just hope one day you'll allow your heart to open a little wider to let others inside." Wynona glanced from me to the flickering candle in the center of the table, the light floating in her eyes. She looked up and said, "That sailing trip we did … Max, you and me. I really got a chance to know you over time in a different world, a different environment. Not the one we'd just left, of pure survival after what happened to Dave Collins and those CIA officers. That trip, maybe it was the boat, *Dragonfly*, like dragonflies in the wild, had a special mystical quality sailing across the sea. Where's the boat now?"

"She's in a slip next to *Jupiter*. I need to decide what to do with her. I thought about selling the boat, maybe giving the money to a children's charity. But since *Dragonfly* was a gift, selling her seems discourteous."

"*Dragonfly* was a gift to you because you saved the lives of two people. You absolutely love sailing. There's no mandate that says you must get rid of things you love, Sean. Why do you feel that way?" Wynona rubbed one finger across the top of her wine glass, leaning back in her chair.

"I don't feel that way. Unfortunately, life has too often made the decision for me, cutting short the people I cherish. It happened in combat. Marriage. In my profession, and in my family. I don't try too hard to over analyze it anymore, not like I used to do. I try to learn from it."

"Are you talking about the meaning of life?"

"Life has real meaning when we bring it to the table. Too often we ask that question when we are the answer. And I use the metaphor, table, because it's better not to dine alone."

Wynona smiled. "I like that metaphor, and I like you Sean O'Brien. I like you a lot. I may even love you. I'm not completely sure because I've never felt like this before I met you. I have had my share of boyfriends. Even a long-term relationship. It was an engagement that dissolved when the FBI required sixty-hour weeks the first year. But I didn't feel for Mark what I feel for you. Maybe it's because you saved my life. I don't know. I respect the privacy you cherish so much. You spend time at sea or sequestered in that quaint old cabin of yours on the river. You're surrounded by your books, by the sound of the birds, the wind off the river, the sunsets on the water, by the isolation of your own form of Eden. But, by surrounding yourself with all that, you do the opposite with people. And the irony is I know how much you care for others—how much you do for others. Your friends, people like Dave, Nick, Joe Billie … would do anything for you. You know I've never pried, but somewhere in your life … maybe it was something that happened when you were in the military or working as a homicide detective, or maybe the death of your wife, Sherri … something, I believe, hurt you deeply. I just want you to know I'm here for you like you've been here for me. I don't find being vulnerable easy either, but love can be worth the risk."

"I agree." I reached out and took her hand in mine.

Wynona lowered her eyes then raised them to mine. She said, "You talked about not being a prisoner in your own castle. That has to apply to you as well. Even in a beautiful place like Eden, a guy called Adam got a little lonely. We all do, especially people with a heart like yours. Can you stay the night?"

"I can."

Twenty-One

Joe Thaxton stood in his kitchen, sipping a cup of black coffee, speaking on the phone with his campaign manager, Larry Garner. It had been three days, and now he had his truck back in the driveway, Jessica's car parked in their garage. He bought new tires, a new windshield wiper motor. A new paint job. And he had a renewed determination to charge ahead with his campaign and his message. He glanced at his watch as Jessica and Kristy entered the kitchen, Kristy dressed for school. Jessica dressed for work. Rodeo, the loveable Lab, following behind them.

Garner asked, "Are you coming to headquarters before you head to the radio interview? Should you grab some doughnuts to take to the radio station?"

Thaxton set his coffee cup on the kitchen table. "Yes. I thought about buying doughnuts, but nothing like feeding our hosts sugar ... sort of an oxymoron, you think?"

"At least you're not feeding them BS like so many other guys in state's races."

"Depends on what BS stands for ... could mean Big Sugar." They both laughed.

Garner stood by his desk in the campaign headquarters, placards and signs all over with Joe Thaxton's smiling face, a half-dozen volunteers working the phones or looking into computer screens, adding material to social media platforms. Garner said, "Remember, you have a podcast to record at one o'clock this afternoon. Carol wrote it for you, but we want to give you time to edit it before we record it."

"Okay. I'll stop in before heading to the radio station."

"Hey, if you get doughnuts, don't forget to bring some for your dedicated staff."

"You got it." He disconnected, turned to Jessica and Kristy. "How are my most favorite people in all the world this morning?"

Kristy smiled. "Good, Daddy. Are you going to take me to school?"

Jessica looked at her husband, lifting her eyebrows, smiling. He said, "Absolutely."

"I'm going to help Mom make my lunch."

Jessica said, "You almost don't need my help anymore. You're getting so good at it."

"Except using a knife to cut the ends off my sandwich. I don't do that."

"I'm betting next year you'll suddenly love all parts of the sandwich."

• • •

A half-hour later, Thaxton and Kristy were almost at her school when the truck's engine made its first sound. It was as if the engine sputtered for a second, quickly correcting itself and then running fine. As Thaxton pulled into the large circular driveway, drove past two parked school buses to the student drop-off area, the engine misfired again. He glanced over at Kristy, buckled in the seatbelt in the front seat next to him, her backpack on the floorboard, lunch pail on her lap, hair pulled back in a headband. He stopped his truck, put it in park, and stepped around to open the door for his daughter. "You have a great day today. Study hard, okay?"

"Okay, Daddy. Is Mama picking me up today?"

"She'll be here. And I'll see you both for dinner. You feel like pizza tonight?"

"Yes!"

"I'll pick one up on the way home." He kissed his daughter, watching her walk toward the front door of the Port Salerno Elementary School. His truck made another odd sound, as if the engine coughed. Thaxton got back behind the wheel and drove off. He didn't get very far. In less than three miles, his truck engine strained, making thrashing sounds, finally quitting. It was all he could do to pull safely onto a convenience store parking lot before the truck died in a short hiss.

"What the hell?" Thaxton mumbled, getting out and opening the hood. There was no sign of smoke or overheating. He tried the ignition. The engine straining but failing to start. He called Larry Garner's phone. "My truck's dead. I'm stranded in the parking lot of a Seven-Eleven store off of Federal Highway."

"What happened?"

"I have no idea. The motor started sputtering, and then it began thrashing and bucking, finally stopping. Battery's fine, but it can't start the truck—the engine is dead."

"I'll call a tow for you. You're close to the Ford dealership. Let's get your truck in there. I'll get you to the radio station. Hey, Joe … you can forget the damn doughnuts."

• • •

Three hours later, Joe Thaxton and Larry Garner waited in the lobby at the radio station. The walls were nearly covered in framed awards and photos of celebrities and politicians who'd been guests through the years. Thaxton was to go on the air as a guest for an entire hour. He'd called Jessica and let her know what happened, telling her that the service manager at the dealership promised to assess the truck's problem immediately.

Ten minutes before Thaxton was to join the host in Studio-C, his phone buzzed. He looked at the caller ID. It was the Ford dealership. He answered, and the service manager said, "It wasn't too hard to find the source of the problem."

"Is there some good news?"

"Good and bad. Someone poured sugar in your gas tank. That's not what did the damage. In addition to the sugar, they put water in the tank. That's where the problem lies the most. Water and gas do not mix. For that matter, neither does sugar. Whoever the jerk is, he or she wanted to make sure you weren't going very far in your truck."

"How much damage?"

"The fuel injector is shot. We'll remove all the water and sugar from your tank, flush the fuel-lines, clean out the carburetor, dry the cylinders and pistons. Then we'll add fresh gas and clean-burning additives to give the engine the boost it needs."

"How long will that take?"

"All of today. You should be able to pick it up tomorrow." The service manager paused, watching a car lifted up on a hydraulic rake. "Mr. Thaxton, you said this happened when you drove away from your home this morning, right?"

"Yes. That's the first I noticed it after getting the truck back from having had all four tires slashed, a wiper blade motor broken, and a keyed paint-job."

"Sir, do you have security cameras on the outside or your home?"

"No."

"Just a suggestion, but you might want to get them. With all that damage you've had to your truck lately, and now the stuff with the engine, somebody's obviously got an ax to grind with you. And they might come back. It'd be good to catch the creeps on camera."

"I'll see you tomorrow, thanks." Thaxton disconnected, turned to Garner and told him what happened. "Sugar and water in my gas tank. Is that sending a message or what?"

Garner said, "Bring this up during the interview. I think listeners—voters, need to know what we're up against and maybe who's pushing back and why."

The producer of the radio show, a tall blonde woman dressed in designer jeans, dark blue blazer and a knit, white shirt entered the lobby, smiled. "Mr. Thaxton, we'll need you in Studio-C now. The program is starting in a couple of minutes. We anticipate that this will be one of our better political shows. You're gaining quite a following, and from what we see on our social media sites, your supporters are passionate. It should make for a lively discussion and debate. You both can follow me, please."

Twenty-Two

Chester Miller led his granddaughter Callie on a journey of discovery. They both wore black rubber waders, suspenders holding them waist-high, as they walked through water and the dense jungle-like terrain of Big Cypress National Preserve. Mottled sunlight penetrated the boughs of tall cypress trees, the odor of decaying leaves and swamp gasses bubbling from dark mud to the surface. Two blue herons stalked tiny fish darting in and out of the submerged tentacle roots of red mangrove bushes.

Chester used a hand-carved, white oak cane for balance, a wide-brim hat on his head, stepping through water up to his calf muscles, the sucking sound of mud coming from each step. Callie followed close behind her grandfather, a camera in one hand, strap around her neck, backpack over her narrow shoulders, long sleeve shirt. "Look," she said, pointing to a fallen log in water surround by lilies, white blossoms like cotton balls in the distance. A young alligator, less than two feet in length, crawled up on the log, settling down in a shaft of sunlight, its yellow eyes glinting like small gold coins.

They'd parked off a dirt road that twisted three miles into the preserve, figure S curves, as if an enormous snake had left a trail through the swamps. They left Chester's twenty-year-old Chevy truck to one side of the narrow road, locked the doors and set out on foot. It was a trip Chester had done before, but never with his granddaughter.

The seasonal rains were gone, water levels dropping enough to make the hike through the bogs and sloughs rather safe.

Chester stopped. "Let's hunt for ghosts."

"You think we'll find some today?" Callie asked.

"I do believe we will. Used to be more out here, way before you were born. Not so much anymore. Like I told that fella, Sean O'Brien, the ghost orchids are one of the canaries in the coal mine in Big Cypress and the glades."

"I know you mentioned that Grandpa, but I'm not sure exactly what you mean."

He stopped walking, the sound of shadowy wings fluttering through the treetops, something splashing in the water farther into the swamp. "Years ago, coal miners in parts of West Virginia and Kentucky would carry a caged canary into the mines with them. It was because the canary would warn them of any poisonous gases leaking in the mine … carbon monoxide was a gas they couldn't smell."

"Could the canary smell it?"

"I don't know. Maybe."

"How'd the canary warn miners? Did it start chirping like a smoke alarm?"

"No. It died."

Callie looked at her grandfather, her eyes widening in surprise. He said, "The canary, with its smaller and a more fragile respiratory system, would be the first to die, giving the miners a warning to get out of the mine. Today, that allusion is sometimes used to give an example of an early warning system in nature."

Callie watched two roseate spoonbills prowling in the shallow water, the birds feeding near cypress knees, the spoonbill's pink feathers reflecting off the water like hundreds of rose petals floating on the surface. She said, "I feel so sorry for the canaries. I know the lives of the miners are vital, but to use canaries as sacrificial lambs seems cruel."

Chester nodded. "The practice is history today, but its use in the past created quite a parallel to what we search for here in the middle of this natural paradise."

"You mean the ghost orchids, right?"

"Indeed." He used the tip of his cane to point toward a large cypress tree. "That tree, for example. Last year a ghost orchid lived its life about ten feet up from the surface, just beneath the lowest hanging limb. Now, the orchid is gone."

Callie focused her camera lens to where her grandfather pointed, took a picture. "I only see what looks like a piece of dried vine. Why'd the orchid die?"

"It wasn't eaten by a predator. It wasn't beyond its life cycle. Its demise, I believe, was accelerated by the changes in hydration within the swamp. Sometimes, it'll be too dry in here, causing the ground-level atmospheric conditions, the humidity in particular, to fluctuate to extremes. It's analogous to the ocean waters warming a few degrees causing the death of coral reefs."

"A canary in the mines for our oceans." She watched the spoonbills thrust their heads in and out of water, looking for food. "This place is so beautiful and fragile. Most people don't have any idea because they haven't done what we're doing. When you take the time to walk through this water, to feel the pulse of the swamp, the birds and wildlife, how it all moves in a rhythm … you can develop a much deeper appreciation for its beauty."

Chester smiled. "I'm delighted you feel that way. Come on, Callie. The visuals are stunning, but I want you to experience something else … the sounds of nature when it thinks no one is listening. I know the perfect spot." The old man led her deeper into the swamp, water bugs moving in elliptical patterns across the surface, like skaters on ice. Chester pointed to a snake up in a tree. "Always remember to look at what's in front of you and what's above you."

Callie stopped walking, lifting the camera to her eye, focusing on a snaked wrapped around the limb of a cypress tree. The snake's body was covered in a variegated pattern of pumpkin orange and black, its belly creamy. She zoomed in, snapping a picture. "Is it poisonous, Grandpa?"

"No. It's a beautiful snake with a name that does not do it justice. That's a rat snake. I haven't seen one that size in quite a while. It's a good sign." He started walking, leading Callie another hundred yards deeper into the preserve, spindly air plants and red and white bromeliads perched on trees and limbs swathed with hanging moss. Leafy ferns, some the size of small cars, grew from the mounds of exposed dark earth, the humid air heavy with the musky scent of life spawning.

When they got to a darker section of the swamps, canopies of cypress trees dimming much to the sunlight, Chester held one finger to his lips. He leaned closer to his granddaughter and whispered, "I want us to stand still for at least five minutes. No talking. Just listening. In a moment, the orchestra will begin."

Callie smiled and said nothing. She looked around at the lush foliage, giant trees with limbs that steepled together in arches above the swamp. Other trees with coal black trunks had rotted or fallen during storms, the branches splayed into the water as if the limbs tried to prevent the fall. She watched a brown spider, the width of her hand, crawl down one of the limbs, the spider stopping at the water's edge. Gnats orbiting. Deerflies buzzing. Minnows swimming around her legs. There was the primordial, haunting cry of a limpkin. Its long shrieks almost human in pitch.

And then the other birds started to join the ensemble. One by one. Chester pointed to three white egrets on a high branch, the birds throwing back their feathery heads and crooning, each trying to squawk louder than the other. Soon, the swamps teemed with birdsong—chirps, hoots, chants, cooing, long melodies of warbling, as if the birds were singing in a frenetic harmony, belting out ballads echoing through the trees and bayou.

Callie closed her eyes for a few seconds and listened to the solos, the choruses, the orchestra of nature in a cornucopia of sounds. She felt like she was being serenaded as she stood in knee-deep water, a bullfrog sitting on a submerged tree limb and joining the choir with its baritone voice.

After another minute, Chester stroked his beard and whispered, "Now you can understand what you can hear if you take the time to listen."

She took a picture of the three egrets. "This is literally, in all sense of the word ... wild. I love it. It seems like these birds and animals were all around us but playing hide-and-go-seek until we stopped seeking.

Then, they came to us. She spotted a four-foot alligator slowly swimming through the water about fifty feet away from them. "Maybe some feel they can come a little too close."

"That gator means no harm. They were here long before us. Okay, Callie ... right now I'm going to show you where to look. But I want you to tell me what you see, okay?"

"Okay."

He used his cane to point to a cypress tree with a base as wide as a round picnic table. "Up there, in the cypress, about ten feet from the water, what do you see?"

Callie looked in the direction he pointed. Two ghost orchids, petals the color of fresh snow, seemed to spring from the trunk of the tree. "I see a ghost, Grandpa. Not one, but two ghosts. That's so awesome. It looks like they're defying gravity, suspended in midair above the swamp."

"They are, in some respects. They're attached to narrow stems, and from this distance it's not that easy to see the stems, giving the ghost orchid the illusion that they're drifting in air ... like a ghost.

"I'm getting a picture." She looked through the lens, zooming in until the orchids filled the frame, taking two pictures. "Did you know they were there, Grandpa, or did you happen to spot them?"

"I knew one was there. The second one wasn't up there the last time I visited the area. Seeing it today is a pleasant surprise."

The sound of a rifle shot echoed through the swamps.

All the birdsong abruptly ended, as if a giant muzzle was thrown over Big Cypress Preserve. Callie, taken out of her moment with nature, looked through the pockets of dappled sunlight deep into the sloughs. "What was that?"

"Gunshot. Sounds like a rifle."

"It seemed really close to us. You think there are hunters in here?"

"Maybe. Poachers more likely."

"Should we be scared, Grandpa?"

"No, don't be scared. Be cautious."

"I think I'm going to be both, afraid and cautious."

"Hunting season has begun, but this part of the preserve is supposed to be off limits. That's what bothers me. Let's walk back to the truck and whistle as we go. We don't want to be mistaken for game and get shot. By the time someone found us, there wouldn't be much left. That's another thing the swamp does well … hides its dead."

Twenty-Three

A week later, one of the most anticipated televised political debates of the season was about to take place. Incumbent state senator, William Brasfield, now facing challenger Joe Thaxton, who was making big waves to unseat Brasfield. Thaxton and Brasfield stood behind podiums, fifteen feet apart in the studios of Channel Seven in Miami. An audience of less than one hundred people sat in portable, hard plastic chairs, watching as the moderator Jennifer Hernandez appeared. She wore a dark blue suit, black hair up, a legal pad in her hands, walking with an air of confidence.

"Hello, everyone," she said to the audience. "Thank you for joining us tonight. I'm Jennifer Hernandez, one of the political reporters here at Channel Seven. If time permits, we'll take questions from the audience. And thanks for submitting some questions in writing." She held up a few dozen index cards.

"Stand by, Jennifer," said a husky floor director who stood near one of the four studio cameras, earphones on his head.

Jennifer stepped to a small table in front of the candidates, smiled and sat down.

"On three … two …one …" The floor director motioned with his hand, and the red light came on above the lens of a camera.

"Good evening," Jennifer said, looking directly into the camera. "Welcome to tonight's political debate for the state senate from

District twenty-five. It's part of a series that Channel Seven is producing live from our studios through the coming weeks. Tonight, we are pleased to welcome State Senator William Brasfield. Mr. Brasfield has served in the state legislature for six years and tonight he seeks another term."

The camera cut to a close-up of Brasfield, he had the lopsided grin of someone who'd just dropped an ice cream cone. Double chin. Narrow, anxious eyes. His small hands gripped the sides of the podium like a man climbing a high ladder. Jennifer said, "Welcome Senator Brasfield." He grinned and nodded at the studio audience. "His challenger, on the left of your screen, is Joe Thaxton. Welcome Mr. Thaxton."

The camera cut to a close-up shot of Thaxton. He smiled, looking directly at the moderator and said, "Thank you. And thanks for having me."

She nodded. "Mr. Thaxton is a fishing guide. He earned a degree in marine biology from the University of Miami. Off camera, the candidates agreed to a coin toss to determine who'll get the first question, and Mr. Thaxton won. In this debate, as all of the debates we host here, there will be no opening statement. We feel the voters hear a lot of statements and soundbites, not only from these gentlemen, but from others running for office. I will ask the questions, some of which were submitted by our studio audience. We're looking for responses of no more than two minutes. You can see the digital clock from your places at the podiums."

The camera pulled to a wide shot, and she said, "Okay, let's begin tonight's debate. Mr. Thaxton, you've never served in public office. You've made a living as a fishing guide. Your slogan is you're an average Joe with an extraordinary message for all of Florida, not just your district. You've taken on the Everglades Restoration Plan as the centerpiece of your campaign. If elected, what do you propose to do?"

"As much as possible as soon as possible. But I know I'll be one of many moving parts in state government. This election is not about me … not about William Brasfield … it's about the health of every man, woman, and child in Florida … and the millions who visit our state each year. Our rivers are sick and getting worse. Some lakes are so polluted even the gators can't live in them. The Everglades is one of a kind in all the world. But the River of Grass is dying, like so many areas in Florida that need fresh, clean water for life. Back in 2014, more than four-million voters in our state, that's seventy-five percent of us, voted to pass a referendum to buy property south of Lake Okeechobee to restore the water flow to the Everglades. Well-paid lobbyists and their politicians on puppet strings have stalled that program indefinitely. The people have spoken, and to be frank with you, career politicians like my opponent, Senator Brasfield, have turned a deaf ear. And the reason is because money from lobbyists speaks louder than four million voters. Is the legislature above the will of the people? No, they are not and never will be."

There was a loud murmur in the audience. Light applause followed. Jennifer said, "Please refrain from applause until the end of tonight's debate. She turned to Brasfield. "Mr. Thaxton is pulling no punches. You each have two minutes for a rebuttal. Your turn Senator."

"Thank you, Jennifer." He looked into a camera. "I really don't need two minutes because simple accusations like that of my opponent can be boiled down in modest but profound statements of clarity." He shook his head, the crooked grin returning. "First, it's painfully obvious that Mr. Thaxton, the neophyte that he is, has done an average Joe's job at best in terms of research. Since the amendment passed in 2014, there have been some purchases of property, and we are on track to restore the waterflow back to the Everglades, to protect our beautiful springs, lakes and rivers. These things take time. One of the first lessons you learn in government is no one is an island. There are no superheroes in Tallahassee as Mr. Thaxton appears to want to portray himself to be. It takes teamwork to get things done. Water restoration is a top priority of mine. Just like my opponent, I enjoy fishing. But I don't fish for public sympathy by exaggeration and misleading inaccuracies. I might as well have 'Henny Penny' and the 'sky is falling' philosophy running against me. The things he talks about, red tide and algae blooms. These have been part of Florida long before agriculture. Just like hurricanes, we can go for years without seeing one and then, out of the blue, we get a hurricane. That doesn't mean the climate is altered."

The moderator said, "Your response, Mr. Thaxton before we move on to other questions."

"Thank you," Joe said, looking at her. He cut his eyes to Brasfield, and then addressed the audience in the studio and at home. "Mr. Brasfield calls it out of the blue. When you see blue-green algae emerge in our rivers and thousands of dead fish wash ashore, you know it's not coming out of the blue … from some blue spot in the universe. I don't mind being called 'Henny Penny' when the scientific data is accurate. Because it is, and the results are frightening. Man-made pollution is the prime catalyst behind these massive slime-green algae blooms that are far too frequent in our rivers and lakes. Yes, we've had red tide outbreaks on beaches for a long time. But now it's happening more frequently. When toxic slime pours from our rivers to our beaches, the result can exacerbate algae blooms along our coastlines. Tons of fish, crabs, oysters and mammals are victims. The stench is almost unbearable. Let me reiterate … in 2014 the people of Florida overwhelmingly mandated that a portion of taxes from real estate doc stamps go directly into the Land Acquisition Trust Fund for water restoration and conservation purposes, including restoring the Everglades. That's not happening. The question I'd like to ask Senator Brasfield is why?"

• • •

Simon Santiago parked his red Ferrari in one of his four private parking spaces in the garage of an opulent high-rise condo overlooking Biscayne Bay. Santiago, late forties, balding, neatly trimmed short beard, wore an Armani jacket over a dark T-shirt and black, designer jeans. He got out in the parking garage and walked to the elevator, the heals of his Stefano Ricci crocodile loafers, tapping the concrete. Even from the open-air garage one hundred feet above the posh landscaping, he could smell gardenias in full bloom.

Santiago got in the private elevator and rode to the penthouse. Inside his four-thousand-square-foot condo, he tossed his jacket on the back of a Tommy Bahama chair, stepped across the hardwood floor to a lavish bar and poured a long shot of Diplomatic Reserve rum over ice in a crystal glass. He moved across the living room filled with expensive designer furniture made with South Beach in mind. Santiago opened the glass doors, stepping out on his terrace overlooking the Atlantic Ocean, the lights of a cruise ship in the distance, the scent of the sea in the breeze. He sipped the rum and thought about calling an escort service. He'd order one of his favorite girls like he ordered food to go from Whole Foods. As Santiago reached for his phone in his pocket, it buzzed.

He set his drink down on an outdoor table, looked at the caller ID and answered. "Good evening," he said. "Are you in New York tonight?"

The man sat in silhouette in a darkened room, a burning cigar in one hand, a gold and diamond pinky ring on his finger. "No, I'm not in New York. I want to sell that condo anyway," said the man his voice soft and tingeing with a hint of sarcasm. "I'm on the island."

"Good, then you're not that far away."

"I take it you did not watch the political debate between Brasfield and the newcomer, Thaxton."

"No, I was in transit."

"You're a high paid lobbyist. It's your job to watch and monitor these things during an election year. Thaxton is making things difficult. He's aligning himself with Hal Duncan. If elected governor, Duncan has suggested he'll replace everyone we had appointed on the water board. He needs a guy like Thaxton to be his cheerleader."

"Thaxton won't win."

"Oh really. Tonight, on television, he cleaned Brasfield's clock. Thaxton said, if he's elected, he'll work with U.S. reps in the house and senate to amend the farm bill's sugar subsidies. That simply cannot and will not happen."

"I wouldn't worry. That's been suggested off and on for years. We've always beaten it at every level, regional state and national. With enough money, we can lead any hack politician to water and teach him or her to drink the Kool-Aid."

"You told me Thaxton turned down offers of PAC campaign contributions. So, how's that theory working?"

"We're just getting started. We'll bury him in attack ads. Voters will think he's a wife beater and pedophile by the time we're done."

"If you fail, and if he's elected along with Duncan, this contract with you and your firm is finished. Is that clear?"

"Yes sir."

The man on the other end of the line hung up.

Twenty-Four

Johnny Nelson looked at the ceiling tiles in his hospital room and whispered a prayer. The tiny holes in the ceiling tile were swimming, going in and out of focus. *Weird*, he thought. *At night the stars are white surrounded by black. In here, the stars are black, surrounded by white.* He laid flat on his back in the bed, his thoughts racing, his right leg on fire from his swollen foot all the way up to his right hip. It was a pain that hurt deep inside his leg, like termites were chewing the bones in search of soft marrow.

Two IV's strapped to his arms pumped powerful antibiotics into his bloodstream. Yet, he could feel something crawling in his diseased tissue that was now growing purple. Oxycodone barely dulled pain. "Where's Amber?" he mumbled. "Where's my wife?" Johnny tried to sit up, tried to focus on the button to call a nurse. He was weak and getting weaker. The call button seemed as if it was across the room.

The door opened, and Amber rushed in, a doctor and a nurse following her. Amber said, "You have to do something! My husband's getting worse."

The doctor, a tall man with a long face, caring liquid eyes, said, "Let me take a look at it." He approached the bed, the nurse standing to his right and moving the sheet from Johnny's leg. The doctor studied the growing infection, some of the skin around the wound now almost black, the foul odor of puss and rot seeping from the dying tissue. He looked up at Johnny and said, "Mr. Nelson, we have given you massive doses of every antibiotic we know to treat an infection like this. Unfortunately, nothing is working well enough. The infection continues to spread. I don't make this statement lightly, but I believe that amputation is the best to arrest it in order to keep the bacteria from moving further into your body."

"Doc," Johnny said, his voice raspy. "If you take off my leg, how will I feed my family?"

Amber said, "Please! Can't you do more? Isn't there a stronger drug … maybe something that's in the testing and research stages that you can use. Please, we have to try."

The doctor nodded. "I wish I had something like that. This infection comes from an extremely aggressive strain of bacteria—a super bug, a fierce form of streptococcus called vibrio vulnificus that's mutated into an even more virulent form of itself. In the past, some people have called it a flesh-eating bacterium. But that's not the case. Bacteria don't eat the flesh; the bug destroys it and the flesh decays. That's what's happening to your husband. We can remove the dead tissue, but I don't think that will contain the infection."

Amber couldn't hide her fear, mouth tight, eyes welling. "I can't believe this is happening. My husband fought in the military against ISIS and now something he never saw is destroying his leg."

The doctor looked at Johnny and then at Amber. "You folks discuss it. Time is of the essence. I know you're frightened, and you should be. I don't want to add to your stress, but I'd be remiss if I didn't let you know that these water-borne infections are getting more powerful each year. Around the state, we've average one fatality a month from this. Please make your decision quickly."

• • •

I stood at the end of my dock on the St. Johns River, thinking about the time I spent with Wynona. It'd been two days, and I already missed her. Max barked once, chasing a large grasshopper around one of the two wooden benches I'd built and placed at the end of my dock. One bench faced east for the sunrises, the other faced west for the sunsets. The sunrises, and especially the sunsets, are some of the best in the world when the large, spherical ball dips behind the wide oxbow in the river, cypress trees donned in hanging moss and standing in silhouette, ospreys making twilight catches, diving into scarlet and ruby surfaces painted by clouds soaked with the same colors.

My dock protruded about sixty feet from the riverbank into the dark water. I set my phone down on one of the benches, sipping coffee, the sun rising over a tree line of live oaks and cabbage palms. The soft morning breeze delivered the fragrance of blooming honeysuckles mixed with the briny scent of the river, the water moving quietly around the dock pilings.

My phone buzzed.

Max looked at it, cocking her head, then glancing up at me.

"Let's not answer it," I said. "We're supposed to spend the morning fishing. There are bass out there bigger than you."

I ignored the phone. Max and I were going fishing. I'd made a thermos of coffee, packed our lunches, set a tackle box, rod and reel in my fourteen-foot Jon-boat. The boat, tied to my dock, was Army green. It drew less than a foot of water and was easily propelled by a quiet electric motor. The St. Johns was one of the slowest moving and perhaps flattest rivers in America, dropping less than thirty feet its entire 310-mile length, from the headwaters to the sea.

I thought about the old river, its history and legacy. It was one of the few in the world that flowed north. Swamps west of Vero Beach gave birth to the headwaters, burping out a trickling of water that meandered north. The stream soon met springs surging from deep beneath the earth, the water flowing into creeks that grew into a river feeding thirteen lakes, creating a long and twisting necklace of water that meets the Atlantic Ocean fifteen miles east of Jacksonville. The river was the first in the New World to have a settlement of European colonists build a village on a high bluff between present-day Jacksonville and Mayport.

My phone buzzed again.

This time, Max ignored it. She was fascinated by a young gator barely moving its tail to zigzag across the river toward the Ocala National Forest. From the dock or my cabin built near an ancient shell mound left behind by Indians, you couldn't see any signs of civilization or people. My nearest neighbor was about a mile way, via the county road. I had three acres and a seventy-year-old cabin that originally was constructed from white oak timbers, cedar and some cypress planks on the porch. The roof was made of tin. The best part was the large, screened-in back porch overlooking the river.

I lifted up a paddle I had propped against one of the benches, setting the paddle down on the floor of the Jon-boat, Max now pacing in anticipation of a morning on the water. She loved standing on the seat near the bow as we explored the river, her ears fluttering in the breeze, nose catching an infinite smorgasbord. I picked up my phone, glancing at the screen, something I didn't want to do. But I thought Wynona might be calling. Before Max and I dropped anchor in a quiet cove, I wanted to see if it was Wynona.

It wasn't. Dave Collins had called the last two times, and he'd left a message the second time. Dave rarely leaves messages. Maybe because of his history with the CIA, he leaves few if any bread crumb trails. Although he's long since retired from three decades as a spy, it's hard and maybe smart not to break an old dog from the survival tricks he's learned during an occupation where plausible denial is career and lifespan longevity.

I played the message he'd left. "Sean, it's Dave. You have some visitors here at the marina. They come from a referral ... someone you know well. Anyway, I told them I'd try to contact you. Not sure how long they'll be here. When you get this, give me a shout. Last time I left a message, it was three days before I heard back from you. I don't think they can wait that long."

The call disconnected.

Max looked up at me. I nodded, sat down, watching a bald eagle circling the river in search of a fish close to the surface. I looked up at my cabin, Wynona's words echoing in my mind. *You spend time at sea or sequestered in that quaint old cabin of yours on the river. You're surrounded by your books, by the sound of the birds, by the isolation of your own form of Eden. But, by surrounding yourself with all that, you do the opposite with people. And the irony is I know how much you care for others—how much you do for others. Your friends, people like Dave, Nick, Joe Billie ... would do anything for you.*

I watched the eagle dive straight from the sky, shattering the calm surface of the river. The eagle's talons locked into the back of a bass, the bird flapping its large wings, the fish struggling, the surface of the water roiling under the beating wind. The eagle rose, the fish writhing in the death grip. Max barked as the bird of prey flew across the river, settling at the top of a tall cypress tree to eat. I looked at Max and said, "The eagle's fishing. I'm not sure we will be. I need to call Dave."

Twenty-Five

When Dave Collins answered his phone, he said, "Well, this is indeed extraordinary. Almost an immediate call back from you, Sean. It will not go unnoticed, I assure you." Dave chuckled, sitting at his table on the cockpit of his 42-foot Grand Banks trawler, *Gibraltar*, moored near the end of a pier at Ponce Marina. He sipped black coffee, eating a bowl of fruit, watching a brown pelican alight on a dock piling near *Gibraltar*. Dave was in his mid-sixties, full head of white hair, neatly trimmed matching beard, broad-shoulders, thick chest. No gut in spite of his love for food and drink, a connoisseur of craft beers and fine gins. His blue eyes had the rare combination of depth and humor. He said, "I hope I didn't reach you at an inopportune time."

"No, I'm home. Sittin' on the dock of the bay, as the song goes. Max and I were about to take out the Jon-boat for some fishing."

"Well, as my voice message alluded to … there are two people fishing for you. Please excuse the analogy, I get better after my second cup of coffee." He smiled, watching a sixty-foot Hatteras enter the marina, moving at a no wake speed, the boat's big diesels burping water. "They're a couple … a husband and wife. The gentleman is running for elective office here in our great state of Florida, a state where so many national newscasters use the word 'another' to describe the next unique event to happen only in Florida. As long as there are no causalities, I'm resigned to those uniquely Florida happenstances. Makes it interesting to live here and simply be a ring-side spectator."

"Are you sure you've only had one cup of coffee?"

"Pouring my second as we speak, Sean. When you live in a state with water on three sides, it draws the crazies like moths to a flame. And, speaking of water, the candidate is trying to ride that wave to Tallahassee where he hopes a win in the state senate will give him the platform for Everglades restoration and a cleaner environment in Florida. His name is Joe Thaxton. Have you heard of him?"

"Yes, I caught him on a radio talk show. He's articulate and seems serious about his crusade, one that's long overdue. Why do they want to see me? Did they say?"

"No, nothing specific. But through the smiles and handshakes, I can detect they're very concerned about something."

"Where are they now?"

"Chatting with fishing guides in the Tiki Bar, maybe getting a bite to eat. Captain Roland Hatter is there with them. It was Roland who referred them to you. He was apparently attending one of Thaxton's political rallies."

I stood and stepped to the side of my dock, looking at my rod and tackle box in the small boat tied to a post. "There was a recent newscast that had video of Thaxton's pickup truck vandalized at one of his rallies. Maybe that has something to do with the reason he and his wife want to speak with me."

Dave sipped his coffee. "If that's the case, it sounds like a criminal act that police need to handle in the jurisdiction where the vandalism occurred. But it could be there's something much more foreboding. Do you want me to walk down to the Tiki Bar to inform them that you're unavailable? Since Joe Thaxton is a fishing guide, if I tell him you've gone fishing, he'd probably be the first to understand."

I thought about the TV news interview Wynona and I had watched, Thaxton answering the reporter's questions and trying to be resolute as the wrecker driver was hauling the vandalized truck away. *We've received threating phone calls. All this means we're pushing somebody's button.*

Max barked at garfish rolling near the surface of the river.

"Sean, I hear Miss Max, but you've gone silent. What should I tell the Thaxton's?"

I watched the garfish for a moment longer. "Tell them I'll be there in an hour. If they have time to wait, I have time to listen. For somebody legitimately trying to help the rivers and beaches … hearing what's on their mind is the least I can do."

Twenty-Six

The lead surgeon glanced at the blood pressure monitor in the operating room near the patient, Johnny Nelson, who was in a medically induced coma. A second surgeon assisted in the amputation of Johnny's right leg ten inches above the knee. After cutting through dead flesh and sawing bone, the OR smelled of burned skin, disinfectant and urine. The surgeons and nurses worked to remove as much of the infected tissue as humanly possible. There were no further visible signs of the infection, but doctors knew that Johnny Nelson's fight had not ended.

Doctors labored close to the wound, grafting skin to the remaining stump that used to be a strong right leg. Twenty minutes into the procedure, Johnny's blood pressure plummeted. His heart raced. Machines sounded alarms. Nurses circled the patient, both doctors fighting to contain the bleeding and stabilize the patient. One younger nurse slipped in wet blood on the floor, almost falling.

"BP seventy – twenty," said a senior nurse, her voice calm but concerned.

"He's in hypotension," said one of the doctors, small flecks of dried blood on his glasses.

And then Johnny's heart stopped.

The doctors looked up at the monitors.

"Flat line!" said the senior surgeon. "Get me the paddles!"

Two nurses moved the defibrillator machine bedside, quickly gelling the paddles and handing them to the doctor. He placed the flat surfaces on both sides of Johnny's chest and pressed the button. The electric shock caused Johnny to spasm upwards, his chest wrenching. The doctor looking at the heart monitor. There was only one elevated line, the single erratic line caused by the shock.

"Come on …" the doctor said, placing the paddles back on Johnny's chest, sending another electrical jolt through the cardiovascular system.

Nothing.

The doctor tried again.

And again.

Seconds seemed like minutes.

Another shock. The heart failed to beat.

Above the surgical masks covering the mouths and noses of the team, their eyes said it all. Anxiety. Maybe an edge of fear. A strong young man, a father, husband, military veteran, had just lost his leg and was less than a minute from losing his life. "Kick in!" said the lead surgeon trying again and again.

Two nurses glanced at each other. They looked at the patient and then to the surgeon, his hands gripping the paddles, knuckles bone white. The doctor stared above the rims of his blood-flecked glasses, up at the face of a large clock mounted on one wall, the red sweep second-hand moving in a circle, the operating room somehow standing still.

"Carl," said the younger doctor. "He's gone. You did all you could. The infection was like a toxic bomb going off inside his body. It was too much and moving too fast. We couldn't knock it down, and we couldn't contain it. This … the stuff out there in some of the waterways is like a horror movie."

• • •

Twenty minutes later, Doctor Carl Quintero made the long walk down the hall to Johnny Nelson's room. He knocked once and entered. Amber stood by the window overlooking a park like setting, a manicured green lawn, oleanders with pink blossoms, squirrels hiding acorns under live oaks. She turned and looked at the doctor.

His eyes said it all. They delivered the bad news.

"No," Amber said, her hand touching her mouth, fingers trembling. "Tell me Johnny is alive. Tell me!"

"I wish I could. The infection hit his organs—heart, kidneys, shutting everything down. There was nothing we could do. It was like fighting a fire with a water gun." He stepped closer. "I am so very sorry."

Amber couldn't think. Couldn't move. Tears spilling from her eyes, rolling down her cheeks. Her legs felt weak. The room spinning. The doctor reached for her, holding Amber up and hugging her. She wept in his arms. Long wails. She caught her breath, standing straighter, breathing through her nose, blinking. A stream of tears fell from her chin to the floor, splashing near the toe of the doctor's shoes.

Twenty-Seven

Max knew we were almost there before arriving. Maybe it's her dog radar. Maybe it's her nose. A mile before we pulled into the Ponce Marina parking lot, Max started wagging her tail, uttering an excited whimper. I didn't think it was the topography or landmarks she spotted because it's a challenge for her to stand on short hind legs and get a good view out of the Jeep's passenger window. We drove south down Peninsula Drive on the west side of Ponce Inlet, heading for the marina.

I turned off the road and headed through the parking lot, driving to the south end, the gravel and oyster shells popping under the Jeep's tires. We stopped beneath the shade of a gumbo limbo tree, dust falling around the Jeep, Max turning a circle in her seat. I thought about the conversation I'd had with Dave Collins before driving from my cabin to the marina. *No, nothing specific. But through the smiles and handshakes, I can detect they're very concerned about something.*

"Well," I said to Max. "Let's go see what the concern is all about, shall we?" She snorted. I scooped her off the seat, checked for the red glow of backup taillights or movement from any of the two-dozen parked cars and pickup trucks. I set Max down, and she scampered directly for the screen-door entrance to the Tiki Bar. "Whoa, kiddo. At that clip, you'll go right through the screen." She stopped at the door, turning to look back at me as if I was stalling, her nostrils catching the smell of fried catfish, steamed garlic shrimp, and beer.

The Tiki Bar was a ramshackle watering hole built atop large pilings ten feet above the marina water. The rambling exterior was made from aged lumber and driftwood, giving the restaurant the look and feel of an abandoned shack that grew on the pilings, like high-rise barnacles. The dried palm frond roof was artistically painted from roosting pelicans. Most of its windows were made of clear plastic isinglass, allowing the staff to roll and tie up the windows, creating an open-air oasis on stilts.

The back door opened to the marina and its long docks that moored a couple hundred boats and the community of liveaboards and weekend sailors. They mixed with the tourists, charter boat captains and crew at the Tiki Bar. It made for spirited conversations. I opened the front door, Max scampering across the pinewood floor, a table of tourists, faces pink from too much sun, pointing and laughing. Max ignored them, trotting over to the bar. Three customers sat at the dozen or so stools in front of the bar, Jack Johnson crooning *Banana Pancakes* from the jukebox.

I glanced throughout the dining area. I estimated that less than twenty people sat around the tables, eating or sipping cocktails, beer, or glasses of wine. Each table had a circular top, made of wood and, at one time, used by the power company as large spools to store electrical wire or cables. Now they were stained the tint of molasses, shellacked, and flipped over in vertical positions. Four adults could easily fit around each table.

I scanned faces, knowing I'd recognize Joe Thaxton and his wife from having seen them on television. And, I knew Roland Hatter. They were not here. I wondered if Dave had delivered my message to them. Maybe they couldn't stay. Pressing appointments. No sweat. From what Dave had shared with me, on first glance, it seemed that the Thaxton's would be better served letting local police conduct whatever investigation needed to be done.

I walked over to the bar, Max camping to the right, quickly getting the attention of Flo Spencer, the owner, who was working behind the bar as two college-aged girls waited tables. "Hey, Sean," she said. "Max beat you to the bar, and it's not even happy hour yet."

"She left her watch in the Jeep," I said. "How are you, Flo?"

"Good. It's been a great season so far. Long as the tourists keep comin' the beer and smiles will be flowin' and that's why they call me Flo." She laughed.

For a woman in her late fifties, I thought Flo Spencer maintained herself well. She wore her dark hair up. Smooth oval face and eyes that usually reflected humor. She'd, no doubt, been striking in her youth. Flo ran a tight ship, giving high school kids their first jobs, and life-skills advice. She was a savvy businesswoman who hired good cooks and bartenders, and she paid them well. There was very little turnover.

She asked, "You and Max eating or getting something to go."

"Actually, we're meeting someone."

She glanced down at Max. "Well, let me give Max a little snack." She picked up a paper plate next to one of the draft beer dispensers, a half-dozen fried shrimp and two hushpuppies on the plate. "Since Maxine is a puppy, she ought to be allowed to have a hushpuppy, right?"

"Sure, but let's keep her to one," I said. "She has to save room for whatever Nick Cronus is cooking."

"When Nick retires from fishing, I hope he'll cook here, even part-time."

A sunbaked fishing guide, whiskers bleached, deep creases around his eyes and mouth, laughed, a smoker's hack deep in his lungs. He leaned back in his stool and watched Flo toss a hushpuppy to Max, the food never hitting the floor. "Does she ever miss a catch?" he asked, adjusting his billed cap.

"Only ground balls. Never flies," I said.

He laughed, lungs wheezing, lifting a sweating bottle of Blue Moon to his parched lips, two fingers on his right hand yellowed from nicotine. He looked at me and said, "Roland Hatter was tryin' to find you a while ago."

Flo popped the cap off a bottle of Sam Adams and set it on one of the server's trays with an order of steamed garlic shrimp. Flo looked at me. "It's a couple, man and wife. I think Roland is givin' them a tour of the marina. Maybe they'll be back. I recognized the guy. He's the fella runnin' for office. Can't remember his name, though."

I said, "Give you a hint. He says he's not your average Joe."

"That's it! Joe Thaxton. He's on a roll, bringing the water pollution in Florida from the back burner to the front, and that pot is starting to boil baby."

The fishing guide looked up at a TV screen above the bar next to a sailfish mounted on the wall. He pointed to the screen. "Speakin' of water pollution, news is on, and it looks like they got a story about that subject. Can you turn the sound up a little, Flo?"

She nodded, reaching for the remote control and raising the volume enough for us in the corner of the bar to hear it. A reporter in her mid-twenties, shoulder-length hair, stood near a mangrove estuary and said, "This is the area where Johnny Nelson was said to have contracted deadly bacteria that took his life. You can see the Sanibel Causeway in the distance. Nelson's wife told authorities that her husband was using his cast net in that water behind me when he accidently cut his leg in the shin area. An infection took hold quickly, and in spite of the doctor's best efforts, Nelson succumbed to the infection, one that's labeled flesh-eating bacteria known as vibrio vulnificus. County and state water quality officials say they periodically test these waters, as well as many of the beaches in the state and put up warning signs if they find higher than safe bacteria levels in the water. There are no danger signs in this immediate area, and we're told its been months since the water was tested. Amber Nelson spoke with us because she wants to warn others, especially parents of children."

The image cut to an interview with Amber Nelson, her eyes reddened, puffy, standing in her front yard, a weeping willow tree in the background. "My husband didn't deserve this. If there are high levels of pollution and bacteria in the water, why aren't there warning signs posted? I will never step into that water nor will my child. My husband survived heavy combat in the marines only to die at home when he was throwing his cast net and got cut in the water. What's in our rivers, bays and estuaries? Why does the water turn green sometimes? Who's responsible? All I know, right now, is my son lost his father, and I lost my husband … forever."

The video cut to a middle-aged man dressed in a sports coat, button down blue shirt, no tie, standing in front of the county health department. The graphic in the lower part of the screen read: *George Tenny - Florida DEP.* He said, "We test as many places as we can with the manpower we have. Conditions for toxic bloom areas are more prevalent in the summer as the water temperatures rise. We advise anyone going in the water to make sure they don't have open cuts or immune systems that may have been weakened."

The reporter asked, "After the death of Mr. Nelson, would you suggest that people stay out of this area where he was cast-net fishing?"

"That would be sound advice, at least until we can finish testing water samples for the bacteria. People should understand that these things are rare and cyclical. There could be one high bacterial count at a certain depth, and on the other side of the estuary the water will be fine. Between the beaches, lakes, rivers and estuaries, Florida has more than eight-thousand miles of shoreline."

The image cut back to the reporter standing near the water, mangrove islands in the background. She said, "Johnny Nelson was a decorated Marine who saw combat in two tours of duty in the Middle East. The tragic irony is that back home, an enemy he could never see, microscopic bacteria, killed him. He leaves behind a wife and baby son. Johnny Nelson was to have turned twenty-six next week. Now back to you in the studio."

I could feel someone walk up behind me. I turned, and the man said, "We couldn't help but overhear that tragic story. That's one of the reasons I'm running for office. I'm Joe Thaxton and this is my wife, Jessica." His wife stood to his left and smiled at the introduction. Roland Hatter stood to his right, arms folded, fishing cap just above his eyebrows. Thaxton said, "Roland here tells me you're Sean O'Brien. We've been looking forward to talking with you."

Twenty-Eight

Within a few minutes, I could see how Joe Thaxton appealed to his supporters. And, after a half-hour, I knew a lot about his personal and professional life. We sat at a table in the back corner of the Tiki Bar, Joe, his wife Jessica, and Roland Hatter. I sipped black coffee and listened to Joe tell me about the reasons he's running for office. His passion for clean water couldn't be faked. His research data as a marine biologist and his practical knowledge as a fishing guide with twenty years of experience brought a convincing package to the table.

"I tried my best to get other folks to run," he said, stirring his coffee. "I was more than happy to work in the shadows if a good man or woman wanted to take the reins. But nobody would step up to the plate. My parents raised me to be part of the solution. And that's what I'm trying to do."

Jessica said the decision for her husband to run for office had been a joint one, and it wasn't reached without a lot of soul searching. "Our daughter almost died," she said, both hands holding a cup of coffee. She motioned across the restaurant to the TV behind the bar. "And now look at what happened to that man who was simply tossing a cast net and caught a lethal infection from a flesh-eating bug in the water. These things can't be ignored anymore. Do you have a card, Mr. O'Brien?"

I pulled a card from my wallet and slid it across the table to her. "Please, call me Sean."

She smiled picked the card up and looked at it. "It just has your name and phone number. It doesn't say what you do. What is it you do, Sean?"

"Fish, mostly." I smiled.

Roland Hatter said, "He fishes for people and stuff that's lost or hidden. Sean's a private eye who keeps a low profile."

I smiled. "That means I'm fairly selective about the jobs I take. Often, the reason is simply that the parameters of the job are beyond the scope of what I think I can do for someone."

Jessica licked her lips. "I hope you can help us. I don't think the scope is too broad."

Roland Hatter tilted forward, his hands splayed on the top of the table. "Sean, you should have seen that crowd down in Stuart. Joe's gettin' one hell of a big following."

Joe smiled. "When we jumped into the race, we had no idea how much this message would resonate with people. In terms of the environmental health of our state, Florida's sick and getting sicker when it comes to its beaches, rivers and lakes. When you mix chemicals in Lake Okeechobee, the decades of pesticides and fertilizers pumped back in the lake from agriculture, when that combines with septic waste and is flushed down river, it can create this toxic soup of a blue-green algae that looks like an alien life form. It becomes a strange, creepy kind of dystopian world where the rivers and beaches are literally dying before our eyes. Somebody has to standup to the status-quo, to the political machine that's fueled by agriculture and Big Sugar money to keep on doing what they're doing. I'm pulling back the curtain on this problem, and the corporate interests want to stop me."

I nodded. "On the newscast, I saw the damage to your truck. Do you think the people you're spotlighting are behind this?"

"Yes. I just don't know who they are in terms of names or how far up the chain it goes."

Jessica said, "We've received threats on the phone. All have come from untraceable phones."

"Are they death threats?" I asked.

Joe's eyebrows lifted. "Not specifically, but that's implied. Stuff like … we're watching you, and now's the time to shut up or get shut up. Does that mean they're going to rough me up if I continue with these issues, or are they going to make an attempt on my life? I don't know."

Jessica said, "The last time, the caller said they knew where Kristy, our daughter, goes to school. That was the straw that broke the camel's back."

Joe nodded. "And our friend, Roland, suggested we get in touch with you, Sean. We need to hire a good private investigator to look under the rocks for us, and hopefully to expose who it is that's doing these despicable things. Would you take the job?"

"What are the police doing?"

"Not enough," Jessica said.

Joe added, "They got more involved when my car was damaged, not once but twice. The tire slashing, keying the paint, and then pouring water and sugar in the gas tank. I've installed security cameras around our home. Hopefully, they won't try that again with our truck. But we're concerned they might try something even worse."

"Was it the same caller each time?" I asked.

"We're not sure," Joe said. "It's always been a man. Some of our volunteers at campaign headquarters have answered the phone and heard the calls. They're brief. Less than ten or fifteen seconds. Just a short, terse, ominous warning. Telling staffers to tell me to back off or else."

"Have you personally received the threats?"

"I received one call on my cell phone. There was no caller ID. The guy said sweet revenge happens when I cross the line. Before he hung up, he said next time it won't be sugar in the tank … that maybe my car might explode. He used the words … 'go boom.' Then he hung up."

I nodded. "You need to work with police … try to get the calls recorded, traced, or both."

"The police tell us the quick calls came from burner phones, making it hard to find the culprits. Police are doing extra patrols around our home, day and night. Yes, threatening calls are a crime, and we've been on the receiving end of vandalism, but it's as if an attempt on our life has to happen before any real investigations will be done by law enforcement."

"In other words, Sean," Roland said, "looks like the cops are too busy with other stuff, and they're not making this a high priority. We can't wait for some knee-breaker to come outta the shadows and attack Joe, Jessica or their little girl."

I said nothing, the unique rumble of Harley-Davidson engines in the parking lot. I watched one of the waitresses deliver tall mugs of beer to three men at a table, charter boat crew members, who appeared to have just returned from a few days at sea. Peanut shells tumbled like confetti from their table to the floor, falling on beer stains long ago etched in the slats of pine as if a drunken artist left discolored knotholes in the wood.

Joe sipped his coffee and looked up at me. "I really need to concentrate on the campaign, the message and the solutions to what's really a state-wide problem. It's especially bad from Lake O south through the Everglades. I have nothing against responsible farming. My grandfather farmed three hundred acres near Thomasville, Georgia. And he did it without polluting the creek that ran through his property. I'm backing all of this up with the latest research and scientific data. Some of it I'm conducting. I fly my drones for visual observations, take water samples for analysis. And, I work with independent labs to analyze results."

I listened to Joe as three bikers took seats around a table. Lots of black leather, tats, fur and girth. One looked at the jukebox in the corner, got back up and fed the machine quarters, punching selections. Before he could sit back down, Creedence Clearwater Revival started belting out, *Have You Ever Seen the Rain.*

Joe said, "I believe farming and clean water can co-exist, we just need to work together to reach an amicable solution that keeps as much pollution as possible from our rivers and beaches. Antiquated septic tanks near rivers add to the problem. Sean, we'll pay you whatever you normally get for your time and expertise. Can you take the case?"

I leaned forward, looked at Joe, Jessica, and Roland, shifting my eyes back to Joe. "First, I'd like for you to understand that I fully support the mission of your campaign. A workable solution to this problem is long overdue. If I lived in your district, I'd vote for you. Based on everything you all have shared with me, I don't think I'm the right guy for the job. You might want to look at hiring a company that can provide security personnel—bodyguards and surveillance. I'm not that person. And, the bottom line is that it really is a police matter on the local level."

Jessica pursed her lips. "But they're not taking us seriously—we can't wait until someone takes a shot at Joe or tries to blow up his truck."

I nodded. "I wish it could be part of an FBI investigation because they have the advanced electronic sophistication to better track criminals who are primarily using digital sources to deliver threats. I will suggest this to you, though ... continue doing what you're doing with the passion you're displaying. The greater your profile grows and the more awareness you bring to the situation, the less likely those people will be able to do something to you because they'd be the first criminal suspects should harm come to you or any member of your family or campaign staff."

Roland blew out a breath. "Damn, Sean. I wish you'd reconsider. I know you're like a bulldog when push comes to shove, at least that's what I've heard."

"I'm sorry. I wish I could offer more."

Joe smiled. "I understand. It is what it is. Do you have children?"

"No. Max is the closest I have to a child." Max cocked her head and snorted.

Joe chuckled. "She's got a fine personality." He stood, glancing out the open window to the marina. "Ponce Inlet may be north of Lake O and a lot of the discharge we're having down there, but if phosphate, pesticides, and waste continues to flow into these estuaries ... this is part of the Indian River waterway. If that happens, I wouldn't let Max go close to the water. She has small lungs. The fish go first. Then the mammals, such as manatees, start going belly up. Max and little animals like her could get awfully sick. And then it'll be our turn. Look what just happened to the man on the west side of the state. He was attacked by something he never saw coming. And, in the art of war, when that wins ... we, the people, are the losers. Dead rivers, lifeless stinking beaches and oceans create a dying planet. Sean, we appreciate your time here today."

I stood from my chair and shook his hand. Jessica and Roland stood as well, Jessica putting her purse strap over one shoulder. They thanked me, turned and walked out the door to the parking lot, the wash of sunshine flooding the door. I looked at Max and said, "Let's head down to the boat, kiddo."

She followed me through the Tiki Bar, the scent of steamed garlic shrimp fanning from the kitchen, the music of CCR coming from the jukebox. The lyrics followed me to the door. *Someone told me long ago ... there's a calm before the storm ... I know it's been comin' for some time ... it'll rain a sunny day ... I know shinin' down like water.*

Twenty-Nine

I unlocked the entrance to L dock, Max patiently waiting until the gate opened wide enough for her to see daylight on the other side. And then it was off to the races. She bolted through the opening like a ten-pound thoroughbred horse, nose in the wind, legs galloping, butt rolling. The dock was her landing strip, her parade route. She loved coming back to L dock to renew old acquaintances, sample grilled fish handouts, and claim her spot, a bench seat on *Jupiter's* fly-bridge, which overlooked the entire marina.

I followed her down the long pier, sailboats, trawlers, houseboats, yachts and everything in between were moored to the fourteen docks, A through N. My slip, L-41, was at the very end. *Jupiter*, my 38-foot Bayliner was there. Max stopped in her tracks and looked up as a brown pelican sailed over her, the bird's shadow gliding down the stained planks. It flapped its big wings and flew toward mangroves near the Halifax River. Max glanced back at me and continued sauntering down the dock, stopping at a thatched roof fish-cleaning station to sniff the end of a rubber hose.

I walked and replayed some of my conversation with Joe and Jessica Thaxton. I thought about what Roland Hatter said, too. My decision wasn't an easy one to make. It seems like there is never a good time to make hard decisions. Many of my values align with Thaxton. But in my gut, I knew he'd be better off working with police and a company that could provide surveillance and protection for his family, around the clock if it came to that. I hoped it wouldn't. In my past as a homicide detective, I've found that most death threats were just that … threats. The real killers, the contract killers hired by deep pockets, never signaled their intent. They took upfront expenses, did the job and picked up the final payment. The last thing they wanted, or their employer wanted, was a dotted line to the source—the motive and the bullet in the chamber.

Max paused and watched a 44-foot Viking fishing yacht enter the harbor and motor toward M dock. The boat was equipped with tall outriggers, deep-sea rods in holders, a brown-skinned man in red swim trunks at the helm, two other men in sunglasses standing in the cockpit, cans of beer in their hands. I could smell the odor of diesel fuel and creosote, the boat's wake slapping against the dock pilings. A white-haired man in his sixties, stepped from a houseboat and poured half a bag of charcoal into his grill on the deck. Japanese lanterns, strung from bow to stern, jiggled in the breeze across the marina.

In another minute, we approached the end of L dock, and I could just begin to hear Greek music coming from *St. Michael.* The boat was tied with its cockpit toward the main pier, the narrow ancillary dock led to the high-pitched bow. It was a bow that came with a Greek sailing design and pedigree. The 40-foot boat could take the brunt of large waves and blow right through the water. Its owner, Nick Cronus, was one of the best fishermen on the east coast of Florida. And he was simply the best at cooking seafood.

Max stopped on the dock near the transom, her nostrils testing the wind, sniffing to see if Nick was in the galley stirring a sauce. She barked twice and waited. Within seconds, Nick lumbered from the salon to the cockpit, like a bear coming out of hibernation. He grinned and lifted both hands, palms up. "Hot Dawg!" he shouted. "Where you been, 'lil gal pal? Come here and see Uncle Nicky."

Max scampered down the secondary dock to the wooden portable steps leading to the cockpit. Nick lifted her up and carried her in one hand like a football. She licked his salt and pepper whiskered cheeks. He grinned and closed his eyes for a moment. Nick had the shoulders and girth of an NFL tackle. He stood in worn flip-flops just under six feet; olive-bronze skin; a mop of windblown, wavy hair; walrus moustache; and eyes that had the humor and charm of a sleight-of-hand magician. "Sean, are you here to pay your boat slip rent and go back to your cabin, or are you bringing Max in for some real quality time with us?"

I smiled. "Both. Rent's now paid, and Max is doing a Greek dance with you. Life is good and complete."

Nick laughed. "I got back in yesterday from a four-day haul. Woke up this mornin' with sore arms. Fish can really fight you, just like bein' in the heavyweight ring. After my trip to the wholesale market, I kept about twenty pounds of snapper. I'll fire up the grill later." He looked at Max. "You hungry, tadpole?"

She barked. "There's you're answer," I said.

Dave Collins stepped to the bow of his trawler, *Gibraltar,* moored across the dock from *St. Michael.* Dave wore a tropical print shirt, beige shorts and sandals. He said, "I thought I recognized that bark. Upon further investigation, I see it's Miss Max. So good to see you Maxie." Dave eyed me and grinned. "Sean, did you speak with Joe Thaxton?"

"Yes. Spoke with him, his wife, and Roland Hatter."

"I know Roland," Nick said.

Dave nodded, then looked up and down the dock. "I have a strong feeling Joe Thaxton has got some serious trouble following him. He's a rare bird. An honest politician. An almost extinct species. And he's stirring a sacred pot that almost all of Florida's politicians shy away from except for Thaxton. Even in my short conversation with Thaxton, I could tell there's a lot of anxiety that he's sharing with his wife. I'd love to hear more about the meeting. Come aboard. I'll pour the drinks."

Nick looked up at me, grinning, scratching Max behind her ears. He said, "Life is good and complete, oh yeah. My man, Sean, now I know the real reason you're here. Sounds like somebody's in some deep shit."

THIRTY

Dave sipped a Hendricks gin over ice with a twist of lime, Nick nursing a bottle of Corona, the three of us sitting around Dave's table on *Gibraltar's* cockpit. Max trotted into the salon and jumped up on a leather couch to sleep. They listened to me fill them in on my conversation with Joe and Jessica Thaxton. When I concluded, Dave cut his eyes over to a 40-foot Sea Ray, diesels rumbling, the captain easing the boat out of its slip at M dock.

Dave looked back at me. "Sounds like you made the right decision. Thaxton and his wife have filed police reports. They said that there will be more police presence in their neighborhood. Surveillance cameras are now mounted on their home. And I think your suggestion for them to inquire about the services of a company that can provide personal protection is a good and prudent one."

Nick used his wide thumb to wipe the condensation from his bottle. "Too bad this shit happens to good people. I make my livin' from the sea, and I can tell you that this guy's spot on with what he's sayin' about the changes. Sure, we've experienced red tide blooms occasionally. But it was sporadic and brief. No more. Now it's like an annual plague. You combine that with the pea-green goo that rises to the surface of a lot of water from the Indian River on the east coast to Pine Island Sound on the west coast, and you know what this guy's sayin' rings true."

Dave nodded. "What I like is how Thaxton is using science—data he's taking, along with statistics from county, state, and federal water monitoring agencies to combine with his degree and expertise as a fishing guide. Too bad it took the near death of his daughter to bring this to the forefront of the campaign."

I said, "Often change boils down to cause and effect. The result of the on-going pollution and authorities looking the other way, is causing severe health problems in fish, wildlife, and humans."

Dave sipped his drink, his eyes filled with thought. He looked up. "There was another casualty today from water-borne bacteria. A military veteran died. He wasn't old, and I seriously doubt if he had a weakened immune system as he stepped in the water to toss his cast net. The news reports indicate the victim grew up boating and fishing those waters, back when he could see his toes in the sand standing in chest-deep water. No more. Sean, do you think Big Sugar and corporate agriculture could, in any way, be behind these threats to Thaxton?"

"I don't know. I do know that when I was a detective, it was usually the cause and effect we're talking about that went into almost every capital crime. In a homicide, you start looking at the family, close friends or business partners. What was the emotional motivation behind the killing? In spite of what we hear in the news, serial killers who murder anonymous victims are rare. The sad normal in murder is the connection between victim and killer, the first person to tip the first domino. Who has the most to lose or to gain? At least one of the seven deadly sins will always be at play. In the scenario with Joe Thaxton, he's following the source of the pollution or the pollution to the source. So, who flipped that first domino?"

Dave said, "I heard a radio podcast, and Thaxton was talking about how federal sugar subsidies hurt the American taxpayers to the tune of two to four billion a year. The feds set prices on sugar, restrict the amount that can be sold and imported, which increases U.S. prices, ensuring artificially higher costs for sugar. And then the feds can sell sugar at pre-set prices to ethanol companies to be made into fuel. Sugar growers are in the catbird seat. Thaxton's calling for an end or substantial reform of the government sugar subsidies, saying the taxpayers don't get a sweet deal."

I said, "That could certainly rattle some cages and pique the interest of some people in the industry. So, there's more at play here than leveling fines for water pollution or restoring the water flow to the Everglades. He's calling attention to a crony capitalist's program worth billions to a few multi-millionaires."

Nick shrugged his shoulders. "How does a guy like Thaxton, a fella I can relate to because we both fish for a livin'—how can he take on those big special interests and win? They're a Goliath, and he's a man who's earned an honest livin' taking clients out to fish the flats."

Dave squeezed more lime in his drink. "Voters like an underdog if the message is real and resonates with them. Voters are hungry for change when they feel they have no voice and lobbyists control the voting booth because money counts more than votes." Dave sipped his drink and then chuckled. "Oddly enough, Thaxton has a colleague in one of the most unlikely of places."

"Where's that?" Nick asked. "Heaven?"

"No, the governor's race. Polls have both candidates in a close dead-heat thus far. They're running the closest races ever seen on that level at this point in the campaigns. But only one is suggesting that the Comprehensive Everglades Restoration Plan is long overdue to be enforced. Gubernatorial candidate, Hal Duncan, is promising to adhere to the tenets of the Everglades restoration mandate and to begin by replacing the South Florida Water Management Board with all new people."

I said, "That's something I heard Joe Thaxton suggest."

Dave nodded. "He and Duncan could make a powerful difference if they can both manage to get elected. In Thaxton's case, if he can manage to stay healthy."

Nick grinned. "Sugar is kinda like the world's cocaine. Most people have an addiction. They gotta have a fix. If someone in the sugar industry is involved, a guy like Joe Thaxton might as well be facing the world's biggest drug company."

Thirty-One

Chester Miller was careful not to touch the deadly manchineel tree, or beach apple as some people call it. He moved an aluminum ladder to the base of a cypress tree near the manchineel, securing the ladder against the cypress, looking up at the orchid plant perched on a small outcropping of weathered board, which Chester had fastened to the tree. He put one foot on the ladder, saw it move slightly at the top, and then adjusted it at ground level.

"Grandpa, are you going to climb that ladder?" asked Callie coming out of the greenhouse.

"Of course. Who do you think originally placed the orchid up there?"

She watched her grandfather, his face filled with excitement. She carefully chose her words. "If you want me to, I can climb up there and have a look."

"Do you know what you'd be looking for?"

"The sign of a bloom."

"That's some of it, of course. But I need to inspect the heath of the plant. See if there is any rot or disease."

She walked over to him. "Okay, but at least let me hold the base of the ladder for you."

He grinned, his white beard parting. "Sounds like a deal." Chester turned and placed his right foot on one rung and started climbing, the ladder shifting slightly. Callie held it tight with both hands as her grandfather took one slow step at a time. After half a minute, he'd made it to the top. He stopped, pulled his glasses from his front pocket, and begin inspecting the orchid. So lovely," he said. "It's like peering into a bird's nest and hoping you'll see cracked eggs and fledglings peeking back at you, their tiny eyes filled with the wonder of a new world."

Callie watched the old man. "I hope it blooms before I go back to school."

He chuckled. "Perhaps it will. It was here when you started high school. I'm hoping it'll be blooming before you finish college. I see what could be construed as a bud. We'll see." He started the slow climb back down.

As he took the last rung before stepping to the ground, Callie said, "Maybe you can add some extra fertilizer—more nourishment to speed up the process."

He stood on the ground and turned to her. "My dear child, there is no speeding up mother nature. She moves at her own pace. What would happen if you watched a chrysalis, such as a butterfly struggling to break out and you decided to help it by taking a knife or scissors to carefully open the chrysalis and free the butterfly?"

"I'd imagine that it would fall to the ground, unable to fly away."

"Indeed. It needs time to open the door, to work its way out … to free itself. The wings have to be fully developed, and they have to dry in the sun as the butterfly sits on the branch and slowly fans its wings, gaining strength and confidence for the leap into the unknown. When the time is right, he'll stop fanning and start flying." He chuckled. "There's a life lesson in there somewhere, I think."

She smiled. "But of course, you're going to let me come to my own conclusion. Just like when you pointed to the tall cypress trees, you showed me where to look, but I had to see it for myself. Did you and Grandma raise Mom with these little lessons you're always helping me to discover?"

"Absolutely. Although, in those days, I was traveling more than I wanted to. A lot of the day-to-day responsibility of child raising fell into the lap of your grandmother. She did an outstanding job. I'm very proud of your mother."

"I know it's been a lot of years since Grandma died. Do you still miss her as much?"

He looked at Callie and reached for one of her hands. "I miss her more than ever. I miss her when I learn something that I want to share with her. I miss her laugh and her wisdom." He glanced at her hand. "But I see her in your eyes, and in your hands. Through your mother and you, your grandmother lives and is still with me in the physical sense. In the spiritual sense, she never left. Above all else, I miss her love, her gentle touch the most."

Callie smiled. "I hope one day I'll find that kind of love. I'm not sure it exists like that when you and Grandma married. Things change."

"But people don't change, not in the depth of our core being. Most of us still want to be loved and to give love." He looked up at the orchid. "Just like that Persephone orchid. When the time is right, it'll grace us with beautiful blooms. When the time is right, when the love is right and real, you will know. Never rush it, Callie. Take your time to savor, to search. Not so much for the right man, but for who you are inside you ... when you discover that, you'll be surprised at how much easier it'll be to recognize the right man when you do meet him."

She put her other hand on top of his. "I love you Grandpa. Can I go up the ladder and see the orchid? I'll take a picture of it, too."

"Of course. I'll hold the base of the ladder for you. But remember this ... when it blooms, you'll be able to see it from the ground. It'll seem like it's springing out of the nest, sort of like the ghost orchid. But this will be no illusion. It'll be one of botany's finest hours."

Thirty-Two

Nick was in his element. White hot charcoal and mesquite glowing in the grill. Sizzling fish on the rack. Smoke, seasoned with Greek herbs, drifting across the marina letting boaters know Nick Cronus was in the culinary wheelhouse. I watched Nick turn inch-thick slabs of red snapper on the hot grill, humming a song. In addition to the fish, he'd marinated lamb shish kebabs with chunks of lamb, tomatoes, onions, and green peppers, three kebabs searing on the rear section of the large grill.

We were in *Gibraltar's* cockpit, Dave making fresh drinks at the bar in the salon. Max near Nick's bare feet, the sun setting over the marina, flat water reflecting cranberry red clouds in the western sky. I could hear a news broadcast on Dave's TV near the bar.

Nick brushed the snapper with olive oil laced in what he calls his secret recipe of select herbs. He sang a Jimmy Buffett song, *One Particular Harbor*, squeezing lime on the fish, turning the kebabs, fanning the smoke with one hand, a beer in the other, closing the cover to the grill. He looked up, grinning. "A few more minutes, and they'll be ready. Yesterday, the fish were swimmin' in the deep blue sea. Hot Dawg … you hungry?"

Max barked once, turning a full circle. "Be patient, Maxie. We got plenty, even for your belly. Hey, Sean, can you tell me how such a little hound dog can have such a big appetite? Are you starvin' her back at your river cabin so, when she comes here, she's out of control?"

"I think it's your cooking, Nick, that attracts her like a moth to a flame."

He popped the rest of his lime into a bottle of Corona and took a long pull. "Yeah, it's gotta be that—even Hot Dawg has good taste."

Dave walked out onto the cockpit, a gin and tonic in both hands. He gave one to me and said, "Cheers, gents." He lifted his glass. "It's a fine evening over Ponce Inlet, stock market is doing well, and football season is just around the corner. We have much to be grateful for in this old world of ours. Sean, have you decided whether you are going to keep and maintain *Dragonfly* or sell her? Or are you going to sell *Jupiter* and keep the sailboat?"

"I was talking with Wynona about that, and she suggested that I don't sell *Dragonfly* because it was a gift from two people who were deeply appreciative to be alive."

"How is Wynona?" Dave asked. "I miss her."

"She's well, and she's working on a case on the rez that's taking a lot of time. Her birthday's in a couple of days."

Nick grinned. "You gonna send her flowers?"

"Already did, but I didn't send them. I delivered them, personally."

"Damn, Sean. You still got the romantic touch. Who woulda thought?"

"I bought some orchids from a grower I know. Guy lives off the beaten path, way back in Big Cypress Preserve. He's probably the world's foremost expert and grower of rare orchids. He's got one that he says may be the rarest and most beautiful in the world, if it ever blooms."

"If?" Dave asked, stirring his drink. "What's the problem?"

"After he did whatever he did to cross-pollinate the hybrid orchid with some of the world's most exotic pollen, he thought the first blossom would appear in ten years. He says it has been fifteen, and he's still waiting."

Dave shook his head. "How old is this gentleman?"

"He looks to be in his eighties."

Nick grinned. "A guy that age ought not to buy green bananas."

Dave said, "I read an article in Smithsonian Magazine recently about the lore and legend of orchids. The story focuses around the bewitching qualities of the flower. In the late 1800s, some of the most intrepid adventurers in England braved faraway jungles in search of orchids to bring them back to a European market that was mesmerized by the beauty of the blossoms. The story indicated many people develop an emotional connection with orchids unlike any other flower, including roses. One grower was quoted as saying it's as if the orchid has eyes that draw us into it."

Nick chuckled and said, "Roses are red, violets are blue, look at an orchid and it looks back at you."

I laughed. "Nick the poet. Chester did say that, because of the flower's bilateral symmetry, to some collectors, the orchids seem to have a human-like face."

Dave sipped his drink and said, "I read that way before Dolly the sheep was cloned, some growers were cloning orchids, which eventually increased production many times over, and they were able to deliver them to most markets. The one you buy in the grocery store may look identical to the one your neighbor buys from Walmart."

"Not so in the wild," I said. "Chester and his granddaughter, who's a college student studying botany and working with him for a few weeks, are venturing into the glades replanting native orchids. They're documenting and inventorying the rare ghost orchids. Looking at natural propagation of the species and how the environmental changes effect these delicate plants that live on host trees, often cypress."

Dave nodded. "Which means water or the lack of it. So, the ghost orchids are the smoke alarms for the swamps and glades."

"Probably one of many."

Nick finished his beer. "If you keep *Dragonfly*, maybe you can rename her Ghost Orchid. Sounds spooky already. I agree with Wynona … keep the boat, Sean. It's paid for. All you got is the boat slip rent and insurance. Maybe you ought to think about leasing her out. There are plenty of good captains who could do that. Split the profits with you. They could take people out for sunset sails. Something to think about."

"That'd still be using the boat, a gift, to make money. If I needed it that bad, maybe I'd consider that, but not now. I'd mull over selling *Jupiter*, but I think Max would give me the silent treatment for days. She has her nooks and crannies on that boat. Maybe I'll take *Dragonfly* out tomorrow. It's been a few months. I can do some day sailing out in the Atlantic for a few miles. I could use the diversion."

Dave nodded. "I sense that you're having second thoughts about turning down Joe Thaxton and his wife, correct?"

"No second thoughts about that. But I have been thinking about his mission and what he's going up against."

"A David verses Goliath scenario, no doubt. However, this can become an oxymoron in that it's called the Goliath Syndrome. It sometimes happens when large corporations become blinded by greed and their own vulnerability because they look at their size as an asset when it can become a liability. Guys like Joe Thaxton, with his 'average Joe' message, can generate momentum through an underdog public persona. It can become a lethal stone in the sling he's carrying. And, when it's flung hard in the right direction and under the right circumstances, the giant can fall to its knees."

I sipped my drink, a soft breeze coming from the ocean across the scent of Nick's grilled fish and shish kebabs, settling its fragrant mist over the marina. "Often corporate greed and political expediencies mix into a cocktail sipped by crony capitalists that can cause a bad hangover when they wake up. I think Joe Thaxton, a man who has nothing against capitalism or entrepreneurship, but has a real problem with wholesale pollution, is going to cause quite a headache for those responsible."

"I wish I could vote for him," Nick said. He lifted the top of the grill and used tongs to put the fish and kabobs on a large platter. "Let's eat, fellas." He glanced down at Max. "You might be one of the guys, Max, but you're always a little lady to us." She followed him to the table in the salon, tail wagging. He set the platter in the center of the table.

We filled our sturdy paper plates with red snapper and grilled lamb kababs. Nick brought a Greek salad from the refrigerator. I made Max a small plate, setting it on the teak floor next to my chair. In the background, I heard a news story begin on television. The anchorman said, "New polls out for some of the hotly contested political races in Florida."

Dave reached for the remote control and turned up the sound. "Let's see if Thaxton is among the candidates polled by registered voters."

I turned and looked at the screen. The anchorman said, "There is a dramatic shift in the polls this week. Fishing guide, Joe Thaxton, has a double-digit lead over incumbent State Senator William Brasfield. In a random sampling of a thousand registered voters in District twenty-five, people were asked, if the election were held today, who'd be their preference for the state senate seat. Joe Thaxton appears to have pulled ahead of William Brasfield, some seven out of ten sampled in the poll giving their preference to Thaxton. With three months before the election, and ads hitting the airways, all of that can change. But, for a newcomer to politics, a man who insists he's the average Joe and speaks for the middle class, it's quite an accomplishment."

The video cut to an interview with Thaxton standing near the waterfront bay in Stuart. "We're thrilled with the news," he said. "I attribute a lot of that to the hard work my campaign volunteers are doing to get our message out to voters. People are tired of misrepresentation or no representation in Tallahassee. It's as if some politicians who were voted in office to represent the people, forgot the people and prefer to hobnob with lobbyists and the money they spend. In a nutshell, that's really wrong."

The video cut back to the live shot of the anchorman who said, "We reached out to State Senator Brasfield. He was said to be traveling and not available for immediate comment. His campaign manager told Channel Three that, quote: 'Pollsters don't decide elections. The voters do, and it's way too early to give polling any real validity.' End quote. In the race for governor, polls indicated that Republican Hal Duncan is in a statistical dead-heat with his opponent, Democrat Antonio Perez. All of that, of course, can quickly change. In other news today …"

Dave muted the sound and said, "Thaxton is doing more than resonating with voters. He's galvanizing them to take a stand against those who willfully pollute Florida's beaches and rivers."

Nick sipped his Corona and pushed back in his chair, his fingertips glistening in olive oil, lips wet. "I can identify with a guy like Thaxton. But if somebody slashed his tires 'cause they don't like want he's sayin,' what's gonna happen now that he's way up there in the polls? Sean, maybe he'll take your advice and hire a company to keep an eye out for his property and family."

THIRTY-THREE

A few hours later, near midnight, I took Max for her last walk of the night before hitting the sack. We were coming back from strolling near the beach, the breakers rolling louder under a full moon and a high tide. We walked down L dock to slip 41. I thought about my conversation with Joe Thaxton, thought about what he said on the newscast, giving credit for the success of his numbers in the polls to the hard work of his campaign staff and calling it like he sees it. *It's as if some politicians who were voted in office to represent the people, forgot the people and prefer to hobnob with lobbyists and the money they spend. In a nutshell, that's really wrong.*

Maybe Thaxton's running for the wrong office, I thought. Davy Crocket was elected to congress, so maybe Joe Thaxton might want to eventually set his sights on the White House. If he had a million people each donating one hundred dollars … who knows. The night air turned cooler, Nick's brushstrokes of flavored smoke long since blown out to sea. I watched the light atop the Ponce Lighthouse punch out into the darkness, boats in the marina rising on the tide, the collective groan of tie-down ropes like the disjointed snore of sleeping marine behemoths.

We walked up to my two boats, *Jupiter*, which I'd bought years ago at a ten-cents-on-a-dollar DEA auction. And *Dragonfly*, a ship of dreams that never materialized for a married couple who'd put their heart and soul into restoring the 42-foot Beneteau and sailing the Caribbean for a year. Max and I stood at the very end of L dock, the marina and its twinkling lights behind us, the Halifax River and its short journey to Ponce Inlet and the Atlantic Ocean in front of us.

The breeze came in from the sea, causing the halyard on *Dragonfly* to tap against the tall mast like a windchime with only one note, the compelling beat of a distant drummer. I looked back at the sailboat in silhouette under the moonlight, Wynona's words soft as the wind across the water. *Dragonfly was a gift to you because you saved the lives of two people. You absolutely love sailing. There's no mandate that says you must get rid of things you love, Sean. Why do you feel that way?* I'd sensed there was something on Wynona's mind that she didn't want to discuss … at least not yet. I would be patient and wait for when she felt like talking about whatever was on her heart.

I walked over to *Jupiter*, Max trotting next to me, her nose testing the wind. I picked her up, stepped into the cockpit and climbed the ladder to the fly bridge, Max tucked under one arm. I'd left the windows open, isinglass unzipped and folded up. I set Max on the bench console and sat down in the captain's chair, the briny scent of the ocean in the air. The marina was quiet, the Tiki Bar closing, no traffic in the parking lot, lights from moored boats swaying off the water.

Max curled into a half circle. I looked at her. "It's been a while since we sailed. Too long. What do you say we take *Dragonfly* out in the morning, catch a sunrise over the Atlantic? That sound appealing?"

She lifted her head, her snort sounding more like a sneeze.

"I'll take that as a yes, little lady."

• • •

Joe Thaxton lay in bed, moonlight coming through a slit in the bedroom drapes. His thoughts raced. The general election was just around the corner, and win or lose, his life had changed. The task is to sustain the momentum he'd built. The attack ads against him had turned his detractors into zealots, posting scathing character assassinations on social media platforms. But his supporters, at least to this point in the race, managed to drown out the shouters who called him an uninformed tree hugger. Joe turned his head, looking at Jessica fast asleep in bed near him. *She is such a trooper. Always has my back. Always there with compassion and advice that helped his message resonate with more women.*

He thought about the news story he'd recently watched on television, a woman interviewed who'd lost her husband to a waterborne bacterial infection that had spread through his body faster than doctors could treat it. *My husband didn't deserve this. If there are high levels of pollution and bacteria in the water, why aren't there warning signs posted? I will never step into that water nor will my child. What's in our rivers, bays and estuaries? Why does the water turn green sometimes? Who's responsible? All I know, right now, is my son has lost his father, and I lost my husband ... forever.*

Thaxton closed his eyes for a moment. Maybe he could somehow help the woman—do something to honor her husband and not let his name be forgotten.

There was a sound.

He opened his eyes, his heart beating faster. The noise sounded like it came from his driveway in front of his home. He looked at his wife. Sleeping. He got up, careful not to wake her. The family dog, Rodeo, slept on the carpet near the bed. He stood, stretching. He walked quietly through the house, barefooted, listening for more sounds, Rodeo behind him.

In the kitchen, the dog uttered a low growl.

"Shhh, boy," whispered, Thaxton. "Let's take a look out the window." He walked through the kitchen toward the living room.

The sound came again. Loud, as if someone was trying to open his truck. He stopped at the blinds, opening one slat at eye level, looking at his truck in the moonlight. He could see no one, outdoor floodlights covering most of the front yard in a bright wash of light. A large raccoon waddled backwards out from the garbage can it had knocked over, a ripped white garbage bag scattered like confetti near the can.

Rodeo growled again. Thaxton petted him. "It's just a hungry coon. I'll have a mess to pick up in the morning. Let's go back to bed. And this time, we'll leave the floodlights on, okay? We don't want the coon or anyone else coming back."

THIRTY-FOUR

Except for the charter boat captains and crew, most of the marina was still asleep when I released *Dragonfly* from her mooring lines, starting the Yanmar diesel engine. The water under the stern bubbled as I pushed off and guided the 42-foot boat out of her slip, motoring quietly between L and M docks. Nick's boat, *St. Michael*, was gone—out to sea for a day of fishing. *Gibraltar* was dark, Dave probably fast asleep. A sliver of pink and orange light emerging in the eastern sky casting off the shrouds of night, draping the marina and its hundreds of boats into a pastel dawn. Beads of dew on the docks captured the morning light into crimson jewels.

Max stood on one of the cockpit seats, watching a white pelican soar over the marina. I made a wide, right turn into the passage, moving through the channel to join the Halifax River and its short run to Ponce Inlet. I sipped hot black coffee from a large mug. It was good to be behind the helm. The tide was flowing out, which would make the run through the inlet even easier, less current, less drag on the boat. Once we cleared the pass, I'd hoist the sails and head south, sailing along Canaveral National Seashore, maybe to Cocoa Beach before returning.

In the receding tide, it didn't take us long to reach the pass. We entered it just as the sun rose over the Atlantic Ocean, a flock of sea gulls soaring in silhouette above the dark blue water. I looked at Max.

"Don't trot up to the bow while we're going through here. I don't want to have to fish you out of the pass." She watched the birds, ignoring me and my warning.

A shrimp boat was returning from sea, it's outriggers straight up, the big boat entering the inlet as we were about to exit. I waved to the captain, a boney man with a cigarette in the corner of his mouth, one hand on the wheel. He waved back and went by us. Within ten minutes, we'd motored through the wide pass and entered the ocean under a glorious sunrise. Max jumped off the seat and trotted to the bow, the wind now coming across the sea and lifting up her ears.

After cruising two hundred yards straight out, I hoisted the sails and let mother nature take the reins. I shut off the engine and steered a course due south. In less than ten minutes, *Dragonfly* was sailing at seven knots, the sea caressing her bow in a soft hush of spray, the main sail and jib billowing. I refilled my coffee cup from a thermos bottle, holding the helm with one hand, *Dragonfly* performing like a thoroughbred.

I kept the course heading south and two hours later, I could see the northern section of the national seashore to the west. I sailed closer to the beach, staying a hundred yards off shore. From that distance, I could see breakers rolling up on the sand, a few people walking on the beach, and less than a half-dozen, large, white cumulus clouds drifting against the indigo blue sky. Max rejoined me, under the canvas canopy, seeking shade from the hot sun. She lapped water from her bowl and jumped up on one of the bench seats.

I felt my phone buzz in my pocket. I was wearing shorts, T-shirt, no shoes. For a second, I debated even looking at the screen. After the third buzz, I took it from my pocket, not recognizing the caller ID. The number started with the area code 772. I knew it was the area code for the Treasure Coast of Florida, covering cities, such as Fort Pierce and Vero Beach. The city of Stuart was in the bunch, too. I hit the green receive button and answered.

A woman's voice said, "Mr. O'Brien, this is Jessica Thaxton. My husband doesn't know I'm calling you, and I apologize for doing so."

"No apology needed. And you can call me Sean."

"I'm sorry, I forgot. My parents raised me to use more formal greetings than are often needed in this day and time." She paused for a few seconds and then continued. "I really appreciate the time you spent with us. I understand your reasonings for not taking the job. Joe and I met with the police again—specifically the sergeant in charge of our case, and we're just as frustrated as ever. He calls the vandalism cheap pranks that will go away and for us not to worry too much."

"He might be right."

"And, he could be wrong. Look, I'm not the type of woman who's ever paranoid. But I know I've been followed. And the weird thing is this … I believe the guy who followed me, as I took my daughter to and from school, knew that I'd spotted him. But, it was as if he didn't care, staying far enough behind my car and, yet, taking all the turns I took. When I stopped at the school, he went down a side street and drove off somewhere—probably didn't want to be on the school's surveillance cameras."

"Maybe you can get the guy's license plate number and give it to police."

"He's crafty that way. He doesn't pass me, allowing me to see it."

"How often have you noticed him following you?"

"Twice now. A police car escorted me a couple of times and then stopped. We looked into hiring a security company like you suggested. Each of the three we spoke with wanted an exorbitant amount of money. I believe these companies are used to dealing with billionaires and millionaires, people who have a lot of money. That's not us. As a fishing guide, Joe's done well, and then the green goo shows up and clients start cancelling the trips they've booked. We've managed to put money away, some of it for our daughter's college fund. The closer we come to the townhall meeting with Hal Duncan, the more worried I get. Joe's doing great in the polls, and that's got his opponent and his deep-pocketed backers, swinging hard at him. Have you seen any of their attack ads on TV?"

"No. I don't watch a lot of TV."

"They're vicious, and it's all lies. They're trying to make my husband look and sound like some deranged, uneducated tree-hugger who's running his race on emotional scare tactics. Would you possibly reconsider? Maybe see if you can find out who's behind this and expose it. That might be the only way to stop it."

I watched the Canaveral National Seashore, the pristine beauty of untouched Florida off the starboard view of *Dragonfly's* bow. "Jessica, I wish I could help. Yes, you've experienced vandalism. And you've had someone try to intimidate you by following your car as you took your daughter to school. What I do best is try to trace a capital crime back to the person who did it or initiated it. Right now, the crime is the damage to Joe's truck. I'm not undermining that. I know it's a hassle to deal with insurance companies and get repairs done. I can't work as a personal bodyguard. And, at this point, I don't think your family needs that."

"Sean, do you believe people are born with gifts?"

"I believe people are born with undeveloped talent. I think that's a gift. The tragedy is often those gifts are never really opened, they're ignored or simply shoved so far on the back burner they're never resurrected. Many people are too afraid to take the risks it requires to live up to or beyond their potential. I think your husband is an exception to that general rule."

"He is, that's one of the things I love and admire about him. I believe I have a sensitivity or a gift to see things … I'm in no way psychic, but I have an intuition that's saved me from many bad things in life. I often see the best and sometimes the worst in people, and I don't mean by being judgmental. In you, I see a decent, caring man—a person not motivated by money or fame, but rather by simply doing what's right. And I think you're not afraid of risks. It wouldn't be much of a risk for you to help us. My perception is hinting at things that scare me. I fear something bad is going to happen to Joe either right before or after the televised townhall meeting. I'm very worried, and I don't know where to turn."

"Jessica, politics can be brutal. Just look at the recent presidential election. In the primaries and in the general election, there are always losses on both sides in terms of reputations tarnished and political scars left from hard-fought campaigns. That's the norm. What you're talking about is a very large exception to the rule. I'm not suggesting that your fears are unfounded, but I am saying I think Joe will get through the election scratched and battered, but most likely a winner."

"I pray that you're right. I'm sorry to have bothered you."

"No bother."

"If you reconsider, please let us know. Good bye, Sean."

I stood, the trade winds delivering the hint of flowers from the islands. I watched the pristine white sand beaches of the national seashore. It hadn't changed much since the Spanish conquistadors saw it when they came ashore in Florida. I recalled the interview Joe Thaxton did when he referred to the European sailors who came to Florida 400 years ago. *When Spanish explorer Ponce De Leon first sailed here and walked our beaches, coves and woodlands, he called this new land La Florida … or a place with flowers. That bloom is in danger of falling off the plant forever.*

I sailed south, hoping Jessica Thaxton was wrong, and that there was no real threat to her husband's life. She was a loving and concerned wife. And she was a frightened wife. This brave new world of politics, especially with Joe's assault on corporate water polluters, was daunting. Jessica said she had a gift to see things. I hoped she was blinded by fear, and after the November election that fear would no longer be a shadow following her.

THIRTY-FIVE

The Joe Thaxton campaign headquarters was alive with ringing phones and excited chatter among staffers. A long table was filled with fruit, doughnuts, yogurt, granola bars, water bottles on ice and gallons of coffee. Joe worked right beside his volunteers, making phone calls and doing live radio and TV interviews from a small room filled with campaign placards. He finished recording a podcast when his manager, Larry Garner, entered the room. Joe removed his headphones, turned off a switch on the audio console and said, "You look happy."

"I am. New poll numbers are in, and we've grown the lead by another five points. And this is coming in spite of Brasfield's barrage of attack ads on TV."

Joe stood. "I believe most people can see through that crap. They're not buying it. He's had plenty of time in office to do something to turn the tide on pollution. But he's been bought and sold by lobbyists working for Big Ag and Sugar. We just have to remain true to our mission and accessible to the public for their thoughts."

"You're doing a townhall meeting with Hal Duncan. To my knowledge, something like that's never happened in Florida politics. A candidate for governor normally shies away from getting directly involved in races for the state house and senate. Not this time. And it's because you're a dozen lengths in front of Brasfield in this horserace. Your message is connecting with people far beyond our district.

The townhall event with you and Duncan will be televised on the public broadcast stations across the state. That's going to help."

"I want to bring more than just the two of us—Hal Duncan and myself to the stage to answer questions and talk about how we can work together to solve water pollution in the state. I want to show the audience more scientific data as well. I want video to help illustrate the various pollution hotspots and areas in the Everglades that are vastly altered. That ought to work well on TV. Some of it I'll capture in the field … just like I've done in the past."

"I'm not sure we have time for you to go slogging across South Florida looking for pollution. We have full schedules planned."

"The good and bad thing, Larry, is I don't have to go very far. Also, a huge part of my mission, as a marine biologist, is for me to be in the field taking water samples, flying my drone looking at the bio-health of rivers and lakes. The base of my supporters like the fact that I don't just rely on others for data, I go get it myself."

Garner shook his head, released a deep breath. "Okay, but on some of your treks into nature, we'll send a photographer with you to get some pictures. It'll make for great visual reminders of the mission. I need to get on the phone with Hal Duncan's people to begin coordinating the townhall meeting. This will be huge." He turned and walked out just as Jessica and Kristy were arriving. After greeting them, he said, "Good news ladies, we're up again a few notches in the polls.

"That's fantastic," Jessica said. "I've been holding my breath because of all the nasty ads the other side has been running."

"Daddy," Kristy said, wide smile, her hair tied in pink bows. "Mom and I have come to take you to lunch." She walked quickly to her dad's side, looked at the microphone and audio gear and asked, "What's that?"

Thaxton smiled. "That, sweetheart, is the equipment needed to record my voice for podcasts. They're sort of like radio messages. I talk to people just like I'm talking to you. And they can hear it on the Internet anytime they want to listen."

"Can I talk on the podcast?"

"That might be a good idea. I want the voters to get to know my family. Let's talk about it over lunch."

"Sounds good." Jessica said. "Where are you taking us?"

Joe smiled. "Wait a second, I thought you girls were taking me to lunch."

"We're driving. You're buying." She laughed.

As Joe reached for his keys, a female member of his staff, a college-aged brunette, hair in a ponytail, jeans ripped at one knee, wearing a *Joe Thaxton* T-Shirt, entered. "Excuse me. I'm sorry to interrupt." She smiled, looking across the room.

He said, "No problem, Caroline. What is it?"

"There's a woman on line four that really wants to speak with you, no one else."

"Can you take a message? I'll call her back."

"Of course. But her name is Amber Nelson. It was her husband, Johnny, who died a few weeks ago from a waterborne bacterial infection he got when he was fishing with his cast net. I thought you might want to take her call."

"Yes ... yes I do." He looked at his wife, Jessica nodding.

Joe sat down and picked up the phone. Jessica turned to Kristy. "Daddy needs to talk to this person. Let's go in the main area and see if we can find an extra-large T-shirt for your Uncle Rob. He keeps asking, and I keep forgetting."

They left the room, and he answered the phone. "This is Joe."

"Mr. Thaxton, my name's Amber Nelson. I guess the lady on the phone told you why I'm calling."

"Please, call me Joe. She told me who was calling, not why. First, Mrs. Nelson, I'd like to tell you how very sorry I am for the loss of your husband. It is a tragedy, something that never should have happened."

"Thank you. You can call me Amber. I buried Johnny almost a month ago, and the pain of his death is unshakable. He's always on my mind, and always will be. He grew up on and around those waters. Fished, swam, boated from Boca Grande to Fort Myers Beach. And now, after he comes home from tours of duty in the Middle East, he's killed by bacteria in the water ... our water. I know I don't live in your district, but you are the only candidate seriously taking on the issue of water pollution. I want you to know you have my support and thousands of people like me. If there's any way I can help your campaign, I'm happy to do so."

"I appreciate your thoughts, support and your offer. There's really not a lot I need except for you to keep us in your prayers. If elected, I hope I can make a positive difference." Joe glanced through the door, watching his wife and daughter interact with campaign staff. "On second thought, Amber, maybe there is something you can do. I'm not the only candidate taking on water pollution. Hal Duncan is, too. We're hosting a townhall meeting together. Perhaps you could attend as our guest. You could tell your husband's story. I think that will further help drive home the seriousness and deadly consequences of water pollution in Florida."

"I'll be there."

Thirty-Six

I could see the iconic Cocoa Beach Pier in the distance. *Dragonfly* cut through the light chop in the Atlantic with a smooth gallop that made sailing what is—a harmony of wind, open water, good weather, a fine boat and someone behind the wheel to choreograph it all. Max and I watched a few surfers riding the breakers on either side of the pier. Dozens of boats, most of them powerboats, bobbed in the swells. To the east, near the horizon, a cruise ship moved like a mirage at sea.

At the end of the pier, under an open-air thatched roof, people leaned against the railing, some with fishing poles in their hands, others with dreams in their hearts that extended beyond the horizon. Ships in the distance do that. They offered dreamers the stowaway's chance to sail into a new world and leave the old one in the past. The pier, and its railing on both sides, jutted more than 800 feet out and above the Atlantic. Far enough for fishermen to catch sharks trolling the waters. Brown pelicans stood on the railing like stoic props, coming to life when a minnow, shrimp, or baitfish were tossed their way.

I watched the waves break against the heavy pilings under the pier, froths of white-water churning in the constant ebb and flow. If I wanted to return *Dragonfly* to her slip tonight, this spot in the Atlantic is where I had a decision to make. Should I sail farther south, I could stop at any of the dozen or so marinas from here to Vero Beach, spend the night and continue the sail the next day … and the next.

But something pulled at me like an anchor caught in rocks on the floor of the sea. It was the words, the angst, that Jessica Thaxton was saying and feeling. *I fear something bad is going to happen to Joe either before or after the televised townhall meeting. I'm very worried, and I don't know where to turn.*

I looked at Max as she stared at the carnival near the end of the pier—Bob Marley's voice on the outdoor speakers singing *One Love*; two little girls in banana-yellow sun dresses dancing to the music; people eating hot dogs and ice cream; a young man in a body shirt, shorts and a top hat juggling four orange balls in the air; fishing poles bending with catfish and sheepshead; and tourists strolling by, snapping pictures.

The last time I'd sailed *Dragonfly*, Wynona was with me. I picked up my phone and called her. She answered, and I said, "At an eleventh-hour invitation for your birthday, I could bring you a sailboat."

"Well, I take it that you've decided to keep *Dragonfly*." She smiled, sitting at her desk in the police department.

"I took your suggestion. I'm sailing *Dragonfly* as we speak, just off Cocoa Beach Pier. Max and I are watching the show at the end of the pier. She seems fascinated that the pelicans sit like statues as the people snap pictures of them."

"I'm so glad you decided not to sell the boat."

"Maybe I'll sail her to Fort Lauderdale and pick you up for your birthday."

"That would be a marvelous and romantic gift. However, I just can't take a few days off right now to go sailing. Can you come here?"

"Last I checked, the water in the Everglades isn't deep enough to accommodate a sailboat, and I don't own an airboat."

"But you do own a Jeep. I was hoping you'd take me to that place where you bought the orchids."

"Why? You want to meet Chester?"

"Of course. But the real reason is I'd like to buy a few more orchids, one for my living room and some I can keep on the outdoor deck.

You've got me addicted to the beauty of the individual orchids. Will you take me there?"

"Yes, but remember, Chester Miller doesn't keep regular store hours, not that he operates a store. It's more of a lemonade stand for some of the world's most exotic flowers. He's gone a lot replanting orchids all over the glades. I'm not sure if his granddaughter is there. We might get to the place and the gate will be closed."

"Let's take that chance, okay?"

I said nothing for a moment, watching the cruise ship vanish over the horizon. "I'll be there tomorrow."

"Sean, are you okay? For a man on a sailboat, your voice sounds out to sea. Excuse my poor attempt at a metaphor."

"I'm fine. Out here on the water, I've been thinking about a job I turned down. The client's running for office, and his wife is afraid there will be an attempt on his life."

"Who is he?"

"You and I watched a story about him on the TV news when I was at your home. His name is Joe Thaxton. He's a fishing guide who's fed up with water pollution and massive algae blooms. He says it's ruined his business, and it put his little girl in the hospital. He's quite outspoken, has the support and endorsement of a lot of people, including one of the two candidates running for governor, Hal Duncan."

"Maybe, when you get here, you can tell me why you turned down the job? It sounds like you're not sure you made the right decision. I'd love to hear why."

Thirty-Seven

Simon Santiago pulled his red Ferrari up in front of a trendy waterfront café in Coconut Grove. The restaurant offered indoor and outdoor seating with unobstructed views of Biscayne Bay. He stopped near a reserved spot, the deep-throated engine rumbling. The sidewalk café oozing with the funky Coconut Grove vibe. Bright, primary colors on the open-air building. Tall royal palm trees.

Tanned diners sat at tables under wide umbrellas, sipping drinks and munching decorative green salads topped with grilled salmon, shrimp, or stone crab. Pink and white bougainvillea wrapped around a wrought iron railing that ran the length of the outdoor dining area, sailboats on the blue water bay. Some of the diners watched the man park the Ferrari. Others ignored him.

A male, college-aged valet in white shorts and matching polo shirt moved two orange cones and directed Santiago to park in one of the coveted center spots in front of the café. A white convertible Bentley GT was in one of the spaces. Santiago got out of the Ferrari, wearing dark glasses, red golf shirt and black slacks. He handed a twenty-dollar bill to the valet and said, "Keep an eye on it for me, all right?"

"Yes sir. No problem."

Simon Santiago strolled through the restaurant like he owned the place. The head server, a man in his forties, greeted him by name. "

Mr. Santiago, your party is here. He's seated at your regular table on the terrace. Is that fine, sir, or would you prefer to dine inside?"

"That's okay. It's a great day. Why eat inside when you have that view, huh?"

"Exactly. Leslie will be your server today."

Santiago nodded, walking through the restaurant filled with nautical motif and fine art oil paintings of the Florida Keys and the Caribbean. At the most remote section of the outdoor dining area, in a corner with an excellent view of the bay, buffered on one side by a terrace of bougainvillea, was a white-cloth table with four chairs. A man sat in one of the chairs, his back to the diners, sunglasses on, wide shoulders and a swarthy face. His head was shaved. Scalp pink. A small white scar crossed the bridge of his nose. He wore a dark blue blazer, white T-shirt and faded jeans. Boat shoes with no socks. Michael Fazio started to stand when Santiago approached.

"Keep your seat," Santiago said. He sat opposite him, back to the corner. He took his sunglasses off, his ferret eyes darting around the outdoor dining area. No one seemed to be watching. Good. It was time to talk business. He looked at Fazio. "Good to see you again."

"You, too. I was in Jersey last week. Nice to be back in the sunshine."

"I need to see your phone."

Fazio lifted his phone from a pocket inside his jacket and slid it across the table. "I should take offense at that. We have a history together. You really think I'd record our conversation?"

"No, but this move is just like putting on my seatbelt. It's automatic, standard procedure at times like this."

Fazio said nothing, moving a toothpick from one side of his wide mouth to the other.

Santiago said, "We have a job for you. My employer is extremely frustrated with what's happening, and he wants to change the course of action before the action of this individual changes the course of his business."

• • •

I left Max with Dave and Nick and drove to Wynona's home. We had a birthday lunch at the Gator Café before driving south for an hour, turning west on the Tamiami Trail and heading to Chester Miller's place. Wynona wore jeans, a long-sleeve, beige shirt, and a touch of lip gloss, her purse on the floorboard. I told her about my conversation with Joe and Jessica Thaxton, the reason I turned down the job, and why I had mixed feelings about doing so.

"That's understandable," she said, looking at the mangroves with their spindly roots like claws dipping into the water of a canal next to the road. She turned to me. "I think it's because you admire what he's doing, Sean. Or at least what he's trying to do. Maybe the best way to help him is to vote for Thaxton or contribute to has campaign."

"I don't live in his district, and he set a one-hundred limit per contributor. He refuses to take PAC or lobbyist money."

She smiled. "Another reason to admire him."

"The guy's about to go toe-to-toe with some of the most well-funded lobbyists in the state, the influencers who are working for Big Sugar and Big Ag. And he's not doing it using hyperbole, or some overinflated exaggerations. He's got credentials, the chops, and he's letting the facts—the data, win debates. His wife said the attack ads that Brasfield is running are landing hard blows."

"Why doesn't he hit back? Surely Joe Thaxton won't have to look far to find dirt on William Brasfield."

"That's not the way he wants to conduct his campaign. He has challenged Brasfield to another televised debate. So far, the incumbent state senator refuses to commit."

Wynona said nothing. She took her shoes off in her seat. "I think you made the right decision. The Thaxton's have suffered vandalism, threatening phone calls, and Mrs. Thaxton believes someone followed her when she dropped her child off at school. Definitely a police matter. Please don't think I'm marginalizing anything, but I believe your skillset is somewhat above solving the push-back the Thaxton's and their campaign staff are getting."

"I wish I could give them more than just advice."

"If someone had stolen a half-million from Thaxton's war chest, you could be the guy to help him get it back. If someone fired a round at Thaxton, you could be the person to track down the shooter. When does Thaxton join Hal Duncan in the televised townhall meeting?"

"Soon. I believe it's on the second."

"That might be one debate I'll tune in to see. Any changes in cleaner water entering the glades or Big Cypress will only be positive for life on the rez and the Seminole Tribe."

I drove a little slower, looking for the spot to turn off the road. "I'm not sure if there's a sign on this side of the road."

"A sign for what?" she asked.

"The entrance to Chester's wild world of orchids. I do know that when you approach it driving east from Naples there is a sign about fifty feet from the entrance. The sign is small, hand-painted, the size of an average mailbox, and its nailed to a cypress post that looks like it's about to fall to the ground."

"What's written on it?"

"Three words … orchids for sale."

She smiled. "Even if there's no sign on this side of the road, I'm sure you can find it again."

"I can, but I have to be ready because the entrance is narrow and looks like a natural gap in the mangroves. It's a dirt and gravel road that's overgrown in weeds."

"Something tells me that Chester doesn't put much priority in retail sales."

"He doesn't. For him, it's all about making the money to put it back into helping replant native orchids in the Everglades." I came around a bend in the road and recognized the ingress. There was no sign on the west-bound side. I turned off the road. "We're in luck. His gate's open. Maybe he's home."

Thirty-Eight

We'd driven less than one hundred feet onto the property, strands of old-growth, virgin cypress on both sides of the trail, orchids growing from clay and earthen pots wedged in tree limbs near the trunks and in the dark earth along the trail. Wynona said, "Oh my God … this is incredible … so beautiful. It takes my breath away. You weren't kidding when you referred to it as Chester's wild world of orchids."

A great horned owl perched on a thick cypress branch opened its yellow eyes the size of quarters, as if it was rudely awakened from an afternoon nap. The bird leapt from the limb, beating its wide wings in silence, fleeing into the dark shadows through the strand of trees. Wynona said, "Not only are the orchids spectacular in their rainbow of colors, the ferns and bromeliads are the biggest I've ever seen anywhere in Florida."

I chuckled. "The man has a green thumb."

"It's more than that. It's as if, when you turned off the asphalt road and entered here, we went through a time warp into a strange, primordial world. Maybe it's the way the glades looked a few million years ago. This is a rare place in South Florida. I almost expect a T-rex to cross the path in front of us."

We drove another hundred yards through the winding trail and came to a drier area. His truck was there. So was the Ford Escape his granddaughter drove. But I could see no overt signs of them. As I pulled my Jeep near the cabin and greenhouse, I said, "Here is the home and research compound where an old man labors to restock the glades with native orchids while creating hybrid orchids from some of the rarest pollens in the world. He is more of an artist than a botanist, a man with a microscope and tweezers that he uses like a sculptor with a hammer and chisel, or a painter with a palette, brushes and a canvas."

"I can't wait to meet him," Wynona said, looking at a dozen orchids set up on a picnic table beneath a live oak tree, a white sheet under clay pots holding the plants.

Callie Hogan walked from the greenhouse with two large orchids in either hand, both plants in full bloom with purple and pink flowers. She looked at my Jeep and smiled, setting the orchids down on the picnic table. Wynona and I got out of the Jeep, and I said, "The orchids I bought from you and your grandfather were a big hit. So big, in fact, I've returned for more."

"Awesome! It's good to see you, again." She made a quick smile at Wynona.

I nodded. "Callie, this is Wynona. She's the one I bought the orchids for, and she's here to pick out some more for her birthday."

"It's nice to meet you," Wynona said. "Are any of the orchids on that table for sale?"

"Some of them are, yes. I'll get Grandpa. He's in his lab working."

She took off a pair of cotton garden gloves and walked past us, entering the vintage Airstream trailer. Less than a minute later, Chester, shoeless, his glasses hanging from black straps around his neck, approached with Callie. He grinned, and his wild, snowy eyebrows arched. "Where's your little dog?"

"Max is back at the marina near Ponce Inlet. Chester, this is Wynona Osceola. I bought the orchids for her, and she liked them so much she wanted to come here and buy a few more."

"Delighted to accommodate you, Wynona. Your last name rings all kind of bells in my old head. May I assume you are Seminole and perhaps related to the famed leader of the tribe?"

"Yes, on both accounts."

He looked away for a moment, his eyes filled with thought. "One of the finest men I've ever met is Sam Otter. Every time I think I know a little something about botany, I find myself humbled in Sam's presence, especially when he invited me into the glades to pick some plants for his medicine bundle. It's as if he has a thousand years of handed down botanical history and expertise flowing through his veins. He knows the flora and fauna on a vascular level, and he views it all on a holistic level. Everything's connected. It's no exaggeration to say he's a true plant whisperer. He's always been generous with his time and knowledge. I hope Sam's well."

Wynona smiled. "I think he's doing as well as can be expected for a man who's lived more than a hundred years. Has he ever been in here to see what you've done?"

"Yes, a few times. Not in the last five or so years, though."

"I've lived on an off the rez much of my life. I've been to many places in the glades and Big Cypress Preserve, but I've never seen anything quite like what you've done here. This is such an oasis for the soul."

Chester's eyes smiled. His beard parted with a wide grin. "Thank you for saying that. I've been out here probably longer than you've been alive. I got lucky when I bought the place. Although, I've let nature continue its stewardship, I took the liberty to add a few orchids, bromeliads and whatnot in here."

Callie laughed. "One of my grandfather's whatnots is growing in that tree behind you." She pointed. "About ten feet up, you can see the plant sitting on that wooden extension. Grandpa's been waiting more than fifteen years for that orchid to bloom. When the Persephone orchid blooms, we believe it'll be the rarest flower on the face of the planet."

Wynona looked at the big plant in the tree. "I would love to see that when it blooms."

Chester chuckled. "Me, too. I had a fella in here yesterday. He said he was representing a buyer in Miami who'd heard about the Persephone from an article National Geographic did on the stuff I do here. He offered me more money than I thought existed for the orchid if it flowers."

"Who is the buyer in Miami?" I asked.

"The representative wouldn't say. Called him an anonymous buyer and a passionate orchid aficionado."

"Would you sell?" asked Wynona.

"No. The plant doesn't belong in some millionaire's house. The public ought to see it. Callie will make sure that happens with her skill at this social media thing."

Wynona said, "I hope it will be spectacular. Something I think is just as outstanding is what you and Callie are doing by replanting native orchids back in the glades. Sean told me about your program. How many orchids have you replanted?"

"Callie has the exact number. It's more than five thousand. And we're delighted to report that ninety percent have taken root and propagated." Chester used his thumbs to hitch up the suspenders that supported his thick dungarees. "Enough about all that. You, Wynona, came here to invite more orchids to join your family. Let's have a look around to see if there's something that catches your eye."

• • •

Simon Santiago finished a phone call in a remote section of the café and walked back to the outdoor terrace. Michael Fazio sat at the table, shifting his gaze from the bay to Santiago. Fazio said, "I'm assuming you've chatted with your employer."

"He's not my employer. He's my client."

"It's only a question of semantics. Tell me more about the person you'd like to see catch a one-way bus."

"Not a lot to tell. The man we're talking about is running for office. The polls show him in a double-digit lead ahead of our guy, and this is coming in spite of all the attack ads we're running against him."

"Give me his name. I'll need to follow him for a few days, get a sense of the strategy for the hunt. Do you want it to look like an accident, or do you want to send a strong message to others?"

"Accident. He's already built such a brand—a profile, that we can't have it remotely traced back to us."

Fazio grinned. "It never has in the past, what makes you think this is any different?"

"Because this guy has become the darling of the news media and the voters. He's poisonous to the industry, from subsidies to tens of millions in possible fines for environmental clean-up that the EPA could slap on them."

Fazio sipped from a Perrier water, looked at the bay, a windsurfer going by, the white sail reflecting from the water. "He won't take money, and he won't back down, huh?"

"Do you think we'd be sitting here if he would. He can't be bought, and he can't be scared. We've tried. We're coming up to our last option."

"Well, since this guy is different—a greater visibility for you and your employer, I have to take greater risks … meaning the fee is going to be higher."

"How much higher?"

"Half a mil."

Santiago said nothing. He watched a young blonde woman in short-shorts and a halter top jogging down the sidewalk lined with tall palms. After twenty seconds, he said, "You've never asked for that much. I need to run that number by my client."

"Just give me your client's name, and I'll let him know what the job will cost."

"That's not gonna happen. As far as you're concerned, I am the client. I'm the one who hires or fires you, and I'm the one who pays you. Period."

"Hey, don't get all territorial on me, all right. I could give a rat's ass who your boss is, as long as his money's good."

"If he agrees, half will go into your Caymans account. The balance deposited there when you're done … if you succeed."

"You oughta be the first to know I never fail."

Thirty-Nine

"Testing … one … two … three. Testing … one … two," said a sound technician in black jeans and a T-shirt, standing on stage and adjusting the microphones on the podiums. He nodded to an audio engineer in a sound booth to the far right of the stage. Techs adjusted lights as a television crew set up three cameras. The event, which had the vibe of a rock concert, was taking place in Port St. Lucie's municipal amphitheater.

It was 6:30 p.m., the evening still warm, palm fronds swaying in the breeze. The audience began taking their seats an hour before the candidates, Joe Thaxton and Hal Duncan, were to appear on stage. Reporters from across the state mingled, sipping coffee from white paper cups, sharing salacious details about some of the more exciting political contests. Because Florida's large population makes it a key state in presidential elections, the governor's race commanded wide national attention, too. The incumbent, having reached his term limit, was running for U.S. Senate. This left the door open for two Republican contenders, Hal Duncan and Carl Fanning.

But it was a state senate race in District 25 that was grabbing its share of headlines, the battle between incumbent William Brasfield and newcomer Joe Thaxton. Tonight's town hall meeting wasn't billed as a debate because of the two different races. It was pitched as an opportunity for voters to see and hear two candidates who shared similar campaign agendas in terms of the environment. The placards, billboards and information on both candidate's websites spelled it out: *An evening with Hal Duncan and Joe Thaxton ... everyone is invited.*

A narrow-faced newspaper reporter from Orlando, sleeves on his white shirt rolled to his elbows, sipped coffee and said, "Rumor has it that Duncan would have picked Joe Thaxton to run as his lieutenant governor if Duncan had known Thaxton earlier in the game."

A female reporter, blonde hair in a bob, iPad in one hand, said, "I can't recall an election in recent years that's generated the interest Thaxton's managed to get so quickly. Some people are saying he has the right stuff to go the distance and beyond."

"And what would that be?"

"He's got the moxie—the chutzpah, the damn balls to kick the leg out of a three-legged stool and see where Big Sugar lands. No one in fifty years of Florida politics has attempted to do that. In Joe Thaxton, I think Hal Duncan sees a bold ally who would do better in the state senate proposing environmental bills rather than as a lieutenant governor waiting patiently in the wings for the governor to serve out his term or terms."

Jessica Thaxton and daughter Kristy took seats in the front row near the center. Jessica leaned down to Kristy and said, "I am so proud of your daddy. This will be an event I hope you remember for the rest of your life."

"I will, Mama. I'm even prouder of Daddy."

The executive producer for the television station, a man dressed in designer jeans, blue T-shirt and a dark sports coat, walked out on the stage, a wireless, hand-held microphone in one hand. "Good evening everyone. Thank you for coming out tonight. This promises to be one of the highlights of this election year. We are thrilled to host an evening with gubernatorial candidate Hal Duncan and one of the candidates vying for state senate, Joe Thaxton."

There was a burst of applause. One man in the third row shouted, "Go Joe!"

The producer smiled. "We'll take questions from the audience. Please remember, this evening is being televised live to every PBS station in Florida, from Pensacola in the panhandle to Key West. Let me introduce you to your master of ceremonies for this evening. He is a retired political reporter and a former columnist with more than thirty-five years of covering politics in Florida, who backstage a few minutes ago, reaffirmed to me that there is no such thing as a boring election in Florida. Ladies and gentlemen, please welcome Mr. Howard Payne."

In the broadcast remote-control room, a balding director stood behind a large electronic console with a half-dozen technicians seated, a wide panel of TV monitors in front of them. He said, "Stand by. Camera one coming to you. In five seconds … four … three… two … and we are live."

A silver-haired man stepped on stage. He smiled. "Welcome everyone here in the audience and to you watching at home. This may be the first of its kind in Florida politics, and that is one of the reasons we are thrilled to present an evening with gubernatorial candidate Hal Duncan and contender for state senate, Joe Duncan. Without further ado, let's have the candidates come on stage for a conversation with us all. As my granddaddy used to say, this ought to be a doozy."

Forty

Max and I were walking down L dock when Dave came from *Gibraltar's* salon to the cockpit. He waved to us and shouted, "Join me for a cocktail with the candidates. The tube is alive with Florida politics at its finest, and I don't mean that as an oxymoron."

Max picked up her step, tail twitching. We joined Dave on his trawler, the sound of conversations coming from the salon. He said, "I've been watching Joe Thaxton and Hal Duncan live on the telly, and I must confess … Thaxton appears more like a candidate for governor rather than the state senate. Both are good, but Thaxton is compelling because he's relatable and a natural born communicator. You and Miss Max come join me. There are a few minutes left. Let's see how they wrap it up. This should be interesting."

I took a seat in one of Dave's canvas deck chairs. He sat on his couch with Max next to him. He used his remote control to adjust the sound coming from his large TV above the bar. The camera was on Hal Duncan who said, "Should I win the governor's race, and should my friend, Joe Thaxton, do the same in the state's senate race, I'd welcome an environmental reform bill drafted by Joe and his colleagues in the senate. The environment here in Florida, especially our precious water, is absolutely on the top rung of my agenda. I have campaigned hard on this issue, and I will be relentless in seeing it through as governor. The first thing I'll do … and it's something I don't need a legislative bill to do … is replace the current members of the South Florida Water Management Board."

The crowd in the amphitheater applauded. The host nodded and said, "We're down to our last few minutes of questions from the audience." He shuffled though some index cards and read. "This question is for you, Mr. Thaxton. One member in the audience asked, 'You've suggested that Big Sugar can hire the most expensive lobbyists, not only because of their deep pockets, but also because of the federal subsidies they receive. Should the subsidies end?"

The camera cut to Joe. He nodded. "Absolutely. In my opinion, they're not fair to the American taxpayers. Here's why …" He paused, glancing at the audience in the amphitheater and the audience through the lens of the TV camera. "The federal program began in 1982, and today it's costing American taxpayers close to three billion a year. The U.S. sugar program doesn't work on a natural supply and demand economy. It is basically a supply control set-up that limits imports using a quota system while restricting domestic production through what the federal government calls marketing allotments. This means that Big Sugar, here in Florida, can reap up to 150-million dollars a year, per each of the big four growers, from the program. Six hundred million—that's a sweet deal, folks. And that's one of the reasons their lobby group is very well funded. It all boils down to plenty of money to give Big Sugar pretty much the run of the table in Florida. This has got to change. Let's do the right thing and demand clean water in our Everglades, rivers, and beaches. I will be taking water samples from the glades and report to you what I've found."

The audience in the amphitheater burst out in thunderous applause, the TV cameras getting shots of people applauding, Jessica and Kristy clapping and smiling.

Dave looked at me and said, "He's done his homework and knows how to articulate in a way that resonates with the crowd."

We watched as Joe Thaxton stepped out from behind the podium, removing the microphone from the stand and holding it. He held up one hand above his eyebrows to shield his eyes from the bright TV lights. "There is someone here tonight I'd like you all to meet. A few weeks ago, her husband, Johnny Nelson—a combat veteran, cut himself on the shin in knee-deep water while he was tossing his cast net. Not far from where he grew up on Pine Island near Fort Myers. Unknown to Johnny, a vicious water-borne bacterium, entered the cut. Ten days later, he died. There weren't any drugs strong enough to combat what some doctors call flesh-eating bacteria. It spread like wildfire through his system. His widow, Amber Nelson, is here with us tonight. She is here to endorse what Hal Duncan and I want to see—clean water in Florida, so people can wade and swim in our waters without fear of having a horrible bug, something in the water that they can't see, end up killing them. Amber, please stand up."

Amber, wearing a dark blue dress, stood from her seat near the center of the audience. The crowd rose to its feet in a loud ovation. Amber smiled, wiping a tear from under one eye.

Joe motioned to Amber. "Thank you so much for joining us tonight." He scanned the audience. "I'm not suggesting that Big Sugar had anything at all to do with Johnny Nelson's death. I'm not putting the blame on agriculture. I'm not even blaming the septic runoff from old and antiquated systems. What I am blaming is the gatekeepers—the water management boards and to some extent … all of us. Why us? Because, for too long, we sat back, complacent, allowing the cronies to control our waterways and beaches, receiving the composite onslaught of pollution from a lot of factors. Lake Okeechobee, with its polluted runoff, certainly adds to this toxic mix, as do failing septic systems. What are we going to do about it?" He pointed to Hal Duncan. "The biggest step is to elect this man as your next governor. He will, flat out, get the job done. If you chose to send me to Tallahassee with him, we'll start the changes. We'll put 'em in motion. And we'll be relentless. That's a campaign promise you can bet the ranch on!"

Dave and I watched the scene on his TV, Dave sipping a gin over ice. He said, "That's powerful stuff. In a way, he reminds me of John Kennedy in front of an audience."

"I'm too young to have seen that." I smiled.

Dave chuckled. "Well, surely you saw some of his speeches on the old newsreels. If not they're available for viewing online. On the Internet, no one stays dead."

"It gives the word obituary a rather expanded definition."

"Do me a favor, Sean. When I shed this skin, remind my daughter not to post the life and times of her old man on the Internet."

"When your rent's up, I'll let her know. Assuming I'm still here after you. In my line of work, longevity can be the first of the conditions that's compromised."

He nodded, looked at the screen. "It appears that the evening's event is done. I see credits rolling over the exterior shot of the amphitheater and the two candidates shaking hands, working the crowd." Dave muted the sound. "You mentioned longevity … I hope that Joe Thaxton didn't compromise his political longevity by drawing a line in the sand with some of the most powerful and politically connected companies in the nation."

I stood and looked out the open sliding glass windows at the harbor beyond the transom. A fifty-foot Irwin sailboat, sails wrapped and stowed, motoring silently into the marina.

"What's on your mind?" Dave asked. "You look like your thoughts are aboard that big sailboat. I forgot to ask you how it went sailing *Dragonfly*."

"It was good. And Wynona is right. I shouldn't sell her."

Dave propped his feet up on his coffee table. "Wynona's right about a lot of things. She's a young woman with an old soul. Smart. Tenacious. Beautiful. And, for some reason that escapes me, she really likes you, Sean."

I turned around. "It's mutual. I'll leave it at that for now."

"Indeed. Is that what hi-jacked your thoughts from my old trawler to that sailboat that just passed?"

"I was thinking about what Joe Thaxton said."

"You mean Thaxton's talent at making environmental science relatable?" Dave grinned.

"Yes, but not that specifically. He mentioned he'd be in the glades collecting environmental data. That could be risky."

"The candidates have their schedules posted online. They zip around their districts. Wouldn't be hard to follow them since they're out in the open."

"In the glades, Joe won't be out in the open like in some shopping center greeting voters. He'll be in the center of a million acres."

Forty-One

Joe Thaxton remembered the first time he "saw" the wind. As he drove east on Florida's Tamiami trail, he started thinking about the first time he looked out from above the Everglades, and it was not from staring out of a window in an airplane. That day in July he could actually look out over the glades. He was high enough up to see the vista, but not too high, giving him a perspective to take in the effect that an approaching storm was having on the sawgrass.

It was his junior year of college. A friend of his, who specialized in landscape photography, Roy Fitzgerald, had secured permission to take pictures from an old fire tower that stood overlooking the headwaters of the Everglades. He invited Joe to join him.

When they climbed the hundreds of wooden steps to the top, a few of the timbers partially rotted and in need of paint, there was sawgrass in every direction. In some areas, he could see palm hammocks of thick vegetation, that looked like small tropical islands in the river of grass. He remembered standing with Roy at the top of the tower's observation deck, the windows propped open, the smell of rain in the distance, a wasp buzzing in a corner of the humid tower. Roy, a lanky man with thick, black eyebrows, pale skin and fingers that seemed to caress his camera, snapped pictures of dark clouds and lightning, rain streaking from purple skies miles away at the horizon.

But it was the wind across the Everglades that Joe enjoyed. It was how the gusts of wind caused thousands of acres of sawgrass to move in waves similar to the swells at sea beyond the breakers. It was as if a hand—a life force, caressed the sawgrass, causing it to bow to an unseen power in long, billowing rows. Joe smiled, remembering how it reminded him of an enormous Van Gogh painting, dramatic brush strokes from the wind whipping a palette of colors, a sense of urgency, that visceral feeling that something was alive above and below the sawgrass, art in motion.

Joe glanced at his watch. *Plenty of time*, he thought. As much as he enjoyed the campaign, the volunteer staff, the difference they were making in drawing attention to water pollution in Florida, he missed being out on the water—out in the glades. He missed the outdoors because of the connection it had to his soul. It spoke to him in the wind, the birdsong, the roll of a tarpon in the bay—its wide scales reflecting the glint of the morning sun. He reminisced about that as he glanced up in his rearview mirror, spotting a dark car a half-mile behind his truck.

He sped up a little, glancing at his drone on the seat beside him, anxious to get out into Big Cypress and the glades. After another five miles, he slowed down and turned north off the Tamiami Trail onto a dirt road that led far up into Big Cypress Preserve. He looked in his rearview mirror. The black car went by, not slowing down. Or at least it didn't appear to slow down. Regardless, unless you had an all-wheel-drive vehicle, something like a Jeep or Range Rover, the trek north on this road would be quite a challenge.

It was called 15 Mile Road. The locals referred to it as Gator Gully. It was carved through the swamps in the mid-forties when lumber companies cut and hauled a million board feet of cypress trees from the area. The road twisted and turned for fifteen miles north of Highway 41 into Big Cypress Preserve. Dirt. Mud. Pot holes. Just wide enough for one vehicle.

Joe's truck had four-wheel-drive, and he figured he'd use it today. The water levels were not what they'd been when he was a young man. He knew the area well—the sloughs, cypress and palm hammocks, the lakes, gator holes and the grassy prairies. His goal today was to get in some of the of most remote spots and use his drone to capture video of the water levels and the condition of the glades, Big Cypress Preserve, and the Fakahatchee Strand if he had time.

As Joe followed the winding trail, he could no longer see back to the entrance through his rearview mirror. He couldn't see that the black car had returned and entered 15 Mile Road. And he couldn't see that the car was an SUV, a BMW X-1 with all-wheel drive.

Joe drove around and sometimes through potholes, many the width of trashcan lids, all partially filled with water. The road was slick with dark mud. He could see deer and wild boar tracks in some areas. He looked to the east, black vultures rode the air currents, circling over the swamps, the sun white hot in the near cloudless sky.

After another six miles, the road meandered toward the west, but just north of the westward turn, was another road. This one was more like a trail. Narrow. Thick brush on each side. Joe pulled his truck onto that path and drove slowly, the scrape of limbs sliding down the side panels of his truck like the sound of fingernails on a chalkboard. He managed to drive a little more than a mile before the route came to an end. It just faded out as if the brush had enough encroachment and reclaimed the land.

Joe picked up his drone and its controls, a bottle of water, still camera, phone, mosquito spray, and a ham and cheese sandwich Jessica had made him at dawn. He put everything into a backpack, got out, locked his truck and began walking through ankle-deep water the shade of sunlit tea.

He could see five large snowy egrets feeding in the shallows, a spit of wet land between him and the birds. One spotted him, made a shrill cry and flew, the other four following, the beat of their big wings making a heavy *whoomp, whoomp*. The sound reminded Joe of his grandmother using a steel road to beat dirt from a small rug she had hung from a clothesline in her yard.

In the distance, beyond expanse of sawgrass, and the final glimpse of the birds in flight, he heard the sound of a vehicle. He tried to see if it was the noise of an airboat or an off-road-vehicle. Like the clatter of the birds in flight, the sound faded. He started walking, mud sucking at his boots. And then he heard the noise again, just barely, engine whining as if it was revved up to get through ruts and mud on a road that led to only one place.

Right where he stood.

Forty-Two

As Joe sloshed through knee-deep water, about a mile from where he'd left his truck, his thoughts focused on the interaction between water and land. One of the many things he loved about marine biology was the symbiosis between land and water. Whether it was studying the beaches where the sea met the coast, the shore of estuaries, rivers or lakes, the relationship between the land and water often revealed the health of both, especially the water.

A red tide literally spilled its guts of dead fish and crustaceans onto the beaches. The banks of winding rivers were often similar to human arteries. Some were partially blocked with trash or tainted from open drainage pipes causing changes in and around the river's path.

But there was no place on earth like the Everglades, aptly called the River of Grass. Nowhere else on the planet, including the vast swamps of Africa, was there a terrain like the one surrounding him. He splashed through it, thinking about how the interface between water and land in the glades was a heart and soul relationship of pure survival. For thousands of years, vast sheets of fresh water constantly covered the Everglades, moving slowly from north to south, supporting plant and animal life unique in all the world. But, when the glades were ditched, drained, flooded, dried, and reflooded with phosphate and nitrogen, heavy water from manmade sources, the delicate balance of water and land, a million-year waltz, dramatically changed as if someone had stopped the music. Stopped the birdsong. Drastically changing the synergy and collective harmony of life in the glades.

He walked north more than two miles, stopping to fill test vials with the water flowing around his high boots. He used his phone to record the stops, hitting the video record button and holding the phone in one hand as he took samples. "I'm about seventeen miles northwest of Highway 41. This is the first of a few water samples I'll be taking. We'll get these to a lab for analysis. I'm seeing more cattails out here than I've ever seen. That's not a good sign because they're an invasive species, sort of like the python. But the cattails don't kill rabbits and deer … they just choke the Everglades to death. Lots of dry areas, too. And that only breeds wildfires."

He ended the video recording, slipping his phone back in his pocket. He marked the vials, date and location, placing them in the side pockets of his backpack. He pushed on, entering a dry area, the former marshland like a ceramic bowl splintered in hairline cracks. The air smelled of dead insects and wood smoke somewhere in the distance.

He walked northwest, the terrain now taking on a blend of the Everglades and Big Cypress Preserve, sawgrass and cypress, water and mangroves, thick growths of cabbage palms and slash pines. He found an area of relatively high ground, about a foot above the water, removed his backpack, setting it in a dry spot. Joe took a sip of water, the air now more humid.

He retrieved his phone again and hit the auto-dial for Jessica. The call didn't connect immediately. He looked at his phone screen. One bar struggling to stay vertical. The cell tower coverage was spotty at best. He thought about the old fire tower he'd climbed twenty-five years ago. *It's probably still there.* He continued walking.

Joe took out his drone, readied it for flight. He hit the start button, the tiny propellers buzzing. But they were not loud. The newest models could fly with relative quietness. He guided the drone slowly above the landscape. Within half a minute, the drone had gained an altitude of three hundred feet. He watched the monitor and flew in a due north direction. After another minute, he lowered the drone and its onboard camera to about two hundred feet. He flew it slowly, capturing the images on video—images of areas almost depleted of water. Dead and dying sawgrass. The bloom of cattails in the glades. A skinny deer bolting through the brush. He monitored and documented the locations with GPS coordinates.

The drone was so far away, it wasn't visible, but the images it recorded and sent back were. In the distance, Joe heard a gunshot. He had forgotten that hunting season started in some areas of Big Cypress. He was glad his backpack was bright red, making him stand out and not be mistaken for a deer.

He used the toggle controls to fly the drone back his way. After lunch he'd wanted to send it farther south, toward some sloughs and lakes to check their condition from the air. He landed the drone on a dry spot about ten feet from where he stood. After the props stopped turning, Joe looked at his phone, spotted the single bar, and redialed his wife.

Jessica answered on the second ring. "I was hoping you'd call near the lunch hour. How's it going in the glades?"

"Good. A lot of the terrain is as I had suspected. Some areas with severe drought. Other areas with a lot of water. I've been taking samples, collecting vials and data. I forgot today is the first or second day of hunting season. So, I'm not seeing the game and birds I'd like to see from the drone or by simply standing still out here. It almost feels like nature is afraid to come out and play."

Jessica held her phone to her ear as she locked her car and walked toward the campaign headquarters. "You be careful out there in the boonies. You certainly don't look like a deer, although you're dear to me."

They chatted a couple of minutes, Joe giving her the specifics of what he'd done thus far before ending the call. He ate his sandwich, sipped water from a bottle and cranked his drone again, unaware that he was about to see his second monster through the lens of the camera. But this one wasn't a green slime over the river. It stood on two legs and was even more deadly as it stalked through the river of grass.

•••

Michael Fazio carried his Remington 700 rifle on a sling around one shoulder, staying a quarter mile behind his quarry. He moved stealth-like through the palmettos and cabbage palms. He stopped in his tracks as a water moccasin slithered across the muddy path in front of him and entered a small lake a few feet away, the water darker than the snake's skin. He watched the cottonmouth swim through the water using S movements with its body. Fazio resisted the urge to shoot the snake in the center of his thick midsection.

He loved the hunt. The tracking. The moment he sighted the prey through the scope. He had paid big money to hunt mule deer and elk in Montana. He splurged after one lucrative job and booked a safari in Africa, killing a cape buffalo with one shot. He took the pictures but left the dead animal's carcass on the African soil to rot. The hunt, stalking and killing big game was in his blood.

But nothing beat hunting a man, he thought.

It was a thrill like none other. With more than seven billion people on the planet, the vast majority are leeches to others in society. Sometimes culling and killing off part of the diseased herd was needed. That was one of the great things about war—a cleansing. Cut the population down to better preserve the earth's resources for those who could best use and appreciate them.

Fazio had tracked his prey for more than four miles, amazed at the man's stamina and steady progress through water and mud that felt like quicksand in some areas. But now it was time to earn the other half of his money from an employer he'd never seen and would never see. That's often the way it goes in his line of work. You are a mercenary soldier, hired to fight wars you never started and didn't really care about the results. It was a job—a job he did well.

He stepped out from a grove of Everglades palms and stood behind a cypress tree that had toppled from a hurricane years ago. He used his bi-pod to prop and steady his rifle. Through the scope it was easy to see the bright red backpack next to the man. He watched the man holding something in his hands. It looked like a control to a video game. *Maybe the guy's taking some air or soil samples,* thought Fazio. He's not a scientist. He's a bullshit politician.

• • •

Joe flew his drone at a height of about four hundred feet in a southeast direction. He watched the monitor, looking at water levels and the color of the water in the lakes and sloughs. He flew over acres of red mangroves, the sun sparkling off the dark surface of a large lake like a million gold coins. He watched dozens of great white herons feeding in the shallows. Across from them, more than a dozen roseate spoonbills stalked the water. Joe liked the fact that the drone was so quiet that its aerial presence wouldn't disturb wildlife. He moved the toggle switch and flew directly south.

Something odd appeared on his video monitor.

A man.

And he was holding a rifle.

Must be a deer or boar hunter, Joe thought. The drone was about fifty yards north of the hunter. Three hundred feet in the air. Silent. Observing. Joe watched for a moment, unaware that he was about to witness his own murder. The man crouched behind a large fallen tree, propped his rifle on the tree and seemed to be sighting in on wildlife.

• • •

Fazio moved the crosshairs from the top of the man's head to his chest. At this distance, he could easily put a round into Thaxton's midsection, blowing out his heart and half his lungs. Or the bullet would hit dead center, exiting through the spine. The man would be dead before he knew he'd be crippled from the neck down, should he somehow manage to survive.

Fazio heard something far in the distance. The sound of an ATV or airboat, maybe. *Got to get it done. Concentrate.* He centered the crosshairs just as a shadow moved across the mire, stopping in front of him. He thought it was a large bird.

But birds don't stop in flight unless it was a hummingbird. This shadow was too large. He looked up from his scope. A hundred feet above him a drone was hovering. "What the shit … " he mumbled. He squatted, aiming for the drone. He tried to find it in the crosshairs, the drone now moving like a bat. He fired. Missed. Fired a second time. Missed. The drone zipped toward the north. Fazio cursed under his breath, squatting back down and quickly sighting the crosshairs on the back of the man who was now running.

He fired, hitting the man in the back. The man fell flat to the ground. Now it was time to walk the 150 yards and put one in the guy's head.

The noise returned.

He looked through his scope. In the distance, he spotted a man on an ATV, the man wearing hunter's camouflage and a bright orange vest. Fazio thought about killing the hunter if he came closer. He looked through the scope and could see the hunter sitting on the ATV, smoking a cigar, apparently unaware that a murder has just occurred. He sighted the dead man back in through the scope. There was no movement. No sign of life. He swung the scope back in the direction of the hunter at the edge of a distant tree line. He watched the man sitting on the ATV. The hunter stood, ground the cigar ash on one of the ATV tires, dropping the cigar. After a moment, he got back on the ATV and vanished deep into the swampy woods.

Fazio picked up his spent shell casing and started walking toward the spot where the man had tossed the cigar.

• • •

Joe fought the urge to vomit. His heart raced. Breathing labored. His right lung gone. The bullet hit him in the left part of his upper back near the spine, exiting through his chest. "Have to call Jessica …" he whispered. He lay there, the hot sun on the back of his neck, blood pumping from two holes in his body, the caw of a crow in the cypress trees, the odor of his urine. He struggled to pull the phone from his pocket. Tried to hit the one button to call Jessica, his hand trembling, bile flowing into his throat.

No cell signal.

Joe fought the pain. The acute nausea. He started crawling. He could hear the faraway sound of an engine. *Was it the shooter or someone else? Maybe I can make it to a road … to find a cell signal.* He managed to slowly crawl more than one hundred feet, his energy fading. He crept under the shadow of three large bald cypress trees. Joe tried to sit, falling over on his back. He looked up to the canopies of the old trees, Spanish moss hanging from the limbs and barely moving in the breeze. The sky was the bluest he'd ever seen. He thought of Jessica, what she said before he'd left. *I've packed your lunch. Don't forget to eat it out there today?* He could feel her warm kiss on his cheek. He could see Kristy's face as he bent down to kiss her before she left for school. *Love you, Daddy.*

Love you, too. His eyes teared.

Joe remembered the time he stood in the old fire tower and looked far out and above the Everglades. It was the first time he saw the wind in all its splendor as it danced with the sawgrass, moving in swells like a golden ocean, as far as the eye could see. He was back there now with a drone's eye-view of the River of Grass. The sawgrass pirouetting. White clouds tumbling in the sky. He watched a flock of roseate spoonbills rise from a lake reflecting the sun, the light the whitest he'd ever seen. The spoonbills beat their wings and then soared over the cypress trees grounded in water, the birds ascending toward the bright light, like pink and white ghosts catching the wind across the Everglades.

Forty-Three

Jessica Thaxton was more than worried. She was fearful. It was almost 7:30 p.m., and she hadn't heard from Joe since their conversation in the early afternoon. He always called her when he was heading home to see if she needed anything from the grocery store. She'd called him once, left a message, then made a dinner of baked chicken, green beans and potato salad.

And she waited.

Her daughter, Kristy, entered the kitchen. "Is dinner ready. I'm starving."

"It's ready. We're just waiting for your dad to walk through the door or call."

"Where is Daddy?"

"He should be home. He went into the Everglades to test the water there."

"Did you call him?"

"Yes. But I'm not sure the call is connecting way out there. I'll fix you a plate. Did you practice your letters in the new workbook I bought you?"

"Like an hour ago."

• • •

Three hours later, Jessica washed all the dishes, put her husband's food in a plastic container and set it in the refrigerator. After she went into Kristy's room to kiss her goodnight, she walked into the living room, sat in the dark and watched the moon through the bay windows. She tried Joe's phone one more time, and then she called the police.

She opened the front door to her home, stepping outside on the porch. She looked toward the driveway where Joe always parked his truck. Crickets chirped in the wooded lot bordering their property, the concrete steps chilly under her socked feet, night air cool and scented with a trace of wisteria blossoms. She glanced up at the security camera mounted near the top of the door. But, at that moment in time, Jessica Thaxton didn't feel secure. She felt exposed and so very alone.

Two hours later, she fell asleep in a living room chair, phone in her lap, her left hand clutched around it, her wedding band reflecting a glimmer of moonlight through arched windows.

• • •

The next morning at 6:00, Larry Garner unlocked the Thaxton campaign headquarters and put on a pot of coffee. Joe was supposed to meet him at 6:30 a.m. to ride together to a Rotary Club breakfast meeting where Joe was the guest speaker. Ten minutes later, Jessica called Larry's cell phone. "I've been up most of the night. It's Joe … he didn't come home last night from his water survey trip into the Everglades."

"Is his phone going to voicemail?"

"I think so. I've left five messages. The last time I called, at somewhere near four in the morning, the call rang through one time and then went to silence. Larry, I'm frightened. I called the sheriff's office to report him missing and to see if they'd heard anything. Nothing was reported. I called area hospitals from Naples to Miami. No one with his name has been admitted. What if something horrible happened out there?"

"I'll work the phones. Maybe he got lost somewhere in the Everglades. Joe's a survivor. I just hope to God he didn't get snake bit. We'll find him. Two days ago, I'd suggested that we send an intern and photographer with Joe, but he wanted to go it alone. That's how he likes to work in the field—him and nature. I'll call you."

• • •

I climbed the steps to *Jupiter's* fly bridge, carrying Max in one hand, the morning sunrise budding in slivers of coral pink and tangerine orange over the Atlantic. At the top, I set her down on the passenger bench and walked over to an area where I was repairing a small tear in the Bimini canvas. I discovered the rip in the fabric after a thunderstorm tore through Ponce Inlet last month, winds gusting at more the fifty-miles-per-hour. From the bridge, I could see Nick's boat, *St. Michael*, returning from a fishing trip, three sea gulls following him, squawking.

I used what was essentially a handheld sewing machine that resembled a screwdriver with a wooden handle. A large needle embedded in the handle looped the stitches as I moved along the canvas. Within three minutes the job was done without removing the Bimini top. I put the tool up and watched Nick back *St. Michael* into her slip, a puff of blueish smoke coming from the transom exhaust pipes as he shut off the big diesels.

My phone buzzed on the console near the captain's helm. Max lifted her floppy ears, tilting her head. I looked at the caller ID, recognizing the number. I was going to let the call go to voicemail. But then I thought about what Joe Thaxton had told the audience in the amphitheater and the people watching on televisions across the state. *We'll put 'em in motion. And we'll be relentless. That's a campaign promise you can bet the ranch on!*

I answered the phone, Jessica Thaxton greeting me. "I'm worried about Joe. He went somewhere in the heart of the Everglades yesterday to do water and soil samples. He hasn't come home. That's not like Joe. Never has he been away all night without letting me know where he was. He'd called around one o'clock yesterday afternoon and said he was taking a break to eat the lunch I'd fixed him. He said he had a few hours left, and he'd be coming home. I'm so scared. I don't know what to do."

"Was anyone with him?"

"No, he went alone."

"Did you call the police?"

"Yes, I called the Collier County Sheriff's Office. I'm assuming that's the county Joe was in when he called. They told me that Joe couldn't be considered a missing person until forty-eight hours after a disappearance. I don't know where to turn, so I called you."

I said nothing, looking over at Nick's slip, watching him tie down *St. Michael.*

"Sean are you there?"

"Yes. When Joe called you … what exactly did he say?"

"He gave me an update on how his day was going, you know things about his observations of the glades, the water levels, arid places where there should have been water. He was excited to fly his drone for aerial inspections."

"Did he seem worried or apprehensive in any way?"

"No, not really. He did say he may not have picked the best day to collect data."

"Why?"

"Because it was the first day of hunting season, and he could hear shots fired near Big Cypress Preserve. That frightens me. What can I do? Not only am I worried, but his entire campaign staff is concerned. Joe missed an early morning speech to the Rotary Club. He never would have done that without letting me know."

"I have a friend who works for the Collier County Sheriff's Office. I'll call him to see if he can speed things up. I'll let you know what he says."

"Thank you, Sean. Please hurry."

Forty-Four

Chester Miller filled a thermos with black coffee, stepped from his cabin and glanced up at the Persephone orchid in the tree. "Maybe today's the day," he mumbled. He walked toward a picnic table beneath the tall oak tree where his granddaughter was photographing orchids set on top of the table.

He quietly watched as Callie stood behind her camera secured to a tripod and focused on one of a dozen orchids she'd brought up from the greenhouse. She was methodical, moving each plant to a separate spot on the table she'd covered with a white sheet. She closed one eye, took a picture, zoomed in from the perspective of the entire plant to capture one of the blooms and took a second picture.

"Oh, good morning Grandpa. I didn't hear you coming. You must have learned something from the ghost orchids. You walk like a ghost."

He laughed. "Now, how does a ghost walk?"

"Silently, that's for sure. I'm almost finished with this group of orchids. Your detailed notes really help give each type of orchid its own unique personality. I'm editing it down to about a paragraph, including the scientific names and a little about the history of the plant. This is going to make a fabulous online catalog for you. People all around the world will be able to see and read about what you've discovered."

"That's magnificent, Callie. I've always wanted my work to be shared beyond some of the information I've offered in scientific journals. I thought it was great when National Geographic sent a photographer out here a few years back. He and the writer did a superb job. The photographer took a few pictures of the Persephone plant and told me if it ever blooms into a 'real orchid,' to call him. His card is on the corkboard in the greenhouse."

"I saw it right next to a dozen other cards, mostly from photographers and people with PhDs behind their names. The only card that doesn't have anything, but a name and number, is the one from Sean O'Brien. It's like a card you want to turn over to see if there's something on the other side. When you do, it's blank, adding to the intrigue and mystery. I hope his girlfriend liked the orchids."

There was a twinkle in the old man's eye under the spotted sunlight breaking through the cypress. "How do you know Wynona is his girlfriend?"

Callie smiled. "A girl can tell."

"Well, enlighten your poor old grandfather. It's furtive to me."

"Grandpa, you know a lot about the mystery of orchids, a flower that I'm convinced has its own cool love thing going, certainly with the bees. Not so much the birds. When Sean glanced at Wynona, he had the look."

"What do you mean by the look?"

"Like the way he smiled at her. The way he listened to her when she spoke. You can tell she's very special to him, and I could tell that she feels special being around him."

"Are you telling me you could tell how they felt about each other in the half-hour they spent here?"

"Of course. The first five minutes, really." She grinned. "I could see a strong affection in those blue-gray eyes of his. And I could see she cares as much, if not even more about him too."

"Really?"

"Yep. He's way too old for me, but that doesn't mean I don't think he's cute."

"And so are you my dear granddaughter."

She smiled and looked at the thermos he carried. "Are you going somewhere?"

"Yes, I wanted to make a run up into Big Cypress to plant three species of Everglades orchids that are almost as rare as the ghost orchid. These include the butterfly orchid, the longclaw and the grass pink orchids. I loaded them into the bed of my truck yesterday. There are only thirty-eight varieties of orchids left in the glades and Big Cypress. At one time, fifty-one species lived here. No more."

"You most definitely are the orchid keeper, Grandpa. And the world thanks you for your dedication."

"It's always about the flowers and the role they play. You want to come with me? We'll pack a lunch."

"I've got errands to run. First, I really need to finish these while the light under this tree is good for pictures. After I'm done, I want to drive into Naples. We need some more bottled water and a few groceries."

He reached into his wallet and pulled out some money. "Here, take this. Do you think that'll cover it?"

"It's more than enough."

He smiled. "Keep the change."

She stepped over to her grandfather and kissed him on the cheek. "Don't forget to take your phone, okay? And don't tell me you don't want to take it because you can't get a cell signal out in the Everglades. Sometimes you can."

"Maybe it has something to do with the weather." He grinned, his bushy, white eyebrows arching. "You be careful on your drive into Naples. There are lots of tourists coming down the pike called the Tamiami Trail. Most of them have their necks craned, looking at the roadside canals, trying to get a glimpse of a gator in the wild. These folks have a tendency to cross the centerline while driving and rubber-necking."

• • •

Chester sipped a cup of coffee driving west on the Tamiami Trail, listening to an NPR story on the radio about the art of handmade cowboy boots and an eighty-five-year-old man who still makes one pair a week for customers from his small shop in San Angelo, Texas. He glanced up in his rearview mirror, put his turn-signal on and made a slow left-hand turn from the highway onto 15 Mile Road or as he called it, Gator Gully.

• • •

Michael Fazio thought about the drone he'd seen. He knew the man he'd shot had been flying the drone, but he had no idea where it had landed. Couldn't find it on first pass. *Was my face on some aerial camera?* He thought. *Gotta go back out there. Gotta find it.* He called Simon Santiago and said, "Job's done. They'll probably find the body in a couple days. It's deep in the Everglades."

"Good. Maybe they'll never find it."

"I gotta take a run back out there."

"Why?"

"There was a drone the dude was flying. I tried shooting it down. It was movin' like a bat outta hell. I don't know if there was a camera on it, but I'm not willing to chance it."

"What if you can't find it?"

"Then we better hope nobody else can either."

Forty-Five

I made the call from *Jupiter's* fly bridge, hoping my old friend was still working at the Collier County Sheriff's office. I hadn't spoked with Cory Gilson in a few years. I'd worked the homicide division with Cory at Miami-Dade PD. He was one of the best when it came to tenacity and perseverance in tracking down killers. After a decade with the force, two attempts on his life, and one justified shooting—leaving the perp in a wheelchair, Cory packed it in and moved across the state to Naples. He'd been with the sheriff's office for about eight years.

"Collier County Sheriff's Department," said the female receptionist.

"Cory Gilson, please."

"He's in investigations. I'll transfer you."

After almost half a minute, he answered. "Homicide, Gilson speaking."

"Cory, it's Sean O'Brien. How are you?"

"Sean O'Brien … how the hell are you? Where are you? Heard you told 'em to basically take the job and shove it not long after Sherri passed. What's going on?"

"That's not exactly what happened, but I like your version even better."

"I heard through the grapevine that you're doing PI work. Is it true?"

"I've done a few jobs, here and there." Cory and I caught up briefly, and then I asked, "How much of Collier County incudes Big Cypress Preserve and a slice of the Everglades."

"A big chunk. Yeah, you're talking about God's country out there. Some parts of those wetlands are nearly inaccessible, I don't care what kind of swamp buggy you drive."

"Yesterday, a guy who's running for a seat in the state house went into the glades or Big Cypress to do water and soil tests. Apparently, he never came out, or if he did, he's off the radar."

"What's his name?

"Joe Thaxton. He's running for office out of Stuart. He's a former fishing guide with a degree in marine biology, and he's taking on big agricultural interests in a fight over water pollution south of Lake Okeechobee."

"I've heard of him. Good luck with that fight."

"Thaxton's received a few threatening phone calls. He's every bit the personification of David verses Goliath. His wife just called me. She's very worried that something happened to her husband somewhere in the glades. She called your office and got the standard definition of the wait time in filing a missing person's report. You know the glades … you wait too long, and the swamps have a way of hiding things."

"Yeah, and it happens fast in terms of decomposition of physical evidence, too. You really think one of those corporate giants put a hit out on this guy?"

"In most circumstances, I'd say no. But this is different because Thaxton is a rare breed. He's definitely not your average Joe, as his campaign suggests when it comes to his gift for relating to people. And I think this might cause a lot of paranoia within large agricultural companies that may have a lot to lose when it comes to changing their farming practices to be more in compliance … not only with the anti-pollution laws already on the books, but the ones that Thaxton will write and propose if he gets elected."

"Sean, happy to speed things up for you. But, before we do a search in the glades, it would be good to know in which general area we might start. Collier County is more than 2300 square miles, and a large piece of that land mass is under water in Big Cypress and the glades."

"His wife isn't sure exactly where he was doing his surveys. But I can text you Thaxton's phone number and that of his wife, Jessica. She spoke with him around one in the afternoon yesterday. You can pull phone records and see where the calls might triangulate."

"We've never done that on something that really doesn't qualify as a missing person's report in the parameters set up for that. But, since I know you, and I know your bird dog sense for crime, I'll do it. That doesn't mean we'll find this guy out there in a million acres of swamps, but we'll start the search."

"Thanks, Cory. I owe you one."

"And I'll collect. But I'm a cheap date … a Sam Adams, a dozen oysters on the half shell and I'm good. Send me the numbers, Sean, and we'll get stuff going. See you." He disconnected, and I called Jessica Thaxton.

Forty-Six

Chester began the slow ramble north up a road he had traveled many times during the last forty years in the Everglades. Although he'd secured the two-dozen young orchid plants in the bed of his truck, he still drove carefully. The least amount of abrupt movement that the plants experienced, the better. Plants, especially the orchids, he believed, did have a sensory capacity that could detect movement not unlike the buds that could sense sunlight. However, that was more visible in a few other plants.

He remembered the first time he watched a Venus flytrap catch a small moth in the wild. He was in the swamps of South Carolina, studying the native flora. He had watched the plant for three hours, sitting in a portable canvas chair he had carried through the bog. When a small moth alighted in the seductive red mouth of the flytrap, the pair of green leaves snapped shut like a clam shell, faster than the human eye could register. The plants have no nervous system. No muscle. No brain, yet they are triggered at the right second to move … to clamp down on prey. Something about carnivorous plants, ones eating meat or protein, appeared to be paradoxical, yet somehow offering poetic justice.

This would be his seventh trip to the area this year. He wanted to make sure the orchids were planted before the cool nights of the winter season, which was not that far away. He glanced into the rearview mirror and could see the orchids in their clay pots braced by a half-dozen sandbags, propped up in the truck bed. "Taking you guys home," he said with a grin. "It's where you belong." He started whistling a tune, dodging a large, water-filled pothole in the dirt road. The wind through his open windows carried the scent of mud, moss, and lichen baking in the sun on dwarf cypress trees that stood in water hunched over like gangly scarecrows in vast fields of sawgrass.

Chester came to one of the remote ancillary trails that snaked off Gator Gully. He eased his truck onto the muddy path, surprised to see what appeared to be fresh tire tracks in the muck. He drove another one hundred yards, around a cluster of tall Everglades palms and saw palmettos. He glanced in his rearview mirror and saw that one of the sandbags had slid to the side panel and one of the orchids had come loose, falling on its side. "Oh dear ... hold on, I'm coming, little fella," he mumbled.

He got out of his truck, walked to the back and opened the tailgate. He stood the orchid up, using both hands to scrape the spilled dirt into the pot. Then he moved the sandbag back in position. As he walked back to the driver's side of his truck, he was almost caught off guard when he spotted another vehicle coming fast around a muddy bend in the road. Rarely, if ever, did he see cars this far out into spur trails that fanned into the glades.

Chester knew there was no way the black car could go around him safely. He stood there, waved to the driver, smiled. "I'll pull over, so you can get by me. There's a spot about twenty yards back that's got enough ground for me to get my truck out of the way."

The driver said nothing, mud-splatter all along the sides of the car.

Chester nodded. "I'm amazed you got your car this far back in here. That's a fancy looking machine. I wouldn't have thought that it could take this country. Mud will come off. Scratches in the paint are a bigger challenge. That's one of the reasons my old truck is the way it is, scars and all. I got stuck out here one summer during the rainy season on 1999. I had to walk out, more than forty miles, some through waist-deep water. And—"

"Move!"

"Sure thing. Out here, patience pays off." Chester climbed back in his truck closed the door, put the truck in reverse and started backing up.

• • •

Michael Fazio opened his glove box, removing a 9mm Sig Sauer. He set the pistol in the console between the seats, watching the old man in the truck. He put the car in gear and slowly followed him. A deerfly came through the open window, alighting on Fazio's cheek, quickly biting him. He slapped the fly, the dead insect falling between his legs in the seat. "Come on, pops. Move that piece of shit," he muttered. "Gotta get out of this swamp."

• • •

Chester looked in his rearview mirror, carefully backing up. He could see the area he had in mind, a spit of land with a slightly higher elevation than the surrounding area, a strand with buttonwood trees and saw palmettos growing near it. He backed his truck onto the spongy soil and waved for the driver to come forward. The man behind the wheel showed no acknowledgement. He drove slowly, one hand on the wheel the other on the grip of his pistol. Even with the truck partially off the trail, there was less than a foot of room for the car to pass. As it came closer, Chester nodding, offering a smile.

The man ignored him. Chester could see the man's profile well, and a red welt on is left cheek.

• • •

Michael Fazio moved past the vintage truck. And then he looked up in his mirror, watching the old man. He whispered, "If you look up … if you look in your rearview mirror and see my license plate, I'm going to park, walk back and shoot you in your ugly head."

• • •

Chester put the truck in gear, pulled back onto the trail and followed the tracks in the path, wondering where the man had been and why he was out there. "Guess I'll be able to see in a little while," he mumbled. "There's only so far a fella can go in a vehicle. After that it's on foot with waders or snake-proof boots. And he didn't impress me as the kind who'd be out here taking pictures in the glades."

Chester drove three-quarters of a mile more into the marsh, the water getting deeper, coming half-way up his tires. The key, he knew, was not to stop until he reached relatively dry land. If he stopped in the quagmire, without the on-going physics of movement, his truck could easily be swallowed to his bumpers in the muck. He steered for a grove of slash pines and oaks. No cypress trees meant less water above ground. He jostled in the truck, the springs creaking, the orchids in the back still upright.

And then something hit him like an off-key singer's voice.

A bizarre illusion of sorts in front of him.

It was a new model pickup truck parked on the edge of the strand of trees. It almost appeared to have been abandoned. There was an eerie silence, a stance—a look and feel about the truck, as if the owner had dumped it and decided to go the rest of the journey on foot. Chester parked, got out and approached the truck. He felt as if he was walking up to a deserted dwelling, the only signs of life were black carrion birds riding the air currents in the distance over the Everglades.

Forty-Seven

I was pouring food into Max's bowl when Cory Gilson called. I picked my phone off the top of the bar in *Jupiter's* salon and answered. He said, "We pulled phone records from Joe and Jessica Thaxton. It looks like the last answered call from Joe Thaxton was at 1:07 p.m. yesterday. He made no other calls. This one pinged from two cell towers. One was a tower northwest of Big Cypress Preserve, at the border of the Fakahatchee Strand. That's panther country in there. Maybe during the call Thaxton was walking or his wife was driving, but the signal also pinged from a tower north of Alligator Alley near the Big Cypress Seminole Reservation."

I said nothing, trying to picture that desolate terrain in my mind.

"You there, Sean?"

"Yeah, I'm here. Can you send a search team out in the general area?"

"That's the problem … it's a general area. Lots of square miles of sawgrass, swamps and some places that look like the Amazon jungles. You're talking about thirty miles between those two cell towers. Thaxton could be anywhere in there. If he's in there."

"You think he's not?"

"Who knows. He and the wife could have been in a helluva fight. Maybe he finished his work and went down to the Keys to put some distance behind things."

"That's a possibility, but I doubt it's the case. I've met him, spent time talking. His campaign has blown up larger than any of the pundits would have ever thought possible. Thaxton's the junk yard dog that's grabbed the legs of corrupt CEOs, politicians and lobbyists, and he won't let go. He's not in the Florida Keys. He's most likely still somewhere in the glades. He told his wife he could hear shots fired from what he believed were hunters on the first day of the season."

"You think someone may have mistaken him for game?"

"That's possible. Or maybe somebody would like for investigators to think that."

I could hear Cory release a long breath. "All right. Only because we have a history together in the trenches, I'll get my guys to dispatch a helicopter to fly the area. That's more effective than taking a dozen men on airboats or ATV's, running through miles of swamps."

"Thanks, Cory." He'd already hung up.

I looked over at Max and said, "Let' go for a walk." She did her dachshund nod and headed out the open salon door to the cockpit, her little black nose capturing the fishy scent of a low tide, barnacles drying on the sides of the dock pilings, and smoldering charcoal from a grill on one of the boats.

• • •

More than three hours later, Max and I walked back from the beach across the Ponce Marina parking lot. We entered the Tiki Bar, Max scampering toward Flo who was using a damp cloth to wipe down a table. I counted seven customers in the restaurant, five at a table and two sitting at the cypress plank bar. Jimmy Buffet was crooning a song from the jukebox, *Something About a Boat*. Flo looked at Max. "Maxine, you wanna seat at the bar or will the table work?"

I said, "She prefers the bar when Nick's with her. When she's with me, it's always the table."

Flo laughed. "I think Nicky has other motives. Max always has the run of the place. She's good for business." Flo neatly folded the cloth in quarters, setting it on one end of the bar next to a spray bottle of glass cleaner. She looked up at me. "There was a couple in here yesterday, both in their late thirties, looking to buy a used sailboat. I don't know if you have *Dragonfly* on the market. The fella wrote his name and number on a napkin. I have it if you're interested."

"Thanks, Flo, but at this point in time, I'll pass. Who knows what the future holds, though?"

"Speaking of future, the fella you met with in here, the guy running for office, Joe Thaxton … a lot of folks think he has a future in politics mostly because he says that's the last thing he wants, but it's a means to an end … an end to water pollution in Florida. Captain Roland Hatter is in here just about every day singing Joe Thaxton's praises. Does he seem like the real deal to you, Sean? Or does he have a silver tongue for talkin' the talk but not so much for walkin' the walk?"

"From what I can tell, he's authentic. I think what you see is what you get."

"The question then is this … can he stay that way when the big money gets waved in his face?" She looked at Max. "Let's see if I have a snack for you back here." Flo walked behind the bar, singing and harmonizing with Buffett on the jukebox. My phone buzzed. I looked at the caller ID and the area code. It was a text, coming from Detective Cory Gilson. He wrote: *We found Thaxton's truck. Call me.*

I didn't like the tone of the text. Not short and sweet, but short and rather ominous. I started to step outside to make the call to Gilson when Flo looked up at the wide-screen TV and asked, "Where'd I put the remote?" She glanced at me, finding the remote control under a menu. "Sean, take a look at the TV. It's Joe Thaxton's face." She turned up the sound. The image cut from a picture of Joe Thaxton, the one most used in his campaign materials, to video scenes of a sheriff's helicopter flying low above vast strands of cypress trees and open prairies of saw grass.

The picture cut to a reporter standing on the side of a road with a Big Cypress National Preserve sign behind her. She wore a Channel Five bright yellow jacket, dark hair up. She looked into the camera and said, "Investigators say that a Ford-150 pickup truck, registered to Joe Thaxton, was found off an old road that was at one time used for lumber and drilling companies when crude oil was pumped from a few designated areas in the Everglades. At this point, sheriff's deputies are taking to the air in search of Joe Thaxton who was reported to have entered the Everglades and possibly made his way into sections of Big Cypress Preserve. Thaxton is a first-time politician, running for state senate from Stuart. Investigators say they were told that Thaxton entered an extremely remote section of the Everglades because he was conducting water and soil sample tests, data presumably he was going to use in his campaign as a champion for cleaning up Florida's polluted rivers and lakes. Reporting live from Big Cypress Preserve, this is Cynthia Martinez, Channel Five News. Now back to you in the studio."

Flo muted the sound and looked over at me. "That's not good news. I hope he's okay and just got lost in the glades."

"Could Max hang here for a couple of minutes? I need to step outside to make a call."

"Of course." Flo shook her head. "I bet his wife's worried sick. She seemed so nice when she was in here."

Forty-Eight

I stood on the main dock outside the Tiki Bar and called Cory Gilson. As the phone rang, I watched a 44-foot Jeanneau sailboat motor quietly through the marina waters toward C-dock, sail covers on, diesel humming. A man with skin dark as a buckeye shell stood at the helm, the boat purring as it passed. Cory answered, and I said, "Got your message. What do you have?"

"Let's start with Joe Thaxton's pickup truck. We found it way the hell off an old oil rig and logging road. Truck was locked. No sign of Thaxton and no indication of foul play either. We've been flying the chopper, crisscrossing the glades and Big Cypress." Gilson stood next to two deputy sheriff's cars, sawgrass and cabbage palms behind him, his tie loosened, tan sports coat slightly wrinkled below the lapels.

"How long can you keep the aerial going?" I asked.

"Until sunset. Spotlights don't do a lot out here. So far, my guys haven't seen anything from the air, at least anything that looks human. Lots of big damn gators, deer, bear, and a few wild boars running for cover. But no sign of Thaxton. We have a search team combing the interior of the area. Nothing so far, and it's a challenge to follow tracks out here. Too much water. It's hard to see tracks; and when you do, they often lead into knee-deep water that goes for miles. That kind of obstacle makes it tough for the dogs to maintain a scent and follow it very far. Remember when we worked homicide in Miami, how many bodies were dumped in the glades. Most were never recovered, at least all of the pieces. At one time, it was the biggest dumping ground for bodies in the nation."

"Let's try not to go there with Joe Thaxton. There are no parallels, at least not yet. He drove into the glades. He wasn't dumped there. Maybe your search team will come across something. Have you spoken with his wife yet?"

"I left a brief message on her phone. Told her that we'd located his truck. I was hoping to call her later with some good news. You know me, Sean, a born optimist in spite of my profession. The news media, of course, are all over this because of Thaxton's notoriety."

"Thanks for getting out there and finding his truck. I hope you can find him, and when you do … I hope Joe Thaxton's alive."

•••

Callie Hogan thought there was a car accident on the Tamiami Trail. Flashing blue and white emergency lights in the distance. Deputy sheriff's cruisers on both sides of the road as she passed Big Cypress National Preserve. She drove her car east from Naples back to her grandfather's property, slowing when she came closer to the emergency lights and commotion. She could see no evidence of an accident. She did see a sheriff's helicopter in the sky, flying low and in a half circle.

She put both hands on the steering wheel, driving slowly through the spectacle, deputies hunched in small groups, looking at maps, speaking into radio microphones. A static crackle of disjointed police commands in the air. Two deputies watched Callie edging by in her car, one deputy using quick hand motions to direct her through the scene. She almost expected them to stop and check her car.

Maybe they were searching for an escaped prisoner or someone who'd just committed a heinous crime. She made a dry swallow, thinking of her grandfather and wondering if there was a crime scene somewhere close.

Once she cleared the area, Callie looked in her rearview mirror, the flashing lights and noise of a helicopter like a movie scene behind her. She drove the speed limit, her thoughts racing, anxious to get back to her grandfather. Wondering if he knew what was happening and why.

• • •

Jessica Thaxton walked into her kitchen, picked up her phone and listened to the voice mail. She immediately called Detective Cory Gilson. When he answered, she said, "Detective Gilson, it's Jessica Thaxton. I got your message. Have you found my husband?"

"No, but we did find his truck."

"Oh, dear God. Where?"

"About twenty-three miles north of Highway 41. The truck was found at the end of a narrow old logging road that's primarily used today by hunters mostly on ATVs. The truck was locked. We found no signs whatsoever of foul play. We're hoping he wandered out and got lost in the glades or those sloughs and swamps in Big Cypress. It happens a lot more than you might think."

"It's getting dark. I'm so afraid for my husband."

"We have search crews combing the area, and we've been using one of our helicopters for aerial surveillance, too. If he's in here, we'll find him. I'll call you the moment we learn anything more, okay?"

"Okay. Thank you." The detective disconnected, and Jessica held the phone to her ear for a few long seconds. Her thoughts jumbled, racing into places she didn't want to enter. She slowly set her phone down, looked at a framed picture on the wall of Joe, Kristy and herself at the beach. It was taken when Kristy was two, a sky the deep shade of blueberries. The sand was white as new piano keys, water clear and inviting. The framed photograph humanized Joe's campaign—no, his crusade.

She thought about one of the last things he said to her over the phone, *I forgot today is the first or second day of hunting season. So, I'm not seeing the game and birds I'd like to see from the drone or just by standing still here. It almost feels like nature is afraid to come out and play.*

Forty-Nine

Max and I walked down L dock, watching the sun set like a red match smoldering in the crevices of dark clouds far beyond the mangroves and the Halifax River. I didn't know if Cory Gilson had spoken with Jessica Thaxton yet, but I didn't envy him, the "eternal optimist," trying to build hope in what could prove to be a false dawn. Maybe I was wrong, and Joe Thaxton would walk out of the glades. But he hadn't appeared to me as a man who could have easily become lost. Too much of a survivalist instinct. He'd clocked too many years guiding people to lose himself.

Maybe I was wrong.

Max strutted ahead of me, her rump swaying like a quarter horse trotting. She made an abrupt stop to sniff a fish scale the size of a quarter near the dock railing. She resumed her parade, scurrying a little faster the closer we got to Nick's boat, *St. Michael*. She stopped near the transom, staring at the open salon door. There was not the usual music or scent of Greek cooking. Max looked back at me, her face and eyes confused or sad—maybe a little of both.

"Come on, kiddo. Let's share with Dave what we know about a non-politician, a non-conformist statesman, who ventured into the heart of the Everglades and has yet to reappear. This is worrying me, Max." We walked down the narrow gangway parallel to *Gibraltar*, the soulful jazz trumpet of Miles Davis coming from the trawler's salon, the poignant song, *Seven Steps to Heaven*.

I could hear Dave and Nick discussing the art of cooking a T-bone steak in an iron skillet, Dave insisting butter was the preferred frying ingredient over olive oil. Nick vehemently disagreeing. "Butter can't handle the heat," Nick said. "You need a very hot skillet to cook the meat the right way to lock in the juices."

Max scampered over the steps from the dock to the cockpit. "Hot Dawg!" Nick said. "Where you come from … outta the blue?"

I said, "She's here to weigh in on the art of pan-frying a steak, something that some carnivores might prefer not to do."

"That's because they're meat snobs," Dave said. "Doesn't matter if it's cooked on a hot grill or a hot pan, the meat will be succulent if the chef knows how to season and cook it."

"There is a difference," Nick said, grinning. "Butter's for bagels. Extra virgin olive oil from Greece is all the grease you'll ever need. That's what I think."

Dave said, "I think it's time for a cocktail. Sun has gone to sleep and so shall I in a few short hours. Join us, Sean." Dave got off his couch and ambled across the salon to his bar. "He poured a glass of Hendrick's Gin over ice and cut his eyes over to me. "You have that look."

"What look?"

"Like you misplaced your cell phone."

"Perceptive of you. I am thinking about cell phones, but not mine."

Nick said, "When I misplace my phone I start to twitch."

I said, "The phones I'm referring to are those of Joe Thaxton and his wife, Jessica."

"What about them?" Dave asked.

"The cell tower ping of those phones may be the best lead police have in locating Joe Thaxton."

"Oh shit," Nick said. "The P—word … police doesn't sound good. What happened?"

"Actually, it's the S—word for sheriff. Thaxton hasn't been seen since early morning yesterday when he ventured deep into the

Everglades to do scientific water and soil sample research. He spoke with his wife midday from somewhere in the glades or the Big Cypress National Preserve." I told them as much as I knew and said, "I feel bad about this because Thaxton and his wife came to me asking for help, and I gave them advice instead."

Dave stirred his drink. "Sean, what the hell else could you have done?"

"I don't know, maybe more than I did."

"It was truly a police matter at that time, and it probably remains so. We don't know if foul play was involved. You said they found his truck, not his body. With all the pressure Thaxton's under, he could have had a heart attack walking through that thick terrain. The muck in some places is like walking through wet cement. A water moccasin or diamondback might have bitten him. There are some big cougars in there, too."

I said, "I doubt that's a factor."

"Okay, putting all the natural challenges aside, the most dangerous thing in the swamps can be an inexperienced or careless hunter on the first day of season. Too often, he's some guy pumped up on caffeine, testosterone, and his perception of his own huntsman prowess. Taking down a big buck or five-hundred-pound wild boar on the opening day of the season earns bragging rights. In the ancestral sense, it establishes who has the best hunting skills to provide for the well-being of the tribe."

I said, "I'd like to think we're not a nation of tribes. Regardless, today you can have almost any food, including venison, delivered to your door. You can shop for wines, gourmet cheese, and meats online, but yet the hero's journey begins every fall from the mountains of upstate New York to the glades and beyond. There is nothing wrong with true hunting. Hunting done responsibly. There is something inherently wrong about killing in the name of hunting. It has nothing to do with putting food on the table. It has everything to do with the thrill of the kill. The trophy. The blood sport of death. Too often leaving the carcass to rot where it fell."

Nick picked at a callus on his thumb and said, "Even if he was accidently shot, or snake bit … you'd think that, with a helicopter, deputies and bloodhounds, they'd have spotted a body out there … if it was out there. I know it's a big damn place, the glades, but the way you described the cell tower hits, seems to narrow it down to maybe thirty square miles."

"Maybe," I said, "but that's still a lot to cover, and much of it is swampy, heavy with a lot of old growth cypress trees with thick canopies of limbs. Makes it hard to see from the air, and difficult to get to on the ground. Could be that Thaxton is injured, a broken leg maybe, and he can't walk back to his truck."

Dave nodded. "Unless he managed to crawl into some kind of natural clearing, he'd be hard to spot."

I mentioned that an old colleague of mine from Miami-Dade PD, now with Collier County, spoke with Jessica Thaxton. She told him that Joe was using his drone to shoot aerial video of the glades and its water levels. "Between that gear and what he was packing with water and soil testing equipment, that's even more material for searchers to spot from the air and ground. Something is not making sense … as if he vanished."

Nick said, "Somebody could have stuck a gun in his back and took him hostage in a separate vehicle, even a helicopter if they had the dough."

Dave stood behind his bar and nodded. "You might be on to something, Nick. The big money Thaxton's up against can afford their own damn rocket to shoot Thaxton to Mars if they want to." Dave stirred his drink. He looked beyond the transom to boat lights reflecting off the dark water. "Thus far, Joe Thaxton has definitely been a burr under the saddle of powerful farming interests, but to my knowledge he hasn't made any personal or direct accusations against those in charge. He hasn't named names in connection to possible culpable or willful and woeful negligence in terms of water pollution. If, as Nick suggests, he disappeared like Jimmy Hoffa did, then that will speak volumes … but there will be no dead body, meaning no proof of murder."

I said, "Thaxton doesn't have to name names. He's zeroed in on an industry that, for the most part, has been off-limits to political criticism and restrictive economic sanctions. It's as if a sacred cow has been grazing for miles on land with no fences. Thaxton's assertions that the sugar subsidies should end thus putting the industry on an even playing field in terms of regulations is probably enough to anger the growers. If he doesn't win the election, his rhetoric goes away. But is that a chance these people will take?"

My phone buzzed. I pulled it out of my pocket, looked at the screen, and answered. Cory Gilson said, "We found Joe Thaxton's backpack and what appears to be controls to an aerial drone." Cory's voice faded, his cell signal weak.

Fifty

I moved from *Gibraltar's* salon to the open cockpit and said, "Cory, you're fading out. Can you hear me?"

"Yes. Sounds like you're shouting, Sean."

"Where are you?"

"Still in the glades. We're calling it a night because a ground fog off the water is making in next to impossible to see ten feet in front of you. We'll resume at daybreak."

"Where'd you find Thaxton's things?"

"About three miles from where we located his truck. No sign of him, though. Before it got too damn dark and foggy, one of my deputies discovered what appears to be blood on the ground near his backpack and drone console. Our forensics guy bagged it. He'll run an analysis."

"Does it look like Thaxton was shot?"

"All we found was the blood. Not much of it. Maybe three spots the size of dimes. If Thaxton was shot, it looks like he might have been trying to put some distance between him and the shooter. If it was a deer hunter, and if it was an accident, nobody's stepped up to the plate to report it. In my book, that's like a hit-and-run."

"You mentioned that you found his drone controls … how about the drone itself. Did you find it?"

"No. No sign of that. If he was flying the drone at the time he was shot, the thing could have flown off to Timbuctoo. If Thaxton was shot, maybe he tried to make it to Alligator Alley to flag down a motorist to get him to the hospital."

"If he had the strength to do that, why didn't he call for help on his phone?"

"Could have been because he was bleeding out, like a deer that's gut shot. He may not have been thinking straight. Probably running from the direction of the bullet. But the biggest reason is because it's hard to get a clear cell signal out here. We'll be back at it in the morning. Looks like your missing person's report has taken a hell of a turn for the worst. When I call his wife, I wish I could give her hope … but that's where my eternal optimistic approach collides with the reality of a bad situation. Get some sleep, Sean. You sound like you just finished a marathon."

• • •

Chester Miller thought about his rather odd experience deep into the glades. In decades of working to restore orchids in the glades and Big Cypress Preserve, he'd seen a lot of unusual occurrences. Most had to do with nature, the fragile ecosystem, and how man's interjection changes the balance in plants and animals. He'd met his share of eccentric people and squatters traipsing through the wetlands on everything from airboats to swamp buggies. But, somehow, they all seemed to mesh and connect with the unique tapestry of the landscape.

Today was different.

The man appeared very out of place. It was more than a deer in the headlights. It was a juxtaposition of sight and sounds as the man drove an expensive automobile around a muddy bend in a trail like a bat trying to find its cave before sunrise.

Chester thought about that image as he sautéed pieces of chicken breasts and sweet onions in a skillet on the propane stove, the cabin filling with the scent of carnalized onions and biscuits.

Callie sat at a small table in the kitchen, sipping a glass of sweet tea, uploading orchid pictures to social media. Chester watched her as he stirred wild rice in a pot. He opened the oven and removed a dozen hot biscuits. "Dinner will be ready in a few minutes. You might want to wrap up your work as we can use the table to eat on, too." He grinned.

Callie turned back in her chair to him. "I can shut down in five seconds. Smells great. Where'd you learn to cook so well, Grandpa?"

"Practice. After your grandmother died, I developed a whole list of new skills. Cooking was one. The honey for our biscuits tonight came from the beehives out back. So, I managed to merge biology and botany with culinary. It's good to experience different things all your life. Take risks." He chuckled, setting the food on two plates.

"Grandpa, you said you didn't see all the police cars and the helicopter flying over the preserve, right?"

"Thought I heard something like a helicopter way out in the boonies, but I didn't make the connection 'till you mentioned you'd seen one. Wonder what they were looking for?"

"Looks like they were searching for someone lost."

"Lost? Who? A child?"

"I'm reading a news story now. Hold a sec …" After half a minute, Callie looked up from her phone screen. "It says that a man has been missing in the glades since yesterday. Sheriff's deputies found his truck. Guy's name is Joe Thaxton. He's running for a seat in the state senate. He lives in Stuart, Florida, and was in the glades doing water samples. He has a degree in marine biology."

"Does it say what kind of truck they found out there?"

"Hold on … I'll read some more … yes. It says his truck was a 2019 Ford F-150. And it was locked. There's been no sign of the man, though."

Chester set the plates on the table, his thoughts focused on what he'd seen in the glades. Callie said, "I hope they find him. It says he has a wife and young daughter. Are you okay, Grandpa? You look tired all of a sudden."

He nodded. "I am tired. Planting orchids in the glades can do that to a man my age. It's not the planting part so much … it's hiking through the elements to find the best places to replant. I hosed down my waders before you got back home. I had mud on 'em up to my hips." He poured sweet tea over ice in a Bell canning jar and sat down across the table from his granddaughter. "Callie, that truck you described. I saw it or one like it out in the glades."

She looked up from her food. "You did? Did you see any sign of the missing guy, Joe Thaxton?"

"No but I did see something odd out there."

"What was it?"

"A man."

"A man? That's not too odd, depending where you were in the glades."

"It was for this fella. He was coming down a very muddy dirt trail in a fancy and expensive SUV. And he was in a hurry to get out of there. I got a glimpse of his face. He didn't look like a typical hunter, woodsman, or even a nature-loving photographer."

"Then what did he look like?"

"A man on a mission. Like someone who absolutely didn't want to be there. I think I surprised him."

"What did he do?"

"Just drove on by without so much of a glance or gesture toward me, and this was after I backed my truck off the trail to give him room to pass."

"Really? That is kind of discourteous behavior considering you two were probably the only humans for miles."

"I don't think so. Less than a half-mile further in the glades I came up on the pickup truck you just described from the news story."

Callie licked her lips, sipped her tea, and looked at her grandfather. "Do you think the guy you saw did something bad to the missing man, Joe Thaxton?"

"I don't know ... but I do know that I feel obligated to call the sheriff. Maybe what I have to say can help them."

Callie said nothing. She searched her grandfather's face, looking deep into his pale blue eyes, seeking something that wasn't there—an assurance that all would be well. He smiled. "First things first, young lady ... we bow our heads in prayer and be grateful for the food on our table and for the two of us having our time here together. You'll be leaving soon to return to college. And I'd prefer not to think about that at the moment."

Fifty-One

Sammy Tiger was legendary when it came to the hunt. For more than thirty years, he'd been supplying local restaurants with fresh frog legs, catfish, and gator meat. At the Gator Café, fried frog legs were a delicacy and one of the most popular appetizers—second to gator tail bites. Sammy, sixty-five-years old, and a full-blooded Seminole, pulled a ten-foot, flat-bottom boat behind his Jeep Renegade. He drove at night into the swamps bordering the reservation and Collier County.

He navigated through muddy trails into his favorite places to hunt for bullfrogs. He parked and got out of the Jeep. Sammy wore a black, wide-brimmed bolero cowboy-style hat, loose blue jeans, long-sleeve shirt buttoned at the top of the collar. His hair, dark as a crow's feather, hung to his shoulders. Tonight, he quickly pulled it back in a ponytail.

He glanced up at dark clouds moving in front of the moon. His round face was saddle leather brown, puffy eyes were guarded, observant, taking in everything. His powers of observation made him an extraordinary hunter.

Sammy could taste the promise of rain in the air. He knew the frogs could taste it, too. This was one of the best times for frog gigging. Right before a rain. The frogs would be out in full force, singing their baritone grunts, waiting for the fat raindrops to fall, soaking their world and refreshing the swamps with a baptism from mother nature.

He decided to use the boat later. He pulled his waders from the back of the Jeep, slipped them on over his jeans, adjusting the suspenders. He'd spend the first half-hour wading in the back water, holding a three-pronged, long-poled gig in one hand, a 454 Ruger pistol clipped to his belt. He carried a burlap sack in the other hand. He'd use his boat in another area he'd visit tonight, a place where the water was, in places, over his head.

Sammy took off his hat and strapped on an LED headlight, the lamp resting on the center of his forehead. He turned the light on, returned the hat to his head and started wading through knee-deep water under massive cypress trees heavy with Spanish moss. He moved slowly, listening for the frogs, careful not to make any noise as he walked through the swamp. But, with each step, the mud under the water burped up gases. He could smell the slight odor of sulfur and plant decay. The breeze carried the scent of spawning fish on shallow beds.

He heard the first croak. A deep-throated bullfrog somewhere along the bank. Sammy walked slowly, feeling fallen limbs under his waders. His light moved across the water and shoreline. He listened again for the croaking. It came louder as the first drops of rain softly fell. Frogs were one of the few creatures that called the hunter to them. Still, it took a sharp aim with the gig to stick a frog from a boat or standing in waist-deep water.

He spotted a large frog sitting on mangrove roots. He steadied the light in the frog's eyes, the creature's face bright green, like freshly washed celery. Its body larger than Sammy's hand. He lifted the pole, the sharp prongs less than three feet from the frog. Sammy waited a moment for the frog to exhale a loud croak and then he struck, pushing the three prongs through the frog's body. In less than five seconds, he'd dropped the frog into the burlap sack. He continued the hunt, the dying frogs thumping against Sammy's left hip where the sack rested. Within ten seconds, there was no more movement.

Sammy walked another twenty feet in the center of the slough. He saw the red reflection from the eyes of an alligator. He looked at the width between the gator's eyes. The wider the space, the longer and bigger the gator. Even from fifty feet, he could tell the alligator was not that large—under six feet. No problem. Should a larger one, especially those more than ten feet in length, become aggressive, a round from the Ruger between its eyes would end it quickly. That had happened only three times in all the years hunting in the swamps. For the most part, the gators preferred raccoons, rabbits, snakes, and turtles.

As he walked, the water become shallower. It was now just below the knee and there were less frogs. He decided to get out of the slough and walk along dry ground to another area less than fifty yards south.

As he approached the bank, a cottonmouth water moccasin slithered from the mud into the water. Its body was as thick as his forearm. Under the bright light, Sammy watched it swim by him, a few feet away. He knew if he tried to gig the snake and missed, it would become aggressive and attack. Its fangs couldn't penetrate his thigh skin through the thick waders, but he preferred not to challenge the snake.

Sammy stepped out of the water, turned the light off, the weight of the dead frogs pulling against the shoulder strap attached to the burlap sack. He walked south, heading to one of his favorite spots to gig frogs. He'd gone less than one-hundred feet when lightning splintered through the dark clouds. In the light from the flash, he spotted something on the ground near old live oaks and lofty Everglades palms. Sammy could tell that the object wasn't supposed to be there. It was incongruous, out of place with the land and trees.

He reached under his waders, touching the grip of the Ruger. But something told him he would be in no need of the gun. The object on the ground was too still, too peculiar in the way it lay out in the open to be a threat. Sammy came closer, and even in the dark, he could tell that the object was a man. Maybe the man was injured.

Sammy walked faster, the waders slowing him down. Lightning popped again, and in the bright white light, he could tell that the man was dead. Sammy stood next to the body, turned on the flashlight. The man had died lying on his back, eyes open, staring at the heavens. Soft rain fell on the body, the water dripping down the dead man's face giving the appearance of tears falling to the ground beneath the boughs of old oaks and cypress trees.

Sammy remembered the tribal elders telling him his great grandfathers hid in this area, behind the trees and palmetto bushes when the army soldiers rode by on horses, hunting them after the final Seminole war, the remaining members of the tribe forced to flee deep into the River of Grass.

Fifty-Two

I fell asleep thinking about the time I met Sam Otter, the most revered Seminole medicine man alive. His creased and weathered face was the color of bourbon, prominent nose, deep-set eyes like black marbles, white hair in braids. It was last year when my friend Joe Billie took me to Sam Otter's home on the reservation. The old man and his wife lived on two acres. Behind their small, concrete block home were two chickee structures. One open-air, palm fronds on the roof, a black, wrought iron caldron simmering chicken stew over a fire.

The other chickee hut was walled with knotty pine lumber pulled from a gnarled barn. It was in here where the old man kept hundreds of unlabeled canning jars on shelves. The jars were filled with twigs, pieces of root, grasses, tree bark, bits of flowers, stems, mushrooms, and dark mud. He was known as the healer to the Seminoles in Florida and Oklahoma.

I remember Sam Otter packing his bamboo pipe with ingredients from five of the canning jars. He led Joe and I through his garden filled with fist-sized tomatoes and tall, green corn. There was a pen for two hogs, the chickens ran loose, and Cracker the dog—part wolf, shepherd and yellow lab, followed us from about fifty yards away where Sam stopped near the base, of the largest cypress tree I'd ever seen. It towered more than 150 feet in the air, and at its base the diameter was larger than the width of a mid-sized car. Sam lit the pipe, chanted in the Seminole language and blew smoke directly into our faces. Joe looked at me, smiled and said, "Just breathe in, Sean. It is an honor that he is doing this for us. It will help bring clarity of thought."

The old man stared directly at me, took a long drag from the pipe and blew thick smoke into my face. I remember the smoke smelling like holly, burnt moss, pinesap, pond muck and tobacco.

I saw a dead man's face under a burst of lightning.

Rain pelting his ashen skin. His eyes locked on the heavens.

I sat up in my bed. I was home, in my river cabin, Max curled in a ball at the foot of the bed. Rain falling on our tin roof. It had been a restless night. Max and I had left Ponce Marina and driven back to the river cabin after talking with Dave and Nick, sharing the information Cory Gilson had given me about finding Joe Thaxton's backpack and drone control. Sleep in the old cabin tonight was restless, mixed with potholes that jarred me awake each time I tried to dodge them.

It was a little after midnight when the rain started, and thunder jolted me from dark dreams. I lay awake, listening to rain playing against the tin roof, thinking about Joe Thaxton somewhere in the glades. Was rain pouring down there? Was he holed up at the base of a large tree to keep the water off his body? Was he even there? And if so, was he alive?

At 5:00, I got up, showered and put on a pot of coffee. An hour later, at the crack of dawn, Max and I walked down my long yard to the dock. I carried a blue ceramic mug filled with black coffee, steam rising. The morning cool and clean after the heavy rain, a crisp scent in recharged air, glossy droplets clinging to pine needles and leaves.

A week earlier, I'd bought four small orange trees in large black plastic pots. I planned to spend part of the day digging holes and planting each tree. Maybe in a couple of years, I could pick fresh oranges and squeeze them for juice during slate gray mornings like this one. A little liquid sunshine when nature refused to provide the real thing.

We walked to the end of the dock, and I sat on the wooden bench facing east. The surface of the river was flat, a dark mirror reflecting darker skies. I lifted Max up beside me. She rested her chin against my thigh. There would be no sunrise to watch this morning. Steely overcast rainclouds covered the horizon in all directions.

I sipped the hot coffee, the steam floating up from the mug seemed to be the only movement around us. It was as if the birds didn't feel an urgency to rise. No sign of fish breaking the surface of the river. Nature was subdued, needing a real reason to get out of bed. A light rain returned. I sipped my coffee and watched dimples pop on the wide surface of the river, listening to a pileated woodpecker drilling into the trunk of a dead cypress. I thought about Jessica Thaxton and what range of emotions she was no doubt feeling. Somehow, the pewter gray dawn was the perfect backdrop for a pale morning of mystery.

A raindrop hit Max between her eyes. With her chin still resting on my leg, she looked up at me. If I could read her mind, she was probably asking why I didn't think to bring an umbrella. When I was first training her to approach the door when she needed to go outside, I often brought an umbrella with us in Florida's rainy season. Dachshunds can be picky where they pee. Max can be downright finicky, often walking in semi-circles until she finds the right spot with all the correct ambiance and smells.

A movement on the surface of the river caught her eye. Max stood on the bench watching a young alligator, no more than three feet in length, swim near the end of our dock. The gator used its tail to leisurely propel it toward the far side of the river, the Ocala National Forest. A white curlew flew to the top of a palm tree and belted out a wake-up call for this section of the river to hear.

Within seconds, an osprey appeared from nowhere and hit the river with a loud smack, the bird's talons sinking into the back of a garfish. We could hear the osprey's wings beat the damp air, the fish wriggling, water dripping from his tail. Ten seconds later, the osprey flew to the top of a bald cypress tree, breakfast at its feet.

The harmony of nature was interrupted when my phone buzzed. Max glanced up at me. Through cause and effect, she learned that the phone was usually a source of intrusion. I looked at the caller ID. It was Wynona, and it wasn't yet seven in the morning. Probably not a good sign. "Good morning," I said.

"I wish it was a good morning, but it's not." She sounded tired.

"What happened?"

"Remember me telling you how long it'd been since there was a murder on the rez?"

"Yes, I remember."

"As of an hour ago, that's ended. Joe Thaxton's body was found on the rez, right over the boundary line. He'd been shot once."

"You're sure he was murdered?"

"He was shot in the back. I'd say that's probably a good sign that he was murdered. Sean, I have to take a call. I'll call you as soon as I can."

Fifty-Three

Wynona parked her unmarked car and approached the body with respect and professional curiosity. She wore her dark hair up, blue blazer over a white shirt, jeans and flat shoes. A half-dozen members of the tribal police department were already there, along with two senior deputies with the Collier County Sheriff's Office, their green uniforms standing out from the blue uniforms that the tribal police wore.

Yellow crime scene tape looped around wooden stakes hammered into the soft earth, marking off a square twenty feet in four directions from the body. Red-and-white emergency lights pulsated on marked SUVs, two ambulances and a fire truck. Three paramedics stood by, idle. A man and a woman from the police department's forensic unit opened containers that resembled fishing tackle boxes. They slipped on rubber gloves, waiting for detectives and the coroner.

"Poor guy," mumbled a slender police officer to another. "Dying out here in the rain and mud." The officers and emergency techs spoke just above whispers. If the man had been murdered, this was the first on the reservation in quite a while. He was non-Indian. A man fairly well-known running for public office in Florida. The monosyllabic communication on the radio channels seemed out of place in a strand of ancient trees and birdsong.

Wynona met with a senior police officer, a middle-aged man in uniform who'd been on the force more than twenty years. His dark face was unreadable. Impassive black eyes that seemed to take in the scene and never blink. He had a serrated scar above his left eyebrow that was slightly raised, resembling a small lightning bolt. It looked like a white tattoo.

He said, "The vic was shot in the upper right section of his back. Probably by a high-powered rifle. The round went through the chest. The exit wound looks to be a few inches below his collarbone. I'm no medical examiner, but I've seen plenty of gunshot wounds during my time in the military, and I'd bet the vic lost his lung right after he was hit. And that must have been a hell of a struggle to get from where we're told Collier County deputies found blood and his backpack. The guy had to have had one incredible will to live, walking this far before falling over and dying."

Wynona asked, "Is Collier County sending detectives?"

"Yes, we've been in near constant communication. Two of their investigators are on one their way."

"Where's the person who found the body?"

The officer motioned to a man who stood alone in black waders, next to a live oak tree. "Name's Sammy Tiger. Says he was giggin' frogs when he saw the body across this open space, and then he approached it. Do you know him?"

"I've haven't seen him in a while, but I recognize him from around the rez. Now, I think I'll get reacquainted."

The officer smiled. "Sammy's the kind of man who doesn't have a whole lot to say about anything. He's a stand-up guy, but you'll have to ask all the right questions to get answers. Otherwise, he won't volunteer much."

"I'm used to it in this line of work. And that response is not unique to the Seminole." She left, walking over to where Sammy Tiger stood, the burlap sack at his feet. His face stoic. She could see a trace of sadness in the man's eyes. Wynona nodded as she approached him. "Did you get any frogs before you stumbled onto this."

"A few."

"I know you're one of the best. Can I see?"

Sammy nodded, opening the burlap sack. Wynona used her flashlight to peer inside. More than a dozen frogs, some still clinging to life, eyes wide in the light, were in the bottom of the sack.

"Sammy, I'm Detective Wynona Osceola. I'm investigating this case. Was he barely alive when you found him?"

"No. He was dead."

"Is the body just as you discovered it?"

"Yes."

"Did you see any indication of anyone ... a person ... maybe a vehicle. Anything that could have been connected to this man's death?"

"Lightning came across, and the whole area lit up just as I walked out of the swamp. If it had not been for the lightning, I never would have seen it."

Wynona said nothing, looking from his face to the body sprawled on the ground, vultures riding air currents in the distance, the call of a crow at the top of a cypress tree. She reached in her sports jacket pocket and handed him a card. "Please, take this. If you can think of anything else that might help us, call me, okay?"

He nodded and took the card, setting it inside his shirt pocket. "Can I go now?"

"Yes, of course. Thank you for calling this in when you came across it."

He said nothing, picking up the gunny sack and carrying it across his left shoulder, heading back to his Jeep, swamp water dripping from the bottom of the wet burlap.

Wynona walked toward the body, lifting the yellow tape and stopping next to the dead man. A woman with the forensics team took pictures of the body. Wynona looked at her and said, "Give me a few minutes, and you guys can finish your work."

"No problem, Detective," she said, stepping back beyond the crime scene tape.

Wynona put on rubber gloves and knelt next to the body, looking at Joe Thaxton's face, his open eyes, the way his legs and arms were positioned. She examined his fingernails, his palms and the back of his hands. She studied the exit wound on the chest, waving away a blowfly the crawled toward the dried blood.

She whispered, "Who did this to you? If it was an accidental shooting, why'd you run so far? Probably because this was no accident … am I right? Help me find the evidence to prove it." She looked at the soles of his boots, examining the moist soil near the body.

The forensics team stood less than twenty feet away, watching the detective. They exchanged glances as she spoke to the body, as if the dead man could hear her. The officers looked at one another and watched how thorough Wynona was, spending plenty of time simply observing the body from the head to the muddy boots. She didn't take notes. Didn't have to. She observed closely, occasionally glancing up and looking in the direction she thought Joe Thaxton had come before collapsing on this spot and dying.

Wynona stood, lifting the yellow tape and stepping under it. She looked at the forensics team. "He's all yours. After that, it'll be an autopsy. I look forward to your reports." She walked around the officers, looking at the damp earth, finding tracks that seemed to match the grooves on the bottom of Joe Thaxton's boots. She followed the tracks south for more than fifty yards before coming to ankle-deep water.

She stopped, looked up from a boot print to the extensive sawgrass in the distance. And then she looked over her shoulder at the crime scene. She wanted to backtrack as much as possible. It would prove hard to do, but she knew one man who had the skill to do it. She would call Sean O'Brien and ask him if he knew how to get in touch with Joe Billie.

Fifty-Four

Max and I walked from the dock back to the cabin. I lifted a white fluffy towel off a hook on the inside of the screened porch and dried the rainwater from her short fur. After I poured some food into Max's bowl, I refilled my coffee cup. I had very little appetite for breakfast. We sat on the porch, soft rain tapping against the tin roof over the porch. The sound reminded me of one of my last sailing trips with my wife, Sherri.

I looked over at a framed picture of Sherri. It had been taken when she was standing next to the wheel on our sailboat—the last time we sailed before her death from cancer. I remembered one morning, the boat anchored in a quiet cove off Cat Island, we sat under the Bimini canopy sipping Jamaican coffee during a rainy dawn. It didn't matter if the rain was falling or the sun was rising—just being with her, and the way she chose to embrace whatever came our way, was the stuff of a good life. Rare and precious as the gift of life itself.

My phone buzzed again. Max, curled in a wicker rocking chair, lifted her head. I looked at the caller ID. It was Cory Gilson. I answered, and he said, "Sean, a body has been found. It's Joe Thaxton. Somehow, he managed to run, walk or crawl across the county line onto Seminole reservation land."

I listened, not mentioning that I'd just heard from Wynona Osceola. Cory said, "We're back out here. My team found what appears to be some deer hunter stuff about 150 yards from where we located the backpack and drone controller. We'll test it."

"What kind of things did they find?"

"For one thing, a stogie cigar and one of those make-up compact's hunters use to apply dark color to their faces and hands to reduce the shine and blend better into the foliage. We'll try to get a DNA sample from that. We found a wrapper from a trail mix bar. We might lift a print off that. And we found a boot print in the mud. If it was a hired gun, why would he be so careless to toss that stuff out?"

"Maybe he wasn't careless. Could have been planned and planted."

"It's a possibility. But we don't know that. We do know there were at least two dozen hunters registered to be in the area the first day of the season. Granted, 150-yards is a helluva shot. And tossing a stogie or dropping the food wrapper doesn't necessarily put the shooter in the immediate scene of where we found the blood. We'll process it all and see what, if anything, we can find. But since the body was found on the reservation, if it is a murder, it'll be in the jurisdiction of the tribal police. To my knowledge, something like this has never happened in Florida, and there are a lot of Native-American reservations. The Seminoles have five, Big Cypress being the largest. And the Miccosukee have a large one less than twenty-five miles from where I'm standing."

"Cory, there is a detective working for the tribal police that I know personally. She's Seminole. Her name is Wynona Osceola, and she's very good. Wynona is a former FBI agent. After eight years, she decided to return home to make a difference locally. Maybe you can team up with her … an inter-police agency operation to see if you can get to the bottom of the shooting."

"Absolutely. We have a couple of deputies there now. I'm heading up there. I don't know her on a personal level, but I've heard some good things about her. She'll take the lead since the body was found on the reservation, but we'll assist in any way we can. Hells bells, I'd like to turn it over to her right now. Maybe she could call Jessica Thaxton. But since I've been speaking with Mrs. Thaxton, I ought to follow through and let her know. Gotta hand it to you, Sean. You were right about this being a lot more than a missing persons case."

"I wish I'd been wrong."

Cory read from his notes. He said, "We may have a witness of sorts."

"What do you mean?"

"A man called dispatch and said he was out in the glades doing some horticulture work and spotted what he believes was Thaxton's truck. But, before that he said he saw someone in a hurry to get out of the area. Could it be related to Thaxton's death? I'll go interview the fella to see what he has to say."

"Do you have his name?"

Cory squinted in the light. "Yeah, his name's Chester Miller. Gotta go, Sean. I'll keep you in the loop." He disconnected.

• • •

Jessica Thaxton had dropped Kristy off at school when she received the phone call as she was parking in the lot of the campaign headquarters. She looked at the caller ID, recognized the number, and said, "Hello."

"Mrs. Thaxton, its Detective Gilson. I'm so sorry to deliver bad news to you."

Jessica felt her throat close. She tried to say something, but the words were trapped. Detective Gilson said, "We found Joe. He'd been shot once. Unfortunately, he didn't make it. The body was found just across the boundary on the Seminole reservation by a member of the tribe—an older man. Joe had already passed by the time the man found him. He'd suffered a single gunshot to the back. I wanted to drive over and meet you in person to tell you, but the news media will be all over it. And I didn't want you to see it on TV or read about it."

Jessica cried out loud, her voice coming in piercing, mournful cries, her hands shaking, chest on fire. She tried to catch her breath, tears spilling down her cheeks and across the back of her hands, gripping the steering wheel. "Was my husband murdered?" she blurted out.

"We can't confirm that right now. We're investigating every lead we have. There are no witnesses that we know of at this time, but we did find material that may be evidence."

"What kind of material?" she cried, her voice cracking.

"A partially smoked cigar, a food wrapper from a trail mix bar, and a make-up compact—the kind used by hunters to darken their faces. We're hoping DNA will be on some of that, maybe a fingerprint or two as well."

"Where is Joe … where is my husband?"

The body is with the county medical examiner. In this case, we have to do an autopsy to help determine the cause of death. We can release his body to you in a couple of days. Again, Mrs. Thaxton … I wish the word sorry could mean more. I understand how painful this must be for you, and I want you to know that we'll do a thorough investigation. If evidence points to the death as a murder, we'll vigorously pursue it until we find the killer. If it was accidental, a hunting accident, then that person could be up for manslaughter charges, too. We can discuss that later. Please feel free to call me with questions or if you need anything."

Jessica didn't respond. She lowered the phone from her ear. She had to use two hands to push open the car door, a mockingbird chortling from a jacaranda tree near the sidewalk. Jessica felt so weak she didn't know if she could stand. She managed to swing her legs from beneath the steering wheel to the open door. She slowly stood on the asphalt and looked at the Thaxton campaign headquarters decorated in American flags, a large banner with Joe's smiling face.

The distance from her car to the front door was only about fifty feet. She managed to take the first step in what became the longest and darkest walk in her life.

Fifty-Five

Chester Miller was thorough, his attention to detail superb. He met with Detective Gilson and a chief deputy sheriff. They'd pulled up in two cars—an unmarked sheriff's vehicle and a marked cruiser. They drove down Chester's long drive, parking near the cabin.

Callie stood next to her grandfather as the men asked questions. When they told him Joe Thaxton had died, she could see a physical change in her grandfather's face, his cheeks losing color, his jar-line popping, eyes narrowing. The chief deputy, a tall man with wide shoulders, military haircut, probing hazel eyes, said, "It may have been an accidental shooting, considering it was the first day of hunting season, or it may have been intentional. That's why we're here today, Mr. Miller, to get your take on exactly what you saw. If you were to see this guy again, the driver, do you think you could identify him?"

Chester nodded. "I certainly could identify and recognize his features. He had a tanned face, thick black eyebrows, an all-business like look to his eyes, shaved head. No facial hair. Large hands on the steering wheel … big knuckles. I have no idea who he is or where he was heading in such a hurry."

Detective Gilson asked, "Did you see the license plate on the vehicle?"

"Yes. I caught it from an angle on my truck's side-view mirror. It was a Florida plate, but I couldn't make out the numbers and letters on it. In my younger days I probably could have, but those days are long gone."

Gilson wrote something on the notepad he carried. "Do you think this guy driving the black car could have been a hunter? We get guys out of Miami who like to hunt, but not all of them own pickup trucks."

"If he was a hunter, he wasn't wearing any kind of camouflage clothes. Looked to be in a dark shirt."

The chief deputy asked, "Did you notice whether he was wearing any hunters' camouflage make-up on his face … you know, like the colors you might see on a combat soldier's face to knock down the shine. Plenty of guys wear that stuff hunting, especially during bow and arrow season when they need to get closer to game."

"Far as I could tell, his face was as clear as yours."

Gilson nodded. He looked across at Callie and smiled. "I think it's great that you're out here helping your grandfather. Do you go with him when he's replanting orchids in the glades and Big Cypress?"

"Yes, sometimes."

"Why weren't you with him when he found the pickup truck and saw the man in the car?"

"I was going into Naples that day to get a filter for my camera and to buy some groceries."

Gilson smiled. "You say you'll be returning to college soon?"

"Yes, winter term. But working with my grandfather, I feel it's as if I'm earning a PhD in botany."

"You can't beat hands-on learning," said the chief deputy. "It's what sticks."

Detective Gilson looked around the property for a moment. "We appreciate you calling the office and volunteering the information. Here's my card. If you think of anything else, please give me a call."

"Happy to help if I can. From what I heard about Mr. Thaxton, I really admire what he was trying to do. I've been an environmentalist long before the term was part of the vernacular." Chester half smiled. "I've been studying the flora and fauna so long in the glades and Big Cypress Swamp I can tell you emphatically and scientifically that the River of Grass is very sick. The orchids I'm replanting are some of the hardiest species. I fear the more fragile ones, like the ghost orchid, won't make it."

Gilson closed his notebook and tucked it inside the pocket of his sports coat. He said, "The victim was shot once, through the back. He didn't die immediately. He managed to walk a pretty good distance from where we believe he was shot. Unfortunately, it appears he bled out. We'd sure like to find and question the man you spotted out there."

Chester used one hand to hold on to the wooden handrail adjacent to the steps leading to the cabin's front porch. "You fellas think the man I saw might have done it?"

"We're following all leads," Gilson said. "If you see his car again, see him, or even somebody who looks like him, give us a call. We appreciate your time." They turned to leave, talking in low tones as they walked toward their cars.

Chester slowly sat down on the wooden steps, watching the men drive away. Callie sat next to him. "Grandpa, do you think the man you saw was the killer?"

He turned to her. "I don't know. I've spent most of my life looking into the faces of orchids. They're incapable of deception. I have a feeling, though, that a man like Sean O'Brien, a former homicide detective, might have a better insight into that human connection. I would imagine that he has stared into the face of evil more than once. For me, it would be akin to looking at something that doesn't exist in the world of orchids … a black orchid, for example. It's neither good nor bad … it just simply doesn't exist. But darkness does live in the heart of man. I do know there was something about the man driving that car that didn't seem right. It was more than him appearing out of place in the glades. It was as if he was out of sync with everything around him. Like a planet knocked from its orbit in the cosmos. I could see it in his face. And, if I ever see that face again … I'll recognize it."

Fifty-Six

It didn't take long for the news media to swarm the Joe Thaxton campaign headquarters. Four TV news trucks parked in the lot, camera operators shooting the exteriors of the building, reporters at the locked door—somber-faced, looking for interviews and over their shoulders at the same time, fueled by competition and deadlines. They learned that Jessica Thaxton had left, picked up her daughter and was sequestered in their home, requesting privacy in their time of mourning.

Inside the headquarters, staffers openly wept, hugging one another, some trying to hold it together as they answered the barrage of phone calls. Many of the calls were from well-wishers. "Anything we can do," was the prevailing sentiment. The rest of the calls were from the news media.

After Jessica Thaxton left to go home, campaign manager Larry Garner, locked the front door and pulled his team of twelve people into a conference room and told them all he knew from speaking with Jessica and the police. He stood next to a white board, Joe Thaxton's schedule in bold black print for the next week. Garner, eyes red and puffy, looked at his staff. They were mostly young, just over the voting age. All volunteers. All teary eyed. All looking for answers Garner knew he couldn't give.

"The first thing Joe would say to us," Garner said, "would be to march on with the message, the agenda, the passion. He'd tell us to further embrace Hal Duncan's campaign with all of the fiber in our bodies. Hal and Joe shared a lot in common. They saw beyond partisan issues to reach a mutual goal. And, if Hal is elected governor, much of Joe's passion will go with Hal to Tallahassee."

Garner paused, licked his lower lip and blew out a long breath. "Joe was out there … down in the glades doing what he always did. He sought definitive proof. He combed the water, ground, and the skies looking for scars to the environment. The facts, he always said, carried the weight in a debate about the earth's environment and removed opinion from the argument. Joe always talked about man's effect on the environment long before most people recognized climate change. He knew that, for our fragile blue-green planet to sustain life a hundred years from now, we must do something today to curb the toxic pollution. And he searched for ways to do it. Joe wasn't just about calling attention to the problem … he was about working together to find solutions." Garner looked out the conference room's open door to the news media in the parking lot.

A young woman, hair in a ponytail, arms crossed, said, "Joe was shot in his back. You said police don't know if it was the result of a hunting accident or murder. Considering the threats, stuff we received on the phone, and the damage to Joe's truck, how can it not be murder?"

"I'd like to think in this day and time, that murder … as in a hitman or assassin, is something used by the mafia and drug cartels to settle scores or eliminate competition. I hope and pray Joe's death was an accident … because, if it was not, what does that say to anyone thinking about running for office in America who has the fortitude to stand up to corporate greed, and to do what's right for the environment and the people who call Earth home."

A woman asked, "Was Hal Duncan notified? With the media frenzy, he shouldn't be caught off guard."

Garner nodded. I spoke briefly with Hal. He's very upset. Hal sends condolences to Jessica and everyone in this room. He said to 'stay strong and continue the fight.'"

231

Another staffer, this one an older man with gray hair, who manned the phones during the meeting, came to the door and said, "Larry, when you have a minute, can you speak to all the reporters. It's quite a scene out there. And the phones won't stop ringing, TV producers with national news organizations are calling … all asking for information and interviews."

Garner nodded. "They can get details from the police. I'll speak with them about Joe. It won't be easy talking about my best friend … but Joe would want us to face the media and continue to tell our story. And the ending is certainly not done."

Fifty-Seven

There's something about planting a tree, hand-digging with a shovel, the organic smell when new dirt is exposed to morning air, that is its own form of physical and emotional therapy. I thought about that as I dug the first hole to plant one of the orange trees—trying to tuck away Joe Thaxton's death in a file I kept sequestered on a back shelf in my mind. I couldn't help but feel some guilt for not taking the job. *If I'd taken it, could I have made any difference?* Even the Secret Service can't fully protect the president. I was shirtless, dressed in a pair of faded, old jean shorts and scuffed work boots.

Max sniffed one of the rubber pots that held an orange tree, sitting next to it and looking over at me. I drove the shovel blade hard and deep into the hole, scooping out black earth, sweat rolling down my face and chest. After it was the depth I wanted, I dropped to my knees and used my hands to smooth out the bottom of the hole, sweat dripping from my chin onto the new soil, a pink earthworm wriggling through the soil. After a moment, I stood and looked at the first tree. They all were less than five feet high, their roots squeezed into the hard rubber pots filled with dry potting material.

"You're up," I said, lifting the first small tree from its pot and gently setting it down in the hole. "I've already watered the ground with my sweat." I had to smile—talking to a tree, using my hands to fan out the ball of roots, covering them with fresh moist earth. I could almost hear the tree sigh. I recalled what Chester Miller had said about the Venus flytraps: *The plants have no nervous system. No muscle. No brain, yet they are triggered at the right second to move.*

As I finished with the first tree, my phone buzzed. I'd set it down on the grass next to a half-consumed water bottle. Max stood, staring at the phone and then cutting her brown eyes up at me. "Yeah, I know." I looked at the screen. Wynona was calling.

I answered, and she said, "Sean, I have more information about Joe Thaxton's death. I met at length with your old friend Detective Gilson and compared notes." She told me they'd sent the cigar stogie, hunter's make-up kit, and trail mix wrapper to the state crime lab for analysis. Cory wanted to wait for the lab to finish before pursuing a homicide case. Wynona didn't want to wait, but she had little to go on until DNA might be extracted or a print lifted.

She said, "It's an odd case, not only in terms of jurisdiction, but in the scope. Here we have a fairly well-known man running for office, shot in the glades as he collects water pollution data, and he manages to make it across the boundary to die on Seminole land—the rez. It's more than a half mile from where they found his backpack and some blood to where we found the body. Cory Gilson and I will work the case as a co-op, inter-police taskforce the best we can. But I'm not going to wait to see if the cigar and other things might be connected to a deer hunter. I'm pursuing it as a homicide until I have proof otherwise."

"That sounds like a good plan," I said. "I'm sure Cory will follow your lead. He's not about ego. He never was a guy concerned with taking credit … but more of an investigator who wanted to flesh out all leads in a case."

Wynona sat at her office desk. "I hope you're right, Sean. But my spidey sense is tingling just a tad. I think Gilson is a straight shooter, but he seems quick to look at the side of the coin that's spinning toward an accidental death. Maybe I'm wrong." She sighed. "I'm at my desk reading a Thaxton campaign flier. After standing next to his body, thinking about how far he'd walked and crawled after he was shot … what must have been going through his mind … and then looking at the pictures of Thaxton and his family, my heart breaks. It breaks for his wife and little girl. Jessica Thaxton needs to know whether her husband was killed in a hunting accident or murdered by a hitman. And daughter Kristy deserves to know as well. If it was a hitman, who sent him and why. That's where I want to go if the evidence opens that door."

"One thing that might open that door is a missing piece of evidence that could hold the key. They've found a stogie, food wrapper, hunter's makeup, Joe's backpack and drone control, but search teams haven't found the drone. If we're lucky, it just might have captured something that could help."

"We think alike, Sean. That's one of the reasons I'm calling you. I'd like to see if Joe Billie would try to find it. Joe knows the area better than anyone I can think of at the moment. He hunted and fished the land most of his life. He cut palm fronds to build chickees for people and businesses. He's an excellent tracker, too."

"I agree, but how do you follow something that doesn't leave tracks? The drone, of course, zips through the air. Joe has enormous talents in the wild, but I'm not sure even he can track a bird in flight."

"Eventually the bird must stop and rest. So, will the drone. I don't have Joe's number. He doesn't come to the rez that often. He has family here. I could ask them, but I know you have his number. Maybe you could give him a call for me."

"That doesn't mean he'll answer his phone. Sometimes it takes him a week to get back to me. I can always go to his trailer. I might have better luck."

"That would be great. Thanks."

"You said that was one of the reasons you called. What's the other?"

"It has to do with Chester Miller."

"What about him?"

"Gilson told me he spoke with him. Apparently, Chester was in the glades, driving out there to replant rare orchids like he does often, but he saw something."

"What?"

"A man in a black SUV leaving the area not far from where they found Joe Thaxton's truck. Chester said he could ID the guy if he saw him again. When we bought those orchids from Chester and his granddaughter, I could tell he likes you a lot, or maybe he respects you. I thought maybe you'd go with me when I interview him. I'd like for you to hear what he has to say—what he saw, and then maybe we can take a ride into the Everglades."

Fifty-Eight

Chester Miller was loading a dozen orchids into the bed of his pickup truck when an unscheduled visitor arrived. He looked up to see a TV news truck coming down the long drive to his cabin. Chester closed the truck's tailgate, wiped his hands with a red rag he had in the side pocket of his denim coveralls, and walked toward the picnic table where Callie was setting up more orchids to be photographed. She looked at him and said, "I wonder how they found us? It looks like they're from a Miami news station."

Chester inhaled deeply and said, "It may be because my name is on a police blotter when I called in to report what I'd seen in the glades. Or maybe after the detective spoke with me, it's on some kind of police report."

They watched as the van rolled to a stop less than twenty feet from them. A blonde woman, late twenties, attractive, dressed in designer jeans and a blazer, got out of the passenger side. She flashed a wide smile. A tall man, balding, wearing a Channel Two polo shirt and jeans carried a video camera in one hand, microphone in the other. He had a tattoo on his right forearm of the cartoon character, Scooby Doo.

The reporter approached first, smiled and said, "Hi, I'm Linda Brown with Channel Two News. My camera operator is Raul Cordero. Are you Mr. Miller?"

"I am. This is my granddaughter, Callie."

The reporter stepped closer and shook their hands. "It's nice to meet you both. Before we left the station, I spoke with our feature reporter, Simon Hernandez. He told me he did a story with you a couple of years ago … about how you replant rare orchids in the Everglades and sell them on the side to support the effort. That's so cool."

Chester grinned. "I remember Simon. We spent a few hours in the glades, and he bought a lavender orchid for his new bride."

The reporter smiled. "I wish we were doing another feature story. It's truly incredible in here. Raul and I were talking about that during the drive in, how you've got so many exotic flowers set next to the driveway and up in trees." She looked at Callie and then back at Chester. "We're doing a story on the death of Joe Thaxton. He'd built quite a following the last few months on the campaign trail. A lot of folks would like to know how he died in the Everglades. We know he was shot once, but detectives aren't calling it a homicide … at least not yet. We understand that you, Mr. Miller, were in the general area where deputies found Joe Thaxton's truck. We're told that you spotted someone leaving the area and spoke with detectives about that. Right now, police have no way of knowing if the person you saw is in any way connected to Thaxton's death. However, if we could do a brief interview with you, perhaps something you say might help investigators."

Chester smiled. "Well, I've told them all I know. There's not a lot more to say."

"Maybe someone in our audience will hear your interview … jog their memory, and perhaps know where to find the person you saw. If the person you saw out there happens to see himself on TV and calls police to tell them whether he, too, saw something in the Everglades. If it was a hunting accident, maybe the hunter who fired the stray shot will come forward. Can we chat with you on camera? We won't take much of your time."

Chester looked at Callie. She said, "It's up to you, Grandpa."

He nodded. "If I can be of help, I don't mind."

"Great," said the reporter. She looked over her shoulder.

The cameraman handed her a microphone and said, "Rolling in five."

She stood next to Chester. "Mr. Miller, we really appreciate you speaking with us today. We know you've spoken with sheriff's investigators in the mysterious death of Joe Thaxton. Can you tell us what you saw that day you were in the Everglades and found the truck Joe Thaxton drove out there?"

"Well, I didn't see much, really. It was a typical day. I'd forgotten it was the first day of hunting season in sections of Big Cypress Preserve. That's one of the reasons I steered clear of that area. But I have plenty of spots in the glades to replant orchids. Like I told police, I saw a man coming out of the glades on a little used trail. If I ever do see folks that far into the glades, they're most often in ATVs, airboats or swamp buggies."

"What was he driving?"

"An SUV. It was black. Mud splattered all over the sides. Looked like he might have become stuck and somehow managed to pull out of the muck."

"What kind of an SUV was it ... could you tell?"

"I'm not that good with the makes and models of cars anymore. But it might have been a BMW. I've never seen one of those in the glades. It must have had four-wheel drive to navigate through that country."

"Did the driver say anything to you?"

"One word. He shouted *move*. I backed my truck up to allow him to safely go around me."

"Can you describe him?"

"To some extent. I'd say he was in his early forties. Dark complexion. No beard. Shaved head. He had what you might call a prominent nose—a Roman nose, if you will. And he seemed in a real hurry to leave."

"If you saw him again, could you recognize him?"

"I believe I could. I've spent much of my life finding, recognizing, and categorizing rare and exotic orchids. You train your mind to remember details. It stays with you."

Fifty-Nine

I didn't expect he'd call for a few days. He rarely, if ever, took his phone with him when he went deep into the Florida wilderness. I'd locked my river cabin and headed to Joe Billie's trailer about twenty miles away near Lake Woodruff, a large lake fed by the St. Johns River.

I remembered the first time I ever saw Joe Billie. He was almost my height, six-three, long salt and pepper colored hair, dark skin. He grew up on the Seminole reservation but chose to leave after he spent two years in the Army, returning to open a business.

I met him two weeks after buying my cabin. I'd been replacing rotten lumber on my dock. Max spotted him first. He was walking in the river, not far from the bank, chest-deep, and he was hunting with his toes and the bamboo pole he carried.

The first time I saw him, I did a double take. He was at least seventy yards away, up river, midday in the heat of a Florida summer. He was in silhouette, the hot sun bouncing off the water in shimmering heat waves, wet hair hanging to his broad shoulders. In the distortion off the water, holding the pole, it gave him the illusion of a sea god emerging from the murky depth.

He walked in bare feet, feeling the river mud with his toes. When he felt something that could be an ancient artifact—an arrowhead or spearhead, he'd use his toes to dig it out of the mud, placing the object in a small gunny sack he carried on his belt.

Sometimes, when the object was too large to lift with his toes, he'd lower his entire body in the river, using his hands to free ancient history from the grasp of the river. His only protection from alligators was a ten-inch knife he carried on his hip. However, in two decades of harvesting from the river, he said he'd never been attacked by a gator. He told me that more than once he'd been approached by them, but never attacked.

He made a living building chickees—sturdy structures with thatched roofs made with palm fronds and cypress poles he harvested from the Ocala National Forest and other areas across South Florida. Palm trees constantly shed and drop old fronds as new ones grow. Joe would only cull a few branches from each tree, careful not to harm the trees.

I pulled off Highland Park Road, following a gravel driveway that snaked around century-old live oaks, through a fish camp filled with cabins for rent, all with screened-in porches. Joe Billie lived alone down by the river in a vintage Airstream trailer. Max's radar kicked in gear. The Jeep's windows were down. She stood on her short hind legs, head out of the window, inhaling the smells of the fish camp—wood smoke from a smoldering campfire, pine trees and damp moss.

I parked in front of his trailer, the silver roof stained dark amber from years of pine sap. A straight-back, wooden chair, its blue paint cracked and fading, was to the right of his front door. He had a small garden to the left of the trailer, a dozen stalks of corn, tomato plants—heavy with tomatoes, tied to wooden stakes. I counted seven watermelons, most twice the size of Max.

But there was no sign of his truck.

I got out and knocked on his front door, Max following me, sniffing the hard-packed dirt path leading to the door. I couldn't detect movement in the trailer, but when it came to Joe Billie, that meant nothing. He could walk through the woods and not make a sound. I wrote a note, asking him to call me, folded the paper and wedged it in the doorframe right above the handle.

Wind chimes, hanging from a low-slung limb on a live oak, played a lonely refrain under the influence of a breeze across the river. "He's not here, Max." She looked up at me as if she knew he wasn't home. "Let's head to the marina. Maybe later, Joe will help us hunt for a lost drone in a million acres of Everglades. If anybody can find it, it'd be him."

• • •

Detective Cory Gilson got a surprise phone call. It came from a friend of his at the state crime lab. Gilson had asked him to please put a rush on the possible DNA samples from the cigar, hunter's makeup stick and food wrapper. Gilson was at his desk in the criminal investigation division of the sheriff's office. It was a sprawling, multi-story complex that housed the jail and many of the county's emergency services departments.

He glanced at a photograph of his wife and two grown sons as he picked up his phone, taking the call. "That was quick," he said. "Whatcha got, Lou?"

Lou Fisher, late fifties, thick hair like gray steel wool, wore a white lab coat, and stood next to an electron microscope. A half-dozen forensic technicians worked in the background. He said, "This one was easy. It makes it a hell of a lot easier when the unknown subject becomes a known subject because he's in two data bases … CODIS and IFIS."

"Tell me more." Gilson sat more erect in his rolling chair, grabbing a pen and paper.

"There was a very clean thumbprint off the food wrapper. Easy to lift and easy to ID. Guy's name is Craig Moffett. He served a dime stretch at Raiford, in for armed robbery. Long rap sheet. One was the time he used his fists to rearrange the face of his former girlfriend, almost killing her. His prints are in IFIS and FDLE databases. The requirement to have all convicted felons submit to DNA samples is paying off when it comes to CODIS. The saliva soaked in that stogie was filled with Moffett's DNA, and we picked up DNA off the makeup stick."

"Do you have a current address for this guy?"

"Thought you might ask that. Cory, I'm always ready to make your job easier." Fisher laughed and said, "He's in your county.

Lives at 1219 Honeysuckle Road. Now, it's my turn. You think Moffett put a round through Joe Thaxton?"

"Probably. The question is this … was it an accident, or did somebody pay him to kill Thaxton? Maybe today we'll know. Also, what's a convicted felon doing with a rifle?"

"Good luck. Keep us in the loop. The crime lab lives vicariously through the criminal investigations you guys do."

Sixty

As Max and I drove to Ponce Marina, I thought about my last conversation with Wynona: *I'd like for you to hear what he has to say—what he saw, and then maybe we can take a ride into the Everglades.* I followed Max down L dock under a sapphire blue sky, the hot sunlight bouncing off the exteriors of boats—most painted white. A tern and sea gull tussled over a sliver of fish on the dock beneath one of the fish-cleaning stations.

We approached *St. Michael*, Nick wearing faded swim trunks and using a hose to wash down the boat's transom. Max watched him for a second. He grinned and sprayed a short burst of water toward her. She barked and chased the stream of water, drops clinging from her furry chin. Nick laughed. "Hot Dawg loves the water almost as much as me. I need to teach her how to dive. We hunt for starfish. They make the best chew bones for dogs."

I smiled and said, "You keep thinking Max is a Labrador retriever. She's too small to take out diving. She'd be an appetizer for a lot of fish in the ocean"

Nick shook his head, eyebrows arching. "I will protect her. I got Max's back. She knows it. We just don't see her enough here at the marina."

"You're in luck. I need to head south for a little while. Maybe you could keep an eye on her. You know where her food is on *Jupiter*. Do you have time?"

"I always have time for my lady, Maxie. I'm not fishing for the next couple of days. I'll buy Hot Dawg a hot dog at the Tiki Bar."

Dave walked to the bow of *Gibraltar*. "Thought I heard Max barking. I'm watching the news, and before the commercials, the anchorman said they have more on the story of Joe Thaxton and a special interview with someone who could be an eyewitness. You might want to see this."

"Okay," I said. "We'll join you."

Nick shut off his hose and followed us to *Gibraltar*. We stood in the wide salon, and Dave used the remote control to turn up the sound after a used car commercial ended. The anchorman said, "Police investigators are still searching for more evidence in the shooting death of state senate contender, Joe Thaxton. They spoke to a man who first located Thaxton's truck far into the Everglades. Channel Two's Linda Brown has more."

The image cut to an aerial shot of the Everglades, miles of sawgrass interspersed with island-like green hammocks of cypress trees, palms and swathes of palmettos. A female reporter's voice-over narrative began. "The Everglades is more than one and a half million acres. In most places, you'd have to use an airboat or what locals call a swamp buggy to enter. Chester Miller knows the area well."

The image cut to Chester loading orchids into his truck. The reporter continued. "Miller, a world-renowned botanist and an expert on rare orchids, has made it his life's mission to replant near extinct orchids back into the Everglades. That's what he was doing when he was the first person to find the truck owned by Joe Thaxton. Thaxton's body was found several miles away, just across the border of the Big Cypress Seminole Reservation. Detectives say he'd been shot once in the back."

The images cut to a Big Cypress Reservation sign and then back to sheriff's deputies searching the wetlands. The reporter said, "Miller told detectives he'd seen a man driving an SUV through a muddy trail

245

in the Everglades, not far from where Miller first saw Thaxton's lost truck."

The image cut to an interview with Chester. "I'd say he was in his early forties. Dark complexion. No beard. Shaved head. He had what you might call a prominent nose—a Roman nose, if you will. And he seemed in a real hurry to leave."

"If you saw him again, could you recognize him?"

"I believe I could."

Dave glanced over at me. The news story continued with the reporter saying, "Investigators are looking for the man, but they don't have a lot to go on at this time." The video cut to Detective Cory Gilson. He said, "We have a general description of the man and the car he was driving, but no license plate number. We believe he was driving a black BMW SUV. No doubt all-wheel-drive."

In a live shot, the reporter, hair to her shoulders, stood next to an Everglades National Park sign. "Detective Gilson said, although Thaxton was shot on the first day of hunting season, they're not calling the shooting accidental or a homicide. He said forensics tests on items found in the area of the shooting, include a partially smoked cigar, are ongoing and he's waiting for the results. In the meantime, since Thaxton's body was found on the Seminole reservation, the tribe's police department has final jurisdiction. I spoke with lead detective, Wynona Osceola, who said it's way too early to label the death an accident."

The video cut to Wynona standing in front of the Seminole Police Department building. Palm trees swaying in the breeze behind her. "We know that Joe Thaxton was shot at least a half-mile south of Seminole land. He chose to run or walk away from the direction of the bullet. I want to know why? Could he have seen the shooter and was the shooter wearing the bright orange vests a lot of deer hunters wear to prevent this kind of thing from happening … or was it something else?"

The image cut back to the live shot of the reporter. She said, "Joe Thaxton was out here collecting water samples. The restoration of the Everglades was one of the central themes of his campaign. Funeral services are planned for next Monday. Now back to you in the studio."

In a split-screen image, the anchorman nodded. "Linda, as we understand it, detectives have a fair amount of forensics evidence that may be connected to this, correct?"

"Yes, Steve ... the state crime lab is processing things, such as a spent cigar and a food wrapper, found about a hundred yards or so from where Thaxton was shot."

The anchorman said, "Linda Brown, reporting live from the Everglades. In other news ..."

Dave muted the sound. "If I were part of Joe Thaxton's family, I'd be most appreciative that Wynona Osceola is part of the investigation. Not only is she tenacious, she's very intuitive. She follows the evidence and her gut at the same time."

Nick nodded. "I'm glad we got to know Wynona. I just wish she had a sister. I know she's Seminole and Irish ... but I gotta think she has Greek blood in her somewhere. I can tell these things."

"I'll ask her," I said. "I'm going back down to the glades. She wanted me to be there when she interviews Chester Miller and to go out in the glades where he found Thaxton's truck. Maybe she thinks Chester will be more candid with both of us present since we bought orchids together from him."

Dave sat on his couch, Max jumping up next to him. "From the interview with Chester, I'd surmise he calls it the way he sees it. My BS meter didn't budge watching him in the interview. I shared with you an article I read about the emotional connection many people have to orchids, one grower saying it's as if the orchid flower has eyes that draw us to it. Chester Miller, maybe because of his age, his command of language, his knowledge of the glades ... he draws people to his eyes, too. They don't seem deceptive and certainly portray the message he's beyond reproach. But, of course, in a criminal investigation that can be a double-edge sword with a witness."

I said, "Agreed. As eager as Chester is to help detectives, I'm concerned about the interview he did."

"If the killing is a homicide," Dave said, standing, "and if the perp was watching or any of his associates were watching the news story, Chester's ability to make a positive ID might make them nervous."

I said nothing, watching a 52-foot Viking sports-fishing yacht, the hull pale blue, rumble past *Gibraltar*. The captain, shirtless, in swim trunks, puffed on a long cigar. The reporter's voice resounded through my thoughts: *Forensics tests on items found in the area of the shooting, include a partially smoked cigar, are ongoing and he's waiting for the results.*

Dave said, "When you see Chester Miller, you might want to caution him to be less forthcoming with reporters. If Thaxton's death is not an accident, an elderly botanist could be a key witness for the prosecution."

• • •

Wynona sat behind her desk in the investigation division of the Seminole Police Department when Detective Cory Gilson called her. She answered, and he told her about the DNA and fingerprint matches to Craig Moffett. "Seems to be a consistent criminal … in and out of prison. Heavy drug use. He's out now. We're told he works as a part-time house painter. After the lab matched his print, it was easy for them to get a DNA hit because his DNA is in state and federal databases."

"Where is Moffett right now?" Wynona asked.

"Don't know for sure. He could be on a job or at his place. We found an address. He lives in Collier County off a rural dirt road in a trailer. After we pick him up, you want to be around for the questioning?"

"Yes. Thanks. In the meantime, I'd like to meet with one of your deputies or a forensics tech who worked the scene in the glades."

"You won't find anything more than we did."

"Maybe. Just the same, I need to see the area."

"Okay. I'll text you a contact and number. You can set it up. I think you'll be wasting your time, but it's your call."

Sixty-One

Craig Moffett was about to have a bad day. He set his can of Budweiser down on the ground at the rear of his double-wide trailer almost hidden behind the tall, skinny pines at the end of a long, rural dirt road. Moffett hoisted a fresh kill, a buck deer into the air using a rope and pully he'd attached to an oak tree limb.

He wore ripped jeans, military boots. No shirt. Chest and arms filled with hair and tattoos. He was under six feet, late forties, thick neck, and bull shoulders that rolled with muscle as he used a serrated knife to slice through the deer's hide. His round face was filled with speckled black and white whiskers, heavy dark eyes that could have been carved from coal.

After a few minutes of skinning, sweat ran down his chest. He stopped for a moment, lifting the can of beer to his small mouth. He drank, right hand stained cherry red with blood. Moffett continued skinning the deer carcass, pausing for a second when he heard something in the surrounding woods. *Probably just a squirrel*, he thought.

Detective Cory Gilson and twelve deputies, five of them SWAT team members, circled the trailer. They'd parked a hundred yards away, emergency lights off, radio communications through earpieces each officer wore. They could see Moffett's rusty Toyota pickup truck under a towering gumbo limbo tree near his dirt driveway.

Gilson and three men approached the trailer's front door. Although they had a search warrant, they knocked. No reason at this moment to kick down a door. There was no response. No dog. No sounds. Nothing but a wasp buzzing by as it flew to a charcoal gray nest under an outdoor floodlight twenty feet to the left of the door.

Gilson started to say something when one of the SWAT member's voice came through the earpiece. "We got eyes on him. He's out back, behind the trailer, skinning a deer."

Gilson spoke into a small microphone on his sleeve. "Keep in position we're coming around there. Is the subject armed?"

"Other than a damn big butcher knife, we can't see another weapon. He's not wearing a shirt. Could be a pistol in his pocket, though."

Gilson and the three deputies walked around the trailer. Moffett's back was turned toward them as they approached. When they got within thirty feet of him, Gilson said, "Craig Moffett, we'd like to have a word with you."

Moffett turned around slowly, pokerfaced, his dark eyes obscure, the knife in his bloody right hand. When he saw the officers and the detective, he dropped the knife next to his right boot—the tip of the blade sticking in the ground. "I didn't do nothin'."

"Nobody said you did," Gilson responded. He came closer, flanked by his men. The other deputies closed the circle from the woods. Each man had his hand on the grip of his pistol. Two deputies carried sawed-off 12-guage shotguns.

Moffett looked around the perimeter. He shook his head. "What the hell's this all about? Why y'all here. I'm clean, man."

Gilson said, "We're not looking for drugs." He pulled out a search warrant and handed it to him. "We're with the sheriff's department. We are looking for other things. Is your back door unlocked?"

"Uh-huh."

Gilson motioned to the three men next to him. "Lyle, Ron, Jason … why don't you fellas give the place a look. See what you can find."

Moffett held up both hands, palms out. "I ain't done nothin' illegal. I learned my lesson."

Gilson nodded. "I guess ten years in Raiford is a learning experience."

"How'd you know I did time."

"That's our job to know." He looked over at the carcass. "Where'd you get the deer?"

"A friend of mine brung him to me. I used to work as a butcher at Tony's Market. We split the meat."

"You say a friend brought him to you?"

"Yeah."

"What's this friend's name?"

Moffett paused a second. "Mark Conway."

"If I call Mr. Conway and ask him if he brought this deer to you, he'd better corroborate your story."

"What's the big deal about a deer anyway? It's in season."

"Handling firearms is not in season if you're a convicted felon … ever."

One of the deputies came back out of the trailer, looked at Gilson and said, "We found a Remington Model 700 rifle in his closet."

Gilson took another step closer to Moffett and said, "Mr. Moffett, here in the great state of Florida, it's against the law for a convicted felon to own a firearm. I'm betting your friend didn't bring you that deer. I think you killed it out in the glades. And not having a hunting license is gonna be the least of your concerns. Let's go down to the sheriff's office. You have some explaining to do." He looked at his deputy and said, "Jason, why don't you go back in there, probably look in the same closet where you found the rifle and get Mr. Moffett a shirt. Judge Hathaway doesn't like people half-dressed appearing in his court of law."

Sixty-Two

Chester Miller was at the top of an aluminum ladder, propped up against a cypress tree, when Wynona and I arrived. I parked my Jeep close to his cabin. Callie held the base of the ladder. She smiled wide when we got out and approached them. Chester glanced down at us. He held a small watering can directly above the Persephone orchid. "Welcome back. Be right with you folks."

"No rush," I said.

Callie shook her head. She blushed, flashing an awkward smile. "Grandpa won't let me feed and take care of Persephone. So, at age eighty-five, he climbs the ladder every other day and does his thing."

Chester used his thumb to tamp the soil and said, "How are you today, Miss Persephone? We'd love to see you soon. Perchance you might emerge before I reach my ninetieth birthday? That's in five years. Maybe you'll surprise us all before my ninetieth."

Wynona glanced up at Chester as he set the small can on a rung of the ladder, took an eyedropper from his kangaroo pocket and squeezed some drops in the soil next to the base of the orchid. "Are you giving it vitamins?" Wynona asked.

Chester smiled, finishing. "The word nutrients is perhaps a bit more applicable. But it's essentially the same. It's a nutritional formula I've developed throughout the years, definitely through a lot of trial and error … and eventually to success. It captures many of the same dietary requirements the hybrid nucleuses would find in their native lands. Here in Big Cypress, we have a lot of the essential elements in terms of the environment, but this plant will need more to bloom."

He finished and began to climb down the ladder, Callie holding it steady with both hands. When his feet were on the ground, he picked up his cane and turned to us. "It's good to see you both again." He shifted his eyes to Wynona. "I trust the last orchids you purchased are healthy and in good standing. I'd so love a good report card."

"They made the grade. All are high achievers," Wynona said. "They're beautiful and seem to be healthy."

"Ah, yes. But remember, a happy orchid is usually a healthy one, too. As with humans, health and longevity are often associated with reduction of stress, diet and companionship. Chat with them occasionally. Otherwise, they can get lonely, shrivel up and waste away. Just like us. Thank God Callie is here."

Callie smiled. "Mom tries to call you."

"I know. Your mother is a fine woman, in spite of me being her papa." He grinned and turned toward us. "It's teatime. Care to join us? Did you come for more orchids?"

Wynona said, "We'd love to have a cup of tea, but we aren't here to buy more orchids. I'm running out of room in my house."

Chester used both hands, gesturing toward his property. "That's why I'm here. I can't run out of room, and by restocking the glades, I'll never run out of room … only time." He looked up at the Persephone plant and chuckled. "It's been said the two most powerful warriors are patience and time. I'm running out of both as I wait for Persephone to rise. Maybe she'll bloom at night when the constellation Virgo is on the rise."

"What do you mean?" Wynona asked.

"You only see the constellation Virgo during certain seasons, rising in spring … just like Persephone, the goddess of spring. She comes and goes, brings the season of growth after the dead of winter. I believe, when the orchid, Persephone finally blooms, it'll be after a dark period. And it'll have been worth the wait." He lowered his gaze back at Wynona. "If the purpose of your visit this time is professional, I sense it has something to do with your profession, working for the Seminole Police."

"It does. We come with questions and a word of advice."

Chester nodded. "That sounds like it could be interpreted as a warning, which at my age, has little weight or consequence. Nonetheless, I would like to hear your questions and suggestion. Let's have some tea and sit in the shade."

Sixty-Three

The four of us sipped tea seated around the wooden picnic table under the moss-draped limbs of a live oak, a scrub jay above us crooning its songs of the swamp. Chester leaned his cane up against the table, glanced at me and asked, "Where's your little canine companion?"

"Back at Ponce Marina. A couple friends of mine take turns dog-sitting."

Callie said, "Watching your dog, Max, made me want to get a dachshund one day. Maybe after college when I'm more settled."

"For the most part, Max is low maintenance as long as she's first in line for dinner."

After the laughter died, Wynona looked across the table at Chester and said, "We saw your interview on TV. That's one of the things we'd like to discuss with you."

"Did they get my good side?" He smiled.

"Absolutely. Also, they broadcast what you said. Chester, I don't want to alarm you or Callie, but you might want to refrain from granting requests from reporters to do interviews. Please consider this at least until the investigation into Joe Thaxton's death results in an arrest, if that's the direction it takes."

"May I ask you why?"

"At this point, we have no idea whether the death of Joe Thaxton is from a hunting accident or from a round fired by a hitman. If it was the latter, the man you saw in that car could have been either directly responsible, or an accomplice to the killing. And if he, or whomever hired him, believes you can make an identification, that could put you at risk."

Callie looked at her grandfather. Chester nodded. "I understand. I don't know the fella's name, of course. But if police managed to locate him and put the gentlemen in a police line-up, I believe I could recognize him." He paused, watching the scrub jay swoop among the limbs. "I was raised to stand up for what's right. I believe we now live in a society that has an allegiance to two things—themselves and their phones. Most young people, excluding my lovely granddaughter, Callie, hardly look up to see what's around them. I've been a proponent of helping neighbors all my life. My neighborhood today is Big Cypress and the glades. When I see something that might be out of the normal, and when I hear there was a death near the place and time that I saw something out of the ordinary, I think it's my civic duty to report it. I'm not accusing the man I saw of anything. He could have been a lost tourist who wanted to get off the highway and experience the road less traveled."

Wynona smiled. "That's admirable. It's certainly the right thing to do in helping police do their jobs. But there's no civic or municipal protocol that says you have to help reporters to do their jobs."

I said, "Too often helping them can hurt an investigation. It can become a liability and certainly a double-edge sword—cutting both ways."

"How do you mean?" he asked.

Wynona said, "As a detective, and before that as an FBI agent, I had to balance the integrity of the case, witnesses and evidence, against what might happen if the information was released prematurely to the media. Often, I had to withhold details of a case from the news media because to release it would compromise the investigation. It could unveil details that should be kept private about a case until charges are filed and often beyond that. We owe it to the victim and his or her family. When the time is right, and the investigation is wrapped, it's fine to speak with reporters. In the meantime, the public doesn't have a right to know if that information allows an alleged killer to go free as it may keep the real killer from falling between the cracks."

Chester sipped his tea, setting his cup on the table. "You offer a persuasive argument, Wynona. I see the value and the wisdom in your reasoning. One day, perhaps you'll share with me why you are no longer in the FBI. I believe you were good at the job." He chuckled. "I may be an old dog, but I can still learn a new trick or two." He smiled at Callie. "From now on, let's offer reporters orchids but that's all."

"Sounds good, Grandpa."

Wynona said, "Chester, because Joe Thaxton's body was found on the Seminole reservation, the tribal police department is taking the lead in the investigation. Before you saw the man in the SUV leaving quickly, did you hear any gunshots?"

"I heard one. Figured it was a hunter. I've heard poachers in Big Cypress out of hunting season, but when the season opens, especially the first few days, I hear a lot of gunfire."

"But you only heard that single shot before you saw the man in the SUV, right?"

"Right."

"Okay, before you saw the man in the SUV, after you heard the gunfire, how long was it between the gunfire and the moment you spotted the man leaving?"

"Oh, I'd say maybe ten minutes."

"Were you driving your truck when you heard the shot?"

He smiled. "No. I'd stopped to pee. Too much coffee and plumbing that's frayed. It was when I was walking back to my truck that I heard the shot … way in the distance."

I asked, "Which way, Chester … north, south, east or west?"

"Definitely west."

Wynona asked, "And that would be the direction the man was coming from, correct?"

"Yes. The topography of the glades is so flat it's easy to hear gunshots. Especially when there's little or no wind."

Wynona jotted down the information on a notepad. "Chester, I know you've given Detective Gilson a description of the man you saw, he shared it with me. I was wondering if there are any other details that you may have forgotten when you spoke with him that you could recall now?"

Chester folded his hands, interlocking his fingers, brown age spots on the backs of both hands, knuckles scarred. "The driver had large hands. I could tell because he was gripping the wheel. I do remember there was a gold hoop earring in his left ear. I couldn't see his right ear. I don't recall if I'd mentioned that to Detective Gilson. In my sideview mirror I could see that the car had a Florida plate, and I noticed something else, too."

"What was that?" Wynona asked.

"Smoke. I'm not sure if it was coming from the car's exhaust pipes or someplace else. It could have been steam because there's so much water out there, dirt potholes filled with rainwater, maybe it splashed up on the engine and created steam."

Wynona's phone buzzed. She looked at the in-coming text, reading it. She eyed me and said, "Looks like we'll be meeting one of Detective Gilson's forensic techs at the scene. From here, we're close."

Chester leaned back, the wooden bench creaking as he reached for his cane. He looked at me and then shifted his eyes to Wynona. "Do you think Joe Thaxton was murdered?"

I said, "That's a strong possibility."

He nodded, watching the scrub jay make a loud cry and fly off through the cypress trees. Then he looked at me and Wynona. "In my gut ... I do too. You two seem to make a fine team. I hope you can locate the person responsible ... even if it was an accident. A man is dead, and someone should be held accountable for his death"

Sixty-Four

We didn't have to wait long. Wynona and I stood next to my Jeep near the spot where Joe Thaxton's truck was found. I could hear a vehicle approaching beyond the twisting, muddy trail leading through an abyss of sawgrass. "We should have company in just a moment," I said. The breeze smelled similar to an oyster flat at low tide in the sun. Protein either dying or procreating.

Wynona looked at me and half smiled. "Let's hope it's the good guys and not the perp coming back to try to find something he left out here."

"If he spotted the drone, I'd bet he might like to find it, or he may have found it."

"I hope Joe Billie reads your note and calls."

"He will, but I never know when. Sometimes he just shows up at my cabin after he takes his canoe upriver and ties it to my dock."

She walked to a grassy area along the muddy path, studying all of the tire tread marks in the mud. "That won't do us much good if you're here, and he's there." She pointed to something white more than ten yards away. "This might be where the forensic techs took the plaster cast of the tread."

She walked in the direction, west, staying on the grassy areas as much as possible. I watched a Toyota 4-Runner approach, the sheriff's star insignia on the doors, engine whining, mud flying from the tires across the door panels. I could see a woman behind the steering wheel, both hands holding tight, her head not far above the wheel.

Wynona knelt by the tire track, touching the white substance with the tips of her fingers, and then standing as the 4-Runner pulled up next to my Jeep, the engine shutting off and ticking in the still air. A woman in a polo shirt got out and smiled. A logo patch of a sheriff's badge was sewn over the left-side pocket. She wore snake-proof boots almost up to her knees. Blue jeans tucked inside the boots. Her light brown hair was pinned back on both sides above her ears, wide smile and dimples. Small build. No firearm visible.

We walked over and introduced ourselves. Her name was Vera Barkley. She told us she'd been with the sheriff's office more than three years. Works forensics only and earned a master's degree in criminal science from Florida State University. Wynona said, "Vera, we really appreciate you coming out here today. Let's get started."

"I hope I can help. The area is pretty picked over. We spent a full day and a half, covered as much as we could—dawn 'til dusk."

"Is that where you guys did a tire tread plaster cast?" Wynona pointed to the tracks, a dried white mortar substance on each side of the track.

"Yes. It was pretty easy to run down the make and model of the tire. We got that information back about two hours ago." She opened a small notebook she carried in her right hand. "The track was made from a Continental tire … a four-by-four Contact tire. All season. It has some tread wear and nicks. That, like the bottom of a shoe or boot, leaves its own distinct tread mark. We narrowed the type of tire down to a 255–50-R-19. If we can find a BMW SUV with those tires, and the exact treadwear, we can place it out here."

"But we can't tie the driver directly to the shooting," I said.

"Correct, but for him to be in the glades, in this vicinity, near or at the time the victim was shot, definitely makes him a person of interest." She looked over at Wynona. "Speaking of a person of interest, we picked up a man for questioning. Detective Gilson asked me to have you call him. Gilson says he'll keep the individual in the interrogation room. He's not charged with anything yet, but his prints and DNA put him not far from the blood we found near the victim's backpack and drone controller."

Wynona said, "That's a good start. How far is the spot from where your team found the cigar and other stuff to where Thaxton's backpack was located?"

"Not too far. I would say the distance between where the cigar and wrapper were found to the backpack and controller is approximately 150 yards. It's a direct line of sight from where we found the things to where we believe the vic was shot."

I said, "You can get in my Jeep, if you want. No need to take two vehicles out there and risk getting one or both stuck."

She looked at a large green and orange grasshopper—four inches long, crawling across her hood. "Thanks."

• • •

After traveling through some extremely narrow and bumpy trails, and through shallow water and grassy areas, we were there. Vera sat in the back seat and said, "Okay, you can stop here. I'll show you where we theorize the shot originated."

We got out and followed her to an area where a cypress tree fell years ago, its root system the size of an Army tank. The tree, which had probably toppled from the winds of a hurricane, had a portion of it roots oddly attached to the earth. It was at least one-hundred feet long. It was a fallen goliath among a sea of sawgrass dotted with a few hardwood hammocks, like mirages in the distance—a random oasis of green in sawgrass the color of hay.

Vera pointed to a spot next to the fallen tree. "This is where we found the cigar, food wrapper, and makeup stick. We pulled a cast of a boot print from here. We think the shooter used the downed tree as a place to steady his rifle. We found two very small marks not much larger than a pea, about eighteen inches apart. The marks could have been made when a heavy rifle rested on a bi-pod."

I looked up from the fallen tree, across the sawgrass to a hardwood hammock about 150 yards to the north. Three snowy egrets sailed toward the vista. I pointed. "Is that the wooded area, where you found the backpack and controller?"

"Yes. It was quite a shot. I'm not sure your average deer hunter would have attempted it."

Wynona said, "I doubt it either. If he had a scope, it's perhaps attainable. But it would require the skills of an expert marksman, someone with the highest rating, I'd think."

I said, "It could be accomplished without a scope by a real pro, depending on the movement of the target and the wind. A deer grazing, or a man standing, relatively motionless, could be hit from the distance. But through a scope, the shooter could easily be able to see the target was a man and not a deer. So, I'd suggest, if the round was fired through the aid of a scope, it was murder."

Vera let out a long breath. "That's the feeling I have."

Wynona said, "What bothers me is the stuff you found here. I'd think a real deer hunter would smoke his cigar at the end of the day, not while hunting. I'd imagine that a deer, downwind, could smell the smoke and run the opposite direction."

Vera said, "Maybe the shot was fired at twilight and the hunter took it because the movement from here to there was all he had before heading home. I'm sure that some hunters spend long, boring hours waiting for game to approach. They get hungry, eat on the trail and maybe are somewhat anxious and careless."

Wynona nodded. "But do they drop trash in a hunting spot? Maybe. It just seems out of character."

I said, "That would be a question to ask the guy Cory Gilson picked up for questioning. Obviously, he must have dumped that stuff out here. The question is … was it right here next to the tree … or somewhere else and brought here?"

Vera looked at me and asked, "Are you suggesting that evidence might have been planted?"

"That's exactly what I'm suggesting."

Wynona's phone buzzed. She read the text and said, "It's from Detective Gilson. He believes the suspect might make a full confession. He's asking me to come to the sheriff's department."

"You can follow me," said Vera.

"Let's do it, but since we're only a little more than a football field away from where Thaxton was shot, I'd like to see the area before we leave."

It took us less than five minutes to walk from the fallen cypress tree to the place deputies had found Thaxton's backpack and drone controller. "Right there," said Vera, pointing to the tall strand of Everglades palms and palmettos. "That's where we found it. The blood sample was lifted from the soil. The controller was less than three feet from his backpack. We managed to follow a few visible tracks in the soil, and then they vanished as if the victim was mysteriously carried out of the area." She looked at Wynona. "Later, the body is found across the border on Seminole reservation land. Considering his condition, it's remarkable he made it that far."

I stared back at the fallen cypress tree in the expanse of glades, the big tree like a twig in the distance. I felt a wind moving across the land, sawgrass just bobbing in the breeze. I looked up at the tops of the palms and tall pine trees, their branches swaying in the gusts. I wondered how much higher above the trees had Joe Thaxton operated his drone. When he dropped the controller, did the drone come crashing down in the dark water of the swamp? Or did it fly until its batteries died … soaring away … maybe a mile before coming down? Before it flew into the bayous, what had Joe Thaxton seen through the drone's single eye over the Everglades?

I wanted to look at my phone, but I knew Joe Billie hadn't called. Not yet.

Sixty-Five

Wynona and I waited less than five minutes in the lobby of the sheriff's office before Cory Gilson arrived. Bone white tile covered the floor of the large reception area. Two ceiling fans. One not turning, the single strand of a spider's web slung between two blades. A dozen hard plastic chairs. A woman and teenager sat in two of the chairs. Neither talking. There was a framed picture of the sheriff and the current governor on the wall behind a receptionist who answered one call after the other.

Wynona said, "It'll be interesting to watch the questioning of this guy, Craig Moffett. Was he simply an indifferent hunter, a man who throws his trash where he hunts … or is he too, a victim?"

"Let's see what he has to say. Do you plan to question him?"

"Yes. Jurisdiction comes with the territory, and since the body was found on the rez, I need to lead this dance. I'm just hoping Moffett doesn't ask for a lawyer before the questions get rather personal."

Cory Gilson came through one of the doors. He grinned at me. "Sean O'Brien … it's good to see you." He walked over and gave me a hardy handshake with a quick pat on the back. He looked at Wynona. "You come with a formidable partner."

Wynona smiled. "Seminole PD doesn't hire consultants. Sean and I are friends. I asked him to join me as we had a look around the glades. Sean knew the vic."

I said, "Thaxton and his wife wanted to hire me to look into the threats and property destruction as the campaign became more elevated. I turned them down."

Gilson nodded. "I know you, Sean. Looks like you regret that decision, but what the hell could you or anybody do at that point?" He paused, glancing through the windows at the parking lot, the sun's heat shimmering off the cars, chrome winking in the light. "I'm not sure Thaxton's death grew from phone threats or some punk twisting the candidate's windshield wipers in knots."

"Let's see where the chips fall," Wynona said.

"We can pretty much put Craig Moffett smack dab in the middle of where the shot was fired. Considering his record as a habitual felon, he could be sent away for years on manslaughter charges. Before he can start spinning lies and bogus alibis, we just need to let him know we have hard, physical evidence that puts him there. Lab says his Remington rifle was recently fired. I wish to God we could locate the round that went through Thaxton. I'd bet the ranch it would match the rounds we found in Moffett's hunting knapsack next to the rifle in his closet."

"Where is Moffett?" Wynona asked.

"Sippin' coffee in interrogation room number three. We have two other lowlifes in rooms one and two. People doing bad shit to pay the pushers selling opioids. One dude in there is the biggest meth dealer in Southwest Florida. Guy reminds me of the actor in that old TV show Breaking Bad. But rather than cook the stuff from a RV in the desert, he cooks it on a houseboat in the backwater bays between Everglades City and Chokoloskee. He used to be a crabber. But that didn't pay as well. I don't know about you, Wynona, on the Seminole reservation, but we're backlogged in criminal activity here. It wouldn't hurt my feelings in the least if I could just put Moffett in the back of a deputy's car and ship him to you."

"He lives in Collier County. You found him. Let's both go have a chat with him."

Gilson nodded. "Let's get at it." He turned to me. "Sean, I'll take you to the observation area. Y'all come on back. Follow me. Let the good times roll." He looked over my shoulder, his eyes following movement. "The news crews are showing up in the parking lot. I'm sure by now they've heard about us picking up Craig Moffett. At this point, I have nothing to say. This is gonna be one damn high-profile case."

• • •

I stood behind the one-way glass and watched as Cory Gilson and Wynona took seats on the opposite side of the table where Craig Moffett sat. I studied Moffett as he watched them. He leaned back in his chair, arms folded across his broad chest. His face bloated. Cheeks flushed. Eyes veiled. Tats on his arms and the left side of his neck. If he were playing poker, his bluff was to look disinterested and then offended. His tell was in the body language. A twitch he couldn't hide, as if people had the nerve to challenge his innocence. There was a sullen swagger to the way he moved and adjusted his body in the chair. I could tell he'd been here and done this … many times. He harbored some of the irritated unconscious movements and gestures I've often seen in repeat offenders—a petulance—a moral superiority. He would become accusatory if pushed in a corner here. In a bar, he'd come in swinging.

Gilson said, "Craig, you and I have already met. This is Detective Wynona Osceola. Before we get started, can we get you something to drink? Coffee? A Coke? Water maybe?"

He shook his head. "Naw, I don't plan to be here that long. Y'all got nothin' on me, and you know it. Way I figure is on account of all the publicity and whatnot, you're in a hurry to pin this on somebody. That somebody won't be me. You got that?"

Neither Cory nor Wynona responded quickly to Moffett's jab. Cory said, "If you're right, you have nothing to worry about, okay?"

"I ain't worried."

Cory leaned forward, placing both hands, palms down, on the table. "Well, if you're not worried, then you ought to be concerned. And I'll tell you why, Craig. We have your fingerprints on a food wrapper you dropped at your hunting spot. We have your cigar, too. The thing is oozing with your DNA. We have the butt from a marijuana cigarette. It's got your kiss on it too. We have your hunter's makeup stick. Again, skin cells from your face and hands are all over that. We know your rifle has been fired in the last forty-eight hours. It all puts you directly at the murder scene—the murder of a beloved and highly respected man well-known across Florida. Imagine trying to find an impartial jury. You can't win against that kind of physical and forensic evidence. But you do have choices. The question is … are you smart enough to make the right one"

Moffett said nothing, his thoughts racing. He made a dry swallow, tried to clear his throat. "That's 'cause I went huntin'. That's what you do when you're huntin,' okay?"

Cory half smiled. "I thought you told me a friend brought you that deer, correct?"

"I didn't say I shot a deer. I said I went huntin'. There's a difference. Missed a couple shots. Deer run off in the brush."

"I'd say there's a big difference in hunting a deer compared to hunting a man."

"I told you … I didn't kill anybody out there. I didn't even see anybody, so how in the hell could I kill 'em?"

"You're a convicted felon with a rifle, and you are a hired gun. Maybe you smoked some weed to take the edge off."

"No! That's bull shit, man. You're makin' stuff up. You mind if I have some water?"

Wynona said, "Of course not. I'll get some for you." She stood, glancing back at the one-way glass. I could tell she wanted to speak with me.

Cory leaned forward on the table top, looking Moffett in the eye. "Physical evidence puts you in the line of sight from bullet to impact. You say you were just hunting deer, but now, Craig, you look like the proverbial deer in the headlights because you got caught. And you know what you did."

Sixty-Six

I walked from the observation area to a hallway, Wynona coming out of the interrogation room at the same time. She looked at me and said, "Moffett's no Boy Scout by any stretch of the imagination. He's got an attitude on his face and ink in all the wrong places. Maybe the teardrop tat in the corner of his left eye, which doesn't mean he killed a man, was inked there to better survive in prison. Sort of a visible bluff for survival. Is he capable of premeditated murder? Probably. Did he shoot and kill Joe Thaxton? Was he a gun for hire? I'm not convinced. Was it an accident? I'm not convinced of that either. I do know that Cory is going to press that direction."

"No doubt."

"What would you do in there, Sean? Do the good-cop-bad-cop grilling or play a different hand?"

"I can only advise you to truly play it by ear. You've got great instincts. If you feel the interview veering off the tracks, change things up. Change direction. It's not the question or intent to get Moffett to admit to manslaughter … it's to assess his culpability or lack of it as a hired assassin."

"Yes, we have a lot of forensic evidence placing him in the shooter's spot and perspective. With the rifle he has, he could have taken a few shots at Thaxton, only one had to connect in the vital areas. What bothers me is the other physical evidence."

"You mean the plaster tire prints?"

"Yes. That's one component. We know they don't match the tires on Moffett's truck. The SUV that Chester Miller saw certainly wasn't a truck and the guy driving it definitely wasn't Moffett. So, who was he? Why was he out there? Was he working with Moffett ... or alone?" She looked around the hallway. "I offered to get water, and I'm not sure where to find it."

"There's a break room the first door on the left. I saw water bottles in there."

"Thanks." She headed that way, stopped and turned back toward me. "I told Cory before we went in there that, unless we get a real confession for murder, I might not settle for manslaughter if the chips just don't stack up right."

"I have no doubt you'll do what you think is right. Cory may not agree with you, but at the end of the day, the body was found on the rez and that trumps every card in the judicial deck."

She smiled. "Why do I like you so much?"

"I have no idea." I smiled and walked back to the observation room.

• • •

Cory interlocked his fingers together, looked at his hands and then up at Moffett. "Shooting a rifle under the influence of pot can cause problems. You shot at a deer and missed. Maybe that's the way it went down. But the fact is, you were so far away from what you thought was a deer, your bullet went through a man. That doesn't mean it was intentional or murder. Accidents happen. Craig, you wouldn't be the first hunter that accidently shot and killed someone in the woods. And, unfortunately, you won't be the last. Sometimes bad stuff happens."

"I'm tired of it happening to me. I took a couple of shots out there. But I sure as hell wasn't aiming for anything walkin' on two legs. How many times do I gotta tell y'all that, huh?"

Wynona glanced at Gilson and then at Moffett. She said, "Mr. Moffett, let me remind you that you are a convicted felon. You have no legal right to own that rifle. You had no legal right to be out there hunting. The rifle you used has a scope on it."

"What's that supposed to mean?"

"Even under the influence of marijuana, using a scope before taking the shot, you should be able to see whether you're shooting at a deer or a man. The fact is, you chose to shoot at a man. And you killed him. We have the physical evidence, and we have the body. What we don't know is who hired you." She leaned forward. "Here's the deal, you tell us who hired you, and we'll reduce charges. Yes, you'll be back in Raiford, but you can keep off death row if you tell us who hired and sent you into the glades to kill Joe Thaxton. Otherwise, Detective Gilson and I will be in the front row when they pump the chemicals into your body, and you start your final convulsing on earth."

Moffett looked as if he might come across the table at Wynona. Even from behind the one-way glass, I could see a blood vein pulse on the side of his thick neck. His mouth turned down on both corners. He looked across the room at the mirrored glass, as if he were trying to look through the glass. He shifted his eyes back to Wynona. "Lady, you may have my cigar and whatnot out there, but you don't have a bullet from my rifle in the dead guy 'cause it wasn't me that shot him. Why the hell would I kill some dude in the glades that I don't know. I hear he was a politician. I couldn't give a shit about politics, or anybody else for that matter."

"I'll tell you why you could shoot him," Cory said. "Because somebody paid you money to do it. Problem is, you don't know what to do with the dough. You were probably paid in cash. You're afraid to put it in your bank … we checked. So, you have to stash it 'til the heat cools down. Did you bury it in the yard behind your trailer? Eventually, you'll spend most of it on booze, pills, gambling, and prostitutes. It's what you do, Craig. You cycle in and out of society, taking. Never giving. You always have … always will."

"You don't know shit."

"I know this … and you'd better listen carefully because I'm not gonna repeat it. You're about to be charged for first-degree murder in the premeditated and planned death of Joe Thaxton. For you, that's a fast-track to death row, because the guy who most people will vote in to be the next governor of Florida is Hal Duncan—a real good friend of Joe Thaxton's. And, if Duncan becomes governor, you can bet your ass he'll do everything in his power to move you to the front of the line on death row. Forget appeals to any state court, and you can damn sure forget a stay of execution at the eleventh hour from the governor. That's what you're up against, Craig. The murder of a well-known and well-liked man running for office to make a difference … and you killed him."

"Man, you got this all wrong. I rode to my favorite hunting area in Big Cypress on my ATV, and I didn't see a soul."

Cory shook his head in disagreement. "Now, you can tell us who hired you, that's the guy we want. Detective Osceola and I can talk with the prosecutor … work out a deal to keep you off death row. It's up to you. But you gotta talk to us. You gotta work with us."

Moffett said nothing. He looked down at his big hands on the table, his jawline hard as granite, deep-set eyes veiled. He released a chest full of air. "Here's the deal, okay? Nobody hired me to do nothin.' At this point, I wish they did. I'd rather have them take most of the heat than me. Fact is, yes, I'm a convicted felon. Yes, I didn't have a license to hunt. But it's one of my passions … one of the things that keeps my head on straight. I'll admit that I might have accidently shot and killed the dude. But it was no damn murder. I never really saw him. It was getting late, near sunset. Lots of deep shadows. I took a long shot at what I thought was a boar or maybe a deer. I fired the round knowing that I'd most likely not hit the animal. I was just tired and bored. A little high. So, I made a stupid mistake. So, what? But I sure as shit didn't murder anybody."

Cory glanced over at Wynona and said, "With your record, it's going to be very doubtful that you or your public defender will ever convince a jury anywhere in Florida of that. There's way too much forensic and physical evidence … and pal, it all points directly to you."

Moffett folded his heavy arms across his chest. "You can't scare me."

Wynona said, "We're not trying to, the evidence will do that. But only if you have a conscience. Craig, we know that Joe Thaxton was making a lot of enemies among the rich and powerful, because that's who he was taking on in his election campaign. You see, he was doing the reverse of what most people running for office do … he was turning his back on the lobbyists hired by the rich and powerful. Thaxton was turning his back on them so he could turn toward and unite the people—the voters, to support the current laws and make sweeping changes in Florida's environmental laws that would cost some of these people big money. So, whoever hired you is going to discard you like the garbage he thinks you are. You're going to be just another bit player in their role to remain superior to you and millions like you. This is your chance … your opportunity to turn the tables. Who solicited your services? We need a name, and you won't face the death penalty."

He slammed his right fist down on the table, the force almost splintering the inch-thick particle board surface. "Stop! Okay? Y'all gotta believe me. I didn't take money from anybody 'cause I didn't kill the dude … at least not on purpose like a murder. Man, if anything … it was an accident … a stupid accident."

"So," fired Cory, "you'd be willing to face manslaughter charges to put this thing to bed as opposed to possibly face the death penalty, correct?"

"Yes … I'll cut the deal. Can't see as I got much choice in the matter. Maybe with manslaughter I can get out before I'm seventy."

Cory stood, turning his back to Moffett and Wynona. Cory looked at the one-way glass and slightly nodded to me. I thought he'd prefer to take a bow. I watched Wynona. She looked at Moffett and said, "I believe you."

Moffett didn't respond, his eyes resigned to his fate. Cory turned back around, looked at Moffett. "You're making a smart choice. We'll get the prosecutor in the state attorney's office to begin the paperwork."

Moffett leaned back in his chair, picked at a callus on the knuckle of his middle finger, left hand. A skull tattoo on the same finger.

Sixty-Seven

We met for coffee in the sheriff's office break room. Wynona, Cory Gilson and I sat in hard chairs around a square table. Coffee in white Styrofoam cups. Wynona's purse hanging from the back of her chair. Cory said, "I spoke briefly with Sheriff Ketcham and the SA's office on speakerphone. With all the news media outside, the sheriff said he'd announce speedy success in the co-op between our department and Seminole PD. Manslaughter charges don't exonerate Moffett or imply it was an accidental shooting. In this case, it means a career criminal is gonna go back to prison."

Cory sipped his coffee and looked at me. "It's almost like old times, Sean. I know you weren't in the interrogation room with Wynona and me, but I could feel you cheering us on through the glass."

I said nothing.

Wynona held her coffee with both hands and said, "Not a lot to cheer on in there. Granted, Moffett is a career criminal, a guy who pops pills chased by twelve-ounce cans of beer, and smokes weed to top it all off. That's a dangerous combo with a hunting rifle in the glades. And, when we factor in his naturally aggressive mental state, it's proven to be lethal in the past."

Cory nodded. "That guy never should have been released before serving out the last seven years of his original sentence. If he was still behind bars where he belongs, Joe Thaxton would be alive."

"Unless," I said, "Moffett didn't do it."

"Come on, Sean. Moffett was tramping around the glades and Big Cypress, drinking beer, smoking dope and shooting at shadows. He may not vividly remember sighting down on Thaxton, but his pile of shit puts him in a direct line of fire to the victim." He chuckled. "The guy's too much of a liability to be a professional assassin. It appears to be a sad set of circumstances … Joe Thaxton being in the wrong place at the wrong time, and Moffett, the careless criminal that he is, packing a high-powered rifle with a low-powered brain. The collision course is when, at twilight, he squeezes off a round or two and one goes through Thaxton. A jury will see it that way."

Wynona said, "Probably, but that's not the way I see it. Not after sifting through everything Moffett said in there."

"Moffett just admitted he fired in the direction where Thaxton was standing or walking. Manslaughter charges will keep him in prison for years, and that's a damn good thing for society."

She looked at Cory, choosing her words with tact. "I think you're right about Moffett being seen as a liability in terms of him possibly hired as a hit man … especially if the order is coming from powerful people and not some jealous or greedy spouse. It'd require a lot of luck for Moffett to hit Thaxton at that distance, and that would be with him completely sober."

"Accidents happen. If he didn't do it, who the hell pulled the trigger?"

"I think it was the guy Chester Miller saw. We just need to find and question him."

Cory looked over at me. "Sean, you've been quiet through most of this. What do you think?"

"I think Wynona has a valid point and a strong argument. Is the shooter the guy in the SUV that Miller saw? I don't know, but I do think it's worth pursuing. And I don't think Craig Moffett killed Thaxton."

Cory leaned back in his chair, his face drooping. He glanced at his watch. "We have a pack of news media right outside. Sheriff Ketcham is gonna want to hold some brief news conference. You know, announcing something."

Wynona nodded. "I can hold it with him, and I should. We can say that Moffett is a person of interest, even a suspect. But we don't have to make an arrest, and later find out that we were wrong."

Cory shook his head. "Later? I don't have time for later when what we have right now is manslaughter beyond a reasonable doubt. Searching for some guy an old man saw in the glades driving an SUV is going to be a futile effort, and you both know that. With the physical evidence, I say we go on and charge Moffett, let a jury decide, and we'll have done our jobs. We don't have time or manpower to hunt ghosts."

"No," Wynona said. "When the effort goes into building a case against Moffett, it quickly subsides from looking at anyone else, and you know that, Cory. The last thing I want to do is put a man in prison for being in the wrong place at the wrong time. I know it happens, but not on my watch."

"Okay. Let's go talk with Sheriff Ketcham. If this thing backfires, and no one is charged in Joe Thaxton's death, it's on you."

"I can bear that accountability. What I can't and won't bear is the responsibility of putting a man innocent of the crime in prison. If the sheriff wants to share a news conference with me on those terms, I'm happy to do so. If not, I'll walk out there and speak to the media alone."

She picked up her purse from the back of the chair and stood. I glanced up at Wynona and nodded. I looked forward to the news conference … with or without the sheriff.

Sixty-Eight

I could tell Sheriff Dwight Ketcham was old school. That didn't mean he wasn't a competent lawman, it simply meant, in his book, that not all suspects were innocent until proven guilty. And when he factored in a preponderance of forensics evidence that placed the suspect at or near the crime scene, the sheriff didn't seem to want any other facts to get in the way of how he saw the story. And, since he was up for re-election next year, I knew that he saw a good opportunity for garnering positive publicity by bringing a man to justice in the shooting death of Joe Thaxton.

I thought about that as I looked at framed photographs on the wall of his office—the sheriff posing with career politicians, including the current governor of the state, a man whom Joe Thaxton had criticized because the governor had appointed his cronies to the various state water and conservation boards.

Ketcham set behind his large, walnut desk, a bronze statue of a cowboy riding a bucking bronco on the left side of the desk. There was no clutter on the desk. Two closed file folders, one with the name Craig James Moffett on it. Ketchum leaned back in his black leather chair and listened to Wynona's argument. The sheriff was in his late fifties. He'd held the top office for sixteen consecutive years. Comfortable. Complacent. He didn't want to turn in his badge. At least not yet. Ketchum was large boned. A narrow, tanned face and long ears. His dark eyes reflected enduring skepticism from a lifetime of dealing with crime and those who caused some of it.

When Wynona finished, Ketcham looked at her, nodded and glanced over at Detective Cory Gilson. After the initial introductions, the sheriff didn't make eye contact with me. He cleared his throat. "Detective Osceola, how is tribal chairman, James Stillwater? He's been a great friend of mine over the years."

"Good. I'll tell the chairman that you asked about him. Now, shall we both go out and hold a joint press conference?"

"I always enjoy working on cases in an inter-agency capacity. It often brings in excellent and additional resources. I think that was evident in how quickly Detective Gilson and our forensics techs got the physical evidence analyzed. I'm not suggesting that the Seminole PD couldn't have done it as fast, it's just that we first found it in the county before the body was discovered across the line. We moved quickly. I don't want to come across as territorial, I just want you to fully understand that this department is vested in bringing to justice the man responsible for Joe Thaxton's death."

"Then you will continue to assist because the man responsible may not be Craig Moffett."

Ketcham leaned forward, his chair just squeaking. He lifted one of the folders off his desk. "Detective Osceola, this dossier is the record or rap sheet, if you will, for Craig Moffett. He's been in trouble since he was fourteen. He's a man very prone to violence. When he was younger, he was associated with a gang—even they kicked him out. He used to beat his girlfriend that finally resulted in a conviction after one of the last beatings he gave her. Just for being out there in the glades with a hunting rifle spells prison time for this guy. When you factor in all the forensics and physical evidence, seems to me like it's a no-brainer. I'd hate to walk out there, speak to the news media, and tell 'em we've cut Moffett loose because we don't have enough compelling evidence. I'm sure you can understand the gravity of that."

"What I understand even more is the gravity of putting an innocent man behind bars for a crime he didn't commit. I don't care what history Moffett has. If he didn't shoot Thaxton—accident or premeditated—he shouldn't be charged."

"We don't know that."

"And we don't know that he committed it, either. What we do know is that there was another man out there at the same time. We have a plaster cast of his tire tread marks. We have an eyewitness description. As the lead agency on this case, I will investigate all of the evidence until there's nothing left to investigate."

He stood from his seat, slightly rocking in his black shoes. "Duly noted." He picked a second file folder. "Detective, I was intrigued with how this thing went down. The shooting happened in my county. The body ended up on the Seminole reservation. That's gotta be a first. When Detective Gilson told me that we'd be working with you, I was pleased. I wanted to know more about you. Seems you have a distinguished and yet somewhat tarnished record in law enforcement. Stellar with the FBI as an agent until you apparently took the law into your own hands and chose to pump several rounds into a man. Even your partner at the time told an internal investigation team that the man you shot was dead after the first round. Great first shot, Detective. But maybe not great judgment since that decision got you removed as an agent for use of excessive force. I'd hope you aren't using the same judgement here. Letting stuff interfere with your judgement." He grinned and set the folder down.

Wynona said, "I'm not going to the low level to dignify or justify that crap with a response. I don't have to."

I stepped a little closer to the big desk. Cory Gilson looked up at me, licked his lips and started to say something before I said, "Sheriff, you question Detective Osceola's judgment. Perhaps we should question yours." His eyebrows arched. "I checked your campaign contribution records thus far for this upcoming election. One of the highest profile lobby firms for Big Sugar and the many in the agriculture industry, has and is contributing to your elections and re-elections. The known amount is close to six figures. The unknown amount, the PAC money, could be a lot more. Joe Thaxton was a vocal critic of these corporations and others. I'm not sure if the news hounds out there are aware of all your connections. You might want to play this one the way the lead agency is requesting. Am I clear?"

Detective Gilson looked at his shoes. Sheriff Ketcham pursed his lips, a small nerve just below his right eyes twitching, looking like he winked. I turned and walked toward the door. "We'll see you in ten minutes."

Sixty-Nine

Sheriff Dwight Ketcham was not a happy man. But as a politician, he managed to disguise his displeasure approaching a podium in the county's media briefing room. Wynona stepped to the left of the podium. A deputy turned on the PA system, testing the microphone. "Check one," he said. Detective Cory Gilson, the chief deputy, and two senior deputies grouped behind the sheriff near an American flag and a Florida state flag.

I stood in the rear of the room and watched as more than two-dozen members of the news media jostled for front and second row seats. Camera operators secured TV cameras to tripods. Reporters prepped recording devices. A few used pens and paper pads to take notes.

Sheriff Ketcham cleared his throat. "Thank y'all for coming out today. As most of you know, this is a unique case." A photographer focused his lens. Cameras clicked. "We believe the shooting of state senate candidate Joe Thaxton occurred in Collier County … however the body was actually found on the Seminole reservation. Thus, we are conducting a joint-agency task force in this investigation. We have yet to determine if it is a homicide or an accidental shooting that happened out there on the first day of hunting season. To my right is Detective Wynona Osceola with the Seminole Tribe Police Department. Detective Osceola is taking the lead in the case because that is where the death apparently occurred and where the body was located. She has the full support of this office. Together, we have questioned and will continue questioning a number of people, including Craig Moffett. Mr. Moffett is a felon who was released from the state prison in Raiford two years ago … his DNA was found on objects our forensics staff discovered at the spot we believe the shot or shots were fired. Mr. Moffett denies any involvement in the death … accidental or otherwise. He is not in custody at the present time. Before we take a couple of questions, Detective Osceola will have an opportunity to make a statement." The sheriff stepped aside.

Wynona stood behind the podium and looked at the reporters. She smiled and said, "Thank you, Sheriff Ketcham. I know everyone here is on deadline and would like as much information as possible in regard to this case. So, rather than make a statement, I'd be happy to answer any questions that I can at this time."

A hand shot up. A female reporter in the front row asked, "Since Craig Moffett's DNA was found where you believe a rifle shot was fired … isn't this enough evidence to charge him or at least make him a suspect?"

Wynona said, "The investigation is still in the preliminary stages. Mr. Moffett is very much a person of interest. Will the status of Mr. Moffett change? Perhaps. But right now, we can only go with definitive evidence that is irrefutable and evidence that the state attorney's office can use to get a conviction from a jury. We are sifting through all of that at this time."

"Are you investigating this as a homicide?" asked an unshaven male reporter.

"Absolutely," Wynona said. The sheriff's eyes narrowed. He scratched the tip of his nose. Wynona continued. "Certainly, it could have been an accident. As the sheriff mentioned, it was the first day of hunting season. However, because it was the first day and there were hunters stalking sections of Big Cypress Preserve, we shouldn't be too quick to write it off as an accidental shooting until we have definitive proof. Let's disprove that it wasn't a homicide before we focus on all the apparent reasons it could have been accidental."

I watched reporters shift in their seats, some leaning forward, hands shooting up. Wynona said, "What we will look at is who might want Joe Thaxton dead ... and why? Who could have the most to gain, financial or otherwise, upon his death? What did he do or what was he going to do that would have caused someone to kill him? If it was a homicide, was the shooting done by a hired hitman? Or was it done by the person who may have the most to lose had Joe Thaxton lived to be elected and make the sweeping environmental changes in office that he promised?"

"Where is that investigation taking you?" asked a reporter on the second row. "Do you think someone, or some company connected to environmental pollution is behind this?"

Wynona shook her head. "I am not suggesting that at all. What I can tell you is, that in my professional opinion, the shooting appears suspicious. That's not saying it was a murder. The facts, as we uncover them, I hope will lead us to what really happened in the Everglades."

"Can you offer more details?" asked a newspaper reporter in a plaid shirt and jeans.

"There are some things we are at liberty to share and others that might compromise the investigation. I would like to say the sheriff's office has been thorough in its initial investigation. The forensic samples give us physical proof that Mr. Moffett was at or near the scene of the shooting. He doesn't deny that, but contends he was hunting and never saw another person out there that day, including Joe Thaxton."

"How far from that point of impact to where you discovered the body?" asked the newspaper reporter.

"Approximately a half-mile." Wynona nodded, glanced at the sheriff and then at the news media. "Our joint investigation goes into full bore now. We're optimistic that, in a few days, we'll have a lot more than we have right now. Thank you for coming." She turned toward Ketcham. "Sheriff, is there anything more you'd like to add?"

"No," he said, folding his arms. "I think you've covered the bases."

A tall reporter in a tan sports coat and jeans stood, holding his recorder toward the dais. "If this was a murder in the glades, and you're not arresting Craig Moffett, can you tell us if he has implicated someone else in the crime?"

"What did Thaxton find out there at the time of his death?" fired another reporter.

Wynona ignored the barrage of questions coming from the media, stepping down from the dais and walking toward me. I couldn't have been prouder of her.

Seventy

Simon Santiago stood behind his desk in his large office on the twentieth floor of a glass and steel building overlooking Biscayne Bay and the Atlantic Ocean. The Miami headquarters for the Carswell Group was opulent. Each office spacious, expensive fine furniture and art. All of the offices had a spectacular view of the ocean. It was approaching six o'clock in the evening and most of the attorneys, lobbyists, and staff had left for the day. Santiago put his feet on his desk, picked up a remote control and turned on a sixty-inch TV in one corner.

He was dressed in an open Armani jacket, white oxford shirt, and a pair of Gucci jeans. He scanned through the channels, going from a business newscast, to national news, to local and state news. And then he stopped. The video showed aerial images of the Everglades, thousands of acres of sawgrass and a large alligator sliding from an embankment into dark water. The images cut to a man in a T-shirt and jeans leaving the sheriff's office, TV news reporters following him.

One reporter shouted, "Mr. Moffett, did you accidently shoot Joe Thaxton when you were hunting in the Everglades?" The man in the T-shirt, tattooed arms, didn't respond. He was annoyed, looking as if he wanted to backhand the reporter.

The man got into the driver's side of a truck and sped away. A reporter's narrative continued: "After Joe Moffett left the sheriff's department with no charges filed, a joint news conference was held by the two police agencies investigating the death of Joe Thaxton—the county sheriff's office and the Seminole Police Department. Lead investigator, Detective Wynona Osceola, said she doesn't have the evidence to charge Moffett with murder or even manslaughter.

Santiago sat straighter as the dark-haired female detective spoke. "Let's disprove that it wasn't a homicide before we focus on all the apparent reasons it could have been accidental. What we will look at is who might want Joe Thaxton dead … and why? Who could have the most to gain, financial or otherwise, upon his death? What did he do or what was he going to do that would have caused someone to kill him? If it was a homicide, was the shooting done by a hired hitman? Or was it done by the person who may have the most to lose had Joe Thaxton lived to be elected and make the sweeping environmental changes in office that he promised."

Santiago cracked his knuckles, looked through his glass doors to see if anyone was still in the office. He was alone. The reporter's story continued. The video was of the Everglades and then images of flowers—orchids. "One of the areas Detective Osceola will look is in the direction an eyewitness gave her and the other detectives. World-renowned rare orchid expert, eighty-five-year old Chester Miller, lives in his cabin on thirteen acres deep in Big Cypress preserve. The day Thaxton died, Miller was replanting orchids in the Everglades and Big Cypress Preserve, something he's done for years, when he said he heard a gunshot. Although it was the first day of hunting season, Miller said he only heard one shot in the area where he was at the time. He was the first to find the parked and locked truck owned by Joe Thaxton. And he saw something else—a man in an SUV, believed to be a black BMW coming from the direction of the parked truck."

The video cut to an interview with Miller. "I'd say he was in his early forties. Dark complexion. No beard. Shaved head. He had what you might call a prominent nose—a Roman nose, if you will. And he seemed in a real hurry to leave."

"If you saw him again, could you recognize him?"

"I believe I could."

Simon Santiago stood from his desk, walked over to the bar in his office and poured two-fingers worth of thirty-year-old Balvenie scotch into a crystal glass. He took the first sip and waited for his personal phone to ring.

He didn't have to wait more than thirty seconds for his client's number to appear on the screen. He took another sip, licked his wet lips, and answered.

Seventy-One

I couldn't remember the last time I attended a funeral. But I felt a need to attend the funeral for Joe Thaxton. The services were being held almost five days after his body was found. Wynona had been following every lead she could uncover. She drove up to Stuart, and I met her in the parking lot of the Unity-By-The-Sea Methodist Church. "Look at the size of the crowd," she said, as we walked through throngs of people outside the church. She wore an indigo dress and, even at a funeral, looked stunning.

I estimated that more than four-hundred people—mourners, came to pay their respects to Joe Thaxton. They packed the large church, some choosing to remain outside in the sunshine and listen to the service from speakers that had been set up near the entrance. In a little while, they would line the long walkway to watch pallbearers carry the casket to the waiting hearse. All of the Thaxton campaign volunteers were inside the church, many softly crying as friends and family delivered heartfelt eulogies.

Larry Garner and his wife sat in the front pews near Jessica Thaxton and Kristy, the coffin open to the left of the pulpit, two large photos of Joe on easels facing both sides of the congregation. Jessica wore a black dress. She wept. Her shoulders spasmed, hands trembling as she held a tissue to her eyes. Kristy sat stoic, as if the little girl could cry no more, her face filled with anxiety. A white-haired man—perhaps Jessica's father, sat next to her. He put his arm around her shoulders and held her.

Gubernatorial candidate Hal Duncan stepped up to the lectern. He looked at the crowd and said, "You all are an example of what I call the Joe Thaxton effect. He was a man who could bring people together … in life and here in death. Why? Because he had the unique ability to put people at ease. To truly listen to them. To engage them in meaningful conversation … to reach for a common and mutual goal. Joe, in a way, reminded me of Will Rogers … Rogers used to tell folks that he never met a man or woman he didn't like. I believe it was the same for Joe. And after a few minutes with him, most folks went away liking him. You see, he wasn't your average Joe … far from it. He was an extraordinary man."

Someone in a center pew sobbed. Duncan paused and nodded. "Although Joe and I differed in some areas of our politics, we shared a lot of the same ideas to move Florida forward to keep it the pristine state it's supposed to be. I am honored to have known Joe Thaxton. My life will be richer for it. I don't make campaign promises at funerals." Duncan looked at the casket, pausing, blinking his eyes. "But I will promise my friend that I will do my best to carry out what we wanted to do together. His family deserves it. You deserve it, and so does Florida."

• • •

At the end of the services, Wynona and I stood in the church lawn with hundreds of other people. There were TV news trucks and vans parked along the perimeter, reporters and camera operators keeping at a respectful distance. Two motorcycle police officers waited to escort the procession. Six pallbearers carried the polished wood casket down the church steps, along the sidewalk to the hearse, the funeral director opening the rear door. They loaded the casket and the door closed. The sound moved across the crowd with a somber note of finality.

The funeral director nodded to a female member of his staff in a dark blue suit. She turned and watched as Jessica, Kristy, and the older man came down the walkway from the church steps to their car, dozens of mourners following behind them.

Wynona and I watched them in silence, the afternoon sun growing warm, the scent of gardenias in the breeze. Jessica stopped near the end of the walkway, looked at the hearse, the heavy weight—the abrupt end of a life, burdened on her shoulders. Her husband, lying in a box in the back of the last vehicle anyone rides in, was about to be placed in a hole and covered with dirt.

She looked at the mourners and well-wishers, like someone at the airport snatching a worn suitcase off the luggage carousel, turning to search the faces in the crowd for the person who was supposed to be there to pick them up … but that person never shows, and the people leave. There was the subtle look of desperation on her face.

She saw me in the throng—her expression, for a brief second, changing from despair to a look of hope. There was almost a plea in her eyes as they welled with tears, lower lip trembling. The older man held Jessica by the arm, leading her to the waiting car.

It was the first car in a line that would stretch the length of two football fields.

Seventy-Two

Wynona and I didn't go to the cemetery. There was no need to. We'd paid our respects, and we'd seen enough—enough pain and suffering. Joe Thaxton was not the only victim. The future of his child, wife, and extended family would forever be altered, And not for the better. Someone stole Joe's life, but they could never steal the memory of him from the people who loved him. That was evident.

We sat under an umbrella at a sidewalk café in downtown Stuart's river walk district. We had a view of the St. Lucie River, marina, and the Roosevelt Bridge. We sipped black coffee and ate fish 'n chips. Wynona said, "I feel bad for Joe Thaxton's wife and daughter. The grieving is so painful. Tomorrow, the next day, and the next week won't be less painful, only a different form of grief that arrives when something Joe did or said is not there anymore. It's often the little things that dig the big holes of pain—the void—that survivors fall into on their way to walk the dog or check the mailbox."

I sipped my coffee and said, "And, when a letter has the deceased person's name on it, that hurts. People think grief can be shared … maybe—to some extent. But, at the end of the day, the end of a life can be grieved in many different ways by mourners. I think each person carries sorrow alone in his or her heart. And I believe there is a different kind of grief that survivors of murdered victims feel. It's not only that death robbed them of their loved one, it's that someone chose to take the life—to play God and steal a gift that can never be returned. Those tears of pain spill into a pool of sacredness that leaves the ugliest stains. When I was a homicide detective, those stains and blemishes forced me to look into the mirror at my own imperfections before I could attempt to speak for the victims."

Wynona said nothing. She looked out the end of the pier and watched seagulls ride the wind. "One thing I've always admired about you, Sean, is your dedication to live life on your own terms, and you've set those terms pretty high."

"No higher than you do. And you're still doing the job—hunting down the criminals. I checked out, at least in terms of going to the office, coming to the CID each morning and having cases assigned to me. Now I can live vicariously in your work and trying not to overstep boundaries." I smiled.

She laughed. "Feel free to overstep anytime you want. I could always use your help. I'm not getting a lot from the sheriff's department."

"That's not surprising. Physical and forensics evidence points to Moffett, but like a weathervane, it doesn't always face directly into the storm. It points in the direction the wind is blowing at the moment."

"It's been a week, and I'm not a lot closer to solving this thing than I was when I drew a line in the sand with Sheriff Ketcham. Speaking of boundaries … the sheriff and his staff are not exactly eager to provide much more than what they've done. Detective Gilson hasn't returned my last phone call from two days ago. It's as if they've washed their hands of the investigation and don't want to dig in the dirt with me anymore." She paused and watched a sailboat on the river. "I just can't be complicit in leveling manslaughter charges at Craig Moffett until we can prove it wasn't murder. Maybe Moffett did murder him. If so … who's behind it? Who was the other man out there that day—the one Chester Miller saw? We have one of the tire molds but no car. There has to be thousands of BMW SUVs in Florida."

"But not all of them have a cracked oil pan."

"What do you mean?"

"I was thinking about something Chester Miller mentioned. He said he saw smoke coming from behind the car as it sped away. New cars don't smoke unless something is wrong with them. What if the driver hit an object out in the glades—a big rock, log, or some of those potholes? What if it cracked something under the engine and oil was leaking on the exhaust causing the smoke? Maybe the SUV is or was fixed at a shop or at a BMW dealer?"

She considered the possibilities. "That's an idea. I like it. Although it'll be an intensive search. The driver could have taken it in for repairs anywhere, assuming that something did break out there. After he left the glades and got back on the Tamiami Trail, did he go west toward Naples, or east toward Miami? There's a big difference between the number of auto repair shops and BMW dealers."

"If I were a betting man, I'd put my money on the Miami area."

"I thought you might say that. I need to get back to the office and work the phones."

"Wynona, something else I remembered in thinking back over the things that Craig Moffett told you and Cory in questioning."

"What's that?"

"Moffett mentioned he'd ridden to his hunting spot in Big Cypress on his ATV. The area where we believe the shot was fired ... the place where the cigar and things were discarded ... there were no ATV tracks that I could see. Was there a hard rain right after and washed the tracks away, or were they never there?"

A breeze moved through Wynonna's black hair. She used her hand to pull a strand behind one ear. "What if Moffett drove his ATV out there, maybe parked it behind a tree to keep game from seeing it. And then he could have walked to the hunting spot next to that fallen cypress tree where the things were found?"

"That might be how it happened. You can ask him. I think he'll tell you only what he wants to tell you if it benefits him. On the other hand, if there was another man in the area at that time, an assassin with his sights on Thaxton, maybe the killer came across the stuff Moffett tossed either while he was hunting or sitting on his ATV. Assuming Moffett had left, the killer could have carefully picked up the cigar and other things, walked back to where he'd taken the shot then left the stuff near there. For law enforcement, it's great forensics, and its excellent physical evidence ... but, if it's been placed there, it means nothing except that Moffett isn't your killer, accidental or murder. It's someone else."

Wynona smiled. "Did I ever tell you I like the way your mind works?"

"Often it doesn't work, at least not before coffee."

She laughed, looking across the river. The sailboat now a white dot in the distance. "I so miss the time we had on *Dragonfly*. I'm glad you decided to keep the boat. Maybe, when this is over, we can go sailing. I hear the Keys are lovely this time of year."

"They're lovely anytime of the year. Sounds like a plan." My phone buzzed. I looked at the caller ID with no intention of answering it unless it was Joe Billie calling. I didn't want to spoil the moment with Wynona. It was Jessica Thaxton's number. I glanced up at Wynona. "I need to take this." She nodded.

I answered, and Jessica said, "Sean, I saw you at Joe's funeral. I wanted to thank you for coming. We buried him, and then, after lots of hugs and tears with friends and family, I returned to an empty home with Kristy. I heard that police are looking at the possibility of charging a man with manslaughter for what they say was an accidental shooting on the first day of hunting season. It was no accident. Joe was murdered. Whoever pulled the trigger intended to kill my husband … and I think, in your heart, you know that."

"The manslaughter charges against Craig Moffett haven't been filed yet. It's not only the county sheriff's department in the investigation. Seminole Police are involved, too."

"I just don't want the police to take the path of least resistance. Joe never did, and I have a feeling you don't either. Can you do something to keep this from becoming a cold case? Not for me or Kristy, but in Joe's memory and everything he stood for. Please, it would mean a lot. Joe liked you, and I think you liked him or at least what he was trying to do. Please don't let them get away with it. One thing I've learned through the campaign is that big money quietly buys people. Joe couldn't be bought. I don't think you can either. In my heart, I believe someone deliberately did this … someone inside the industries Joe threatened by standing up to them. Can you please help?"

"Jessica, I need to make something clear to you. I'm a PI and not part of the police or sheriff's unit investigation teams. From the sidelines, I'll do what I can, but I can't make you any promises. Also, anything you can think of that Joe or anyone from the campaign headquarters may have said, please call Wynona Osceola at the Seminole PD. She's the lead investigator on the case."

"I understand. But, anything you can do might help, too; and maybe, in some way, the results might influence the upcoming elections. Thank you, Sean. God bless you." She disconnected.

Wynona said, "Sounds like you've decided to step over those boundaries. Welcome to the wild side. As I mentioned earlier, I could use your help. But it seems like it takes two women to convince you." She laughed and sipped her coffee.

"You heard me tell Jessica that I can't make any promises to her. That applies to you as well. I have no illusions. This is a tough case. I'll do whatever I can to help."

Wynona smiled and reached for my hand. "That's enough, and that's all I ask."

Seventy-Three

Sheriff Dwight Ketcham didn't expect the call, at least not yet. He looked at his phone screen, got up from behind his desk and closed his office door. He answered and said, "Good morning. How's the view of Biscayne Bay."

"I don't know. I haven't had time to look out my damn window since Thaxton's funeral. You're supposed to squelch this, and now it's got more national attention. This train is out of control. That Seminole bitch detective is on a freakin' warpath. You need to get this back under your wing."

"What the hell do you want me to do? I can't exactly tell her to go away."

"Grow some balls! You're the damn sheriff. A lot of my client's support and money has helped put you there and to keep you there. You need to perform."

"I'm hoping that Wynona Osceola gets frustrated, sees the wisdom of a second-degree manslaughter case against Moffett, and goes along with filing the charges."

"You're hoping she gets frustrated? That could take months. We don't have that kind of time … nor do you. Am I clear?"

"Yeah. I can only do so much. She's tenacious, and she's got a witness. Those kinds of circumstances don't leave me a lot of wriggle room. I'll do what I can."

"That's not good enough. You're the sheriff. At least for now." He disconnected and called his most powerful client for the authority he needed to do what must be done. After that he'd call Michael Fazio and schedule another meeting.

• • •

Wynona couldn't remember the last time she'd made as many calls in a brief period of time. She sat at her desk in the tribal police department, scratching notes on a yellow legal pad, marking through names and numbers, circling some. She'd worked her way through every BMW dealership on the east and west coasts of Florida. There were plenty of black SUVs in the service departments getting everything from an oil change to engine overhauls. But no one had repaired a cracked oil pan.

She called repair shops that specialized in servicing BMWs, Mercedes, and Jaguars—expensive cars. Nothing. Her final call of the day was to a BMW dealer that had recently changed locations, buying a larger property with an expanded showroom. She was transferred to the service manager's phone. When it connected, she heard, "This is Rusty Davidson, service manager." Then there was a pause.

Wynona said, "Mr. Davidson, my name's Detective Wynona Osceola with the Seminole Police Department—"

The voice continued. "I'm away from the phone, but your call is important to us. Please leave a detailed message, and I'll call you back as soon as I can. Thank you."

At the beep, Wynona pursed her lips and said, "Mr. Davidson, my name is Detective Wynona Osceola. I'm with the Seminole Police Department. We are looking for some help, actually. Recently a BMW, we believe it's one in the X series, black, probably all-wheel-drive. It was last seen in the Everglades and there was smoke coming from the vehicle. Maybe it had a cracked oil pan. We're hoping you made the repairs or are repairing the car. Please call me. It's urgent." She left her number and said, "Thank you."

Wynona picked up her pen, putting a check mark next to the name of the dealership and then writing down the name of the service manager ... *Rusty Davidson*. She leaned back and shifted her eyes over to a single orchid she had in a small ceramic pot on her desk. It was one of the orchids that Sean had given her—lavender and white blossoms. She thought about him, wished he were here to go to dinner. To talk. To simply be near her. Her head pounded and a slight wave of nausea moved up into her throat.

...

Michael Fazio, dressed in a tight-fitting black T-shirt, shorts and soft-leather loafers, sat at the bar in the rec room inside his complimentary ground-floor level condo. The rec room featured a top of the line Brunswick pool table, large-screen TV, overstuffed chairs and two couches. Music pulsed from hidden speakers, Bob Seger singing *Night Moves*.

Fazio used a credit card to make two short lines of cocaine on the top of the bar. He reached into a small crystal bowl and lifted out a plastic straw trimmed short, about three inches. He placed the straw in his right nostril, pushed a finger against the side of the other nostril, leaned forward and snorted the drug.

He did the same thing in his left nostril, sat straight, his hands tapping the bar like he was playing the drums. He picked up his laptop computer from the adjacent barstool and went online, his fingers pounding the keyboard. "What the shit …" Fazio mumbled. He re-entered his account information and got the same results. "Better not have cheated me, ass wipes." He lowered the top to the laptop and pinched his nose, eyes dilated, jawline hard.

He picked up his phone and made the call. When the man answered, Fazio said, "Santiago, where the hell is the second half of the money you owe me? It was supposed to have been deposited in the Caymans account two days ago."

Simon Santiago stood on the balcony of his high-rise condo overlooking the Atlantic, a white cruise ship returning from the Bahamas. He said, "I was about to call you."

"Heard that before."

"Chill, all right. We've never cheated you. You're actually in luck."

"Don't play me, dude."

"Listen! Okay? I spoke to my client. He spoke to his cartel. We have the go ahead to nip all of this shit in the bud."

"What is *this* shit?" Fazio stood from his barstool, pacing.

"The extenuating problems stemming from the removal."

"Problems? What the hell are you talkin' about?"

"Somebody saw you out there. A witness—"

"No way! Give me a break. Nobody saw shit—"

"Here's what we're gonna do. We're gonna retain your services for more work. The price will remain the same. By this time tomorrow you will have one half deposited in the Caymans account. The rest when the job is done."

"Who is the lamb?"

"There may be more than one. You know I never discuss those specifics over the phone. Meet me at the same restaurant tomorrow at one o' clock. I'll have my table reserved. After these are dispatched, my client has agreed to have you flown out of the country to Argentina … Buenos Aires. They have a large ranch and other properties down there. You'll have your own hacienda for a few months 'till this shit has faded away. It needs to happen quickly."

SEVENTY-FOUR

The next morning, I met Dave and Nick for breakfast at a corner table in the Tiki Bar, Max leading the way across the restaurant as we arrived, Dave and Nick just taking their seats. Flo came around from the bar with three laminated menus in her hands. She smiled and said, "I can't remember the last time all four of you were in here for breakfast, and I'm including Max because she has her one scrambled egg on a paper plate, and she never leaves a mess."

"I do," Nick said, grinning. "But, since your food is so good, I leave nothin' on my plate, just like my gal pal, Max."

"Nick, you get a pass. Y'all have a look at the menus. Lisa will be over in a few minutes to take your orders." She smiled and left, greeting a family of tourists that just walked in, their pink faces glowing.

Dave said, "If Charlie's cooking, I'm ordering the stone crab omelet."

Lisa, a college-aged girl in a blonde ponytail, took our orders and filled mugs with steaming black coffee. I brought Dave and Nick up to speed with the investigation. I told them how my former colleague, Detective Cory Gilson, seemed quick to push for manslaughter charges and how that was bothering me. "When I knew Cory, he'd hold out until all the evidence was available. He hated to lose and wanted to give the prosecutor everything he had to win for the victim and the family."

"Sounds like the guy is overworked," Nick said. "Too many cases. People on opioids causing all kinds of crime. Collier County is a damn big county. He's got people cookin' meth out in the sticks, the huge influx of seasonal tourists, and homeowners in the mix. Joe Thaxton's death is probably one he'd like to see in his rearview mirror, if he's got the physical evidence that points to this guy, Moffett, the dude they've questioned."

Dave sipped his coffee and said, "But knowing Wynona, the last place she wants to look is in her rearview mirror. She wants this thing in her high beams and driving straight for it. I concur with her. She's got a witness who saw a person of interest retreating from the glades like the proverbial bat out of hell. What's he running from or to? Who the hell is he, and what was he doing in the glades?"

"We're hoping the tire tread cast will answer questions if Wynona can find the BMW."

"Good luck with that," Nick said, leaning back in his chair.

Dave nodded. "That won't be easy. The death of Joe Thaxton, if it was murder, is one of those unique cases where there is more than enough ample evidence to convict a convicted felon. Most of the time, detectives are thrilled to find small clues, such as carpet fiber, skin cells under the victim's fingernails, a trace of blood. But that's not the situation here. Lots of physical and forensics evidence. The possible perpetrator, Moffett, has no alibi because he's there in the swamps allegedly hunting deer. Rather than prove a case, it's as if Wynona has to disprove one that the sheriff is building so she can truly get the right guy."

Nick sipped his coffee. "I got a ton of respect for Wynona. But man, she's up against some big obstacles, and Thaxton's followers are anxious for somebody to be charged with his killing."

"No doubt," Dave said. "They'd like to see a head on a spike."

"I'm helping Wynona," I said.

"You are?" asked Dave.

"Actually, I agreed to help Jessica Thaxton … well, sort of agreed. She saw me at Joe's funeral, after the church service. Wynona and I didn't go to the cemetery. It was later that day when Jessica called and asked me to help because she doesn't want to see the wrong person charged with the death, and she's afraid it'll turn into a cold case."

Dave exhaled and looked toward the kitchen. He turned toward me. "Sean, where are you going to begin? You don't even know if the guy that Chester Miller saw in the glades was out there to dump a body from a separate killing. You told us that, when you worked with Miami-Dade PD, the glades were where a lot of contract killers dropped bodies for two reasons—it's a million-and-half acres, and the swamps have a way of decomposing human remains quickly."

• • •

Chester Miller leaned over a microscope in his workshop and examined pollen on a slide. He did the same thing with another slide, sitting on a wooden stool at his rustic work bench and writing notes on three-by-five index cards. He paused to sip sweet tea from a canning jar when Callie stuck her head in the open door. "Grandpa, I'm riding into Naples to buy a small storage drive. I'm almost out of room on my other two drives. Shooting pictures and video takes a lot of space. But the good news is I'm just about done. The new website will be so cool when it's live."

The old man turned around on his stool and smiled, sunlight streaming through two windows near him, a dozen tall orchids in clay pots. "Tell me this ... how in the world does something digital be called live? I can see it with plants, mammals, humans, even with our stubborn Persephone on her perch in the tree. She's alive, just slow to develop. But how is a website live, or for that matter, how is anything on the world wide web live unless it's a live event streaming?"

Callie grinned. "A website going live is just a figure of speech. I'm not sure, but I think it was a phrase coined in the wild west days of the Internet, before I was born."

"Oh, so last century." He chuckled. "While you're in town, young lady, can you pick up a few groceries? I'll make a list. You can add to it if you want. I know you have a sweet tooth." Chester used a lined index card to write out a short list of grocery items. He signed a check, removed it from a checkbook and gave it to Callie. "I left the amount blank. Try not to buy out the store, okay?" He gave her the check.

"Okay. You know me, Grandpa. I'm fiscally responsible."

"I'd have to agree with that." He stood, reached for his cane, and went outside with Callie, walking over to her car. "You drive safe. I'll see you in a few hours." He glanced at the Persephone orchid in the cypress tree. "You think our website will go live before we see live blossoms on our shy goddess up there?"

Callie laughed. "Don't take me wrong, Grandpa, but you've been waiting more than fifteen years for that one to bloom. I was just out of diapers when you started your vigil … your Persephone watch. I know you've grown some of the world's most beautiful and rare orchids in that time, but nothing is as stubborn as our friend in the tree."

"You too, Callie, had a rather stubborn streak at one time in your life. For the most part, you grew out of it. I think our indomitable lady in the tree will do the same."

She put her hands on her hips. "For the most part, I did grow out of it. If I have one smidgeon of stubbornness in my body, though, I get it from you." She hugged him and got in her car, windows rolled down. "Are you doing any replanting in the glades or Big Cypress today?"

"No. I'm going to be here all day. I set today aside to do research and pollination."

"When I leave, do you want me to lock the gate? If you're working inside the lab or greenhouse, maybe you don't want to be disturbed."

"You can swing it shut, but you don't need to lock it. If it's dark or getting dark when you return, I don't want you to have to use your headlights to unlock the chain. If we get a customer, maybe they'll blow their horn, and I'll grab my cane and come as fast as a three-legged man can walk. Love you."

"Love you, too."

Seventy-Five

Joe Billie pulled his ten-year-old, black Chevy truck into his hardpacked dirt driveway next to his Airstream trailer, parked and got out. The bed of the truck was loaded with palm fronds he'd cut deep in the wilderness on property east of Inverness, Florida, near the Withlacoochee River. It was land that, two-hundred years earlier, Seminole leader Osceola used as his last refuge from U.S. Army soldiers. Billie felt a peace there, often eating his lunch atop an earthen mound left behind centuries ago by the Calusa, a race of people long extinct from Florida.

In his mid-fifties, Billie stood over six feet, dressed in jeans and a black T-shirt. He was thick in the chest, olive skin face, with creases around the eyes from spending most of his life outdoors in the sunlight. His shoulder-length hair, gray mixed with the black, was pulled back in a ponytail. He leaned over the truck panel and picked up a machete that was wedged between the palm fronds and the interior side of the truck.

Walking to his front door, he could sense the recent presence of a visitor. Maybe it was one of his fish-camp neighbors. He looked down at the soil. No visible tracks. Nothing looked disturbed. The garden appeared as he'd left it a week ago. The chair near the door had not been moved. And then he saw the paper sticking out of the doorframe. Billie removed and read it. The note was from Sean O'Brien, requesting that he call him. Billie unlocked his door, walked inside the trailer, finding his phone on the kitchen counter. He looked at the screen. Dead. He plugged a charger wire into the base of his phone and set it in the corner.

• • •

Returning from Naples, Callie Hogan slowed her car as she approached the entrance to her grandfather's gravel driveway. She glanced in the rearview mirror, the last deep orange tinges of sunset in the west behind the jagged tree line. She put on her turn signal even though there was no car behind her, turning off the Tamiami Trail onto to the driveway. She drove a few feet, stopping to open the gate she'd closed but not locked six hours earlier.

The gate's open.

She played back the conversations with her grandfather. She didn't recall him saying he was leaving the property.

Are you doing any replanting in the glades or Big Cypress today?

No. I'm going to be here all day. I set today aside to do research and pollination.

Callie licked her lips, turned on the car's headlights in the murky darkness as twilight descended over the cypress and oak trees, a full moon rising in the east. She drove across the entrance, stopped her car and got out. She closed the gate, locking it. A mosquito whined in her face, the deep-throated bellow of a frog coming from the canal that ran alongside the paved highway, the heat of the day quickly fading.

She got back in her car and drove down the gravel road, her headlights raking across the trees and orchids Grandpa had planted through the years along both sides of the driveway. There was a movement up ahead, near the first bend in the drive. A young deer stood and stared into the lights, the deer jumped over two orchids and was lost in the veil of darkness.

Callie turned the car radio off, the rock music suddenly distractive, almost alien in the primal environment. She kept both hands on the wheel, the sound of gravel and small sticks under her tires. For some unknown reason, her heart beat a little faster. There was no real reason for her to be anxious. Maybe her grandfather had gone somewhere and left the gate open for her when he returned. Maybe he'd had a customer.

She drove the last fifty yards as the driveway made its final twist and led to the compound. Her grandfather's truck seemed to be exactly where it was parked before she left. But something didn't feel right. She realized there were no lights on in the cabin. Grandpa always turned on the flood lights when she was coming home after dark to make it easier for her to park and see around her car. Not tonight.

But there were lights coming from the greenhouse.

She parked and got out, putting her purse strap over her shoulder, leaving the grocery bags in the car. "Grandpa!" She waited, the only sound coming from cicadas in the woods. "Grandpa!" Nothing. She put her car keys in her purse, leaving the headlights on as she walked down the gravel path to the greenhouse. The door was partially ajar. She reached for the handle and opened the door. "Grandpa … are you in here?"

No response.

She entered, quickly looking at the length of the long greenhouse. Some of the LED grow lights were on, casting shadows among the hundreds of orchids. She couldn't see her grandfather anywhere. She walked down the center aisle, toward the workbench where he'd labor to cross-pollinate plants.

Her heart beat faster, the heady scent of the flowers was thicker than usual, less perfumed and now muskier. It was an odd odor. Something she had never smelled in the greenhouse before now. Callie knew that dogs can smell fear from other animals and even humans. Could flowers—orchids do the same thing? It was as if they'd secreted pheromones of distress, the heavy collective smell of gloom … maybe death.

She spotted his hand first. It was clenched in a fist. Just visible on the floor in a short aisle leading to the workbench. "Grandpa!" She ran the rest of the way, stopping to look down at her grandfather's body lying on the old wooden floor.

Callie froze. She held her hand to her mouth. She couldn't speak. She stared at her grandfather's body, his eyes open, face ashen, a dark stain of blood near his heart, soaked into his khaki shirt. Finally, her vocal cords opened. At the top of her lungs, she released a long, primal scream.

Her eyes filled with tears. She dropped to her knees. Reaching for her grandfather. Blood on her fingertips. Her mind numb, lips trembling, a stream of saliva falling from her lower lip. "Grandpa … oh dear God no. No! Please, God!" She sobbed, chest heaving, tears rolling down her face and falling onto her grandfather's beard. She lowered her head to his chest and wept.

Callie fought back the strong urge to vomit, somehow finding the strength to stand. She stared at the hundreds of orchids, the bright blooms appeared drained of color under the white lights. She almost fell, stepping to the workbench, holding onto the back of her grandfather's high-back chair. She looked up at the corkboard, her vision blurred by tears. She wiped her eyes with her hands and scanned the dozens of business cards on the board.

Callie found the one she remembered. "Sean O'Brien …" she whispered, reaching into her purse for her phone. Her hands and fingers trembling so much she could barely touch the correct numbers on the keyboard, stopping when she touched a wrong digit, looking at the card and starting over again. On her third try, she did it. The phone rang.

And on the third ring, he answered.

Seventy-Six

I had just finished a long walk with Max, coming down L dock, when Callie Hogan called and said, "My Grandpa ... he's dead. Please help me." She continued talking, hysterically, sobbing so loud and hard I couldn't understand most of what she was trying to say.

"Callie ... stop. Take a deep breath through your nose and release it through your mouth. After that, try to slowly tell me what happened, okay?"

I heard a muffled, "Okay." A few seconds later, she told me what she'd just found, her voice raspy, filled with sobs.

"Here's what I want you to do, Callie. Call 9-1-1 immediately. Your grandfather's cabin is in Collier County. They'll send sheriff's deputies and detectives. Tell them exactly what you found, okay?"

"Okay."

"After that, stay on the line with the dispatcher. Don't hang up. Turn around and leave the greenhouse immediately. Don't touch anything. Door knobs. His work place, the body ... nothing more than you've already touched. When you are out of the greenhouse, don't enter the cabin. Go to your car. Remember to stay on the phone with the 9-1-1 operator until your car door is locked, and you've turned the motor on, okay?"

"Okay ... but can you come, too, please. My Grandpa really liked you, he said he thought you had been a good detective. Please help ..."

"Yes, I will come to you. And I'll have my good friend, the woman who was with me the last time you saw me, Detective Wynona Osceola, come as well. She'll be able to get there sooner than I can. Because she's investigating the death of Joe Thaxton, she'll want to speak with you, too. Do you understand?"

"Yes. I'll call 9-1-1. But please hurry."

• • •

I called Wynona, told her what Callie told me and said, "I'm leaving the marina now. I'll get there as soon as I can. You might want to arrive when the sheriff's office is investigating. I know it's out of your jurisdiction, but this has to be connected to Thaxton's death. It also will be a comfort to Callie to have you there as you'll be the only one she'll recognize."

"I'm on my way as we speak. Chester never saw Craig Moffett in the glades that day. Maybe Detective Cory Gilson will see the light and drop his insidious effort, suggesting Thaxton's death was an accident and pursuing manslaughter charges against Moffett. I'll see you when you get there, Sean. I know you're going to ignore what I'm about to say next, but I'll say it because I care about you. Please don't drive too fast. Your Jeep is great for the glades, not so great at a hundred miles an hour on two-lane roads."

"I'll be cautious. See you soon." I disconnected and looked down at Max. "Gotta go. Who do you want to do the sleepover with, Dave or Nick?"

We walked quickly toward *Jupiter*. I packed an overnight bag, putting my Glock in the pack. When I walk out to my Jeep, I'll place the Glock in the special place I have between the front seats, close to where my right hand could reach.

I locked *Jupiter*, turned to Max and said, "Let's go." Nick was walking across the dock to *Gibraltar*, an open cooler of stone crab claws on ice.

"Sean, look at this treasure chest. I'm gonna be steamin' these puppies later. Sorry, Maxie. Then we put the claws back on ice, let 'em cool down for the full flavor. Dave says he'll make some of his German mustard. Why don't you and Hot Dawg come over? We got plenty.

I traded a crabber pal of mine a dozen red snappers for these. I think I got the better end of the deal."

"I'd like to, Nick, but I have to go. I'll walk with you to Dave's boat and explain what's happening."

On *Gibraltar*, I told Dave and Nick what Callie had told me. Dave said, "What a damn shame. I'd spent some time reading some of the articles about Chester Miller and his research. From Smithsonian to National Geographic, he's been there. That gentleman and scholar is taking sixty-plus-years-worth of orchid research to his grave. The deaths of Joe Thaxton and Chester Miller have to be connected."

Nick said, "This kinda shit sounds like the mafia, Sean. The old man was the only eyewitness, somebody comes and kills him while he works in his greenhouse. Looks like a contract killer is on the loose. How the hell do you find him without putting your hand into a hornet's nest?"

"Best time to hit a hornet's nest is at night. When they're not active. Not on guard. I'll work with Wynona and Detective Gilson. Do whatever I can to help."

In the dock lighting, Dave watched a brown pelican alight on the transom of a 61-foot Bertram sports fishing yacht in the slip opposite *Gibraltar*. He cut his eyes over to me. "I hope you can work within the law enforcement system. You've been out quite a while. I know you're close to Wynona. That could complicate things even more. Like Nick said, it could be a far-reaching hornet's nest. And, if you get there, you might not have the cover of darkness on your side."

Seventy-Seven

I knew there'd be no access. Rarely do officers at an active crime scene allow a private investigator beyond the yellow tape. A mile before I arrived at Chester Miller's driveway, I called Wynona. She met me at the entrance. Two TV news trucks were there. The reporters speaking with deputies, trying to gain further access to the crime scene. I saw one taller deputy shaking his head. No admittance, at least not now.

Another deputy had given Wynona a ride in his car. She thanked him and got in my Jeep, the taller deputy waving me through. As I drove down the driveway, she said, "You got here a lot faster than I thought you would."

"Wasn't much traffic. What's the situation?"

"It appears to have happened in the greenhouse. It looks like Chester was shot once in the chest, the round most likely entering his heart. The ME arrived about forty minutes ago. He's still here. Forensic techs are dusting for prints, pulling every visible sample they can. Maybe they'll find something."

"When did you get here?"

"Not long after the first responders."

"Any chance you saw tire prints that might not be from Chester's truck, Callie's car, an ambulance or sheriff's cruisers?"

"No. It was dark. As you know, most of the driveway is gravel. It might be hard to find a spot of soft dirt to lift a tire impression. And now that the cavalry's arrived, it'd be next to impossible."

I said nothing, driving around the last twist in the road, blue and white lights pulsating against the old bark of tall cypress trees. I counted six deputy sheriff's cars, two unmarked vehicles, an ambulance, a coroner's dark blue van, and the medical examiner's white van.

A deputy stepped from the shadows, near the crime scene tape and held up his hand, like a crossing guard. Wynona rolled her window down. "He's with me. We'll park next to my car."

The deputy looked at me, nodding. "No problem."

I parked and asked, "Is Cory Gilson here?"

"Yes. He's examining the scene, and he's spoken with Callie."

"Where is she?"

Wynona pointed over to the cabin. I could just make out a silhouette sitting in partial darkness, the blue and white lights bouncing off the cabin's tin roof, the foreign light punching into the knotholes and crevices of the dark exteriors.

Looking at Callie alone, sitting in one of her grandfather's antique rocking chairs, I wanted to immediately go to her, her pain and horror palpable even from the short distance. Wynona said, "Before I spoke with Callie, I just held her. She pretty much fell into my arms, crying. After a while, I sat down beside her, and we talked. She called her parents. She told me how she found her grandfather, lying on his back in the greenhouse, blood on his shirt near the heart. She said her mind went blank, remembering nothing until she got you on the phone, Sean. Whatever you told her seemed to help. Deputies found Callie locked in her car, curled up and crying. Her phone in one hand.

I looked toward the greenhouse, crime scene tape around the perimeter. "Is the body still in there?"

"Yes."

"Let's take a walk."

Wynona nodded, and I followed her past deputies and investigators, the stammer of police radios was a strange language on an island in the stream of nature—a place of blooming flowers and life. We ducked under the yellow tape and entered the greenhouse. I counted seven people near the body. Forensics techs, two deputies, and one woman with letters CID on the back of her shirt.

I could see Cory Gilson speaking with the ME, an older man with a white beard and ruddy cheeks shining in the warm air, his corduroy pants held up on his beanstalk frame by red suspenders. Cory was taking notes on a pad, the overhead LED lights casting his face in strong shadow.

Another detective, a taller man who appeared to be Hispanic, spoke with one of the forensics techs, the other taking pictures of the body. I followed Wynona as she walked through the greenhouse, the heavy scent of flowers and pollen mixed with human sweat, floating in the motionless air. Cory looked over at us, nodding once, continuing his conversation with the ME.

We approached the body, and I felt like I had always sensed when investigating homicides. The deep feeling of loss that stayed behind after a life was taken. It started when I looked into the victim's eyes. I never thought there was a moral dispatch or message left behind. But there was a death mask of terror.

The eyes were often the twin portholes to the horror the victim faced at the hands of someone who was intent on killing them. The eyes always drew me to them, forced me to look into them, to try and see what the victim had seen—had suffered at the tragic end of his or her life. It was what stayed with you long after the autopsy, the burial, and the photographs in the news.

It's what haunted you during the night when an investigation had stalled. When everyone but the victim's family had moved on with their lives. When holidays and birthdays came and went. Place settings no longer set. Cards no longer sent or received. It was the silent human misery, the hole in the heart of the victim's family cut with the dull knife of sorrow that left scars of grief ... forever.

I thought about Callie sequestered up on her grandfather's front porch, staring through the blue and white lights, watching a murder investigation happen on the hallowed and safe grounds of a home she temporarily shared with a grandfather so dear to her. I knelt down beside the body, looked into the pale blue eyes of Chester Miller and wanted to see what he'd seen. What had he said to the killer? What, if anything, had the killer said to him? I could see how it happened. Why did it happen?

I saw potting soil under the fingers of his left hand, the same hand that still wore a thin gold band on his left finger. I studied the body down to the bare feet. Among the thick silver beard, I saw a reddish tint to one whisker under his chin. "Do you have gloves?" I asked Wynona.

She nodded and lifted a pair of plastic gloves from a cardboard container near the metal coroner's gurney a few feet away. She put the gloves on and knelt down beside me. I pointed to beneath the chin. "There … take a look. Maybe a speck of blood."

"Could have happened when he was hit by the round."

"I don't think it came from blood splatter. Can you part the beard in the area?"

Wynona used both hands to part the thick whiskers. We could see what appeared to be a cut under the chin." She looked over at me and said, "I wonder how he got that?"

"Did the perp strike him under the chin, or did he get it from somewhere else?"

"Good question. I'm sure the ME would have found it during the autopsy, but I'll mention it to him and Detective Gilson before the body is loaded."

I thought about what Chester had said to me the first time I'd stopped in to buy orchids for Wynona. It was after he'd asked for my card. *That's noble, and about all anyone can ask of a person. I have a feeling that you might solve more than you don't.*

Wynona said, "It was obviously done at close range. Large caliber gun. The ME says the round exited Chester's back. Forensic techs are searching through all of these orchids, trying to see if the bullet is lodged somewhere in one of them. There's no indication it went through any of the greenhouse walls."

I nodded and stood, studying the immediate area. It looked like the last time I'd seen it. Potting soil scattered in areas up and down the long workbench. Small tools, knives, tweezers and a magnifying glass on the bench. A half-consumed cup of black coffee. Wynona said,

"He probably faced his killer at the time of the shooting. God only knows what was said, if anything."

A perspiring man wearing a dark blue windbreaker with the word *Coroner* on the back of it approached and said, "If you folks are done with the body, we'd like to move it at this time."

Wynona said, "We're done. Thanks."

He said nothing as he gestured for two other men to help him with a metal gurney and white sheet.

Seventy-Eight

Two members of the coroner's staff wheeled a gurney outside. The body was covered with a white sheet. They pushed and pulled around large clay pots filled with orchids. The techs finally collapsing the gurney. They lifted it from the ground and carried it at least seventy-five feet to the waiting van, the emergency lights reflecting from the white sheet, one of Chester's bare feet partially showing.

I looked toward the cabin's front porch. Callie had pulled her feet up and onto the chair, she hugged her knees, her head down. Wynona said, "I mentioned the cut under the chin to the ME. He said he's doing the autopsy in the morning."

"I want to go up on the front porch and talk with Callie, but before we do that, let's go around to the back."

"You mean to the lab?"

"No, I'm thinking about the big cypress tree where the rare orchid is growing."

We walked to the left of the cabin and approached the cypress tree. The ladder was down, the first time I'd seen it on its side. I used my flashlight to examine it.

"What are you looking for?" Wynona asked.

"Something I probably won't find … blood. What if Chester hit his chin on one of the rungs on the ladder? Forced off of it and maybe slipping."

"Possibility. But why do you think that might have happened?"

"Because this ladder is always propped up against the tree. Chester climbs it every day to check on that rare orchid, Persephone, he calls it." I moved the light to the orchid. "It's perched up there on the wooden plank that looks like a bird feeder." I looked at the beach apple tree not far from the ladder. "That tree—it's a beach apple. Chester called it a manchineel. He said it was derived from the Spanish word manzanilla which means little apple. It's a little apple with a big punch—one of the most poisonous trees in the world. It's more like a large bush. It would be a good place for the perp to hide if he snuck up on Chester, marched him into the greenhouse and shot him to death. And, if the perp touched parts of the tree, it may have touched him back—and not in a good way."

"That's a possibility, unless he was already in the greenhouse when the perp got here."

"Maybe. I want to talk with Callie. Maybe Cory's done by now, too." We walked to the front of the cabin. I could see Cory and another detective talking with the coroner near the blue van. I motioned to the front porch, and we climbed the three wooden steps to the porch.

Callie looked up from gripping her knees. "Sean, you came." Her face was stained in tracks of tears. Some dried. Some still wet. She stood, and I gave her a hug. She started crying in soft sobs.

"I'm so sorry, Callie. We'll find the person who did this."

She said nothing, her tears dampening my shirt. After a moment, she stood straighter, taking a half step backwards, her eyes roaming my face. "Why did Grandpa have to die? He could never hurt anything or anyone. He was a pacifist who loved nature and people."

"Did it look like anyone had entered the cabin?" I asked.

"No. I checked the door when I came up here to sit. It was locked. I unlocked it for the police and detectives."

"How about your grandfather's workshop lab behind the cabin?"

"I unlocked it for them, too."

Wynona said, "Nothing appears to have been stolen or moved out of place. It looks like the perp entered the property and quickly did what he came to do."

I looked down the yard toward the greenhouse. "Callie, did your grandfather have any security cameras out here?"

"No. He was a trusting person. He didn't feel that people would steal his orchids, even though some are worth a lot of money. He'd give orchids away to people he felt couldn't afford to pay for them. I saw him do it twice this summer. I'm not sure how Grandpa knew these people didn't have the money to pay. And the people were always so grateful. Usually retired couples in older cars." She watched the coroner speak to his staff. "Where are they taking Grandpa?"

Wynona said, "The medical examiner will do an autopsy. It's the law in murder cases."

She folded her arms across her breasts. "It's pretty obvious what killed him. Some evil person shot my grandfather in the heart."

"Yes, but there could be other things, other forensic evidence the medical examiner might find."

Callie looked from Wynona to me and asked, "Do you think Grandpa was murdered because he saw that man in the glades at the time Grandpa found the dead man's truck? Did that person come here, come to our home, and shoot an eighty-five-year old man in his heart?"

"I don't know. But I do think there is a connection."

Wynona said, "Callie, do you have someplace to stay tonight, a friend or family? You shouldn't stay here tonight."

"My mother has a close friend in Naples. I could probably stay with her. My parents will be down here in the morning."

I could see that Cory was done speaking with the coroner. Cory jotted another few words in his notepad, blue lights raking across his chest and face. He started to make a phone call when I walked to the front steps and asked, "Got a minute?"

317

Seventy-Nine

The phone vibrated twice in my pocket. I ignored it as Wynona and I walked from the cabin porch toward Cory Gilson. He said, "Sean, good to see you, although I wish the circumstances were better." He cut his eyes up to the porch.

"I agree. Chester Miller was a fine man."

"You knew him personally?"

"I first bought orchids from him when Sherri was alive. And I recently bought some more. What do you have?"

"Not a lot. Gunshot wound to the chest. Looks to be a powerful caliber … maybe a .45. No spent shells to be found. Nothing seems to have been taken. No attempt to make it look like a robbery. The perp was probably in and out in minutes. Way back here off Highway 41, nobody could hear it. No obvious tire tread marks. Unfortunately, his granddaughter came home and found the body." He paused, angling his head, waving a mosquito out of his face. "Go on and say it, Sean. I know you're thinking it."

Wynona said, "So am I … so I'll say it. This has nothing to do with Craig Moffett. It, most likely, has everything to do with whoever Chester Miller saw out there in the glades when he found Thaxton's truck."

Cory took a deep breath and exhaled. "I think you're right. What looked like manslaughter on the surface, due to the strong evidence, has turned into a double murder." He glanced over at the coroner's van. "And, the one person who could ID that guy is dead. Now, all we have is a tire tread impression and a possible make of the vehicle."

"Maybe that's all we need," Wynona said. "If we can find the vehicle, match the impression, we can make an arrest."

"That's a big if."

"It'll take time, but I think it can be done."

"I've had a week's vacation scheduled for almost half a year. My wife and I are supposed to be on a cruise ship next week."

"Take your vacation," Wynona said. "I'm sure the investigation will not be solved before you can return."

"I'm partnering with Jose Garcia. He's one of the best detectives in the department. I'll introduce you. He's here tonight. You'll like working with him. Maybe not as fun as working with Sean, but Jose is a close second." He smiled and looked toward the yellow crime scene tape in front of the greenhouse and then to an approaching TV news truck. "Somebody let the news hounds from hell in here. I'm glad the body's bagged and in the coroner's van."

I said, "We need to make sure the reporters don't try to interview Callie. She's in no emotional shape for that."

"Agreed," Cory said. "I'll run interference. Let 'em get their video shots, keeping out of the greenhouse, cabin and that lab out back. We'll confine them to the parking lot."

Within a half-minute, three other TV news trucks arrived, and four cars behind them. The reporters and camera operators got out. Cory said, "Excuse me for a few minutes. I need to go over there and establish some ground rules. The public's right to know doesn't compromise a crime scene. I don't care if you're NBC news, CNN, Fox or the Miami friggin Herald. It is what it is." He walked away, mumbling, quickly corralling three deputies to help him coordinate with the news media.

I turned to Wynona. "Are you going to do any interviews tonight?"

"I never come to a crime scene planning to do that, but I don't mind because I refuse to answer subjective questions or questions that might in any way hamper the investigation, but I've found that we can use the media to get our message out. I had a mentor with the FBI, he was a former police chief before growing bored and applying to the Bureau. He used to say, and I'm quoting here: *'Somebody knows something. Somebody's seen or heard something. The news media is the best way to reach those somebodies.'*"

I managed to smile, remembering the phone call I'd received when I first arrived. I pulled my phone from my pocket and looked at the caller log. I recognized the number of the last caller.

Joe Billie.

I looked over at Wynona. "Joe Billie called me. Let's see if we can reach him."

Eighty

I made the call from inside my Jeep. With the news media descending on the scene, the interviews going on, I wanted a quiet place to speak with Joe Billie. I made the call and waited. As it went through, ringing twice, I watched Wynona being interviewed by a blonde reporter, hair bobbed just below her ears. I kept my eyes on the cabin's front porch. We'd asked a deputy to stand vigilant, keeping any media away from Callie. On the fourth ring, Joe Billie answered. "Hey, Sean."

"Hi, Joe. It's good to see that you're using caller ID."

"Your number is one of five I have filed in my phone. It's not hard to remember." Billie stood on the outside of his Airstream trailer, moths circling a flood light near him. "Sorry I didn't get back with you sooner. I was over near the west coast. You know the area well, close to the Flying Eagle Preserve. I have an order to build a chickee for a hotel on the bay in Naples. I cut a truck load of fronds for the job."

"I'm close to Naples right now. As a matter of fact, Wynona and I will be escorting a college student from Big Cypress to her friend's house in Naples. The girl's grandfather was murdered today. It's a very bad scene. Did you know a man by the name of Chester Miller?"

"Yes. Not too well. I'd met him a couple of times. He used to visit Sam Otter. Was Chester the one killed?"

"Yes." I told Billie the story and brought him up to date with the investigation into the death of Joe Thaxton. I concluded by saying, "I believe Thaxton's drone is somewhere in the glades or maybe Big Cypress Preserve. I was hoping you might help Wynona and I look for it. We can show you exactly where Thaxton was last when he flew his drone. Maybe you can see something deputies and searchers missed out there. Can you meet us?"

Billie looked at the moon coming up over the canebrake, the buttery reflection shimmering across the black belly of the river, a bat chasing moths and gnats. "I'll do what I can. Can't make any promises."

"I'm the first to understand. When can you come? We can meet you at the entrance to 15 Mile Road off Highway 41."

"Today's Tuesday. I'm supposed to visit the rez on Thursday. Would Thursday morning work?"

"We'll make it work. Thanks, Joe."

"Save the thanks for if and when we're successful. I've tracked a lot of things in my life. Drones don't leave tracks. Should make it challenging. See you Thursday at around eight in the morning."

• • •

Two hours later, Wynona and I watched Callie park her car in the driveway of a two-story, Mediterranean-style home near Pelican Bay in Naples. The house appeared to be larger than five-thousand-square-feet. Pitched gables. Clay tile roof. Pockets of soft light showcasing the home's exterior. The verdant yard was landscaped with Canary Island date palms and sabal palms.

Wynona said, "I'm going to go with her to the front door. If I detect the smallest hint of deception in whomever opens the door, Callie can stay with me or I'll get her a hotel room."

"Good idea."

Wynona got out of my Jeep and walked with Callie over a sidewalk adjacent to the front yard, leading to the door. Callie pulled a suitcase on wheels. The front porch light came on and the door opened. From where I sat, I could see a middle-aged woman step out and give Callie a long, heartfelt hug. Wynona smiled, chatting with the woman briefly, and then Callie stepped inside the home, the door closing.

Wynona got back in the Jeep. "The lady's name is Janice. She and her husband, Charles, have known Callie since she was in diapers. Apparently, Janice and Callie's mom attended the University of North Carolina at the same time. Her parents will be coming here in the morning."

I started to put the Jeep in gear when Wynona looked over at me. "I feel so bad for Callie. She was as devoted to her grandfather as he was to her. They shared a bond that was sweet to watch. In a way, Callie reminds me of myself when I was her age. Focused. Dedicated to learning as much as possible about what she loves and wants to do with her life. Sean, we have to find this killer. Thank God Callie wasn't there when he entered the property … or we would have three homicides."

"She's lucky, and I think she knows it. Doesn't take away any of the pain from her grandfather's death, but she's still here to carry on his legacy and build one of her own."

"I have no doubt that she will."

"I wonder if the perp was watching Chester's place, saw Callie leave, and entered. He could have driven onto the land with the intent to take out Chester; and if anyone else had been there, they could have been killed, too. That was risky, considering the fact that Chester sells orchids to the public. There could have been customers at the time or any time during …" I backed out of the driveway.

Wynona said, "If there were customers present, all the killer had to do was stay in his car, lie low until they left. Don't make eye contact. Then do the hit and leave."

"You said hit. Do you think that's what it was, a contract hit … or was the perp coming back to take out the only witness who could ID him?"

"I don't know. I do know that, if Chester had never done those TV interviews, chances are the killer would not have a clue that Chester thought he could recognize him."

"Maybe."

"Maybe? Sean, what do you mean?"

"Unless the sheriff is somehow connected to all of this and might have relayed Chester's name to whomever is responsible for Thaxton's killing. If the sheriff hadn't leaned in so hard on pushing for manslaughter charges against Craig Moffett, I wouldn't be saying that."

"But you smell a rat, right?"

"I detect police behavior that's not consistent with the known parameters of an investigation. I think he's too eager to wrap it up without tying the loose ends. And, now, there are a lot of loose ends."

Wynona was silent for a long moment. "If you're right, do you think that Cory Gilson is complicit? You know him. I don't."

"I don't know. I do think he wants to keep his job at least until his daughter is out of college. The sheriff's ultimately calling the shots. It's sort of a good cop—bad cop, with Cory trying to run a joint investigation with you when his boss is more impatient than the circumstances require. Chester's murder will remove the heat from Craig Moffett. I just want to find out who is ultimately responsible for the death of Thaxton, because that person is now responsible for Chester's murder. And, if this goes way up some corporate pedigree, we have an executive who is fundamentally no different than any serial killer, only worth more money."

"I wonder how many degrees of separation—the handlers, managers, the PR people … all the built-in buffers there are between him and Joe Thaxton. And now, Chester Miller."

"Maybe we'll find out."

Wynona said nothing, watching traffic coming out of an upscale shopping mall. "I have to get my car."

"We'll head back that way."

"I wish I hadn't left it parked near Chester's cabin. That's the last place I want to return to right now. But I need to get it." She looked across the seat at me. "Are you going back to the marina or your house tonight?"

"I haven't decided yet."

"Well, maybe I can help you with your decision. My house in closer than yours."

"Good suggestion."

• • •

After a light dinner of turkey sandwiches and potato salad, Wynona and I sat outside on her deck in Adirondack chairs, the moon almost full and breaking through the clouds. We could hear the hoot of a great horned owl in the adjacent woodlands. She looked over at me. "Ever since I was a little girl, I loved the call of the owl."

"I hear it occasionally at my cabin on the river."

"I remember hearing it there the last time I was with you. In the Seminole culture, the various clans are named or derived from animals. There were many, including the alligator, deer, panther and fox clans. Ours was the owl. And these are inherited from the mother's side of the family. Members of the tribe were forbidden to marry within your particular clan."

"Are you still a member of the owl clan?"

"Yes, but now it's so far removed from the culture, it's pretty much mostly history and not actively present. There are exceptions, of course. People like Sam Otter and the older members of the tribe practice what they were taught. Sam will probably light a special fire for Chester and grieve in the ways of the elders." She was quiet for half a minute. "I know you still grieve for Sherri and always will. I hope one day your heart will have room for someone who loves you as much as you loved her. I can't compete with your memories of her, Sean, but I can and do love you."

The owl made a long hoot into the night. Wynona took my hand and said, "There's something I need to tell you."

"Okay ... what is it?"

"I'm pregnant. The child is yours ... or ours might be the better word. I just wanted you to know."

She looked over at me, her eyes roaming my face and slightly welling. She was radiant in the soft moonlight. I leaned closer and kissed her lips, using my thumb to wipe a tear from her left cheek. She smiled and took a deep breath. "I'm only telling you that because I wanted you to know. That's all. No obligation. No commitment if you're not ready. Because, for me, Sean ... you have to be fully committed if we're going to have a family together. If not I will raise the child on my own. I won't abort a gift, especially one conceived in love. It's too precious."

I smiled. "I don't do things partially. If I commit, I'm fully committed. And I am."

She said, "I know that love comes with risks of allowing yourself to be vulnerable. To take emotional chances. And I know, for whatever reason, that's difficult for you to do. But for me, guarded as I've always been all of my life, you are more than worth the risk of failure at this thing called love."

"Sometimes the biggest risks are those we take with our hearts. I've never been one for playing it safe only cautious in finding what matters. Rather than think of what if it doesn't work out … let's focus on what if it does, okay?"

She nodded. "Okay."

I kissed her again, warm tears spilling from her gorgeous brown eyes.

"I love you Sean … and I always will."

Eighty-One

It was almost nine in the morning the next day when I arrived back at Ponce Marina, Max greeting me like I'd been gone a year. Dave ground Blue Mountain coffee beans and made a pot of coffee. I sat with him and Nick around a table on *Gibraltar's* cockpit and told them what we'd found on Chester Miller's property. Dave sipped his coffee and said, "Sadly, I think this definitely confirms the connection between the unknown suspect that Chester saw in the glades and Joe Thaxton."

Nick said, "Who would shoot an eighty-five-year old man—a kind, old scientist, in the heart like they were shooting a rabid animal?"

"Whoever killed Thaxton," Dave said. He looked across the table at me. "Now that Chester is gone as a prime witness, all that you and Wynona have is a tire tread impression."

"At this point, yes. Maybe the forensic reports from Chester's greenhouse will come up with something else. We may have something else."

"What?" asked Nick.

"Joe Billie. He's going with us to the area spot where Thaxton was shot. Not the place where he died, but to where he was flying his drone at or near the time he was shot. If the drone is somewhere out there, we're hoping Joe can find it."

Dave grinned. "Even for a guy with Joe's talents, that will be a hell of a challenge unless he's using a drone, an eye-in-the-sky, to hunt for the one that could be lost in the glades."

"I know he has a few tracking tricks up his sleeve, but I don't think a drone is part of Billie's arsenal."

Dave nodded. "The Everglades is about a million and a half acres in size. Big Cypress Preserve is well over 700-thousand acres. I'd say Joe Billie will have his skills tested to the limits. On another note, you mentioned the hesitancy of the sheriff to pursue this beyond Craig Moffett and manslaughter charges. Chester's death seems to exonerate Moffett. Do you believe the sheriff is on the take?"

"I know he's taken campaign money from some of the industries Thaxton was targeting. Is the sheriff complicit in the deaths? I don't know. I think he's too close to the special interests, and that's a dangerous relationship when it comes to enforcing the law."

Nick pursed his lips, exhaling. "How do you deal with that?"

"You try to keep him out of the way until the evidence pushes him into a corner. Although he was running interference, Wynona and Detective Cory Gilson want to put cuffs on the guy who actually pulled the trigger … twice. And they'd like to get him to tell them who hired him."

My phone buzzed on the table. "Speaking of Wynona. She's on the line." I answered, and she said, "I got a Miami address for a guy who recently had the oil pan in his X-1 BMW repaired. The BMW service manager returned my call, and according to him, the car had a lot of mud, twigs and what he said looked like sawgrass beneath the undercarriage. He said the owner, Michael Fazio, had it towed to the dealership and told him that the car had been stolen."

"Is the car fixed?"

"Yes."

"Do you know if, when the car was being repaired, the service department offered this guy a loaner car?"

"I did ask that. The rep said Fazio declined and called for an Uber."

"What do you want to do?"

"Question the guy. At this point, I may not have probable cause to get a search warrant, but I can knock on his door. I called Cory Gilson and his partner, Detective Garcia. Both are up to their eyeballs in the Chester Miller investigation. Cory said he could go over there with me on Thursday, but that's the day we meet Joe Billie. Do you want to go with me to talk to Fazio?"

"I do. I'll drive down ninety-five south."

"Can you meet me in the parking lot of the Seminole Hard Rock Hotel? It's close to I-95 near the Florida Turnpike."

"What's this guy's name again?"

"Michael Fazio. I ran him through every database we have. He's a bad guy. I'll tell you how bad when you get here." She disconnected.

I looked up at Dave and Nick. "Wynona managed to find the needle in the haystack—a BMW that fits all the criteria down to the sawgrass stuck to the undercarriage. She's going to pay the guy a visit. I'll join her. I have no official capacity … no more than a bounty hunter would have. But that's all I need." I paused and watched a man fishing from M dock, the man dropping bait on a hook near the underwater pilings covered in barnacles. "I may need something else."

"What's that?" Dave asked.

Do you happen to have a spare GPS tracker on *Gibraltar* … maybe one with a magnet that would adhere well to the underside of a car?"

"I do have one. Still in the box. It's yours if you want it."

"Thanks." I leaned over and lifted Max to my lap. "Gotta go again, kiddo. Could you hang with Nick and Dave for a little while until I get back?"

Max licked my chin and then looked across the table at Dave and Nick as if she was about to choose.

Eighty-Two

I drove faster than the speed limit south on I-95. Wynona, dressed in a black blazer, pale gray shirt and black jeans, left her car in the parking lot and got in my Jeep. She said, "I have Fazio's address on my phone's GPS. Let's just hope he's home when we arrive."

"Maybe we'll get lucky."

"I called Miami-Dade PD and let CID know I'd be in their neighborhood. Not only is it a professional courtesy, I want a contact if push comes to shove, and we need backup. Also, I called a contact of mine in the FBI's Miami office, just to let him know we're here."

"My former partner, Ron Hamilton, is a senior detective. I'll call him, too. What do you have on Fazio?"

"Although I now longer work for the FBI, I still have contacts in the Bureau who can put their fingers on the latest criminal data. Early in his criminal career, Michael Fazio served seven years out of a ten-year sentence for armed robbery, aggravated assault and second-degree manslaughter. In an Irish bar called the Shamrock in south Boston, he hit a man one time in the face during an argument over a debt. The guy died on the way to the hospital. Fazio said it was self-defense, and he was only standing his ground. Fazio was a soldier, an enforcer, on the Jersey waterfront for the Genovese family. After his boss was killed, Fazio went freelance. He worked as a contract mercenary in Iraq for almost two years. When he came back to the states, it seems he refined his skills that he learned in the Middle East, sniper skills as well as teaching hand-to-hand combat."

"Who's he working for now? Who owns the condo?"

"This condo unit is owned, or allegedly owned, by a multi-national company called Triton Worldwide. They appear to be in shipping, construction and agriculture. They have offices in Athens, Greece; New Jersey; and here in Miami."

"Sometimes things aren't as they appear."

Wynona glanced between our seats, the grip of my Glock just visible. "Did you bring anything more than a handgun?"

"You mean something like a 12-gauge shotgun?"

"That's always a show closer."

"No, but I did bring a GPS tracker."

"Not nearly as intimidating."

"Maybe this guy will get the urge to take another field trip into the glades. We can tag along at a distance. We know he won't have much if anything to say. We can read his body language to see if our initial questions elicit a response."

"For a guy like Fazio, a hired gun, there's little human response in the eyes of a psychopath."

"Depends on how fast and hard we can sting him. If we can be a rock in his hoof, maybe he'll lead us to a blacksmith. In this case, the person he's working for."

Wynona smiled. "I like your western metaphors. For a Florida boat kind of guy, I think you'd make a good cowboy."

"I always liked John Wayne movies."

We followed the GPS voice directions through neighborhoods I knew well from my time working as a detective from South Beach to Aventura. The directions were taking us to an upscale area of condos and single-family homes near Surfside Beach. "Your destination is on the left," came the computer-generated voice.

We drove another two-hundred-feet down Collins Avenue. "There it is," Wynona said, motioning toward a beachfront condo. "It's a ground-floor unit, number 129."

I drove by slowly, scanning the building and the parking areas, and then I turned around, pulling into the parking lot that ran adjacent to the high-rise condo. I said, "There's a black BMW X-1 near unit 129. Looks like it's been washed and waxed."

"No doubt." She glanced down at the paper she held in her lap. "The tread impressions came from a Continental tire, a four-by-four Contact all season, and it's a 255-50-R-19. The wear and tear marks are distinctive as well. Before going in, let's surveil the place for a little while. We may see movement."

"If nothing happens, we can quickly identify the tires. You said the impression was believed to have been made by the left rear tire. I can drop down, snap a picture of the tread, and slap on the magnetic GPS tracker at the same time in probably eight seconds, the time it takes to ride a bull."

"Okay … I'll go with that analogy."

We parked across the lot, the BMW and front door to the condo in our line of sight. We watched an elderly couple come from the condo's main entrance. The older man, dressed in an ill-fitting, plaid sports coat, salmon pink shirt, thin black tie and neatly pressed gray slacks. He held the woman's left forearm, helping her get inside a new model Cadillac. Wynona watched, smiled and said, "That's sweet."

"Yes, I have a feeling he'd open her door even if she wasn't physically challenged."

Movement to the right of the parking lot, toward Collins Avenue, caught my eye. A Toyota with a plastic Domino's Pizza sign on the roof, entered the lot. The driver didn't seem to be searching for numbers on the doors. He pulled in next to the black BMW as if he'd made the delivery more than once. He got out with a pizza encased in a zipped black warming container. He stepped up to number 129 and knocked. I could see the blinds in a front window barely part, seconds later the door opening. The man at the door spoke with the deliveryman, glancing around the parking lot, and then paying in cash.

I looked over at Wynona. "Can you recognize him from the distance?"

She studied the man as close as possible before the door closed. "I think so. Same general build and facial features."

"Well, now we know he's in there. Right after the pizza guy leaves would be a good time for us to knock on the door. Fazio may think the guy forgot something, and that just may cause him to jerk open the door without taking the time to peek through the blinds on the window."

"Let's go."

I wedged my Glock under my belt in the small of my back, keeping my shirttail out. Wynona wore her Beretta in a holster under her blazer. We walked across the lot, strolling like a couple on vacation. When we approached the BMW, I squatted down by the left rear tire. I snapped a picture of the tread and one of the sidewalls, getting the brand—a Continental and the tire size: 255-50-R-19. Then I lifted the GPS tracker to the undercarriage, the powerful magnet holding the device in place. In less than eight seconds, I stood.

I nodded at Wynona, and we approached the door. She knocked. We could hear movement inside. In a few seconds, the door opened wide. The smell of pepperoni and onions greeted us—so did Michael Fazio.

He was surprised, looking at Wynona and then eyeing me. He was my height. Entire head freshly shaved. A crescent moon scar on the bridge of his nose, the scar resembling a frown. It matched his downturned mouth. A spot of red pizza sauce on his lower lip. Wynona said, "Michael Fazio."

"Who wants to know?" His voice gruff.

She lifted her badge and ID. "I'm Detective Wynona Osceola with the Seminole Police Department. Our department is working in a joint-agency task force with the Collier County Sheriff's Office."

"What do you want?"

"To talk with you."

"About what?"

"We'd like to start with your car, that BMW. According to the service department at the dealer, you brought the car in because of a damaged oil pan. Can you tell us how the vehicle sustained that damage?"

"I didn't bring the car to the shop, I had it towed. The car was stolen. Highway Patrol found it off the road near Highway 41 and Krome Avenue. Check with them."

"We will."

He eyed me, his blue-green eyes flat. "You people, your joint agency, investigating stolen cars? Must be a slow crime period."

"No, the murder rate is up. In the glades, where your car was seen, and in Big Cypress Preserve, where a man lived who saw you and your car." Wynona went for it. "Who paid you to kill Joe Thaxton?"

I could see a vein in his forehead bulge slightly. "This conversation has officially ended. You want to talk with me, you'll do it through my attorney. His name is Julian Braverman. You can call him at his law firm in downtown Miami. We're done here."

As he started to close the door, I motioned to his left hand and arm. "Looks like you got a burn on your arm. Better check it out. White, puss-filled blisters can get infected. That's what can happen when you brush up against a manchineel tree. It's one of the most poisonous in the world. The sap from one of its little green apples killed Ponce De Leon. He was here in Florida searching for the fountain of youth. What he found was death at the end of a Calusa Indian arrow dipped in the sap from the same species of tree that you hid behind when you first ambushed Chester Miller."

He looked at me as if the pepperonis in his gut were about to come through his flaring nostrils. "I didn't get your name, dude. Why don't you give it to me, so I can give it to my lawyer to file charges against you and your department."

I smiled. "Name's Sean O'Brien. I don't work for a department. Like you, I'm freelance. And like you, I have no boundaries. Now, you can point us to the people who hired you ... then your life will go considerably better."

"Sean O'Brien ... I'll remember that. You got no jurisdiction here. Now, go fuck off."

He slammed the door.

I looked at Wynona. "Let's walk around the building to get to the Jeep. No sense in letting him know what we're driving because I'd bet that we'll be following him soon. And I don't think it'll be to his attorney's office."

Eighty-Three

Three hours later, Michael Fazio was on the move. I'd called my former Miami-Dade partner, Ron Hamilton, and brought him up to speed. I had the GPS tracker app loaded on my phone. Wynona held it in her hand as we followed the pulsating blip on the map screen. She said, "He's continuing to make all kinds of turns, backtracking, even going down what appears to be a one-way side street. I bet his eyes are almost glued to the rearview mirror."

"Of course. He's doing what he can to shake any tails. That would work if we had to rely on a visual pursuit. But he can't escape the satellite."

"I need to get a warrant to have his car impounded. The photo you took of the tire will help, but we need to do a forensics match with the tire."

"I have no doubt it'll match."

"Agreed. But, as you know, we have to stack the evidence. He's turning off Bayshore to Charthouse Drive."

"That's Coconut Grove. I know the area well. We're less than two miles from there."

"He's slowing down."

Wynona studied the phone screen. "There are restaurants in that specific area. Most with waterfront views. Looks like he's stopping the car."

"Where?"

"At the end of Charthouse. I'll get my camera ready."

"That's the Dinner Key area, near the marina."

In a couple of minutes, we were tuning into Charthouse Drive, tall canary palms lining both sides of the street. The Bohemian charm of European sidewalk cafes in a tropical setting. A young, auburn-haired woman jogging in short shorts, pink sneakers and matching halter top, her ponytail bouncing shoulder to shoulder.

I drove slowly, past boats stored in a fenced-off lot next to a three-story marina building. As we approached a waterfront restaurant, we looked for Fazio's BMW. Wasn't hard to spot. It was parked in the valet section behind a convertible F-Type Jaguar and a red Ferrari.

Wynona said, "There's his BMW. What a lovely day for dining outside."

"Let's hope our guy is under one of those colorful umbrellas."

I took a right, the bay in front of us, another section of the restaurant directly facing the waterfront view. There were lots of tanned bodies around the tables. Many the product of good genes and even better plastic surgeons. Wynona said, "There he is … in the corner. He's sitting across the table from a man." She raised her camera lens, taking two pictures in less than five seconds. "I wonder if that's his lawyer, Julian Braverman?"

"Maybe. Somehow, I doubt it."

"I'll have the photos run through a face-recognition database. The guy's got the exaggerated language of a player in the sense of being in control, but with the inflated moves of a Hollywood agent who hasn't made a sale in months. Maybe he is the lawyer."

My phone buzzed. I drove by the restaurant, glancing at the caller ID. "It's Joe Billie."

"I hope he isn't cancelling our meeting in the glades."

I pulled my Jeep into the marina parking lot, hundreds of boats tied to the docks, lazy gulls riding in the wind above Biscayne Bay. "Hey, Joe." I shut off the motor.

"Sean, I know we weren't supposed to meet until tomorrow, but if you want to get an earlier start, I can do it this afternoon. I came in earlier. Sam Otter is sick. His wife said he was asking for me. I just finished visiting with him."

"I hope he gets better."

"I think the death of Chester Miller has upset him."

"Did you tell him about Chester?"

"No. He already knew. I didn't ask him how. Sam doesn't leave his house often. Are you in the area?"

"We're in Coconut Grove. Wynona is with me. Can you meet us at Gator Gully Road off the Tamiami Trail in about ninety minutes?"

"I'll be there. We'll have a few hours of daylight left."

"Maybe that's all we'll need."

Eighty-Four

On the road to meet Joe Billie, Wynona transferred the pictures she'd taken of the man meeting Michael Fazio and emailed them to Cory Gilson. She called Cory with a detailed update of what we found. "If you have a few minutes," she said, "maybe you can check with Uber. Fazio says he heard from the Highway Patrol that his car had been found. What we'd like to know is who left it there and when he reported the BMW stolen? Maybe Fazio pulled it off the road, smoke billowing from under the hood, walked back to the intersection and called Uber. Later on, calling a tow truck to have his car hauled to the dealer."

"I can check with Uber. They'll have the pick-up records. I'll call the FHP, too."

"Thanks."

"No problem. I wonder who Fazio was meeting at that restaurant in Coconut Grove?"

"The photos I sent to you, I'm sending to a former colleague of mine in the FBI's Miami office. I'm hoping he'll run it through facial-recognition databases. I'll let you know what he finds. Shouldn't take long."

"Good. Is Sean doing okay?"

"Yes. Do you want to speak with him?"

"Not at the moment. I'll get back with you." He disconnected.

She looked at me. "Cory's checking with Uber and the FHP. It helps to split up the workload." She looked at her phone, scrolling through her contact list. "With the remaining friends I have left in the Bureau, I prefer to speak with them on their cell phones rather than call through the switchboard. Makes for better communications."

"No doubt."

"My friend's name is Eric Valdez." She made the call and filled him in on the investigation. "Great. Thank you. I'll shoot over the pictures. It shouldn't take you long to get a match. I have a feeling he's some kind of player in the Miami area."

"We'll see what we can find," said the agent, a man in his forties, short dark hair, sleeves rolled up, tie loosened, sitting at his desk in the FBI's office.

"Thanks, Eric. I owe you a lunch soon."

"No sweat." He disconnected.

Wynona put her phone back in her purse. "We should know who our mystery man is soon. And I hope Cory can get what we want from Uber."

• • •

Michael Fazio put his elbows on the table and leaned a little closer to Simon Santiago. Fazio lowered his voice, the shade from the umbrella over the table falling across his face. "You have to get me the hell outta here, you understand?"

Santiago said nothing. He lifted a plastic stir stick from the table and twisted it between two fingers. "And you need to be more cautious. How did they find and track you to the condo?"

"I wasn't in a position to ask them. But let me assure you of this ... I did everything humanly possible not to leave a trail."

"The old man saw you."

"That was because he was out there. Now, he's gone. I did the job, and that means that you and your client are more, shall we say ... secure. You need to get me to the place in Argentina."

Santiago tilted forward, his eyes drifting across Fazio's face. "I detect a veiled threat. You were spotted. The witness had to be eliminated, and now you have the security of my client to leverage a safe house for you in South America."

"You made the offer. I did the job. The heat is rising, and I need to get out, okay?"

"Yes, you did the job. But there's one more thing that needs attending. After that, your ass is on a plane."

• • •

Joe Billie was sitting on the fender of his truck when we turned off the Tamiami Trail onto Gator Gully. He was whittling a stick, slivers of bark between his high boots. He stood and greeted us both with hugs. Wynona looked at him and asked, "How's Sam Otter?"

"I wish I could give you an accurate answer. When the top medicine man in the tribe gets sick, who does he see for a second opinion? Nobody. His coloring is off. Eyes not as bright as they used to be. But shoot, he's a hundred years old." Billie chuckled, a breeze tossing his long hair. "I remember his eyes when I was a boy. When Sam would take a group of us boys out in the glades for his fabled walks and talks, I always felt his black eyes could literally see through me, at least into my heart. He taught us a lot." Billie reached in the front seat of his truck and picked up a leather satchel, the exterior worn and soft from years of use.

"Is that what I think it is?" Wynona asked.

"What do you think it is?"

"Is it a medicine bundle?"

"No, at least not the kind Sam Otter uses. It's more of a natural tool kit."

"Did Sam give it to you?"

"He loaned it to me."

"What's in it?" I asked.

Joe smiled. "I'm really not sure of all the things. Sam tells me what he wants me to know."

"I remember meeting him. Although he spoke very little English, he communicated well." I glanced at the satchel. "If it weren't for Sam Otter, I'm not sure we would have seen or at least understood the nature of the juvenile vultures we saw that day. We didn't find the body. They did."

Joe looked up at the sky, toward the northeast. He watched two carrion birds ride the air currents. "Maybe today they can help us find what's left of the drone."

Wynona glanced at the sky, nodding that she understood the undertone in Billie's statement. He lowered his eyes to both of us. "You two want to climb in my truck and we'll head out there?"

"Sounds good," I said.

• • •

A half-hour later, we stopped at the fallen cypress tree and got out of the truck. The afternoon sun was hidden behind steely gray clouds in the west, a light breeze stroked the sawgrass. Wynona said, "This is where we believe the shooter took the shot."

Joe looked at the ground near the toppled tree, walking up close, his eyes searching. Wynona said, "It's been gone over here with a fine-tooth comb. Outside the things I mentioned to you, the cigar, food wrapper and whatnot, we couldn't find any ATV tracks in this area."

Joe said nothing. He knelt down, using his fingers to touch the earth. He stood and looked at the fallen tree, the two small marks on the trunk. He raised his eyes and stared into the northwest. "How far in that direction was the man who died?"

Wynona glanced at me, arching her eyebrows. "About 150 yards."

"Show me."

Eighty-Five

We got back in his truck and drove the distance. When we parked, Wynona led him to the area where Thaxton's backpack and drone control were found. She pointed. "This is where he dropped them, or at least it is where we found the things. A blood sample was removed from here. The sample matched Thaxton's blood type and DNA. Somehow, he managed to run, walk, or crawl the distance to the reservation where the body was found."

"The man had a strong will to live," Joe Billie said, looking up at the ashen sky, the wind playing in the leaves atop the cypress trees. He watched an Everglades kite fly low over the sawgrass. He set the leather satchel on the ground and carefully opened it. Joe lifted out a small pouch, about the size of a change purse. He reached inside and used his fingers to pinch a yellow powder that looked like oak pollen. He turned, tossing it up in the air. He studied the way the powder drifted.

Wynona said nothing, watching Joe. He set the small pouch back in the satchel and removed what looked like a large wing feather from an eagle. He opened the door to his truck and removed a tarnished brass Zippo lighter, using his thumb to turn the wheel, striking the flint and igniting a yellow flame. I could smell the brief odor of lighter fluid in the wind.

Joe lit the tip of the feather, watching the flames grow as the fire devoured the feather, the smell was like hair burning. He looked in the direction the smoke rose, watching it snake up through the cypress trees, and drift toward the west. He said nothing, simply watching the smoke and leaves.

Wynona motioned toward the south. I saw what I assumed was a vulture until it flew closer, still at least a thousand feet above the glades. Then I spotted the white-feathered head. A bald eagle rode the air currents, turning its head and looking down on the earth. Wynona smiled, her beauty even more radiant in this environment. She looked over at Billie. "Did you somehow call that eagle?"

"I did nothing. Only what Sam Otter instructed me to do." He observed the eagle for half a minute, watching the bird surveying the Everglades. "We're looking for a manmade object … a drone. For the most part, something with an engine on it is usually pushing against the wind." He looked over to me. "I know you're a sailor, Sean. Against the wind can work both ways on a sailboat. But if you're an eagle, you look not to fight the wind, you want to ride it. Burns less energy. Not as tiring, and the wind will take you places it wants you to go. The eagle just soars. Watch him."

There was no wing movement, only the large bird's outstretched wings, soaring. Billie nodded and said, "If the drone was flying about as high as the eagle is now, and it was close to the same time of day …" He paused, watching the bird ascend in a westward direction. "Then the drone—if, at that point, the propellers were not pulling it in the opposite direction, it may have flown off toward the west." He grinned. "Let's hope it didn't fly all the way to the Gulf of Mexico." He started walking in a westward direction.

Wynona looked at me. She pulled her hair back and fastened it into a ponytail. "I'd suggest we follow him."

"Good suggestion."

Joe Billie led us through hardwood hammocks filled with oak, slash pines and palms, into wetlands, the water up to our knees. He stopped about every one-hundred feet or so and simply stood in silence, watching movement in the sawgrass or the leaves, listening to the rustle of palm fronds. Wynona didn't ask him questions. I wasn't sure what questions he could or wanted to answer.

We walked. We sloshed through brown water. Mosquitoes following us. Joe stopped abruptly. He pointed to a motion in the sawgrass. Whatever was causing the tops of sawgrass to tremble, was much larger than a rabbit, and longer. He walked closer, quickly rushing but not touching whatever was moving. A large Burmese python emerged from the grass, crawling down the same trail we followed. Its mid-section was as thick as my thigh, the skin a perfect checkered camouflage of brown, olive green and yellow.

Joe watched it as if he was watching an alien life form. "They were never in here when I was a boy. People, many from the Miami area, would buy the snakes as pets. But when the animals got too big to care for, they'd bring them out to the glades and release them. Except for large gators, the python has no natural enemy here—not good for the glades."

Wynona said, "We didn't grow up with giant pythons crawling through the reservation."

I watched the snake slither off into the grass. "I'd estimate that one would be at least fifteen feet long, maybe closer to twenty."

Joe looked up to the sky. The eagle was no longer visible. "Come … I think we are getting closer."

We followed him less than one hundred yards, moving away from the trail, wading through waist-high sawgrass. We walked through a piece of Florida that was vanishing. It was the River of Grass in its most primal embodiment, flat as a prairie. Above us, a sapphire blue bowl stretched to the ends of the glades, cotton white clouds the size of the Himalayas drifting in the sky. The warm breeze across the land frolicked with the sawgrass, in fields of motion like swells on the surface of the sea.

We came closer to one of the islands in this ocean of grass, a grove of old-growth cypress trees, the wind causing Spanish moss to sway from the limbs. I estimated the strand of trees was not more than five acres. Joe stopped, turning back to us. "Perhaps the reason the search teams didn't find the drone is because they were looking on the ground and not in the air." He motioned toward the trees. "Look up at the tallest one in the center, the old man of the group. You can just make out the drone on one of the lower branches. Sean, I think you are probably tall enough to reach the branch and shake down the drone."

Wynona and I looked in the direction Joe Billie pointed. Near the end of a low-hanging limb, there it was, like a silent bird roosting. The black drone tucked at the end of the branch. He was smiling. I looked at him thinking what an amazingly skilled tracker he was. "I think you're right. I can probably reach it. You want to stand under the limb to catch the drone?"

"Let's do it."

The three of us waded through water a few inches above our ankles. We walked around cypress knee roots that protruded up and out of the murky water like wooden spikes on the floor of a murky cave. When we got to the base of the tall tree, I stepped up on its massive, gnarled roots and reached for the limb. Joe stood in water directly below the drone. Wynona said, "Please try hard not to drop it. If there are images on the video card, being submerged in the water won't help us."

He stood with outstretched arms. "Okay, Sean. Give it a little shake."

I grabbed the limb with both hands and shook it. The drone immediately fell into Joe's arms. He caught it and grinned. "This is no diving bird. Its plastic feathers are not wet. Maybe it has something to show us."

Wynona said, "Nice catch. I so hope there are images on the video card that will help us."

Eighty-Six

The three of us stood under the branches of the deep-rooted cypress tree, a tree that Joe Billie said was tall when Sam Otter was a boy. It wasn't the tree of the knowledge of good and evil but, in a remote sense, it felt like there was a forbidden trait to it with tap roots that began in the soil of Eden. I thought about the huge snake we'd just seen. The great tree was a standing monument to time itself. When I shook the limb, the mechanical fruit that dropped from the branch had an ominous feel to it.

The drone, with its four rotors, jet black aluminum body, was foreign to everything around us, yet it might unveil evil walking in its most visual form. Joe handed the drone to Wynona. "It's all yours."

She drew in a deep breath. "Let's cross our fingers, hoping there is something we can use." She opened the slot where the micro SD card was stored. "It's in here. My laptop is back in Sean's Jeep. I wish we had an airboat to get us there sooner."

• • •

An hour later, just as smoky embers of a crimson sun were shut out through the blinds of lead colored clouds, Wynona set her laptop on the hood of my Jeep and lifted the screen. She inserted the SD card and waited a few seconds for the file to load. Joe Billie and I stood beside her, me on the right, Billie on the left. She said, "There are a lot of video files on here. But the one we're most interested in seeing is the final file … or at least the last couple of files. So … let's scroll down to that area and see what we see."

She started the playback at the beginning of the video frame. The image was on the full-screen. The footage was of the Everglades, maybe five-hundred feet above the sawgrass. I could tell that Thaxton had been an excellent aerial photographer. The video scenes were all smooth. Nothing jerky, the movements fluid and with a cinematic look and feel. We watched a deer on the ground run, zig-zagging through shallow water and sawgrass.

The drone flew over a flock of roseate spoonbills feeding in the shallows of a mangrove framed estuary, golden sunlight reflecting from the water. More than two-dozen of the pink birds wading. None looking up at the drone. It moved away from that perspective, back over the sawgrass, this time gaining altitude. Within a minute, I began to recognize some of the area because it was what we'd just been walking through on the way to finding the drone.

The next image also was recognizable. We could make out the fallen cypress tree lying on the ground in the distance, the drone beginning to descend as it approached. "Check that out," Wynona said.

Joe looked the screen. "The man in the video is attempting to hide behind the toppled tree."

I nodded. "But there is no place he can hide from the aerial advance. He's standing, and from that distance, I recognize him."

"You do?" Billie asked.

"Yeah, we do," said Wynona.

The drone moved closer. We could see the fear in the face of Michael Fazio.

"Looks like he's going to shoot at it," Billie said.

We watched as Fazio aimed his rifle in the direction of the drone and fired shots directly at it. We could see the puffs of white smoke at the end of the barrel, the anger in his face.

But it was the next shot that I felt in my heart.

Fazio crouched back down next to the tree. He took careful aim, not at the drone ... but rather at the man flying the drone. He sighted through the scope, taking his time. One shot. One final puff of smoke. "That's it," I said. "From the camera on the drone, Thaxton saw his own killer aiming at him and taking the fatal shot."

"Incredible," whispered Wynona. "What a horrible way to see your assassination in a video monitor you're holding. Almost like watching fate or the future a split-second before it happens. And no way to prevent or change the consequences."

We watched the drone from that point, quickly gaining altitude. Maybe now at a thousand feet above the sawgrass. In the wide angle, we could see Fazio scatter something in the area where he stood.

Wynona said, "He must have picked up the cigar stogie and food wrapper from some spot where he saw Craig Moffett siting on his ATV, drinking beer, smoking weed and leaving a trail."

I said, "All Fazio had to do was carefully pick up some litter and deposit it where he wanted. Planting physical evidence. But he never bargained for an eye in the sky that caught it all."

The drone ascended a little higher, now flying erratically. Twisting over the Everglades. The camera picking up more of the horizon, the sun setting far in the distance where the sawgrass merged into a vista of purple and golden clouds. We could see a flock of white pelicans beating their wings, moving from north to south, toward the Ten Thousand Islands.

And then we saw an eagle. Not beating its wings, but rather spiraling over the Everglades. It seemed to eye the drone as a curiosity in the shared sky before catching an updraft and soaring toward the sunset.

The drone did the opposite. It descended, snaking its way over the wetlands like a chaotic bird not sure where to alight. It dropped lower, now maybe two-hundred feet above the ground. The drone seemed to pull out of its aerial freefall, climbing up for a few feet before fluttering back toward earth. Out of energy. No gentle hand to guide it. But the boughs of an old cypress tree were there to catch it, the drone falling through the limbs and Spanish moss. The eye of the camera capturing it all. Finally, the drone came to a rest, the leafy moss-laden branch catching it. In the breeze, the tip of the limb barely moving, left to right, like an unseen hand rocking the cradle.

And then the camera eye closed and faded to darkness..

Eighty-Seven

Joe Billie stepped back from the computer screen, his dark eyes unreadable. He looked across the glades. "That camera on the drone, like the eye of an eagle, caught it all." He turned back to us. "Now, what can you two do?"

Wynona closed her laptop. "We can arrest Michael Fazio and charge him with first-degree, premeditated murder."

I picked up my phone, scrolling to the app and looking at the digital map. I could see Fazio's car was back at the condo. "Looks like he's home, or at least his car is back there."

Wynona's phone buzzed. She glanced at the screen. "It's Eric Valdez, FBI."

She answered, and he said, "Wynona, we have the guy's ID."

"Who is he?"

"You were right about the player part, at least in terms of South Florida politics. Guy's name is Simon Santiago. He's a former lawyer, disbarred seven years ago after his third DUI, the last one crippling a young mother in a car accident. Santiago is one of the partners in a national lobby firm called the Carswell Group. Its corporate offices are here in Miami. The company leases two floors in one of the most expensive office towers overlooking Biscayne Bay."

She drew in a deep breath and released it. "Well, the person he was meeting with is Michael Fazio. He's a hitman. And we just watched aerial video shot by a drone, capturing Fazio shooting Joe Thaxton." She gave Valdez more details including the murder of Chester Miller. "So, what we're looking at is an assassin who shot and killed two people in the glades. And we believe the guy Fazio was meeting … this Simon Santiago, is complicit in the murders."

"Do you need the Bureau's help in apprehending the suspect?"

Wynona, cut her eyes to me. "FBI backup would be great, but since I'm such a persona non grata with the current assistant director, I don't want to jeopardize your career by having you going to bat for me."

"Wynona, it's not about you. It's about taking a dangerous perp off the streets."

"Somehow, it will become about me … especially if things don't go well. I don't want that to haunt you and your career. You have two small children. All I have to worry about is old ghosts, and I can see through them. Besides, the sheriff's office has my back. We'll call Miami-Dade PD and see if they can spare a posse." She smiled. "Thanks, Eric." She turned to me. "Sean, I think it's time to call your old friend again with Miami-Dade PD."

"I'll update Ron Hamilton. Before I make the call, how are you feeling?"

"Fine. The nauseous part went away a few weeks ago—at least in the intensity of it. Now it's occasional."

"You don't have to make the arrest. You've tracked him this far."

"I can't step aside. Not now. I'll be fine, and the baby will be fine, too." She smiled.

"Are you sure?"

"Yes. Stop worrying, okay?"

"It's not that easy. Not now."

Joe grinned. "Baby?"

Wynona smiled, and I said, "I just found out, too."

Joe looked at me and then at Wynona. "Well, congratulations to you both. Do you know if it's a little girl or a boy?"

Wynona said, "No, not yet. I'm not sure I want to know … at least not yet."

I smiled. "I don't mind surprises. We can wait and see."

Joe touched Wynona's shoulder. "I'm happy for you. Boy or girl, the child will be loved and very special."

"Thank you, Joe," Wynona said.

"Okay … now, we need to get back to business," I said. "Wynona, what's next from your perspective?"

"I'll call Cory and let him know what we found. We'll get the arrest warrant and plan the take-down." She leaned up against my Jeep and made the call, the wind over the glades blowing her hair. She brought Cory Gilson up to speed. "This guy is beyond armed and dangerous. He's a hired-gun—a ruthless killing machine. We think he's working for Simon Santiago. The question is: Who is Santiago working for?"

Cory sat at his desk in his wide office. Four other detectives shared the office, working phones. He looked across the hall and into a large glassed-in office, the sheriff talking with the chief deputy. "That's a great question. I checked with FHP and Uber. The Uber record indicates the driver picked up Fazio at a Seven-Eleven store parking lot at 11:17 a.m. The lot is about two blocks from where his BMW was found by FHP six hours after he called it in to them, and that was seven hours after he took the Uber ride from the area to his condo."

"Bingo. Great work. Now we know he left the car off the side of the road, took an Uber home and faked the whole stolen car scenario to give him an out if his car was ever connected to his trip in the glades. Can you get the murder warrant?"

"Yes. Send me a copy of the drone video. We can pick Fazio up in the morning."

"Are you bringing backup?"

"Yes. Two to three deputies. I don't think we need to bring in SWAT. We have the element of surprise."

"Maybe not. After Sean and I paid him a visit, his radar will be on guard. I believe he's a flight risk, and we need to arrest him as soon as we can get the warrant."

"The good thing is that it's not a hostage or stand-off situation. Fazio doesn't know we're going to be there to arrest him."

"Considering this guy's track record and the fact that we believe he just shot and killed two people, I'd feel better with some backup. Let's plan on arriving there first thing in the morning."

"All right. We'll work out the logistics and form a plan. We can get a no-knock warrant. Break through the door and arrest the guy. I'll call you back. By the way, I know Sean is aware of this, but it's worth mentioning. He's not in law enforcement. The PI thing doesn't cut the mustard when it comes to arresting people. Bounty hunters operate by a whole different set of loose guidelines. We can't afford to risk this arrest going south or the case becoming compromised. Sean is a friend of mine, too. It's just the way it is."

"He's not a bounty hunter. But I understand. And he does as well."

...

For Callie Hogan, it was surreal. Her parents speaking on the phone to a funeral director, the medical examiner's office, the sheriff's office, and the news media. She overheard the stilted phone conversations with other members of the family scattered across the nation. Everyone talking about her grandfather, but few seemed to know who he really was and what he'd accomplished in his lifetime.

He was known as the "orchid man," the eccentric family member who was more of an illusionary figure—an explorer who traveled on expeditions rather than vacations. Few seemed to know or care that he was, first and foremost, a staunch conservationist who looked at the world's plant life as the first alarm to the health of earth.

She was in the backseat of the car her parents rented while they were in Naples to make funeral arrangements for her beloved grandfather. Her father, Stan, drove slowly, turning from the Tamiami Trail onto the property. He was in his mid-fifties; narrow-set, hazel eyes; wire-rim glasses; prominent forehead; and pale skin, driving with both of his hands on the wheel.

Callie's mother, Barbara, was still attractive for her age, long neck, a few lines around her eyes and at the corner of her full mouth. She said, "I wish I'd come out here more often. Dad turned this place into quite a nature preserve. When I was your age, Callie, he didn't have so many orchids lining the driveway to the cabin. And, when I was your age, he was often away on some adventure deep in the Congo or Malaysia, searching for the world's rarest orchids."

"He found them," Callie said.

"Oh, where?"

"All over the world."

Her father said, "It's the sacrifice he chose to make. It's sad and ironic that he spent a lifetime visiting some of the most treacherous places on earth, dealing with hostile tribes, jungles, dangerous animals, and he dies here at his home."

"Dad, he didn't die at his home like he had a heart attack or some other natural cause. He was murdered here. That's a big difference."

"I know. That's what your mother and I have been talking to the police about almost since we arrived. That's what I was referring to … the tragedy of circumstances in all this."

"Grandpa used to say that we should never be a sum total of our circumstances. He said that a positive attitude will rise above hard times. He told me that it's okay to make mistakes in situations as long as I tried, I would learn from those circumstances … and that's never failure."

Barbara said, "I'm glad you got to spend so much time with your grandfather."

Stan pulled the car up in front of the cabin. They all got out, quietly closing the doors. Callie looked across at the greenhouse, the yellow crime scene tape still there, a piece down and barely moving in the breeze.

"This is so heartbreaking," Barbara said, her eyes welling. "I can feel Dad all around here."

Callie looked to the left of the cabin, the orchid plant beneath the lowest limb on the cypress tree. She walked over to the ladder, positioning it back against the tree. She picked up a small watering can, used a garden hose to partially fill it. Callie climbed the ladder, like her grandfather had done so many times before. She used her fingertips to test the soil. She poured a small amount of water into the base of the plant, staring at it. "Grandpa didn't make it to see you bloom. That's not your fault. But I think where he is now … he can still see you. So, whenever you're ready, you have his permission to bloom and become ... Persephone."

She wiped a single tear from her cheek.

Eighty-Eight

I was the one man out, and it wasn't a problem. Only Wynona knew I was even there, following not far behind the team that was positioned to knock down a door to evil. *But could it be contained?* That's what I was thinking when Detective Cory Gilson, Wynona, and two sheriff's deputies arrived in the predawn hour at Michael Fazio's condo. Wynona rode with Cory in an unmarked cruiser. The two deputies drove together in a separate marked car.

They parked in a back portion of the condo lot, behind a row of other cars. I drove my Jeep, staying out of direct sight around the perimeter of the tall condo, a hint of sunrise changed the skyline over the Atlantic. I parked on the street with a view of the parking lot and the entrance to the condo. But I couldn't see Fazio's BMW. I checked my phone and got a strong signal, the pulsating dot appeared to be emanating from the parking lot.

I scanned the area, finally seeing the black BMW parked on the street between Fazio's condo and another matching high-rise, this one named *Neptune II*. But there was no sign of Fazio in or around the car. I looked back at the condo entrance. The two deputies were both large men, wearing uniforms and bullet-proof vests. Wynona and Cory wore body armor, too. Every member of the team had a gun visible. The largest of the two deputies carried an iron battering ram in one hand, his pistol in the other. I watched him holster his pistol. They stood at the door for a few seconds, whispering. Cory nodded, and then the deputy used the ram to knock the door open.

"Police!" I heard them yell as all four entered the condo. "Police!"

I got out of my Jeep, instinctively touching my Glock under my belt. I wanted to be with them as they entered, but I was forced to keep the boundaries. I knew all the reasons, but the reasons mean nothing when bullets start flying and officers begin falling. I could just here them yelling, "clear," as they searched the condo. I couldn't take my eyes off the doorway, waiting for Wynona and the others to emerge with no shots fired and Michael Fazio in handcuffs.

It didn't happen.

The largest deputy was the first to walk back outside. I watched him holster his gun, bend down and lift the battering ram off the concrete porch. The other deputy came out next, and then Wynona and Cory walked outside, all talking. It was obvious that Fazio wasn't there.

I looked at his car and then lifted my eyes to the roof of the adjacent condo. The sunrise was a little brighter. There was a figure in silhouette on the rooftop.

A man was aiming a rifle.

The next ten seconds were the longest in my life. The deputy holding the battering ram fell, his head almost blown off. In less than two seconds, the second deputy was shot in the neck. Cory took a bullet and fell to the ground.

Wynona fell, holding her leg. As she lay on the pavement, a second bullet ricocheted off the sidewalk and went under her vest. I used the hood of my Jeep to support my arms as I stood, aiming at the man on the roof. I shot three times, his body flinching at the third round. He disappeared from the roof. I didn't know if he was dead, wounded or running away.

I called 9-1-1, gave the dispatcher the address, and then I ran through the parking lot, keeping the cars between me and the shooter on the roof. I ran toward Wynona and the other downed officers. Both deputies were dead. Most of their heads gone. Cory bled from the neck, his eyes open, staring at the wisp of pink clouds in the sky.

I knelt down by Wynona, blood squirting from the femoral artery in her left thigh. I held my hand to it, looking back up at the roof. The shooter not visible. "Hold on, Wynona. Help is on the way."

"Sean, he knew we were coming. How?"

"Don't talk." My hands were covered in her blood. I could see blood coming from under her vest, the bullet having entered her lower stomach. I took off my belt, ripped the sleeve from my shirt, then folded the cloth and placed it under the belt, tightening. "You're going to be okay. Just take slow breaths." I could hear sirens in the distance.

She coughed, her eyes growing vapid. "I'm cold, Sean. Just hold me."

I held her in my arms as a new day rose over the Atlantic. "Stay with me. I won't let you go." My eyes welled. Tears spilling onto her cheek. She tried to smile, her lower lip trembling.

The sirens were closer. Maybe a minute away.

I heard a noise. Someone running in hard sole shoes. I looked to my far right and saw Fazio running from the building across the street to his parked car. I lifted my Glock off the pavement next to Wynona and aimed. My eyes were too filled with tears to see clearly. He looked at me for a half-second before jumping behind the wheel and speeding off, knocking down a green plastic trash can as he swerved over a sidewalk and into the intersection, driving away.

I cradled Wynona in my arms, her pulse growing weaker, breathing shallow. "Stay with me, I whispered."

"Sean … I'm afraid … our baby."

Eighty-Nine

I refused to leave the hospital. I knew that Michael Fazio was probably out of the country by now. Didn't matter. I'd find him. There was no place on earth where he could crawl and hide, at least not for long. Wynona was still in surgery. There was no way I'd leave her. I stood in the hospital waiting room and looked up at a wide-screen TV mounted on the wall between plastic ficus plants and award plaques the hospital had won and displayed on the wall, magazines held vertical in plastic containers.

There were three other people in the room. All had their eyes on the TV where a female reporter stood on the street with the condo in the background and said, "Again, three people are dead, another critically wounded in Parkview Memorial Hospital now undergoing surgery. We're told that 38-year-old Wynona Osceola was part of the police raid before dawn at Atlantis Condominium behind me. She and the other officers were serving a warrant for the arrest of Michael Fazio, a man wanted for two recent murders in the Everglades. Detectives say Fazio is believed to have been the shooter this morning, taking shots from the roof of a condo across the street, giving him a clear vantage point to pick off the officers as they came out of his condo. Miami-Dade PD detective, Russ Delgado, said it appears they walked into an ambush."

The video cut to a detective in a tan sportscoat. No tie. He had a long face, and eyes filled with fatigue. "The officers were shot after they came out of the condo, not before they entered. We are doing our best to cover the airports in the area and major highway exits. We know the suspect was driving a black BMW X-1. The license plate is registered in Florida."

The reporter asked, "Do you think Fazio was tipped off about the raid?"

"We don't know at this time."

The video cut to a split-screen between the reporter live on the scene and the anchorman back at the TV studio. "Carolyn, do you have an update on the condition of the fourth and last person to have been shot, Detective Wynona Osceola?"

"The last time we checked, she was in surgery and listed in critical condition."

I walked out of the waiting room to a glassed atrium overlooking a park-like setting of palms and jacaranda trees budding with purple blossoms. I looked down at my hands. Even though I'd washed them, I spotted some of Wynona's blood under my thumbnail. I thought about the night when Wynona told me she was pregnant. *The child is yours ... or ours might be the better word. I just wanted you to know. I love you, Sean ... and I always will.*

"Mr. O'Brien?"

The voice sounded far away. I turned around. A man stood in front of me in green hospital scrubs, a small bloodstain near the chest. He was lean. Dark skin. Maybe originally from India. He wore black-framed glasses, a tiny blood speck on the left lens. "I'm Doctor Patel. Miss Osceola is stable. We'll be moving her to a room in critical care for the next few hours. She lost a lot of blood, and we had to remove part of her lower intestine. The bullet did a lot of damage. The child she was carrying, unfortunately, did not survive."

The statement made me stop breathing for a moment. I felt my heart hammering in my chest, could almost hear the blood rushing through my veins. "Can I see Wynona?"

"She's not conscious. Probably won't be for hours. She's heavily sedated. You may see her, though. Give us a half-hour, okay?"

"Yes. Thank you for saving her life."

He looked at me, making a dry swallow. "I wish we could have done more."

He started to turn. "Doctor …"

"Yes?"

"The baby … could you determine if it was a girl or boy."

"Yes. A girl. I am very sorry." He sighed, shook his head as if he was going to say something more, turned and left, walking down the long hallway.

As I watched him leave, I took my phone out of my pocket, looked at the GPS satellite app. I could see that the BMW was stationary. Still at the last place, the parking garage of the Seacrest Towers, the building where the Carswell Group had its national headquarters. I thought about calling the police, letting them know they might get two birds with one stone by blocking the exits to the building and bursting in Simon Santiago's office, arresting both of them.

But they'd have nothing concrete on Santiago unless Michael Fazio would cut a plea deal for life rather than the death penalty. There wouldn't be much deal room after killing Joe Thaxton, Chester Miller and three members of law enforcement.

Santiago would lawyer up, deny any criminal association with Fazio and toss him to the wolves. I remembered an old Cherokee proverb, the one about how each of us has two wolves always fighting inside our hearts … one evil and one peaceful. The one that wins, of course, is the one you feed. Today, I wanted to feed both of them equally because I knew I'd need the savage aggression to do what had to be done. Maybe, at the end of the day, the good wolf would prevail. At this point, I didn't much care.

Beyond Santiago and Fazio there was someone else. He or she was the one pulling all the puppet strings. That's the person I would find. Beyond that, even I didn't know what I'd do after I cut the strings.

• • •

I stood by Wynona's bedside. I almost didn't recognize her. Her face was bruised and swollen from falling on the pavement. Tubes and IV's ran to multiple parts of her body. Heart and vital signs monitoring machines beeped. Screens moved with digital calibration of life. Her wounded left leg was elevated on a pillow. Her arms and hands were folded across her stomach. Although she was unconscious, it was as if she was holding her stomach and her ovaries, feeling for the child inside her. My heart sank.

I leaned down and kissed her forehead. "You get well. When you open your eyes, I will have orchids in your room. They can only add to the beauty that I see now."

Ninety

I was within three blocks of the Seacrest Tower when I saw an assassin move across the screen of my phone. I sat in my Jeep at a traffic light, almost running the light. "Come on," I whispered under my breath. I looked at the phone again, the dot now exiting the building. I had a gut feeling that Fazio would head for the airports, but I didn't know if it would be the closest, Miami International, or the four-hour drive north to Orlando. Both airports have large numbers of international flights. The Miami airport would be under heavy police surveillance.

The dot moved north from downtown, up Brickle Avenue and then on to Biscayne Boulevard. I followed as close as possible. The dot was going the opposite way from the airport, turning instead toward the Port of Miami, a place I knew well. Within a few minutes, I drove over Port Road, gleaming white cruise ships visible to the right and left. Fazio wasn't driving toward any of the commercial cruise docks. He was driving to the cargo area.

I followed the moving dot to a remote parking lot at the southeast side of the port. I could see three large container ships, each one being loaded and unloaded with container boxes the size of trailers that semi-trucks pulled down the highway. The tall cranes slowly lifted and set the big boxes from ship to shore and then the opposite, from the shore to the ships.

At this point, I assumed Fazio's escape plan was on a freighter bound for a distant nation. He most likely had a couple of different passports and enough cash in a briefcase to buy his way just about anywhere. The largest ship was called *Athena*. I could see it was registered in Argentina. I was within five-hundred feet of Fazio's BMW, watching it moving from the main road onto the parking lot. It was a lot where sea captains, crew members and dock workers parked. The area was where a vehicle could be parked for weeks, even months, without raising suspicion. Fazio parked between a Dodge Ram pickup truck and a Subaru.

I stopped two rows away in a spot where he couldn't see me in his rearview mirror. I looked around the property for security cameras. There were none close by that I could see. I knew that the closer we got to the docks that would change. He was standing behind the back of the BMW, rear hatch door open when I approached, walking quietly. A sea gull squawked overhead, the long blast of a ship's horn coming from the Atlantic-side entrance to the port. The morning was hot and humid, a drop of sweat tricking down the center of my back.

Fazio lifted his right foot, moving it under the rear bumper to close the rear door. Any man has a compromised balance standing on one foot. I kicked him in the dead center of his back, his head and face smashing into the closing hatch door. I started to pull my Glock from beneath my belt. But something in his face, his startled yet arrogant look, changed my mind. I hit him hard and fast in his mouth, my knuckles smashing lips and teeth. Blood pouring from his crooked mouth. He charged me, swinging with his right fist. The blow connecting against my shoulder. I countered, delivering my left fist to his jaw. The sound of bone cracking was like an egg dropped on a tile floor. He fell back against his BMW.

I looked at him for a second. "What'd Santiago pay you to kill Joe Thaxton and Chester Miller? Beyond Santiago, who's calling the shots?"

He said nothing, his chest heaving, blood running out of his mouth. "I'm going to give you the chance to live the rest of your miserable life in prison. Who tipped you off to the raid?"

"Screw you!"

"You make the decision to shoot four police officers. Three are dead. One, the woman, is clinging to life. But you killed her unborn child. My child …"

His expression was of instant fright and hate. He rolled away from the SUV, reaching for his left shoe, pulling a small pistol out of an ankle holster. Before I could draw my Glock, he managed to get off one round, the bullet grazing my left shoulder. I shot him in the chest. He fell on his back, breathing heavy, a flower of blood staining his shirt." His eyes locked on mine. I stood over him, my heart pounding.

"You won't kill me. They got cameras out here. And these people are big money people … they'll come after you." He grinned.

"This is for Joe Thaxton, Chester Miller, three police officers, a severely wounded woman and her dead child." His grin faded. I shot him between the eyes, the round leaving a hole in his forehead the size of a nickel. I pulled his phone out of his back pocket, looking at some of the last numbers called and received.

I left the body where it fell, between his SUV and the pickup truck, used a napkin to detach the GPS tracker, then turned and walked to my Jeep. When I got behind the wheel, I scrolled to the last few numbers called on Fazio's phone. I took a gamble, hoping that one of the numbers was directly to Santiago's cell phone. I wanted to get him anxious. Frightened. Moving quickly and making mistakes. Getting sloppy. Calling his contacts.

As I started my Jeep, I hit the call back on the last number called on the phone. A man answered. His voice in quick bursts. "What now? I told you not to call me until you're out of the country. Are you on the ship?"

"It seems like Fazio missed the boat?"

He was silent for a long moment. "Who the hell is this?"

"Someone who is about to become your worst enemy. Here's why, Simon. You're an accessory to murder. Not just one, but a whole string of them. Fazio is going to cut a plea, and you'll wind up on death row. Bribing and buying politicians, maybe a sheriff or two, will get you time in prison, but murder—you hiring a hitman, well—that just sent you to the top of the stupid criminal food chain, and you're about to be eaten alive."

"Who is this? Don't you threaten me!"

"You're about to meet me. It'll be rather informal. But, before we have our little chat, you can call the man who paid you to have Thaxton killed, and you can tell us all about it. That way, you are truly the middle man or the man in the middle. So, what are you going to do? If you're smart, it'll be Simon says who did it. See you soon."

Ninety-One

People who buy red Ferraris want to be seen, at least they want to be seen behind the wheel of one of the most expensive sports cars in the world. Simon Santiago was no exception. As I drove into the ten-story parking garage next to the Seacrest Towers, I was glad that earlier Wynona and I had seen Santiago get into the red Ferrari parked at the Coconut Grove restaurant. The car would be easy to find in the labyrinth of the parking garage.

I took the ticket from the automated machine and began the slow access from the ground floor all the way to the top floor. I anticipated that by poking Santiago's psyche on the phone, he would move at a speed of carelessness. Call his lawyer. Call his contacts. Making arrangements for meetings. And, hopefully, be leaving the parking garage soon.

As I ascended through the levels of concrete floors, I looked for cameras. Most were always in the same place on each floor—near the exits, the elevators and stairwells. I was hoping Santiago had not parked his car in a direction that would be easily picked up on a surveillance camera. If so, I'd have to deal with it.

When I finished driving around the ninth floor without seeing his car, I was a little worried. And then I drove to the tenth and final floor. Parked by itself, in a premium spot, was the red Ferrari. It wasn't next to the elevator or the stairwell. But it was in a choice corner space with a view of the Atlantic. It was the first thing Santiago saw when he parked in the morning and the last thing he saw in the late afternoon, assuming he worked late.

I parked my Jeep in a spot directly across from the Ferrari, turned off the engine and waited. I looked at my watch. I had just enough daylight left if my plan was to happen the way I wanted. As I waited for Santiago to come running from the elevator or the stairway, I called the intensive care unit at Parkview Memorial. I was quickly put through to the nurses' desk. "ICU, can I help you?"

"Yes, this is Sean O'Brien. I'm calling to check on the condition of Wynona Osceola."

"Hold on, please."

I waited, watching the elevator doors and the entrance to the stairwell. A statuesque woman in a business suit walked to her car, high heels echoing off the concrete walls and floor. She got into a silver Audi and left. The voice came back on the phone. Sir, doctor Patel is in there with the patient now."

"Is she doing better?"

"She's still unconscious. Her condition remains the same, critical and guarded."

I could hear a doctor being paged over the hospital intercom. "Thank you." I immediately called Detective Ron Hamilton. He answered quickly. "Any update on Detective Osceola?" he asked.

"She's still listed in guarded condition."

"Where are you?"

"I'd rather not say, specifically."

"Listen to me, Sean. I know you're angry that this happened, but you can't become a vigilante and hope to have a snowball's chance in hell of bringing justice to people like Fazio and Santiago." Hamilton, tie loosened, pinched the bridge of his nose.

"Depends on what you define as justice. Fazio is dead."

"What? Oh Christ."

"He pulled his gun on me, and he fired a round. All I did was protect myself. Ron, we're up against people who believe the rule of law is beneath them. Our serial killer is a billionaire who gave the nod to have people eliminated that could change the way he does business.

And you know that kind of money their defense will buy. They'll lawyer up so hard and fast it almost becomes impenetrable unless you have absolute proof that they're complicit. Santiago hired Fazio because of direct orders from someone. I don't think Fazio knew who the lead dog was. We have to get Santiago to tell us. We need proof from him, a direct bread crumb trail to the person or persons calling the lethal shots."

"Unless you have something on Santiago, he's not going to sing. He'll get the best attorneys and wind up suing the city for false arrest."

"No problem. I don't have the authority to arrest him. But I can have a man-to-man chat with Santiago. When I'm done, I want to deliver him to you with his confession."

"Just tell me where you are, and we'll come get him."

"I'll call you in a couple of hours. Trust me on this one, Ron, there is no other way. They've killed three officers, two men in the glades, and they murdered an unborn baby. Wynona was carrying my child."

"Oh, dear God ... I had no idea."

I saw the doors open and Simon Santiago walk from the elevator toward the Ferrari. He had a phone in one ear. Mouth moving.

"Gotta go. Call you soon. When I do, Santiago should be ready to talk to you."

I slipped off my boat shoes and walked up behind Santiago as he was disconnecting and putting the phone inside his suit jacket pocket. When he unlocked the door to the Ferrari, I said, "Fazio did miss the boat, but he sends his regards."

Santiago whirled around, and I slammed my right fist into the left side of his jaw. He fell to the floor of the garage. I picked him up, opened the back of my Jeep and then went to work, covering his mouth with a thick piece of masking tape, put his arms behind his back, and wrapped his hands and feet in tape. He was curled in the fetal position as I reached inside his suit pocket and got his phone.

And then I left the parking garage and headed to a scenic and remote spot in the Everglades.

Ninety-Two

It didn't take me long to leave the urban jungle of Miami and enter a whole different jungle near an area of Lostman's River. In some areas of South Florida's Ten Thousand Islands, there are places that both alligators and crocodiles co-exist. And it happens nowhere else in the world but here. I drove my Jeep through wetlands for a few miles south of the Tamiami Trail. I kept checking my rearview mirror to see if Santiago was moving, lifting his bruised head over the back seat. So far, nothing.

Soon the cypress trees melded into mangroves, their spindly prop roots like claws grasping the dark water. I pulled my Jeep as close as possible to the brackish estuaries and parked, rolling my window down. There was a low tide smell of salt, seaweed and mud. I reached in the console for my Buck knife and rope that I always carry. I cut off two pieces, each about four feet in length. I strapped the knife to my belt along with the rope pieces and stepped outside to open the rear hatch door.

Simon Santiago moaned. His jaw was red and purple, swollen. He opened his eyes and stared at me. I pulled the knife out of the leather sheath on my side. His eyes opened wider, the tape across his mouth preventing him from yelling. I grabbed his feet and used the knife to cut through the duct tape. "Get out!" I pulled one of his legs, dragging him to the end of the floorboard. "Stand up!" I yanked the tape off his mouth.

He sucked in a chest full of air. "You're a dead man!"

"Not yet."

"Who the fuck are you?"

"Watch your language."

"What do you want?"

"The truth! I know in your line of work, that's not a prerequisite for the job. But I think that'll change in a few minutes. Walk toward the water."

"What!"

"Now!" I shoved him in the back. He stumbled and got up. I grabbed him by his collar and pulled him closer to the estuary. There was no wind, and the water was dark as onyx stone. The surface appeared polished. A hundred feet across the estuary, a snowy egret stood motionless, its white feathers so reflective off the water it looked like two egrets connected at their gangly legs. The ripe scent of oysters rose from a mud flat at low tide.

Santiago looked back at me like a condemned man. "What are you gonna do?"

"That, pal, depends on what Simon says."

"Let's go for swim."

"Come on man!"

"You won't drown. It's shallow. Probably not over our waists in most places. But there is something unique about the area. It's called Lostman's River. Guess how it got the name?" I smiled. "We're not here to talk history. We're here to talk the future—yours specifically. You see, Simon, this is brackish water. It's one of the few places on the planet where alligators and the fierce crocodiles live and thrive in the same area. Some of the crocs here are almost twenty feet long. Can you imagine the crushing power of those jaws? Walk into the water!"

"You're crazy!"

"You're right. Walk!"

I pulled the Glock from my belt, pressing the end of the barrel hard against his forehead. "It doesn't matter to me if I shoot you here and roll your body into the swamp. They won't find your big toe after the gators and crocs move in." I pulled out one of the pieces of rope from under my belt, quickly made a noose and slipped it over his head. I tightened the rope around his neck and led him into the dark water. "You scream, and I'll crush your larynx."

I pulled him through hip-deep water to an area of large red mangroves lining the bank. I used the other length of the rope to run around his wrists and tied him to the thick prop roots. He stood there in water up to his waist looking out into the long and winding bay bordered by mangroves and cypress trees.

"It shouldn't take too long," I said. "Once the first croc or gator hits you, it'll be a feeding frenzy. It's time I step out of the water and let mother nature take over."

"No! You can't leave me tied up here."

"Watch me." I walked out of the water, about fifty feet, and stood to his left on the embankment.

"You can't do this! Just shoot me!"

"No, that's way too quick. As the crocs are feeding on your entrails like eating pasta, you may still be alive. And I want you to think about all the people you've killed."

"I didn't kill anybody!"

"You didn't pull the trigger, but you paid the triggerman. Shhhh!" I stopped speaking. A hundred yards out near the opposite bank, a big gator or croc slid into the water with a loud smack. That reptile was followed by another. "Now, all you have to do, Simon, to come out of there is to tell me who sanctioned Joe Thaxton's death."

He stared at the water, the knotted eyes and snouts of the animals coming closer, the water behind their big tails rippling. "Please! Don't let me be eaten alive."

"I need the information. You don't have to die here or on death row ... I want to know the name of your boss, who he works for, and why he wanted Thaxton, Chester Miller and three police officers killed." I glanced at the V-shaped ripples coming closer.

"Okay! I'll tell you! Cut me loose."

I took my phone out, punched the video record button and stepped back in the water. "Look at me and start talking. You leave anything out ... I leave you out here. It's time to come clean and don't even think about trying to lie to me. Who ordered the death of Joe Thaxton and why?"

"His name is Timothy Spencer. CEO of Heartland Sugar Corporation. His family has owned the company for decades. And that's one of many companies they own. Nobody took Joe Thaxton serious as a candidate … and then he did those TV interviews, and they caught on like wildfire. The environmental laws he was talking about pushing through, combined with a threat to reduce or end sugar subsidies, made him public enemy number one."

"How much did Timothy Spencer pay to have Thaxton killed?"

"A half-million."

"Who killed Thaxton?"

"Michael Fazio." He looked at the water, the gators and crocs coming closer, the shrill sound of a limpkin in the bush. "Get me outta here!"

"Did Fazio kill Chester Miller?"

"Yes!"

"Why?"

"Because the old man could identify him."

"Did Timothy Spencer pay for that one, too."

"Yes."

"How much."

"A quarter million."

"Who killed the two sheriff's deputies and Detective Cory Gilson and severely wounded another detective, Wynona Osceola."

"Fazio."

"How'd he know about the raid?"

"The sheriff tipped us off."

"Name! I need a name!"

"Sheriff Dwight Ketcham!"

"Why?"

"Because he's in Tim Spencer's pocket. Dozens and dozens of people are, too. Mostly politicians. It's just the way it is, man. He buys people like cattle. That's the system we've created. Don't shoot the messenger!"

"What was your role in the killings?"

"I hired Fazio to do the jobs, at least the first two murders. I had nothing do to with the shooting of cops."

"Is everything you told me true, and will you tell the same story to the state attorney and Miami-Dade police?"

"Yes!"

"Yes what?"

"It's all true … I swear to God! Come on! Get me out of here!"

"Where does Timothy Spencer spend most of his time?"

"He's got a half-dozen houses that I know of—probably more. He owns one of the biggest houses on Fisher Island."

I slipped the phone into my pocket, still recording audio. The two gators and one crocodile were less than fifty feet away, the croc and one of the gators broke out of the pack, forming a half-circle. I pulled my Glock out and fired three quick shots. A round a few feet in front of each reptile. Not to harm them, but to frightened them. They vanished, dropping below the surface. I knew they wouldn't be gone long.

I walked into the water, cut the ropes and pulled Santiago out, tears streaming down his unshaven face. His knees were so weak he dropped down, almost unable to walk. He looked up at me and said, "They'll come for you. There's nowhere on earth you can hide. You have no idea who you're messing with."

"Let 'em come. I'll put out the welcome mat. Now, stand up and start walking to the Jeep." I made a call to Detective Ron Hamilton. "Ron, we have a full confession from Simon Santiago on tape. I'm emailing it to you now."

"Where's Santiago?"

"He's a little wet. I was showing him around the glades. Looks like he lost his balance. I'll bring him to you. Where do you want to meet?"

"Someplace where there are no cameras. There's an abandoned airstrip off forty-one and fifty-seventh street. This will be one of the oddest prisoner exchanges in my career."

"Bounty hunters do it all the time, but I'm not doing it for money. It's justice. Santiago said the man who commissioned the hit on Joe Thaxton is Timothy Spencer. He's—"

"I know who he is. He's a billionaire. Big Sugar—big sugar daddy. Once he hears we have his primo lobbyist in custody, he'll be on one of his private jets and out of the country. He'll bring in an army of lawyers to bury this."

"Maybe not."

"Sean, you can't step over more boundaries and expect this to stick."

"What sticks is the truth. There's no better glue. I stayed behind the boundaries and three members of law enforcement are dead. If Wynona dies, it'll be four. When you count the baby ... as I do ... it's a serial slaughter. It's time that the guy at the top is held accountable."

NINETY-THREE

The airstrip looked more like a dirt road. When it was in use, most of the planes that came in and out of the area were crop dusters. There were two abandoned hangars, corrugated aluminum tarnished, looking more like elongated barns than places for planes. Ron Hamilton was already there when I arrived. I had retied Santiago's hands behind his back, using the rope and binding his feet together. He sat in the rear seat and didn't say a word during the hour drive back toward Miami.

I pulled closer to the hangar, Ron standing by his unmarked car. He had another person with him, a dark-haired woman dressed in a business jacket and black pants. I could tell she was carrying a handgun. She wore a badge on her belt. Ron said, "Sean O'Brien meet Rita Rodriguez. She started with the department a few months after you left. Rita came up the ranks quickly."

She extended her hand. "I've heard a lot of good things about you."

"You know none of that came from me," Ron said.

"I know." I smiled.

"I assume that's Santiago in the back seat?"

"He's all yours."

Rita said, "We checked in with Parkview Hospital. Detective Osceola is still in guarded condition. My prayers are with her."

"Thank you."

She glanced at Santiago in the Jeep. "We watched the video a few times. Santiago will try to say he was coerced into a confession. But the information he gave is too compelling."

"That's because it's true."

Ron said, "Your extraction methods are rather unorthodox, but under the circumstances ... five people are dead."

"Six ... six lives taken."

He nodded. "You're right. You know that you're bleeding from your shoulder?"

"It's a bullet graze. Fazio pulled on me. I had no choice. As long as Santiago thinks Fazio is alive and willing to testify against him, you'll get more from Santiago."

Ron looked from my Jeep to me. "Why don't you go be with Wynona? We'll take it from here."

"One of the houses Timothy Spencer owns is on Fisher Island. I have a feeling he's there. But he won't be when the news media break the story that you've picked up Spencer's right-hand pimp."

"At this time, all we can do is take Santiago in and interrogate him, using the interview you already did to corroborate and establish facts and timelines. We'll build the case as quickly as we can. Much of it will probably come from any emails, phone calls, and texts between Santiago and Spencer. We'll follow the money trail. Spencer paid a hefty price to have Joe Thaxton eliminated, and he had to follow up by agreeing to have the only possible witness, Chester Miller, killed. Maybe we can get Santiago to wear a wire and meet with Spencer. An oral admission of complicity, if it could be obtained, would nail it."

"Let's see if Santiago will cooperate."

"Rita and I we'll take him in, do what we can to convince him that wearing a wire would be in his best interest."

• • •

I went to a CVS pharmacy and bought antiseptic and a three-by-three gauze bandage to cover the bullet scrape on my shoulder. I entered a restroom at a convenience store, locked the door, removed my shirt and applied the medication and bandage, the round had grazed the bone. Later, in the parking lot of a McDonalds, I sipped black coffee and used my small laptop to go online. Checking county records, I quickly found the location and address of the house owned by Timothy Spencer and his wife Delores.

I looked for other property he owned—companies under his umbrella, any affiliation with corporate and non-profit boards. And I found more. Seven years ago, when Spencer was between wives, he was questioned when a twenty-seven-year-old model was discovered dead in one of his homes. This one was in the Hamptons of New York, the model found dead in one of the nine bedrooms. An autopsy revealed no apparent foul play, but the toxicology report indicated high concentrations of cocaine and oxycodone in her system. Although no criminal charges were filed, the dead woman's family brought a civil lawsuit. Spencer's attorneys settled the suit for 1.7 million dollars. I dug deeper, looking for clues into the psychological profile of Timothy Spencer.

The Hamptons estate was one of four homes I could find owned by Timothy Spencer. The others were in Aspen and Malibu. I downloaded satellite photos of Fisher Island and the house, looking for the best access and exit points. The home was on the northeast section, with a direct view of the sunrises over the Atlantic.

There were no bridges to the island. Only a ferry boat that I knew would be too risky to take. There'd have to be pre-arranged security clearances. Surveillance cameras. People who would make TSA screeners look like amateurs.

Maybe I wouldn't have to make a midnight run to the island. Maybe Simon Santiago would agree to wear a wire and meet Spencer at some members-only club for a new talk over old scotch. But would he say anything that might later incriminate him?

I thought about that and Plan B as I drove to a Whole Foods Market and bought a half-dozen colorful orchids. And then I headed to Parkview Hospital. I entered Wynona's room with the orchids sitting on a tray I carried. Joe Billie stood by her bedside. He looked up at me and nodded. "She'll make it, Sean. Her will to live is too powerful, and she has a lot to live for."

I tried to smile, the pulsating sound of the machines, heartbeats, breathing—made a real smile tough to do. "I'm still worried." I put the orchids as close to her bed as possible.

"I know you are afraid for her. Sam Otter wanted to come. He's a little too frail to make the journey. But he's doing what he does back at his firepit and chickee to help from a distance."

"We can use all the help we can get."

"I heard about the three police officers who died in the hail of bullets. Wynona is lucky to be alive. Is the baby okay?"

"She lost it."

A sadness instantly filled Joe's dark eyes. He stared at one of the orchids then looked up at me. "I'm so sorry to hear that."

"There will be retribution."

My phone buzzed. I looked at the screen. Ron Hamilton calling. I answered, and he said, "We've been working with the state attorney. Santiago doesn't know Fazio is dead, so Santiago is hedging his bets. After your interrogation, Santiago believes that Fazio holds the trump card against him so he's willing to talk, and the state's open to cutting a deal. No death penalty for full disclosure. But Santiago isn't willing to wear a wire. He says Spencer's house is set with hidden metal detectors. When we suggested for him to meet Spencer at a club or restaurant, he said Spencer is too leery to let one small detail about the killings slip out of his wealthy mouth."

"Then what's left?"

"Following the forensics, evidence, and money trails the best we can."

"Has Santiago asked for a lawyer?"

"No, not yet. I think he's still in such a state of shock after you two went for a swim in the glades, it's as if he has a mild form of PTSD. He's rather subdued. Maybe his meds are really kicking in now. Where are you?"

"At the hospital."

"How's Wynona?"

"Serious but stable condition."

"If there is anything that I can do, don't hesitate to ask. I was telling Rita that I'd lost count of the times you had my back."

"We had each other's backs. We made a good team, Ron."

"Yes, we did. I was stunned to hear about Cory Gilson's death. I didn't know him that well when he was with the department. I know you knew him a little better."

"Remember that the guy Cory worked for, Sheriff Dwight Ketcham, has to be complicit. Santiago said it was Ketcham who tipped off Fazio."

"We have two detectives en route over there to arrest him. This is gonna be one helluva case. The question is …who do we put on trial first?"

"The guy who first ordered the hit."

"We gotta get him on something. He's the great white shark circling beyond the perimeter. And he uses people like chum bait. Stay with Wynona, Sean. Don't do anything that might come back to haunt us for years."

"If Santiago won't wear a wire, then I will."

"Spencer will never speak with you. Don't even try."

I looked down at Wynona. "I'll bring you something you can use. Expect a video call around midnight. And please be where you can record live video. Thanks, Ron."

"Sean—"

I disconnected and looked across the room at Joe Billie. "Do you happen to have your canoe in the back of your truck?"

"No, it's at home. Why?"

"Because I need to make a midnight run by water. And it must be quiet like a canoe."

"How far do you need to travel by canoe or boat?"

I found the satellite images of Fisher Island on my phone screen. "About three hundred yards." I walked around the bed to Joe, held the screen so he could see it. "This is Virginia Key in Biscayne Bay … and right to the immediate northwest is Fisher Island. The eastern tip is where I need to go."

"I have an idea. A two-man raft with an electric motor. It's quiet, and it'll do well in those protected waters. I know a marine store close by."

"Do they sell hunting equipment?"

"You mean guns?"

"No, crossbows."

"I think so." Joe glanced down at Wynona, touching her hands. "She's a special one. In the language of the Seminole, she is called Cho-se." He looked up from Wynona's face to mine. "I have an idea what you're planning, Sean. I suggested a two-man raft. I could be your second man."

Ninety-Four

When I used to sail out of Miami, Virginia Key was one of the islands in Biscayne Bay that intrigued me the most. Before the Spanish arrived with galleons and greed, the Tequesta Indians called the island home. It's close to 900 acres in size, filled with palm trees, a county park, the Miami Sea Aquarium and marine research facilities. But the north end of the island is rustic, remote and undeveloped. It is laced with bike trails that lead up to white sand beaches. Wide bike paths make easy access in a Jeep.

Joe Billie sat in the front seat, silent, as I drove the trails by the light of the moon, the Jeep's headlights off. I told him everything I knew about Timothy Spencer, and Spencer's connection to the murders. He looked over at me and asked, "You think you'll get him to talk?"

"It's worth the gamble. Too many deaths. Too little accountability. There's too much money to bring this to justice through the conventional method. It needs leverage."

He said nothing, watching the moon through the gaps in the palm trees, the sound of the surf coming through the Jeep's open windows. After a moment, he said, "This island is a spiritual place. When the ships from Europe arrived on these shores, the native people had no idea what was coming across the horizon and descending upon them. They were curious, greeting them with peace but with suspicion.

This big island and the others in Biscayne Bay, a place where the natives fished and gathered clams and lobsters for centuries, was decimated in less than fifty years."

"And there was no gold to be found in Florida, only a lot of flowers." I pulled up to the beach on the northeast side of Virginia Key, the moon shimmering over the Atlantic, a massive cruise ship coming around the tip of South Beach in the distance. I looked across the inlet to Fisher Island, lights from expensive condos and multi-million-dollar homes twinkling.

We unloaded the raft from the Jeep, inflated it with a plug-in pump, attached an electric motor and batteries. We brought two fishing rods and a crossbow with five arrows. I locked the Jeep, and we carried the raft to the surf, both Joe and I were shoeless. We pushed off through the breakers, a small amount of sea water coming over the bow. Billie piloted, and I sat near the bow with a pair of binoculars, watching the island. I propped the rods up against the side of the raft. And then I looked for marine patrol in boats.

I didn't have to search long. Through the binoculars, I spotted a private security boat. It looked to be at least twenty feet long. Two men aboard. Both sitting near the stern, one man behind the wheel. The words on the transom read: *Bayside Security*.

I turned to Billie. "It's good they have their tail feathers pointed toward us. I don't think we've been spotted. Regardless, we look like a couple guys doing some night fishing on an in-coming tide."

A smile worked at the side of his mouth. "Maybe we should have bought some bait."

"I'm hoping they won't get close enough to inspect us. From what I was able to gather, nighttime security makes a loop around the island from ten through daybreak. Spencer's mansion won't be hard to find. Maybe we can tie up where the patrol can't spot the raft the next time they circle around the island."

Billie studied the shoreline as we approached the center of the inlet, the small electric motor pushing us in silence, a breeze blowing from the east. "I don't think it'll be hard to hide our little boat among the mega-yachts."

I watched the patrol boat disappear around the tip of the island, the two-man crew heading northwest. We moved within a hundred yards off shore and set a course that looked like we were heading to South Beach. In reality, as soon as we spotted Spencer's mansion, we'd make a sweeping left and set a path directly toward the house.

As the moon slipped behind dark clouds, we watched heat lightning reverberate in the distance where the inky sky met the sea. We were about two-hundred yards off shore. There was a mega-yacht docked out front, a dozen or so lights glowing from the yacht. It was sleek and sexy, Italian lines, all 150 feet in white with blackened windows.

I saw two people in silhouette moving on the long deck. I looked back at Billie. "The mansion will be loaded with surveillance and motion detection cameras and alarms. But maybe not so much for the yacht. Someone is on it. At least two people. If we're lucky, Spencer will be one of them."

He watched the yacht. "One could be Spencer. What will you do with the one who is not?"

"Nothing. Maybe encourage him or her to remain silent."

"What are you thinking?"

"I'm thinking that you get me to the stern of the yacht, I'll jump onto the swim platform and work my way through the decks, hunting for Spencer."

"And if you don't find him on the big boat, what?"

"I'll have whomever is on the yacht escort me inside the house."

"I have a better idea. I'll board the ship with you. We'll search it together and have each other's backs."

"The number one thing we have going right now is the element of surprise. I can move faster and stealthier on foot by myself. Regardless, if all hell breaks loose, I don't want you going down and being sentenced to prison. You'd never survive it living in a cage."

"Would you do any better, Sean?"

"I hope I don't have to find out. The moon's behind the clouds. Let's head to Spencer's play toy."

With an in-coming tide, it took us less than five minutes to get within one hundred feet of the yacht. The words on the stern read: *Sweet Dreams*. It was secured to a long concrete dock, soft lights coming from globes at the top of each piling. Ropes coiled to perfection, the hull gleaming in the subdued lights and shadows. The sloping yard leading from the dock to the mansion was dotted with expensive canary date palm trees, each lit from the base. A winding brick path from the waterfront up to the estate was lined with small white lights on both sides of the walkway. The night air carried the fragrance of sweet acacia, lilac and jasmine blossoms.

I heard laughter. Maybe from a woman or a girl.

I signaled for Joe to cut the electric motor, allowing the raft to drift in the last fifteen feet. I whispered, "You can tie up to the platform. It's in subdued light. If the patrol boat comes by again, just lie down flat. They won't see you from the distance, and a dinghy tied to the aft of a boat won't raise suspicions."

"I still don't like you going it alone."

"If I haven't returned in thirty minutes, you head back and take my Jeep. Go to the rez and just lay low."

"I don't like the sound of that. I won't leave a man behind. I didn't do it in the military, and I won't do it here tonight. If you aren't back in thirty minutes, I'll come looking for you, Sean. So, don't screw up."

"Don't plan to." When we were close enough, I jumped from the raft to the swim platform. My Glock wedged under my belt, the ten-inch serrated knife in a sheath strapped to my right leg. I watched Billie tie the raft to the swim platform, and then I spotted trouble. Two men coming down the stone path from the mansion to the yacht. There were dressed in black pants and black polo shirts. Lots of steroid induced muscle. The waddle of gym rats who spent more time lifting than doing cardio exercises. Each wore an earpiece. They were armed. Both men with powerful, tactical flashlights in their hands.

I crouched down on the massive swim platform. Looked at Joe and gave him hand signals, indicating two men were approaching. He nodded, picking up the crossbow. The guards were heading toward the yacht. A sense of urgency in their step. I didn't know if they'd seen us I arrive. Maybe we triggered some hidden alarm near the yacht. They were less than fifty feet away, and both men were reaching for pistols clipped to their belts.

Ninety-Five

They hit their flashlights, the twin beams were powerful searchlights along the perimeter of *Sweet Dreams* and across the surface of the dark water. I hid in the shadows, near a staircase on the yacht's transom leading to the deck above me. I watched the shafts of light crisscrossing in the night sky. The men were now within twenty-five feet of reaching the yacht. Out of the corner of my eye I saw Joe aiming the crossbow. He shot the arrow into the limbs of a palm tree, the arrowhead embedding into a coconut knocking it to the ground with a thrashing noise.

The men turned, whispering and walking in the direction of the sound. I climbed off the yacht and followed them, wondering if I was on surveillance cameras and my every move seen in a guardhouse near or on the property. At this point, it didn't matter. Timothy Spencer didn't play by the rules. He believed he was entitled to whatever he desired, damn the little people and the collateral damages. I thought about Wynona lying in the hospital bed, now pulling my Glock, less than twenty feet behind the men.

They used the flashlights to scan the area, their talk in brief whispers. "What the hell is that?" asked the taller of the two, a rawboned warrior who looked like he trained Navy Seals. He shone his light on the arrow embedded in the center of a green coconut, the red and yellow feathers like a tiny bird caught in the beam of light.

The other man said, "It's a damn arrow. We have hostiles on the property!"

Before they could move, I slipped behind the taller of the two and drove my fist into the back of his neck. He collapsed on the spot. The second man reached for his pistol. Before he could pull it from the side holster, I dove into him, grabbing his gun arm and wrenching it behind his back. There was a soft crack of bone. He swung at me with his good arm, the blow hitting me in the mouth. I saw the lights in the distance go off for a half second, the taste of blood instant.

I slammed my forearm into his nose, blood spurting on impact. I released his broken arm, drew back and hit him as hard as I could in his lower right jaw. His eyes dimmed, and he toppled to the ground, his head resting next to the coconut with an arrow dead center in it. I removed the pistols from their holsters and tossed them into the shrubbery. I turned and ran toward the yacht, giving Joe the thumbs up sign, the music from the top deck loud—the song *Whipping Post* from the Allman Brothers Band in the night air.

I spit a mouthful of blood into the water below the yacht, two teeth loose. I climbed back onto the transom and entered *Sweet Dreams*. I pulled on rubber gloves, moved through the salon and felt as if I'd walked into a deserted billionaire's club. It was all light woods, dark leathers, an opulent bar that covered more than twenty feet of one wall. A large saltwater aquarium was behind the bar, exotic fish swimming around pink coral and eel grass. Seven posh seats were in front of the bar. Expensive original paintings hung from two of the walls, the paintings softly lit. I walked through the salon, entering a labyrinth of rooms—mostly guest cabins, all decorated like bedrooms in a Manhattan penthouse. There was no master's berth on this deck. A blue backpack was on one of the beds.

I found a carpeted stairway and climbed to the second deck, looking for security cameras along the way. This deck was teeming with expensive toys. Two wide-screen TVs, a sunken conversation pit filled with a leather, half-circle couch and wide chairs. A backgammon board was atop a small glass table in the center. A regulation-sized billiard table was near the rear of the room. A chef's galley at one end with a winding bar. Two empty bottles of champagne were on one of the mahogany dining tables.

I followed a hallway, walking over thick carpet past a head that can only be called a luxurious bathroom. There was no one in it. I moved toward what I assumed was going to be the master berth. The door was closed. I pulled my Glock, using my left hand to test the door. It was unlocked. I slowly turned the handle and opened the door, immediately extending the pistol.

The berth was larger than the master bedroom in many expensive homes. But no one in it. The bed was not disturbed. A small dining area was near a walk-out veranda. A large, polished-brass telescope on a tripod next to one of the windows. A glass-enclosed fireplace stood less than twenty feet from the king-sized bed. There was a massage table adjacent to a private bath, a spa and glassed-in shower at the far end of the room. I approached the balcony, the sliding glass doors open, translucent curtains billowing in the night breeze.

I pulled back the curtains. No one. Only two thick-cushioned chairs, center table, an umbrella that was closed and tied at the base. From the veranda, I could hear the music. It came from the upper deck. I left the master and headed up through a half-circle staircase. As I approached the top couple of steps, I stopped and listened. A man said, "Turn around, I want to see more."

Ninety-Six

I slowly rose, keeping to the shadows. A blob of a man sprawled naked in a lounge chair. His walrus skin was pink, and it looked like layers of soft ice cream on a cone. He had little hair on his round head, dark fur across his back. I knew I was looking at Timothy Spencer. In front of him, two young women danced naked to a pulsating beat. There was a swimming pool and hot spa built into the expansive deck. An outdoor bar. Lots of chairs and colorful umbrellas.

I put the Glock under my belt beneath my shirt and approached them. The girls saw me first, not sure if I was crashing the party or an invited guest. Spencer answered the question on their faces when he looked up under heavy lids and asked, "Who the hell are you?"

"I'm the dream-weaver. It's good to be aboard *Sweet Dreams*. But in a few minutes, it will become a nightmare."

The girls both gasped, searching for panties, shorts and tops. I looked at them. "How old are you two?"

"Eighteen," blurted out the blonde.

"Tell me the truth."

"Seventeen."

I eyed the dark-haired girl. "And you?"

"Seventeen."

"How'd you get here."

"We were forced to come here. Both of us left bad stuff at our homes. She's from Atlanta. I'm from Milwaukee. We lived on the streets until … we like can't get away. One of his men met us at the ferryboat."

"I will get you help, okay?"

Both girls nodded. "Who owns the blue backpack in one of the state rooms?"

The blonde raised her hand, her lower lip trembling. "It's mine."

"I want you and your friend to go back to that room and lock yourself inside. Don't open the door for anyone but me or the police. I will get you out of here and into a safe place."

Tears were filling the eyes of both girls. I said, "Go on and get your clothes and stay in that room." They grabbed their clothes, dressed in seconds and left the top deck. I turned to Spencer. "It's just you and me now."

He pulled a white towel over his gut and crotch, looked up at me. "You'll never get away with this."

"Wrong. I've already gotten away with this. I'm here. And you're sitting there. I have a nine-millimeter that will blow your head off your hairy shoulders. Two of your guards are sleeping soundly in your yard. It's just you and me, Timmy. I can find you and penetrate your security anywhere you run, but you won't run. Not now. Not ever."

"Who are you? What do you want? Money? How much? Name your price?"

"You can't afford me."

"A million? How much?"

"You can't buy me."

"If you don't want money, what do you want?"

"The truth."

"Truth. What truth?"

"I know the word is hard for you to pronounce. Work on it because your life depends on something called the truth."

"What are you going to do?"

"That's up to you. I may kill you."

"What? Why?"

"I'm going to kill you if you lie to me. You're going to walk the plank. You have all these nautical toys, but you are deathly afraid of the water. It's from a near drowning as a child in Lake Michigan."

He pushed back in his chair. "How do you know this?"

"I know a lot about you, Timothy. I know that you were a trust-fund baby for years until you could leverage your way into a company your grandfather built. Your older brother, Ron, died hunting big game. It was from an apparent stray bullet. Convenient for you, eh? You leveraged full control of Heartland Sugar. From there you used that power to buy and sell people like pawns. And then along came Joe Thaxton, threatening to make a big change in your narcissistic world."

Spencer's eyes opened wide. There was a slight twitch from a nerve in his left jowl, his pink face growing hotter. "I had nothing to do with that."

"You had everything to do with that. Thaxton was an anomaly, a non-politician who amassed a statewide following because he had the balls to stand up to corporate greed. You couldn't buy him. You couldn't compromise his ethics. You couldn't stop him from rocking your boat. Then you killed him. And now your boat is about to really rock. Stand up!" I pulled out my Glock and shoved in under his bulbous, triple chin. "Stand up!"

He grabbed his towel, struggling to stand, his shoulders slouching, his pale blue eyes fearful. I said, "We're going to go for a little stroll on *Sweet Dreams*. This yacht draws at least fifteen feet of water, meaning that off the port side it's very deep. It's pure Atlantic Ocean on this side of the island, and it's the season for the bull sharks to come into the channel as the mothers enter Biscayne Bay to birth their young. And those mother sharks have quite an appetite, especially at night. You're going for a midnight swim."

"No! I can't swim."

"That could be a problem."

"Please!"

"Let's go!" I shoved him hard in the center of his back, his towel flapping behind his large butt. "Move!" I pushed him toward the bow and, in less than a minute, we were standing portside, a railing between him and the dark water. I slipped my knife from the leather sheath and touched his stomach. "A quarter-inch cut about here will create a slow bleed. Not enough to kill you, but more than enough to call in the sharks. It's amazing how far they can smell blood in the water."

"No! Don't! I'll give you ten million. You name the bank account to have it deposited."

"You and the cronies you hire, people like lobbyist Simon Santiago, just don't get it. You can't buy your way in and out of everything. You turn Florida's beautiful environment into a cesspool, and you couldn't care less. Chaucer said all things must come to an end. Someone later added the word *good*, as in all good things must come to an end. But there's nothing good about you, Timmy. This is one of those life changing events. You tell me the truth, or you tread water. The tide is going out, so I'd expect they'll never find what's left of your considerable body." I held the knife against his gut. "Last chance, Timmy."

"Okay! I'll talk. But this will never stick. I'll never be prosecuted."

"Don't bet the yacht on it, pal."

I lifted my phone from my pocket and hit the live video feed. Detective Ron Hamilton answered. I said, "Detective Hamilton, you can see Timothy Spencer, the CEO of Heartland Sugar Corporation. He's more than willing for you to question him."

Hamilton cleared his throat and said, "Mr. Spencer, we're investigating the murders of Joe Thaxton and Chester Miller as well as the killing of three police officers in Miami yesterday. This video questioning is being recorded. Do you understand that?"

Spencer pursed his lips, goose bumps rising on his hairless, flabby arms. "Yes."

"And you are willing to speak to us without a lawyer?"

"Do I have a choice?"

"Yes, you do. What will it be?"

I looked hard at Spencer. He cleared his throat. "I'll speak with you."

"All right. What role, if any, did you play in the death of Joe Thaxton?"

Spencer looked at me and then shifted his eyes to the screen on my phone. He said, "I hired lobbyist Simon Santiago to deal with Thaxton."

"What do you mean deal with Thaxton?" asked Hamilton.

"To make him go away."

"As in to kill him, correct?"

"I didn't specifically order his death."

"But you knew it was going to happen, right?"

"I assumed they'd do something bad. I don't like to get into those details."

"You paid Santiago to hire a hit man, correct?"

"I paid him to hire what he called a fixer."

"Fixer and assassin are the same in terms of killers. And you knew the money was being used in a murder-for-hire scheme, correct?"

"I assumed, but I never asked or got into the specifics."

"Who was the hit man hired?"

"I never met him."

"What was his name?"

"I don't know … Fazio something, I think."

"Why did you want Joe Thaxton out of the picture?"

"Because he was a threat to our business interests."

"How about Chester Miller? Why have him killed?"

"I didn't want to do that, but Simon insisted that it be done. He said Miller could identify Fazio and the connections could come back to us. I didn't condone that killing."

"But you knew it was going to happen, correct?"

"I assumed it would."

"And you did nothing to stop it, right?"

"I didn't order it, so I wasn't going to stop it."

"Why ambush the police raiding the place where Michael Fazio was staying—a building owned by one of your companies?"

"I had nothing to do with that. I wasn't aware it was going to happen. That's the truth."

Hamilton released a deep breath. "We will have officers at your home in less than thirty minutes. You will be placed under arrest at that time and brought in for further questioning. Is that clear?"

"Yes, and I'll have my lawyers with me."

I placed my phone back in my pocket, allowing the audio recording to continue. I stared at Spencer. He crossed his arms and said, "I won't do a day in jail."

"No, but you'll do years in prison."

"That's not going to happen."

"You might as well have pulled the trigger. You're the money guy, the one who hired the people to commit the murders. You're as complicit, if not more so, because it would never have happened had you not ordered and paid for it. You wanted Joe Thaxton dead. He's dead. You wanted to have Chester Miller killed because he was an eyewitness, and you were afraid Fazio and Simon Santiago would cop a plea and point their dirty fingers at you."

He grinned. "Sure, but you'll never prove that."

"It's already happening. You dump on people like you do with the environment. You could care less that those police officers died in the line of duty and one is left in critical condition."

"I can't control the actions of a hired hit man. Stuff happens. I'm done talking with you."

I backhanded him hard across the left side of his face. The blow knocked him to the deck. I pulled Spencer up and propped him against the yacht's railing. I grabbed him by the back of his thick neck and pushed his head down, the swirling dark water directly below us. "Stuff happens," I said. "I want to make this clear to you, Timmy. I found you on your big boat. I'll find you anywhere. You'll do a lot better serving time than facing me again. Because if you do … there will be no negotiations. No compromises. No second chances for you." I leaned down toward his ear and whispered. "Do you understand me? Do you understand what will happen to you?"

"Yes! Let me up! Please!"

I pulled him straight and placed the serrated knife blade against his throat, staring at him. He averted his eyes. "Look at me!" He glanced up at me. "Take a good look at my face. If you ever see it again, it will be the last face on Earth you see. That's a promise." I dropped him, and he fell to his knees coughing, face strawberry red.

I turned and left, the wail of sirens coming across the channel at the Port of Miami. In less than thirty seconds, I was back in the dinghy with Joe Billie. "Let's get out of here."

We pulled away and rode across the water for half a minute in silence. I called Ron Hamilton and said, "Ron, there are two underage girls, victims in a sex trafficking ring. They've locked themselves in a stateroom on Spencer's yacht. Please see they get to a safe place tonight. Maybe we can get them back to their families."

"Will do. Are the girls okay?"

"No—at least no physical bruises. But the internal ones can last the longest."

"Unfortunately. Nice work with Spencer. He'll lawyer up, but the video is so self-incriminating, so far beyond a reasonable doubt, he'll pay the consequences. Let's talk in the morning." He disconnected.

Joe Billie looked across the bay to Virginia Key, his right hand on the electric motor controls. He looked up at the moon and then at me. "How'd it go?"

"We have a confession. It's on video and audio. Spencer admitted his involvement in the murders. He thinks he'll lawyer up and beat it. But the video interview is a strong admission of guilt because of the level of details. Conducted by a homicide detective, it'll be admissible in court. A jury will see it and decide. I doubt Timothy Spencer will have sweet dreams the rest of his sorry life."

"Good."

"By the way, nice shot with the crossbow. Dead center into a coconut. It proved the perfect distraction at the right time."

"I got lucky. It was a ripe one and fell easily. Gravity gets the credit."

As we came closer to the dark beach on Virginia Key, I looked back at Fisher Island, the blue, red, and white pulse of police lights descending on the mansion and yacht. Toward the northeast was South Beach, the neon glow of nightclubs and posh condos. And then I looked directly east into the dark of the Atlantic Ocean, the salty and floral scent of the trade winds in the night air.

The stars hung low, a flicker of heat lightning where the sea meets the sky. I thought about Wynona, looked up into the heavens, spotting the glow of a bright star that I knew was Venus. The constellations twinkled like holiday lights. I found the constellation Virgo and thought about something Chester Miller said, *'You only see the constellation Virgo during certain seasons, rising in spring ... just like Persephone, the goddess of spring. She comes and goes, brings the season of growth after the dead of winter. I believe, when the orchid, Persephone finally blooms, it'll be after a dark period. And it'll have been worth the wait.'*

From the heart of the constellation, a fiery meteor ripped across the night sky in a long arc, vanishing over the horizon in a dimension somewhere between land, sea and night sky.

Ninety-Seven

A week passed, and Wynona was ready to leave the hospital. It was a little after 9:00 a.m. when I walked down the corridor toward her room, the medicinal smell of bleach and antiseptic recycled in the canned air. A middle-aged janitor was pushing a damp mop at the far end of the hall, orange headphones strapped to his ears. I went around him as I moved toward the nurses' station. One nurse looking into a computer screen, two more updating digital patient charts. "She's been waiting for you," said the head nurse, looking up from the computer. "She wants to go home."

"Thank you all for taking such good care of her."

"You're welcome. She's a strong woman … but right now she's hurting inside."

I nodded and walked past a half-dozen partially opened doors until I came to room 910. The door was closed. I gently knocked and entered. Wynona was standing by the window, looking at the traffic nine floors below the room. Her blue suitcase was packed and set on the floor at the foot of the bed. She turned toward me when I closed the door. She managed a half smile, her eyes not reflecting pain, but rather sorrow.

I walked across the room. She said nothing, extending her arms, her eyes searching my face. I took her and held her close, her face buried in the center of my chest, her silent tears absorbing into my shirt. After a moment, she said, "I'm so tired. I feel more vulnerable now than at any other time in my life."

I held her close, the morning sunlight coming through the sheer curtains. We stood there for a few minutes, holding each other in the solitude of shared, heavy grief and love. She looked up at me, her dark hair matted to one side of her cheek, eyes red and still brimming. "I've always wanted to be a mother. The career came, and I threw myself into it with passion to help right the world a little more." She used one finger to wipe the tears from beneath her eyes.

She took a deep breath and released it. "I always thought I'd make time for a family. But time doesn't play favorites, and the years clicked away. I was okay without having a family of my own … and then you came along, Sean. The pregnancy simply happened in the emotional and physical act of our lovemaking. When I found out, my whole world and priorities changed. I wanted to tell you sooner, but that vulnerability thing keeps creeping into my head. And now …" Her voice choked, tears rolling down her cheeks, her eyes filled with the pain of a mother's mourning.

I held her and said, "I'm not sure we can sustain true love without allowing our souls to open—to become vulnerable because that is love's dance partner. Being vulnerable doesn't mean being weak. It means you're willing to take the risks of love's joy and bruises because, in the end, it's what we're here for. I'm taking you home … to my river cabin. You need the solitude and peace. It'll help, and I'll be there with you for as long as you'll put up with me."

She closed her eyes, nodding her head. "Take me there—that would be good. I need to be in nature and with you right now. Being by the river will help."

• • •

It was almost three weeks later when the family and friends of Chester Miller gathered in the heart of the Everglades to spread Chester's ashes. Wynona walked with me down a narrow dirt road as mourners convened in a picturesque spot of cypress trees and a vista of sawgrass. The blue sky was so hard and deep, it felt as if you could hit a tennis ball against it. A flock of white ibis appeared from the heart of the only cloud in the sky, a towering cumulus, rising in a vertical, massive column.

There were more than fifty people taking their places near an ancient Indian shell mound that was slightly elevated above the sawgrass. Callie Hogan, wearing a dark blue sundress, held the urn with her grandfather's ashes. She was flanked by her parents. The people gathered in a half circle. Joe Billie stood next to Sam Otter, the oldest living Seminole. The old man's deeply creased face was stoic with the enduring strength of worn saddle leather. His cotton white hair was braided. He wore a traditional Seminole multicolored, patchwork jacket, white scarf and dark pants. His black eyes filled with wisdom, depth, and sorrow.

Wynona whispered, "Sam Otter asked Joe to bring him here today. I know that Sam and Chester were friends, but I think they shared a common bond in the glades and respected each other more than any of us knew."

"I agree."

We watched Callie look at the immense expanse of sawgrass for a moment before turning around to speak. "My grandfather loved the Everglades so very much. He said, of all the places on earth he visited, and he was well traveled, this land held the most special place in his heart. He loved the environment—the birds and animals, the wetlands, the towering bald cypress trees, the almost imperceptible change of seasons. But, most of all, he loved the flora and fauna." She paused, her eyes roaming across the faces of those in front of her.

"As many of you know, one of my grandfather's life's missions was to help restore the native orchids into the glades, Big Cypress, and the Fakahatchee Strand. At last count, right before he was killed, he'd restored more than seven thousand native species of orchids. I think the ghost orchids were his favorite. He used to tell me they grew up on the trees to keep an eye on things. Rarely seen because you have to look up to see them and, when you do, it's like they're jumping out to you. He said the ghosts were the canaries in the coal mines. And, when they disappeared for good, the glades would go with them. He wasn't a pessimist or doomsayer. He was the opposite—convinced that, when people truly had the facts and understood the consequences of our actions, they would come together to make a difference." She paused, her eyes welling with tears.

Wynona held my arm and took a deep breath. Sam Otter stared across the sawgrass. A woman in the congregation softly cried. As we all came to honor the life of Chester Miller, I thought about the events of this last month and tried to get a perspective I didn't have even two weeks ago. An assassin, a man who made a living killing people, took his last and youngest victim from Wynona's womb. I tried to delete the sickening image of Michael Fazio aiming his pistol at me. His flat eyes, every pore in his face filled with the mask of evil.

Wynona and I had days and weeks of talking, hours filled with emotion, trying to come to terms with the death of our unborn child. Although unborn, there had been a heartbeat, a pulse of movement near Wynona's stomach, the chance of a future, the lease on this thing called life that is the greatest unwrapped gift. I knew there was no promise of tomorrow. Life, or even birth, had no warranty. No guarantee. Only an expiration date. But our child didn't receive that. The powerful desire for retribution was still palpable in the back of my throat.

Simon Santiago was the state's star witness in the upcoming trial of Timothy Spencer. Even with a small army of lawyers, Spencer's bond was denied as a flight risk. The video confession and level of detail he knew about the murders were more than enough for prosecutors to build a strong case and take him to trial.

Joe Thaxton may never have served one day as an elected member of the state senate, but his efforts to get there—his grit and determination to speak the truth about those assaulting Florida's fragile environment, would leave a positive and lasting difference.

Callie's mother spoke for a few minutes about her father, Chester, telling those in attendance that he was a man with an insatiable curiosity for the world around us and that humanity's options and collective decisions should not be out of sync with the rhythms of nature. He wanted us to be good stewards of the planet. She turned to her daughter. "Callie, I think it's time to release your grandfather back to the place he felt most at home."

Callie nodded, pulled a strand of hair behind one ear. She looked at the polished, white urn in her hands. "My grandfather told me when he died, he wanted his ashes released here. He said it was because of the splendor you see all around us. He wanted us to remember him and think of the beauty here ... and to know he saw that beauty in all of you."

She turned to face the horizon, removing the lid from the urn. An east wind came in from behind us as Callie released the ashes, the wind carrying them over the sawgrass. Some in the congregation wept as the urn emptied and the ashes disappeared into the surroundings. I saw Sam Otter slowly lift his head toward the sky, his eyes following something. I watched an eagle come from the north, dip down, make a circle high above us, turning and soaring in the direction the wind carried Chester Miller across the Everglades.

Ninety-Eight

After the crowd had dispersed, and after the extended hugs and condolences, Callie invited Wynona and I to follow her back to her grandfather's cabin in the Big Cypress Preserve. "There's some unfinished business at his cabin," she said, getting into her car. Wynona and I rode in my Jeep east on the Tamiami Trail until we came to the near hidden entrance and into the world Chester Miller created and left behind. It had rained, and the dirt and gravel driveway had the fresh-washed scent of pine and blooming jasmine.

We parked near the picnic table beneath the old oak. Callie's car was in front of us. She got out first, smiled and gestured for us to follow her. We walked in her direction, the grounds and place had a different feel. It was still beautiful with the gardens of blooming flowers tucked everywhere, but the larger-than-life presence of Chester Miller was gone, one of his canes propped up next to the hand railing by the wooden steps leading to his front porch. His spirit could be felt among the flora in terms of what he left for others, but the locked cabin, greenhouse, and small lab seemed deserted and somehow abandoned.

We approached Callie. "I'm gonna miss this place," she said.

"I can see why," said Wynona. "It's special. Nothing quite like it anywhere on earth."

THE ORCHID KEEPER

"In my grandfather's will, he left the entire thirteen acres to the Nature Conservancy to remain as is … in perpetuity, and to be used as a place of study for university graduate students majoring in environmental sciences and botany."

"Your grandfather was a generous man," I said. "Not only did he leave a legacy in the world of plant sciences, he was making sure others would be able to carry the baton to the next level."

She nodded and smiled. "I just wish I could have had a few more years with him." She motioned toward the cypress tree near the small lab, a wide smile forming. "It bloomed! Persephone has finally bloomed. I wanted the two of you to be among the first to see it. My mom and dad saw it yesterday. I'm going to take it down from the tree, photograph it, and tell the world on my grandfather's website and social media sites the amazing story behind it."

Wynona grinned and said, "This is one of the real OMG moments."

Callie led us to the base of the tree where we could see two blossoms protruding from the clay pot perched on the wooden support that Chester had built and attached to the lowest tree limb. "Sean, can you hold the ladder?" Callie asked, as she started up the rungs.

I held the ladder and watched her stop near the top and simply stare at the orchid with a reverence taught by her grandfather. She carefully lifted the pot with both of her hands. "You need some help?" I asked, hoping she wouldn't drop the pot.

"No thanks. It's not too heavy." She gripped the pot with both hands and used her forearms to balance as she carefully backed down the ladder, her red sneakers stepping in the center of each rung. In less than half a minute, she was on the ground holding the clay pot for us to see. "Isn't it the most beautiful orchid in the whole world?" Her eyes beamed, filled with pride and joy.

Wynona said, "I've never seen any blossoms like those anywhere. The colors are by far the richest and most vivid I've ever seen."

"They're beautiful," I said. "Maybe worth the long wait of fifteen years." The blossoms were about the size of my palm. The petals were ivory white speckled with light lavender and pink dots in a graduated intensity. The edges of the petals were bordered in a soft crimson. The center portion of the flowers had a delicate look as if they were patterned from the lips of a woman, blood red with specks of yellow that carried the iridescence of solid gold.

Callie said, "I'm going to set the plant on the picnic table and take pictures of the lovely blossoms from every angle I can. Come on."

We went with her to the table under a large oak. She set the clay pot down on a black cloth and stood straight. "My grandfather said, when it blooms, it'll be the rarest of the rarest, a hybrid with the DNA of the Shenzhen and Kinabalu orchids along with an exotic pollen mix from the Cattleya. He would have been so proud. I wish he was here to see them."

"I think he sees them," Wynona said. "And I feel that the thing he would be most proud of is your joy after they bloomed and the way you'll help take care of them."

Callie smiled and looked from Wynona back to the blossoms. I said, "Here on a picnic table, under a century old oak tree, we have the rarest, most exotic orchids on earth. What we're looking at is visible proof of a hybrid. Not so much in the orchid, but in the partnership your grandfather had with nature as they worked together to create beauty for the world." I looked over at Callie. "Now, after all these years, after it has finally bloomed, what will you do with it?"

She didn't respond immediately. She thought for a moment, her eyebrows rising. "After I photograph and shoot video of it, after I write a new species document to be shared, and after I give the world the opportunity to see the blossoms on the Internet, maybe I'll work in my grandfather's lab to take stems and produce more. As part of the Nature Conservancy's inheritance, grandfather's Last Will and Testament gave me that option. Persephone was born here in the Everglades. I'll replant any reproductions in the wild, in nature. Maybe some of my grandfather's ashes will eventually land on their petals, and his creativity will continue." She grinned.

I said, "His creativity has already landed. It did so when you were born. This is your time, Callie ... your new adventure. Share it with the world, as your grandfather wanted, but keep the roots of all of this here close to you. You are the new orchid keeper."

She beamed, her eyes tearing. After another half hour, we hugged Callie and said goodbye. Wynona and I slowly drove back up the driveway that Chester built, orchids and bougainvillea hanging from weathered fence posts and the trees themselves. It was a unique world. A slice of Eden tucked away on the threshold of the Everglades. I looked in my rearview mirror and saw Callie carrying the orchids to the greenhouse. They were in good hands. I glanced over at Wynona. "Callie will do well."

"She's already doing well. She'll make a difference."

"Let's go home. The river awaits us. I don't know if wild orchids grow there, but there are some beautiful yellow and purple trumpet flowers that are in bloom near the water."

Wynona reached for my hand and smiled. She said, "Don't forget about all of my wild orchids on the porch. However, trumpet flowers make music without having to sound a note. New flowers growing next to the old river will be music to my soul."

The End

Made in the USA
Monee, IL
15 March 2020